Praise for
The Spanish Brand Series

PALOMA AND THE HORSE TRADI

4 1/2 stars, Top Pick: "Kelly knows ⟨barcode D0871094⟩ knows how to reel readers in from the get-g[o] [ ] away with the deep, emotional romance and highly likable characters. The story is adventurous and totally out of the ordinary, which makes it a splendid read and a completely satisfying experience."
—*RT Reviews*

"I am totally captivated by this series. Marco and Paloma have formed such a strong love, that it's breathtaking. The descriptions of the characters and places are vivid. The plot is riveting and the action is exciting. I am totally invested in this couple, and I'm thrilled to hear that there is at least one more book coming in the series. I would recommend reading the first two books of this series to get the maximum enjoyment. *Paloma and the Horse Traders* is pure artistry and a sheer delight. I give it my highest recommendation."
—Lady Blue, *Romantic Historical Reviews*

Editors' Choice: "Set in the 18th century in what is today New Mexico, the novel is much more than a romance. It is, in fact, a rousing and exciting Western that will appeal to all readers.... Kelly knows her subject matter; her historical research is impeccable. But her research never gets in the way of her spinning a good yarn. This is a great read, and it is highly recommended."
—The Historical Novel Society

"This is truly some of the best historical fiction I have read.... The Spanish Brand Series weaves a lot of historical information into Marco's and Paloma's love story. Carla Kelly doesn't shy away from the harsher aspects of life, yet these stories are fast paced and exciting and beautiful. There is subtle humor as well, the kind I enjoy, humor that doesn't hit you over the head, but nibbles at you, causing you to smile. Every book here is a winner, and a keeper. All receive my highest recommendation."
—Roses are Blue, *Romantic Fiction Reviews and Discussions*

"Carla Kelly proves a later book in a series can outshine its predecessors with *Paloma and the Horse Traders*. Bringing back the authenticity of the old Spanish West and the hacienda of Marco and Paloma while introducing additional enemies and newfound friends, Kelly turns Paloma and the Horse Traders into a must-read.... Marco and Paloma open their hearts and their home to a cast of characters that bring smiles, tears and life-changing surprises and revelations in this series set at the end of the 18th century."
—Tara Creel, *Deseret News*

MARCO AND THE DEVIL'S BARGAIN

"[There are] powerful themes of disease, infertility, strength in the face of loss, and kindness between individuals whose cultures are at war. Though la viruela is, in some ways, the story's main character, the love between Marco and Paloma, equal parts strong attachment and mutual high regard, takes emotional center stage, a satisfying oasis of beauty in the midst of stark harshness."
—*Publishers Weekly*

Grade A: "There are some series which need to be read in order if they are to be understood. Carla Kelly's Spanish Brand series is not one of these. Although I didn't read *The Double Cross* first, as I should have, I still managed to fall head over heels for Marco and Paloma. To me, that is a good testament to Ms. Kelly's amazing writing. I can't wait to get my hands on another one of her books."
—Alexandra Anderson, *All About Romance*

"I found this book a pleasure to read, the characters well-formed and credible. Her knowledge and understanding of the era are excellent. I look forward to her next in the series. Highly recommended."
—The Historical Novel Society

"Kelly's ability to transport the reader into the unsettled Spanish territory of New Mexico is remarkable. From the daily life on the ranch to the travels into the wild, every word and action is well researched and natural.... With historical events such as smallpox and Native American threats and alliances driving the plot, *Marco and the Devil's Bargain* is a well-rounded story that is sure to please."
—Tara Creel, The *Deseret News*

"A fascinating and different premise, with an arrogant English physician

as the antagonist, and Comanches as surprising allies—a romance in the middle of a really good Western novel."
—*Roundup* Magazine

THE DOUBLE CROSS

"[*The Double Cross*] packs a full story with plenty of frontier action and believable, sympathetic characters. I'm already looking forward to the next entry in the Spanish Brand series, but until then I will content myself with rereading *The Double Cross*."
—Heather Stanton, *All About Romance*

5 Star Top Pick: "Life at this time was hard and unpredictable, and this beautiful love story interwoven with history makes for an outstanding read."
—Lady Blue, *Romantic Historical Reviews*

"Kelly skillfully invites readers to share in this romantic adventure that is played out amidst scenes depicting the harsh landscapes and living conditions on the frontier–all punctuated with an assortment of unsavory characters pitted against the heroic."
—*ForeWord* magazine

"Each of these characters' personalities are portrayed so endearingly that at the end of this unforgettable story of honor, love and redemption, we are sad to let them go, making us eager to see what is in store for the next installment of the series."
—The Historical Novel Society

"Engaging and highly entertaining, *The Double Cross* is Carla Kelly at her best. I can't wait for the next book in what promises to be an amazing series."
—Carla Neggers, *New York Times* bestselling author of *Saint's Gate*

"The characters, even the secondary ones, are real and lovable. Even through some darker themes, Kelly's smart writing breaks through and the adventurous heart triumphs."
—Tara Creel, *The Deseret News*

"One of the things Ms. Kelly does best is show ordinary people living lives of extraordinary grace, and that's a treat."
—Darlene Marshall's Blog

"Carla Kelly's vivid storytelling plunges the reader into a tense, hypnotic tale of love and courage in *The Double Cross*. A dangerous land filled with memorable characters springs to life and stays with you long after the final paragraphs."
—Diane Farr, bestselling author, Regency Romance and Young Adult Fiction

THE STAR IN THE MEADOW

THE STAR IN THE MEADOW

THE SPANISH BRAND SERIES

CARLA KELLY

Seattle, WA

CAMEL PRESS

Camel Press
PO Box 70515
Seattle, WA 98127

For more information go to: www.camelpress.com
www.carlakellyauthor.com

Cover design by Sabrina Sun

Cover photograph by Diana Powell, www.mountainparkphoto.com
Cover design by Sabrina Sun
Map and brands by Nina Grover

The Star in the Meadow
Copyright © 2017 by Carla Kelly

ISBN: 978-1-60381-992-3 (Trade Paper)
ISBN: 978-1-60381-993-0 (eBook)

Library of Congress Control Number: 2016953597

Printed in the United States of America

10 9 8 7 6 5 4 3 2 1

To Nancy Laing, Eric Laing and Johnny Laing—

friends, good ones.

Books by Carla Kelly

Fiction

Daughter of Fortune
Summer Campaign
Miss Chartley's Guided Tour
Marian's Christmas Wish
Mrs. McVinnie's London Season
Libby's London Merchant
Miss Grimsley's Oxford Career
Miss Billings Treads the Boards
Mrs. Drew Plays Her Hand
Reforming Lord Ragsdale
Miss Whittier Makes a List
The Lady's Companion
With This Ring
Miss Milton Speaks Her Mind
One Good Turn
The Wedding Journey
Here's to the Ladies: Stories of the Frontier Army
Beau Crusoe
Marrying the Captain
The Surgeon's Lady
Marrying the Royal Marine
The Admiral's Penniless Bride
Borrowed Light
Enduring Light
Coming Home for Christmas: The Holiday Stories
Marriage of Mercy
My Loving Vigil Keeping
Her Hesitant Heart
Safe Passage
The Double Cross
Marco and the Devil's Bargain
Paloma and the Horse Traders
Season's Regency Greetings
Regency Christmas Gifts
The Wedding Ring Quest
Softly Falling
Doing No Harm
Courting Carrie in Wonderland

Non-Fiction

On the Upper Missouri: The Journal of Rudolph Friedrich Kurz (editor)
Louis Dace Letellier: Adventures on the Upper Missouri (editor)
Fort Buford: Sentinel at the Confluence
Stop Me If You've Read This One

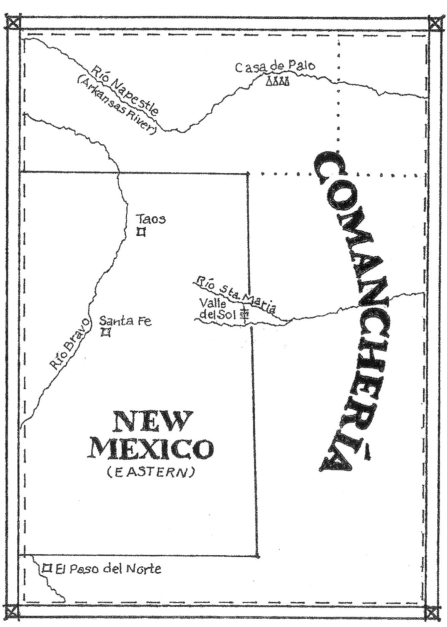

Map by Nina Grover

Juez de campo

An official of the Spanish crown who inspects and registers all brands of cattle and sheep in his district, settles disputes, and keeps a watchful eye for livestock rustlers. In the absence of sufficient law enforcement on the frontier of 18th century New Mexico, a royal colony, he also investigates petty crime.

Contents

Chapter One

In which disturbing news upsets a timid accountant and his daughter

Santa Fe, *Febrero* 1785

Catalina Maria Ygnacio hated winter in Santa Fe with all the venom she could muster, which was quite a lot. Ten years they had been exiled to this godforsaken bit of impoverished real estate—ten years of chilblains, a cold bed at night, ink freezing in the bottle, and no one to complain to, not even in jest.

Her cross might have been easier to bear if the Mendozas had not moved in next door. Carmen and Luis Mendoza were newlyweds, the curse of the earth. Their houses connected, a common fact in this poorer side of town. Long after she was in bed, stockings on her feet, mittens on her hands, Catalina heard them laughing together. Later, the bed began to squeak rhythmically as her neighbors warmed each other up in time-honored, legal fashion.

At first the creaks and moans had embarrassed Catalina. Now they just made her sad, and more fully aware nearly every night just how lonely her life was. She would end up drawing herself tight into a little ball, wishing the Mendozas would move somewhere else, wishing for a man of her own, wishing for something as simple as spring.

She knew better than to trouble her father about what was missing in her life, for he was worse off. Leather satchel slung over his increasingly stooped shoulder, Fernando Ygnacio left the house every morning at half seven o'clock. He never returned before six o'clock and generally was later. Though older than most of the governor's accountants, *los contadores*, he was the one who bore the stains of scandal and imprisonment, which meant last-minute work fell to him. A scapegoat he was, and a scapegoat he would always be, world without end, amen.

Too bad no one knew the father he was, kind and courteous, with a generous heart. She stifled whatever discouragement she felt, even as the practical side of her nature yearned to know how she was to support herself and make her solitary way through life when Papa finally shuffled off this mortal coil.

Those were the worries tormenting Catalina Ygnacio as she waited for her father. She sat in their cozy *sala*—some might call it small—and waited to hear the day's news from one of the Spanish empire's more timid functionaries.

There came his knock. Catalina remained in the *sala* and listened for the quick footsteps of the all-purpose girl. She heard them speak in low tones and knew the servant had relieved him of his hat, coat, mittens, and muffler, which went in a small chest by the front door.

She rose when he entered the *sala*, not one to forget the honor owed him, even if the nagging reality of his shame dogged him like a bad odor. He was still Papa, and she loved him.

Usually his tired eyes brightened when he saw her, but not this evening.

Accustomed from youth not to encourage bad news, she waited for him to speak. Perhaps his complaint would be as simple as wet boots. It could not be as bad as fifteen years ago in Mexico City, when the magistrate had hauled Papa away in chains to make him answer accusations that ultimately boiled down to his becoming the whipping boy for cost overruns on a simple bridge project. Five years in prison had followed, only to be compounded by exile. No, bad news could wait, and so Catalina waited.

With a sigh, Papa handed her a single sheet of paper with the seal snapped. "I'm too old for this," was all he said before she started to read.

Catalina brushed through the flowery first sentence, typical of all Spanish documents, and went right to the second paragraph. " 'When the mountain passes are free of snow, you are required to travel with a small guard to Valle del Sol, where you will conduct the seven-year audit,' " she read out loud. "You've done these before."

Or rather, *they* had. The fact that she checked and double-checked the columns of figures was their little secret. She had no doubt that she could handle an audit as easily as Papa. He had taught her well.

Papa nodded, his eyes full of enough worry to move her to sit by him. She looked closer, seeing his resignation, as if he had been waiting for such an order.

"Yes, but ... but Valle del Sol!"

She didn't understand. "You've done many audits in many places. What is wrong with Valle del Sol?"

He took the orders from her hand and looked at them again, as if seeing them for the first time. "Valle del Sol is on the edge of *la frontera*, my child," he said. "Comanches, thieves, and murderers live on frontiers." He snapped the paper with unaccustomed venom. "This is an assignment for a young man. They're finding a new way to kill me."

"Oh, Papa," she said, loving the man but wondering why he continued to see himself as a victim. "I do know it's been safe to travel in recent years. Don't worry."

He nodded, but the frown did not leave his face.

Catalina took his hand, rubbing it between her warmer ones. "Papa, let's have supper. "

He let her help him to his feet. The kitchen was but a few steps away, so she had no trouble keeping up an inane conversation she forgot as soon as the words left her mouth. She had become good at inane conversation, so good that it should have distressed her. So many things should have distressed her.

Papa rallied during supper, a modest meal in the kitchen, the warmest room in the house and the place where their servant slept, curled up on a pallet. More than one or two nights this winter, Catalina had wanted to join her in the kitchen, simply for warmth.

"Winters are getting colder here, Papa," she said, not even trying to disguise her wistful tone.

She had retired to her frigid bedroom when she heard a quiet knock at the door, then another. Catalina scuffed her feet into slippers and pulled a shawl around her shoulders, but Papa reached the door first, throwing the bolt and stepping back as a poorly clad man came inside and closed the door behind him.

"Pablo," Papa said, and ushered the man into the kitchen, rather than the *sala*, telling Catalina volumes about his modest status. Of course, the kitchen was still warmer.

Papa did not indicate that he required her presence, but Catalina tagged along anyway. Nothing ever happened in her life, so the prospect of an unexpected late-night visitor intrigued her. Enough hot water remained in the iron pot inside the fireplace, so she made him a drink of watered-down wine.

"What brings you here so late, Pablo?" Papa asked.

"Papa, who is—"

"Oh, my manners! Catalina, Pablo cleans the offices in our wing of the governor's palace. Pablo, this is my daughter, Señorita Ygnacio."

The servant ducked his head in subservience, and returned his attention to Papa. "*Señor*, I overheard something tonight."

Papa tsked with his tongue. "Pablo, it's not wise to carry tales from the governor's palace. Your exaggerations have gotten you in trouble before."

"Please hear me!" the man exclaimed. "I didn't come all this way, avoiding lantern lighters and thugs, to waste your time."

"Very well," Papa said, putting up a hand to calm the man. "Tell me your news." He looked at Catalina, but she was seated by now, too.

"*Señor*, you know I work late cleaning the office."

"You do a fine job, Pablo," Papa said. "Señor Moreno is the governor's chief *contador*," he told his daughter. "I, uh, believe you know his daughter, Maria Tomasa."

She did, and made a face.

"What happened?" Papa asked.

"Remember this afternoon, when your office partner dropped that box of pens? He told me to pick them up after he left. I crawled under his desk to look." He darted a quick glance at Catalina. "We can trust her?"

"She is my daughter!" Papa exclaimed. "You need not fear, Pablo, and the hour is late. Tell me."

"While I was under the desk, I heard someone next door with Señor Moreno, who spoke first. 'I can solve your problem, Miguel,' he said."

"Miguel?" Papa asked.

"You know. The young man who shows up there now and then. I believe he is trying to get a position in your department."

Papa nodded. "He is newly affianced to Señorita Maria Tomasa Moreno." He turned to Catalina. "That one."

Don't remind me, Catalina thought. Tomasa Moreno was stuck up, silly, and condescending. Theirs was a mere nodding acquaintance, which was precisely the way Catalina wanted it, after watching Tomasa slap a servant around for dropping a hairbrush. "She had an older sister who married a man from Valle del Sol, didn't she? I believe they all died in a smallpox epidemic," Catalina said. "There was someone else: a servant girl who stole money and ran away."

"I am not certain how much to believe about that tale," Papa said. He shrugged. "It was four or five years ago."

He returned his attention to Pablo. "I know the man you speak of. His name is Miguel Valencia, and he took it badly when the governor himself assured him that there were no openings in the accounting department."

"The very one," Pablo said. He cleared his throat. "Only a half hour ago, I heard Señor Moreno assure Miguel Valencia you would never return alive from Valle del Sol, and that your position would become his." He sat back with something resembling relief, now that the bad news was someone else's burden.

Catalina reached for Papa's hand. "He would *do* this?"

Poor Papa. He had turned so pale. "I believe he would do anything to accomplish his goals, my dear." To Pablo, he said, "What else did you hear?"

"They both laughed, as though it was a good joke. Someone slapped someone on the back and I heard the *contador principal* say, 'Never you worry about who will do the deed. The less you know, the better.' Then they left the office."

"Did anyone see you leave?" Papa asked, his voice soft, as if spies might be lurking behind the cistern.

"Oh, no!" Pablo declared, pounding on his chest. "I stayed still as a mouse until everyone was gone. Then I came here."

"You were brave, Pablo. I can't think of anyone else who would have bothered."

"You stood up for me when all that ink was spilled in the oak cabinet," the servant said quietly. "I didn't do it."

"I know, Pablo, I know," Papa assured the fellow. "Now I think you had better leave us as quietly as you came, to be safe."

Señor Ygnacio walked with Pablo to the front door. Catalina heard the bolt slam into place. Back in the kitchen, Papa sat down heavily.

Silence claimed the room for a long while. Catalina finally asked, "What can we do?" She wanted to sound calm and rational, but her voice shook.

After another long silence, Papa shrugged. "Go to Valle del Sol when the passes are open," he said. "Knowing the *contador* as I do—*hay caramba*, what a man!—he won't strike until the audit is done."

"We go to Valle del Sol?" Catalina asked. "That's *all*?"

"Yes, when the passes are open. Let us hope someone will help us in that godforsaken place."

Chapter Two

In which the Mondragóns receive a sweet reward for last summer's fooling about

Abril, 1785

"SANCHA, MAY I HAVE a warm blanket for Paloma?" Marco asked from the foot of their bed, where the smiling midwife was tidying up his wife. "She's shaking."

The same thing had happened after Claudito's birth nearly three years ago. Eckapeta had put a piece of sagebrush between Paloma's breasts to remedy the shakes. Eckapeta was not here this time, but Marco was nearly certain the warm blanket was preferable to sagebrush for calming his wife and putting her to sleep.

When Sancha returned with the promised blanket, Marco sat in the chair next to the bed, holding Paloma while another servant replaced stained sheets with clean ones. He kissed Paloma's cheek and put her back in bed, standing aside for Sancha to apply the warmth Paloma craved.

Paloma's sigh of relief melted his already tender heart. Marco looked away to regard his newest son, who gazed back at him with what appeared to be considerable interest.

You have such old eyes, son, Marco thought, enchanted with this new arrival, who came into the world quietly, compared to Claudito. He seemed content to observe his new surroundings in silence.

"May I pick him up?" Marco asked the midwife, who nodded and stepped back respectfully, her work done.

Father and son regarded each other solemnly. To Marco's further delight, the baby's eyes were dark blue, like his mother's beautiful eyes, half closed now as she snuggled down into the warmth.

Careful to hold his son's head, Marco rested the baby against his shoulder and enjoyed the peculiar fragrance of an infant newly eased from the womb. He knew the scent would fade soon, never to return. Amazing how a bit of afternoon fun near the hayfield last summer had led to a new person, bone of his and Paloma's bones and flesh of their flesh.

He perched on the edge of the bed and held their son closer to Paloma, whose eyes opened, her interest overruling her exhaustion. Without a word, she made a crook of her arm and he placed the baby with his mother.

Her free hand went to her buttons and stopped there; she was too tired. "Could you?" she asked. He obliged her by unbuttoning her nightgown and spreading the fabric away from her shoulder and breast. With practiced fingers, Paloma held her nipple close to the baby's cheek and brushed it until he turned his head and latched on.

She lay back with a sigh that went straight to Marco's heart as their son nursed, with the instinct of all newly birthed creatures. Marco smiled when *chiquito* patted his mama's breast, his little fingers digging in.

"He looks like you, my heart," Marco said, his face close to Paloma's. He kissed her and she returned his kiss with more fervor that he would have thought she possessed, considering her long night's work. He whispered, "Paloma, how do I break this to you? Too much of this causes babies."

She laughed softly, the intimate laugh uniquely hers that he had heard many times, and God willing, would hear many more. The Lord had been good to them both.

If it were June or July, the sky would already be light. Since it was barely April, their bedroom was still cloaked in shadows. The midwife and her apprentice had left. Sancha made the sign of the cross over them and left, too, closing the door behind her.

"Get in bed," Paloma said. "Let's share this wonderful blanket."

It took him no time to shuck his moccasins and pull off the breeches he had yanked on so quickly when Paloma had awakened him before midnight and told him to fetch the midwife. He surrendered to the mattress and the warmth and the love that surrounded the three of them. Claudito had been born in the middle of the day; this was better.

"You know, you could request a warm blanket anytime you want," he said to his wife, who was examining their son's fingers. He remembered his dear Felicia counting the fingers and toes of their twins, as if she had a mental list of what a baby should arrive equipped with, and would not be satisfied until she completed the inventory.

"I know I could, but I think of this warm blanket as my reward for a job well done."

They lay close together, Marco adding his warmth to the blanket, until his wife stopped shivering. Practiced himself, Marco took their son from her slack arm when he started to move about restlessly. He raised him to his shoulder for a burp, which came out so emphatic that the baby jerked in surprise, his eyes wide open.

"You'll get used to it, *mijo*," Paloma told her new son. "Soon you will make as many noises as your father and brother, and Soledad and I will have no peace."

"Paloma, you slander us," Marco teased back. "I know I warned you about cooked onions even before we married."

He handed back their son and settled him in her other arm. More experienced now, the little fellow went right to work. His quiet suck put a half-smile on Paloma's face. She closed her eyes and her head drifted toward Marco's shoulder. In a moment, she slept, weary of labor and content to be warm.

Marco stood the watch, his eyes on the dearest wife a man could have and this new child of theirs, who had found his way into the Mondragón family. For now, his cradle would occupy a spot close to the corner fireplace. Perhaps Claudito and this newest arrival, small but a brother, could occupy the room across the hall recently vacated by Marco's brother-in-law Claudio Vega and new wife Graciela. They were finally in residence on the old land grant belonging to Soledad's father and mother, who had died of smallpox.

A house for Claudio and Graci had been started immediately, to replace the one he and Toshua had burned to the ground to avoid contagion. The mild winter meant construction went faster than usual, freeing up the bedchamber across the hall.

To think there had been a time when Marco had walked the halls of his house alone, groaning in grief and wondering if he would ever recover from the shocking loss of Felicia and the twins to cholera. Now his house overflowed with children. *God is good*, he thought, as he closed his eyes, too.

He woke before Paloma and slid out of bed carefully, determined not to interrupt her hard-earned slumber. The baby slept, too, so Marco picked him up, touched as Paloma's fingers tightened around her son in what had to be a reflexive movement, because her eyes remained closed. He carried their baby to his cradle, the one Soledad had used first, and then Claudito, and laid him down.

Hands on hips, he stood there looking down at what he and Paloma had created. "Juan Luis," he whispered. "For my little brother, gone these many years. Juanito." He made the sign of the cross over the infant, then tiptoed to the *reclinatorio*, where he knelt and prayed. When he finished, he closed the door behind him and walked to the kitchen.

Her eyes bright with happiness, Perla *la cocinera* put before him well-frothed hot chocolate along with a bowl of mush and chilis, which she followed with anise bread slathered with butter.

Sancha and her husband Lorenzo came into the kitchen through the door that led to the kitchen garden.

"Fair morning, you two," Marco said, feeling shy about the recent birth. Everyone in the earthy colony of New Mexico knew where babies came from, but he had never been one to brag about his obvious fertility.

Trust Lorenzo, that newly reformed horse thief—redeemed by Sancha's love—to make mention. "*Señor!* Two sons now! Such prowess." He laughed. "Sancha tells me that your first wife—God rest her—gave you twin sons. Has no one ever written *una canción* about the stallion of Valle del Sol?"

"Lorenzo, enough," Marco said, grateful he and Paloma had told no one of his Kwahadi name, Big Man Down There. "We have been blessed and that is sufficient."

Sancha gave her husband a good-natured shove while he laughed and tried to shield himself from her harmless blows. Marco watched them, pleased—and relieved—that Lorenzo had remained true to his promise not to thieve or steal anyone's livestock. Even Emilio, Marco's *mayor domo*, had to admit that the man had become an exemplary stockman.

He was useful in other ways, too. "Lorenzo, would you go to the presidio and see if there is any official mail for me?"

A year ago, Lorenzo wouldn't have ventured near a presidio unless forced. Now his herder looked up and nodded. "I'll go now," he said and touched his finger to his forehead.

"Sancha, your husband is no longer a rascal," Marco teased, after Lorenzo blew a kiss and left the kitchen. "I hope you still love him anyway."

Sancha pinked up and shook her finger at him. They sat in mutual friendship, discussing the day's plans, which included keeping little Soledad, four years old now, and Claudito, nine months younger, from disturbing their mother's needed rest. "You let the children look, then I'll keep Soli occupied," Sancha said. "If you send Claudito to the horse barn, Emilio will do the same. What will you do?"

She knew him well, and had every right to ask. "Look in on my dear ones now and then, and try to clean up the mess that used to be my desk."

"And try to stay awake yourself?" she asked gently. "*Señor,* if there is a better husband and father than you, I can't imagine where he is to be found."

God forgive him for allowing his emotions to be so close to the surface this day. Marco wiped his eyes and said nothing, which made Sancha get to her feet and touch his shoulder, a liberty she had only begun to take after the death of his first family. She gave him a little shake, then went about her duties.

Hearing his children speaking in loud whispers, he joined them in the hall in front of the closed door. He knelt beside them, Soledad—the daughter of his heart but actually his wife's cousin—and Claudito, the child he and Paloma thought they would never have.

"Your mama had a baby early this morning."

"A sister for me?" Soledad asked hopefully.

"Ah, no. Will another brother do?" he asked, pleased when her arm went around his neck. *Por dios*, he loved this child.

Soli gave him a wry look, which turned quite serious, because that was Soledad. "Next time it must be a sister for me."

"There is never a guarantee, *mija*," he said. "You will come to love this little Juan Luis."

"He'll play in the *acequia* with me and I'll teach him stuff," Claudito declared.

"We'll give him a little time to be a baby before he does that," Marco replied. He stood up and opened the door. "Be very quiet. Your mama is worn out because having babies isn't easy."

He took their hands and walked them to the bed, where Paloma was starting to open her eyes. How did she do it? He knew how tired she was, how she had clutched him during the delivery, and here she was, her smile as radiant as any he had ever seen. She patted the bed and Claudito, with Marco's gentle caution, climbed carefully into her arms.

"Soli, you and Papa go to the cradle and see if your new brother is awake."

He kept Soli's hand in his until they reached the cradle. Soledad knelt by the cradle and looked into Juan Luis's wide-open eyes.

"*Hola, hermano*," she said softly as she touched his cheek. "You will like it here."

Ay de mi! His traitor eyes! Marco hadn't bothered to tuck in his shirt, so he used it to wipe away his tears and reflect on the reality that he was turning into a soft old man.

"Is he awake, my love?" Paloma asked.

"Yes, and probably hungry," Marco said, pleased to have a task that he enjoyed. He picked up Juanito, breathed in that new-baby fragrance again and brought him to his mother, who was already unbuttoning her nightgown. In another moment, their son was nursing quietly while his brother and sister watched.

"Does he get lots and lots?" Soli asked.

Paloma nodded. "Lots and lots." She touched Soledad's hair. "Have Papa brush your hair and tie it back with a ribbon, then see if you can help Sancha today." She tugged playfully on Claudito's ear. "I imagine Papa will find something for you to do involving baby animals. He is good at that."

Marco blew her a kiss as he led their little family from the bedroom. In the nick of time Sancha saved him by brushing and braiding Soli's hair herself. Once the children were fed, he took Claudito to the horse barn, where Emilio had a bum lamb to feed.

Marco watched a moment, then went to his office next to the horse barn, the free-standing building that his friends Toshua and Eckapeta shared when they visited.

He stood in the doorway, missing his Comanche friends, who had been away most of the winter. Their sleeping bundles were stowed neatly by the fireplace, put there by Eckapeta, who was as tidy as Sancha, although he would never share this observation with his housekeeper.

Marco leaned against the doorframe, wondering when Eckapeta would appear. The Comanche woman knew roughly when Paloma was due, and Marco had witnessed her territoriality as far as Soli and Claudito were concerned.

"And what about you, Toshua?" he said out loud as he shut the door and sat at his desk. During a brief solo visit after Christmas, Eckapeta had told him that the Kwahadi and many Comanche tribal leaders to the east had gathered in Palo Duro Canyon to discuss the idea of a treaty with the royal colony of New Mexico.

Marco leaned back in his chair and thought of the last five years when he and others on the frontier had done their cautious diplomatic *paso doble*, hoping for just that. Maybe this would be the year, maybe not.

He turned his attention to the paper on his desk. Within a minute, he rested his head on his arms and slept.

Chapter Three

In which the Mondragóns need to remember just who is listening

"S*EÑOR? SEÑOR?*"

Marco opened his eyes and sat up, his hand going immediately to his back. *I want my own bed*, he thought as he stood up and stretched and winced. "*Entra, por favor*," he said.

Lorenzo crossed the threshold, but not before taking a careful look around to make sure no Comanches were in residence.

"You should be at peace with Toshua," Marco replied, amused. "You cannot deny that he saved us last year when we attacked Great Owl with our minuscule army."

"I will *always* check first," the reformed horse thief said with a smile.

"I am expecting Eckapeta any time, though," Marco told him. "She has a sixth sense about babies."

"I'll look out for her," Lorenzo assured him.

"You'll never see her," Marco said and laughed. "Nor will I. I only hope she doesn't embarrass me by sitting by the cradle some early morning in my very own bedroom, and I none the wiser. Do you have letters for me?"

Lorenzo handed over the battered pouch. "Lieutenant Gasca sends his greetings and congratulations on the birth of your son. Says he will be around soon to see for himself."

Once he was alone again, Marco checked his timepiece, amazed that he had slept a major portion of the day away. He picked up his official correspondence and hurried from his office, his conscience smarting because he had promised Paloma he would check on her.

The kitchen was empty and a cosmic thumb and forefinger smacked his skull. He had promised Paloma she could rest. Where would the children be, but with her?

He opened their bedroom door quietly and peeked inside. All was quiet and orderly. Soli looked up from the end of their bed, where she sat cross-legged, playing with her dolls, and put her finger to her lips.

Pillows behind her, Paloma slept, with Claudito cuddled against her thigh, his eyes closed, too. Relieved, Marco glanced at the cradle to see Juan Luis bright-eyed and wide awake. Happy for a chance to hold the little one, he went to the cradle and picked up his son, who stared at him through crossed eyes. In another moment he was nestled in a tidy package against Marco's chest.

Marco eased himself down on the floor at the end of the bed, close to Soli. "Thank you for watching everyone so diligently," he whispered to the child who had captured his heart the moment he held her four years ago. "I look at Juan Luis and I look at you, and suddenly you seem so much older than you did yesterday, before Juanito came. Why is that?"

Soledad gave him an indulgent glance. "We are all growing up, Papa."

"Don't grow up too fast."

Content to sit there holding his newest child, he thought of his own childhood, so much of it spent in terror of Comanches and Apaches. He recalled long nights under the chapel floor, waiting for the Comanche Moon to set. And here sat Soledad, knowing little of such terror, although she had spent a few nights below ground herself.

He looked down at his son, who continued to regard him as though memorizing his face. "*Ojalá, mijo*, you will never know such days," he whispered.

PALOMA WOKE SLOWLY, HER leg extra warm where her son Claudito still nestled in slumber. She raised up slightly to see Soli, and then her husband's broad shoulders as father and daughter chatted together. A glance toward the empty cradle told her precisely in whose capable arms her son was cuddled. Her womb contracted painfully, but she knew the ache would pass, as would the soreness between her legs, since babies came out the same way they went in.

She touched her breasts, which were already beginning to swell. By tomorrow, she would be engorged with milk, and Juan Luis would get the surprise of his young life. She would be milky and sticky, and not the wife of any man's dreams, except Marco never said that. "I love you however," he said simply, the first time they made love after Claudito, and her milk came in at a most inopportune time. She smiled at the memory, grateful for a flexible man. She could probably even get him to change a diaper.

"Marco, is he wet? The diapers are in the chest by the cradle."

Her husband looked over his shoulder. "So is my shirt, but I didn't want to bother him."

He kissed Jan Luis on the top of his head before laying him down next to Soledad. The diapering followed, promptly and professionally, all the time her breasts began to yearn for the infant. In another moment Juanito latched onto her nipple.

Marco lay beside her, sharing her pillow, as Claudito slumbered on and Soledad returned to her dolls. "I was going to spend only a few minutes in my office, but I slept half the day away," he confessed. "Some champion I am!"

"You were awake all night, too," Paloma pointed out.

Marco took off his wet shirt and found a dry one. He came back to bed with his correspondence, which he rested on his chest as he lay down. Picking up a letter with a heavy seal, he snapped it.

"From our esteemed governor," he told her, and held it open. He read quickly. "He is wondering if I know anything about the Comanches gathering to discuss peace."

"Eckapeta will tell us when she arrives," Paloma said. "She will be here soon."

"Tonight?" he asked, putting the letter aside.

"Would you be surprised?" she questioned in turn.

He shook his head and went to the next letter, this one with a seal she was more familiar with, even though it still made prickles run down her back. She had seen this seal often enough in her uncle's house in Santa Fe.

"It is from *el contador principal*, your favorite uncle." As he read, he swore under his breath. "Flowery words! And here at the bottom, as I expected, the seven-year audit."

She put Juanito to her shoulder for a burp. "I recall curses and a cuff or two from my uncle during the days when he was organizing his minions to make those audits. Every year, different ones went to different districts."

"It's our turn. He is sending Fernando Ygnacio."

Back went Juanito to the other breast. "Wake up, little man," she crooned, flicking the bottom of his feet with gentle fingers. "Don't fail me now. Ah, there."

Her husband was still looking at the letter. "Odd. He doesn't call him Don Fernando, or even Señor Fernando, just … Fernando." He folded the letter and searched through the remaining messages until he came to another one with the same seal. "Here is a letter from Señor Ygnacio himself. Or is it?" He read the letter. "No, it is from his daughter, Catalina, stating that she will accompany her father, and that she requires no special favors."

Paloma's eyes had started to close. At the mention of Catalina, she opened them. "Let me see that," she said, and took the letter from him before he could hand it over. " 'I will accompany my father, as I have through many audits. All I ask is a place to sleep that is safe.'" She handed back the letter. "Marco, I know her."

"Good or bad?"

Paloma shrugged. "Hard to tell, but I can say this: Señor Ygnacio is a meek little man dogged by years of misfortune." She sighed. "His daughter has been forced to bear it with him."

"You have met her?"

Paloma was silent, remembering a shy girl a little older than her. "Only once, and we were never introduced. She was quiet and my cousins Teresa and Tomasa were rude."

"Why?"

"A few weeks earlier, my uncle announced that Mexico City was sending him a miserable felon who had served five years in prison for accounting errors he never could explain," Paloma said. She lay back, trying to recall the details from a time long ago. "When his prison term ended, he was ordered to Santa Fe to work for the rest of his life."

"One would think five years in prison would be enough."

"Not when you misplace government money, or so the story went," Paloma told him. "Poor man! He came to the house to present a paper of some sort to my uncle. Uncle sent Catalina into the courtyard where his daughters were sitting." She closed her eyes, remembering. "I watched from the shadow as they teased her about her father. Danced around her and poked her. Poor thing. I wanted to do something, but we know how little power I had in that household."

"Yet another reason to wish your uncle to perdition," Marco said.

"Perdition? Where is that?"

Paloma looked down to see Soledad watching them. "Little ears," she whispered to Marco, then held out her hand to Soli, who came closer. "It is a bad place for people who are unkind to others," she told her cousin, the granddaughter of Felix Moreno, the worst man she knew.

"Mama, you look so sad."

"I have never liked watching bullies hurt people who have committed no offense," Paloma said.

"You know bad people?" Soli asked in surprise.

"Very few, and they are far away," she replied, grateful again that Marco had made certain her uncle would never know that Soledad was the surviving child of his daughter Teresa. She rested her hand on Marco's knee. "All the people I know in Valle del Sol are good."

"Sometimes I am not kind to Claudito," Soledad admitted. "I won't go to perdition, will I?"

Oh, heavens, Paloma thought. *We must be more careful.* "When Claudito tries your patience, what do we do?"

"I sit quietly in the *sala*," Soledad said, "and you remind me to be kind."

"When Claudito is unkind to you?"

"He sits in the *sala*, and you remind him," Soli told her with a smile, "and then we forget and play together."

"Exactly. Over and done." She thought about her uncle. "Sadly, some people never forget a wrong, Soli."

"They are never happy?"

"Never, my love. Never."

She glanced at Marco, who was beginning to doze off. Soledad, her eyes bright, put her hands up to catch the official correspondence dropping from his hands. She wrinkled her nose at Paloma, who wrinkled her nose back, pleased with her almost-daughter.

"You know your face will stick like that if you keep it up," Paloma heard from the doorway, followed by an after-the-fact tap on the frame.

"Claudio!" Paloma said, as Marco stirred and looked around. "Come see our latest Mondragón!"

Her brother Claudio Vega came to her bed, kissed her forehead and nodded at Juan Luis, sound asleep.

"Good work, Sister," he whispered. "I'll be quiet so I don't wake up this *juez de campo* who needs a shave and looks so undignified."

Marco chuckled as Paloma patted her side of the bed, inviting her brother to sit down. Watching his dear face, which bore such a resemblance to their father's, she wondered if she would ever tire of seeing the brother she had thought dead for so many years, married now and living on his own land grant close by.

"Paloma, you're looking at me all sentimental," he teased, as he touched her little one, smiling when Juanito's hand grasped his little finger.

"Can't help it," she admitted. "I am surrounded by tender mercies."

She asked after Graciela, who was getting closer to confinement with their own baby, and lay back to listen as her brother and husband, awake now, discussed new calves and the endless lambing going on now. The talk turned to a quick visit to Presidio Santa Maria. She closed her eyes with gratitude at the new life in her arms, and the family talk swirling around her.

She thought of her uncle Felix Moreno. *No, Soledad. Some people are never happy. We are, though.*

Chapter Four

In which Joaquim receives his own letter and wonders

I T IS A GREAT pity that a man in power sometimes finds himself with less time to do what he wants. Or so El Teniente Joaquim Gasca, *capitán* of Presidio Santa Maria, had quickly discovered when his lieutenancy was restored last fall and the presidio at Santa Maria handed to him like the prize it wasn't.

He complained to Marco, who assured him it wouldn't hurt him to set a good example and spend less time mooning over women. Joaquim could have asked, "How would *you* manage without Paloma?" but he knew better. After their nearly foolhardy expedition to rid the world of Great Owl, Joaquim knew Marco's heart. If ever a man deserved a comfortable, intelligent wife, it was Marco Mondragón.

"Your turn will come," Marco had told him.

If Joaquim wanted to blame someone for his new status—he had gone from lowly private to commanding officer—he could point to Marco alone. After the death of Great Owl last fall, the *juez de campo* had insisted Joaquim accompany him on a quick trip to Santa Fe. Joining them also was Claudio Vega, Paloma's long-lost brother, as a claimant to the open Castellano land grant vacated by the smallpox deaths of Alonso Castellano and his wife Maria Teresa.

Joaquim couldn't help but be impressed with Marco Mondragón's reception by Governor Juan Bautista de Anza. With admirable aplomb, Marco had set Great Owl's scalp on the governor's desk and leaned the renegade's lance against the wall. When Marco finished his narrative, Joaquim found himself a lieutenant of the royal engineers again, and commanding officer of a faulty, shabby presidio in the worst part of New Mexico. He couldn't have been more pleased.

He still was, mainly because Governor Anza gave him full rein, plus ten more troops, to turn the sow's ear into a silk purse. Anza included a small bonus that Marco augmented without saying a word. The coins were enough to pay for materials to whitewash the inside of the presidio and burn sulfur to fumigate it. Daring him to object, Paloma had a Tewa servant weave a rug and two blankets for his spartan quarters. He hesitated over a similar rug in his office, wondering if it was military, but succumbed when she gave him her hard stare.

He mentioned that stare to Marco later, over wine in his quarters. "The first time she did that to me, I never again forgot to pick up my clothes from the bedroom floor," Marco said and they laughed together.

I could use someone like Paloma in my life. The thought had been filtering through his brain all winter, as he trained his raw and stupid troops into something resembling soldiers. He did not envy Marco—not too much—because he knew that was folly. The more he saw Paloma and Marco together, the more he wanted a marriage like theirs, and not an endless cycle of women. That habit had only gotten him in trouble in garrisons from La Havana to St. Augustine to Mexico City, putting him at his lowest ebb ever, broken down to private and living in Santa Maria.

He had cemented himself firmly to his men by sitting down with them in the mess hall—unheard of in a commander—and telling them precisely what he intended. He assured the men who knew him from his earlier devil-may-care days that those times were over. He told the soldiers new to the presidio about his former life, minimizing none of his sins and misdemeanors. He told them they would train together and become the best presidio in all of Carlos the Third's New World possessions.

He noted the men who shook their heads, and those who nodded them, which allowed him to focus on the skeptical. Joaquim was a Catalonian, and therefore too great a realist to suppose everyone would see things his way. He surprised himself. By the time the meadowlark was heard in Valle del Sol, a reminder of spring coming, he saw improvement.

He walked into the presidio's courtyard, remembering with painful clarity his first glimpse of the shabby place. At the time, he had been forcefully reminded of how small the simple square fort was, with offices, barracks, mess hall, garrison chapel, storerooms, and artisan's shops lining each interior wall.

The fort hadn't grown any; it was still a miniscule display of Spanish might on the edge of the vastly more powerful Comanche domain. Even last year, it would not have surprised him if Indians had overwhelmed the presidio and Santa Maria and called it a job well done before noon.

Now he wasn't so certain. His men were alert and able, steadily walking the terreplein as he knew Marco's servants and personal guards did at the Double Cross. True, there were only two small cannon, but each was ready, and between the two of them could be aimed at any intruder. As the cannoneers said, at least they made a damned noisy impression.

He looked at the red and gold flag snapping in the stiff wind and felt a level of pride that had begun with Marco Mondragón's ridiculously tiny but determined army of three—augmented by a handful of fierce Utes—that had set out to destroy Great Owl, renegade, troublemaker and all-around nasty man.

"We claim this in the name of Spain," Joaquim said softly, and meant it.

Nodding to his men on duty, Joaquim strolled across the courtyard and up the stairs to the terreplein, that top deck where his men stood guard. He walked to the southwest bastion and looked toward the not-so-distant Sangre de Cristo mountains, towering and purple in the afternoon sun.

It was about time for him to visit the Double Cross, preferably near dinner, and see the newest Mondragón Lorenzo had mentioned. The thought happily coincided with the sight of two horsemen coming from that direction.

He watched as they materialized into Marco himself and Claudio Vega, Paloma's brother. Both men carried lances, of course, and Marco had slung his bow over his shoulder as usual. Joaquim compared the sight before him to earlier, more perilous times, when no one dared travel alone or by twos. He wondered where Toshua was, and even Eckapeta, realizing how much he also liked them.

Someone—he couldn't remember who—had told him, probably in jest, that Valle del Sol had a way of working on a needy person lacking friendship, or courage, or any number of admirable traits. He had scoffed at the time, but El Teniente Joaquim Gasca didn't doubt it now. There was an empty spot in his heart, but only there. He watched his friends approach with a feeling close to joy. The amazing part to him was that he still recognized the emotion.

He stood a while longer, elbows on the parapet, arms dangling over, so casual because there was no current danger. He watched his friends approach, then waved when they were close enough to see him. Clambering down the stairs, he stood by the slowly opening gate to receive them. One of his earliest orders had been to keep the gates closed always, and only to open them upon recognition or password.

Marco handed Joaquim his lance before he dismounted, the lance from old Kwihnai that Governor Anza had returned to him last fall. The *juez de campo* grasped his friend in a warm *abrazo*.

"Good news from my world, although I know you have already heard,"

Marco said into his ear as he pummeled his back. "Paloma was brought to bed with another son. God has blessed us."

Giving a friendly nod to Claudio Vega, Joaquim walked arm in arm with Marco as the three of them let the horses be led away and headed for his office.

Marco looked around appreciatively. "I obviously haven't been here in a while," the *juez de campo* said as he removed his cape. "And look here ... Paloma's rug!"

"You told me I had better accept it," Joaquim reminded his guest.

"You are wise beyond your years," Marco said, his eyes lively.

"*Al contrario, amigo,*" Joaquim said. "Sometimes I come in here early in the morning with bare feet, just because it feels good. Wine?"

Both his guests nodded, and he poured small amounts into three goblets, wine gifted to him from Santa Maria's cobbler and occasional winemaker, who had a daughter of marriageable age.

Small talk seemed in order, so he turned his attention to Claudio. In Joaquim's estimation, Paloma's brother had changed this winter, too, from a suspicious, tight-lipped man who rode with horse thieves to a contented husband. Joaquim had attended Claudio's wedding to Graciela Tafoya, the part-Ute former Comanche slave. The man's eyes were calm now, his hair cut and combed, his entire demeanor relaxed. Joaquim thought again of Valle del Sol's magic.

"And you, sir, I hear you have a house of your own, and cattle."

Claudio glanced at his brother-in-law, and the look was most affectionate. "Indeed we do. The land grant is now in the Vega name, and I am again using the Star in the Meadow brand of our father—Paloma's and mine."

Joaquim nodded. "That is entirely as it should be," he said politely, wondering why they had come.

He hadn't long to wait. Marco reached into his doublet. "Here is the reason for our visit. Read it."

Joaquim did, then handed it back. "You know I am a royal engineer, without much understanding of district policy. A seven-year audit is typical?"

"Most typical," Marco said. "My records are up to date, with a few exceptions from some *rancheros* who never tell me the truth, and a pair of total idiots I will continue to ignore as long as I can."

Joaquim chuckled at that. "Every district has them."

"These two are more stupid than most," Marco said. "As for the audit, I am a little surprised by the inclusion of the *contador*'s daughter. She sent us a separate letter announcing she could come, too."

Joaquim reached behind him to his desk, where he found his own letter with the governor's seal. "I received my own letter from Santa Fe regarding the audit. Apparently I am to have one soldier from the presidio sit with the *contador* and make sure you do not threaten or try to bribe him."

Marco nodded, his expression merry. "Especially threats! I don't know if the auditor will come here first, or to the Double Cross. We're on the way, so we'll likely see them before you do."

"This extra note might surprise you." Joaquim reached behind him again for a smaller letter. "It's from … from la Señorita Catalina Maria Ygnacio. I don't know what her game is."

Marco read the note, frowned, then handed it back. "Paloma knows the auditor's daughter, and something of the man's history, which I will tell you before we leave this afternoon." He tapped the letter in Joaquim's hand. "This puts a new complexion on their visit, eh?"

"We'll find out when the mountain passes between here and Santa Fe open and disgorge a *contador* and his daughter," Joaquim said.

"Death threats, she says? *Dios mio*, this man is an accountant. Can you imagine anyone less likely to bring drama and death threats along with his quill pens and double entries?"

The men laughed at Marco's joke. "And I thought living here on the edge of Comanchería was enough danger," Claudio said and rolled his eyes. "At least we are not accountants, too!"

Chapter Five

In which Catalina worries,
something she does well

As much as she loved her father, Catalina Ygnacio wondered how much longer she could continue to travel with him. She seemed to have no other prospects, so the answer brought no joy: forever.

Two weeks ago, the passes opened between Santa Fe and points farther east. That meant they'd had no choice but to go about the Crown's business, even if it came with a threat. Catalina wondered if she had been wise to slip that little note in with the letter bound for the commanding officer of Santa Maria's presidio, but it was too late to retrieve it. She was used to having her fears ignored or mocked, so she knew a skeptical look from El Teniente Gasca would roll off her back.

They had left Santa Fe in late March and endured two weeks of hard travel to arrive at this point, where they gazed upon a view of the sun-speckled valley wide open to distant Texas.

A view is only a view, though. For two weeks, she had watched the four-soldier escort, wondering which one would suddenly strike her father dead, once the audit was done, and kill her as well.

She discounted the coachman of the shabby carriage with the royal crest on the door, a silent mestizo who continually hummed the same five notes under his breath, when he wasn't hawking and spitting through the spaces in his teeth. From sheer boredom she had tried to talk to him once, and got no response. "*Tanto*," one of the soldiers told her, as he spun his forefinger beside his ear.

Each night when they made camp, she longed for them to get where they were going, even if it was to the edge of danger this time. Maybe someone would help them, she reasoned, then reminded herself that no one had ever helped them before.

By the time they finally left the last pass and enjoyed the sight of Valle del Sol spread out before them, Catalina knew as much about this particular *juez de campo* as she ever had. Their audits had introduced them to many brand inspectors, some coarse and ill-equipped, others organized and efficient. The one quality they all possessed was a vast disdain for her father, whose sad story must be known from Santa Fe to Alta California.

She expected nothing better from Señor Mondragón, but she couldn't deny the more vulnerable part of herself that continued to hope. Maybe Papa knew of the man.

Papa merely shrugged. "All I know about Señor Mondragón is that some twelve years ago he succeeded his father as *juez de campo* and that he is efficient in his duties. Beyond that, he has done much to foster our current good relations with our noble friends, the Comanche."

Papa had a surprising sense of humor, considering all he had been through. *Noble*, indeed.

She was silent, wondering about their reception, and steeling herself for the worst. She liked it best when she was ignored and allowed to work silently with Papa, checking his numbers because he had lost all confidence in himself. She could immerse herself in numbers and documents and for a moment forget their precarious lives. It wasn't much to ask, and she did like numbers.

She sucked in her breath and gripped Papa's arm when the corporal in charge of the escort waved the driver to stop. Maybe he hadn't understood. Didn't he know that Felix Moreno wanted the audit done *before* their deaths?

Papa opened the door. "Yes, corporal?" he asked, without a single quaver in his voice. Sometimes Papa was positively brave.

"We will be at the Double Cross soon. We could go on to the presidio and Santa Maria, but they are probably expecting us here," the corporal said.

"Then we will remain here."

Interested, despite her fear as they approached each new assignment, Catalina admired the solid stone walls. The guards who had been pacing as they approached had stopped, lances ready. She knew this was no place anyone, good or bad, would be able to approach unannounced, which reassured her.

She noticed a tall man standing next to a guard. He gestured to the corporal, who waved back. The gates opened and soon they were inside a spacious courtyard. As she watched, the tall man came down the stairway, a child riding on his hip. He came close to their dirty, shabby carriage and she saw his welcoming smile.

"Do you think he knows who we are?" she whispered to her father, who looked as surprised as she felt.

"I don't know," he whispered back.

The man opened the door and let down the step. Catalina admired his light brown eyes. The boy in his arms had similar eyes—father and son, no doubt.

"Welcome to the Double Cross," he said. "I am Marco Mondragón and you must be Señor Ygnacio and … and …."

"Catalina Ygnacio," she said, in her most business-like voice.

"Oh, yes. The letter said there would be two of you for the audit," he replied. He set down his son and pointed him in the direction of the hacienda. "Go to Mama." He helped Papa from the carriage, then held his hand out for Catalina to step down. "Our house is your house," he said most formally. These were words she had never heard before, coming from a man waiting to be audited, a man who surely knew of Papa's past.

He spoke to the soldiers and gestured to an older man with a bunch of keys at his belt who must be the *mayor domo*. "Soldiers, Emilio will show you to the stable and the wagon yard, and then your quarters. Mind you, it's nothing fancy, but you will be comfortable and the food is good."

Señor Mondragón turned to Papa. "Now let us find you what is surely a softer bed than that carriage." He regarded the ramshackle conveyance with some disdain. "One would think Governor Anza capable of providing better transportation."

I am certain he is, Catalina thought, *but Señor Moreno prefers humiliating arrangements.* "Señor Moreno, chief *contador*, makes these arrangements," Catalina told him.

She nearly smiled at his wry expression and wondered if word had got out about how unpleasant the man could be.

"Señor Moreno? I should have known," Señor Mondragón replied. "In that case, I am surprised he did not make you ride a hobby horse."

Catalina laughed out loud, which startled Papa. Had it been that long since she had laughed in his presence?

A menacing man much like a pirate came from one of the large outbuildings and took their luggage from the back of the carriage.

"Thank you, Lorenzo," their host said. "Just set them in the hall."

Señor Mondragón must have noticed her expression. He gestured toward the man's retreating back. "Lorenzo was a horse thief and a scoundrel. He married Sancha, my housekeeper. I trust him now. In fact, I will send him for El Teniente Gasca. We have been expecting you." He called back the rough-looking fellow, who headed right for the horse barn.

Kindly anticipating that Papa would be stiff from all that time knocking about in a carriage, Señor Mondragón walked them slowly toward the house. He pointed out a small building standing by itself between what he said was the horse barn and the house. "My office," he said. "We will conduct the audit there, where you will be more comfortable. I'll move in a table so you can spread out my records easily."

Catalina glanced at her father, who stared back at her. She could almost hear him thinking, *When did anyone care about our comfort?* She blushed because Señor Mondragón must have seen the look that passed between them. He made no comment, choosing instead to talk about the length of the winter and the coming of spring. Hadn't they heard a meadowlark only yesterday?

Señor Mondragón deferred to an older woman with keys at her waist who met them at the door. "Sancha, please take Señor Ygnacio to his room, and I will take Señorita Ygnacio to meet my wife. We will eat in about an hour, so you may rest."

There was no mistaking Papa's bewildered look as Sancha led him down the hall. Señor Mondragón tapped on the door on the opposite side of the hall. "Paloma? Would you like to renew an acquaintance?"

What was Señor Mondragón talking about? Catalina followed him into a whitewashed room with colorful rugs and a massive Spanish wardrobe that seemed to fill half of one wall. The corner fireplace gave off welcome warmth, certainly for the benefit of the woman and baby seated close by.

"I fed him within an inch of his life, Marco," the woman said to her escort.

Charmed, Catalina watched as the *juez de campo*, a powerful man in any district, claimed his son and patted his back, obviously in expectation of a burp, which wasn't long in coming. A few more pats, another burp, and Señor Mondragón, like a well-seasoned father, settled his son in the cradle. It was homely duty she never expected from a man, and it charmed her.

He gestured toward the sleeping infant, and Catalina saw all the pride and love on his face. "Our son, Juan Luis. He is two weeks old."

He put his hand lightly on the woman's shoulder. By instinct it seemed, she inclined her cheek toward his hand. Catalina could have sighed with the loveliness of it, but she was long past such sentimentality.

"Señorita Ygnacio, let me introduce my wife, la Señora Paloma Vega y Mondragón."

Catalina turned her attention to the young woman in the chair, with her light brown hair and blue eyes lively with recognition, and wondered for only a few moments just where she had seen her before. It wasn't a pleasant memory—so few of her memories were pleasant—but ten years dropped away like a window struck by a hammer.

"I remember a courtyard and the *contador's* daughters teasing me about my father," Catalina said finally, the words coming out easier than she would have thought possible. How was it she could speak so freely with near-strangers? "You were there, too, weren't you, standing in the shadow, rubbing your arms."

Paloma Vega nodded. "I was there."

"I wondered why you didn't come to my aid," Catalina said quietly, unsure of herself, but compelled by some imp to say something.

"It would have been worse for me later," Paloma replied, her voice equally soft. She patted the chair beside her. "Sit with me."

Catalina sat and looked from Paloma to her husband, whose eyes were watchful. She could tell he would not allow anyone to slight his wife, not that she had any such plans. As she recalled the long-ago incident, Catalina did not remember there being any animosity in Paloma's eyes. There was certainly none now.

"I've sent Lorenzo for El Teniente Gasca," Señor Mondragón said. "It's not far, and he wants to hear your story. That way you need tell it only once."

Catalina's head went up. "I sent you a note, and I sent him one also, but it was different. He probably thinks I am crazy."

"Don't underestimate Joaquim Gasca," the *juez* told her, then turned to his wife. "My love, you should probably show our guest the chamber we have arranged for her." His face filled with apology. "We're crowded here, what with little ones, but we manage. Paloma?"

Paloma stood up carefully, with Marco's hand at her elbow. She wrinkled her nose at Catalina, who nearly smiled at the woman's charm. "This baby business! I am perfectly sound, Marco."

"I can give you a hand up if I feel like it," her husband replied, "and I do."

Paloma led the way down the hall, past the guest room. Catalina paused there and tapped lightly on the door. When no one answered, she peeked inside to see her father sound asleep.

"It is a long journey from Santa Fe," Catalina whispered to Paloma.

"Would you believe I thought I could make that trip in a mere few days and return a foolish pup to that man back there with the light brown eyes?" Paloma said as they continued walking. "I'll tell you the story some day. Here we are."

Paloma opened the door on a room both tiny and furnished with meticulous care. The colorful rag rug matched the one in Paloma's bedroom. There was a plump pillow at the head of the bed and no one had skimped on a mattress. Catalina suddenly wanted to lie down, too.

"I think Marco is making mental plans to enlarge our hacienda," Paloma said. "Hopefully this summer they will turn into physical plans." She opened the door wider and ushered Catalina inside. "At night, a servant will move in a charcoal brazier, so you will have to leave the door ajar to be safe from bad fumes."

"It's a lovely room," Catalina said, and meant it, thinking of the mean little spots allotted her because she insisted on going on Papa's audits with him. "I'll just lie down for a few minutes."

"Someone will tap on your door before supper," Paloma said. She touched Catalina's arm. "I am glad you are here. I have thought of you through the years, and truly, I wanted to help you that day." She shook her head. "They could be so mean."

Catalina nodded, happy for such a gentle reminder that matters weren't always as they seemed. Through the years, she had forgotten that.

After Paloma left the room, Catalina sighed and took off her shoes. She was about to unbutton her skirt when she heard a gasp in the hall.

Startled, she opened the door and peeked out to see Paloma Vega in the tight embrace of an Indian woman. Catalina held her breath in fear until she heard laughter from both women. She closed her door, thought a moment, and threw the bolt as quietly as she could.

"What kind of a place is this?" she asked herself.

Chapter Six

In which El Teniente Gasca decides to end any nonsense

ALTHOUGH LORENZO ASSURED HIM Señor Mondragón said his own arrival at the Double Cross could wait until tomorrow morning if he was busy, Joaquim Gasca's careful nature insisted he ride back with the herder.

Not that he believed a word of the frantic letter some overwrought daughter of a disgraced man had sent ahead. Better he show up tonight and put his own official stamp on whatever silliness this was. Besides, there was a new baby to admire, and maybe, for just the smallest moment—too small even for a careful husband to observe—he might pretend *he* was the lucky father.

Lately, he had been mulling over his matrimonial prospects and coming up short. If only there were a woman for him—not a once a week, occasional woman, but a woman who would stay around and scold and argue and see some good in a threadbare man. Fixing a garrison was one thing; changing a life was another.

El Teniente Gasca notified his trustworthy *sargento* that he was in charge until tomorrow at least and selected one volunteer from among his privates to accompany him to the Double Cross. Everyone wanted to go, mainly because of the good food found there. The selection made itself, when he walked to the stables and found one determined fellow saddling his horse for him. Joaquim never argued with initiative; he had seen too little of it in himself.

Dusk was settling over the Sangre de Cristo Mountains when the two soldiers arrived at the Double Cross. The guards on Marco's parapet strained to see who wanted admission, until the quietly spoken saint's name "Santiago" told them the riders were colonials, using the centuries-old password of Christians.

Emilio himself greeted Joaquim and pointed to the gate that led through the kitchen garden. Joaquim sent his private with Emilio and the horses and walked through the kitchen garden, which looked to have been newly plowed if not yet planted.

A tap on the door brought Sancha to stand before him and grasp his hand. He kissed her fingers, which made her laugh, and found himself among friends. He looked first for Paloma and frowned when he did not see her. Marco caught his glance and seemed to understand his first concern.

"We wore her out and she is dining in our bedchamber with a handsome young fellow named Juan Luis," Marco said. "Both are well. Sit, friend, and eat. I'll take you to them later."

He did, accepting the bowls passed his way and piling a plate, too. He reached for the bread handed to him by a woman he had not seen before, likely the author of the ridiculous note. A small older man with what appeared to be a perpetual worry line between his eyes sat next to her. Their clothing branded them as city dwellers and they looked exhausted. Joaquim smiled to himself; that first trip through the passes from Santa Fe could do that to a person.

"Pardon my country manners," Marco said, and indicated the woman. "This is Señorita Ygnacio, and her father, Señor Ygnacio, here for the audit. This is El Teniente Joaquim Gasca, commander of the presidio."

"We will need to talk about this audit, won't we?" Joaquim said, surprised when Señorita Ygnacio nodded instead of the auditor.

"Eat first," Marco said.

He did, enjoying every mouthful. The Ygnacios ate silently, their eyes on their plates, as if unused to the reception they had found at the Double Cross. A glance at Sancha from Marco produced two dishes of flan, which Marco accepted.

"Marco, this handsome young fellow named Juan Luis is already eating flan?" Joaquim teased, as his friend went to the door.

"There is another friend in the room, one you will like to hear from, too."

"Oh?"

"She could hardly stay away from a Mondragón baby. It would be easier for her to gut and skin you, if she felt like it," Marco replied, and left the room with dessert.

Joaquim couldn't overlook the gasp from Señorita Ygnacio. So Eckapeta was here, too? Hopefully she brought news with her. "Bravo," Joaquim said under his breath, and turned his attention to the flan.

"Bravo?"

Joaquim looked up at the woman, noting her fear. "Things are different here on the frontier, *señorita*," he said formally. "We have some Comanche friends and we treasure them."

He laughed inwardly at her skeptical expression and wondered how long *she* would last on a frontier.

She startled him by skewering him with a look of her own that equaled his in skepticism. This woman had clearly never suffered a fool gladly in her life, no matter how precarious her own standing. And how could that standing be high, considering her habit of sending panicky notes?

No sense in wasting anyone's time. "Señorita Ygnacio, you and I and the *juez* have a lot to talk about. When he returns, you'll explain the note you sent to me."

"Daughter, you didn't!" her father said.

"I did, Papa," she said calmly, as if she was used to managing him, but in a kindly manner, which impressed Joaquim. Perhaps he should alter his first impression of her. "Maybe someone will help us."

Help them? Joaquim wondered again what sort of people these were, and addressed her one more time.

"We don't turn away people here in the valley," he said, raising that first quivering mouthful of flan, "nether do we send hysterical little notes. When the *juez* returns, we'll discuss this."

He concentrated on Perla *la cocinera's* divine dessert, at the same time glancing at the lady across the table from him, disconcerted to find that she was watching him, too.

They regarded each other, brown eyes assessing brown eyes, Joaquim certain he was coming up short. He admired her flawless white skin, whiter even than Paloma's, and her remarkable control, even though he had referred to her "hysterical" notes. He looked away first, and then back. She was no beauty, but there was something about her dignity that caught his attention. He saw no animosity in her expression, only sadness, as though she knew already that no one in Valle del Sol would hear her out.

Thank God Marco returned to the kitchen, all smiles, the kind host. The only problem was that Marco the kind host was also a most discerning man. His smile faded as he sensed the tension, then gave Joaquim the slightest warning—the smallest shake of his head. How did that damned *juez* know that he, Joaquim el teniente, had been less than polite? *Ah well.* Joaquim knew he could apologize later.

Marco stood there, regarding them. "We have a matter to discuss," he told them in his polite but adamant way. "Paloma will make me sleep in the *sala* if she is not included, so if you do not mind the informality, may we adjourn to my bedchamber?"

"Is the Comanche woman there?" Señorita Ygnacio said quickly, and Joaquim heard her fear.

"She is, and you will be most polite to her," Marco said, in his special way. "You needn't be afraid." He chuckled, and Joaquim understood the humor. "That is, unless you make a sudden move to threaten Paloma or Juan Luis."

"I would never!" Señorita Ygnacio had the good grace to smile. "I see how things are."

"Good! Follow me, please."

Joaquim watched with more sympathy now as Señorita Ygnacio helped her father to his feet, her arm around his shoulders.

Señor Ygnacio hesitated at the door to his guest room and spoke quietly to his daughter. She nodded, and turned to Marco.

"*Señor*, he is tired."

"We need to talk."

"I know," she said, "but I can tell you anything you need to know. Please."

Marco considered the matter, then nodded. He opened the door to the guest room and Señorita Ygnacio took her father inside.

"I do not think I have ever seen such a broken man," Marco whispered to Joaquim. "What mischief has our favorite *contador* Felix Moreno been party to?"

Chapter Seven

In which Catalina pleads their case and everyone listens except the baby

"Papa, I do not know if we are among friends at long last, or more enemies," Catalina whispered to her father, as she helped him lie down. She removed his shoes and covered him. "The lieutenant is belligerent, but that might be all show. I cannot tell."

"*Hija*, you are good at discerning," her father said. His eyes closed and he turned over the problem to her, as he always did.

She stayed beside his bed a moment more, wishing she had a champion. Just once, someone to defend her; just once wasn't too much to ask. Then she had to be honest and ask herself if she would recognize that sort of kindness. *I honestly do not know*, she thought, as she joined the others.

A glance at the lieutenant told her he had certainly never been in the Mondragón's bedroom before. He looked around, as she had done, perhaps admiring the marvelous wardrobe that must have come from Spain, who knew how long ago.

Hands on hips, he spoke to Señor Mondragón. "How did that ever arrive here in one piece?"

"Family legend claims that many bribes were involved, and not a few prayers. But here is the reason we assemble in my bedroom." Señor Mondragón nodded to the Comanche woman Catalina had seen in the hall earlier with Paloma Vega. "Dear friend, you must share a little. Thank you."

The Indian held up the baby in her arms, and Marco made his claim. He held out his son to the lieutenant, who nodded, and looked from the child to Paloma, who lay back in the bed beaming at them all.

"Looks like you, Paloma," El Teniente said, and gave her a little bow. "Well done."

Marco kissed his sleeping son, then handed the baby back to the Indian woman. "Eckapeta, here you are. We knew you wouldn't stay away long." He motioned to the lieutenant, and the men moved the chairs by the fireplace closer to the bed.

"*Señorita*, you sit here, please," he said, and she did as he asked. "Joaquim, this one is for you." Señor Mondragón sat down in his bed next to his wife, and she shifted slightly to share the pillows. "*Señorita*, forgive our vast informality. I do not usually interview people in such a casual way, but you understand us."

"I do," Catalina assured him, as she wondered at the catch in her throat. "You ask yourself what kind of crackpot female would write you frightening notes before something as ordinary and boring as an audit."

"Basically, yes," Señor Mondragón said. "Tell us more."

She already knew enough about this man with the light-brown eyes to get a glimpse of his kindness, but he had a way of demanding results in a polite fashion. She also sensed that what she said had better be the truth.

"I must begin this story in Mexico City fifteen years ago," Catalina said, thinking of the times she had tried to tell her father's story to uninterested audiences, or people who had reached their own conclusions before she even began. "Please hear me out before you judge us."

The *juez* frowned. "That has been your experience?"

"It has," Catalina told him. "Please surprise me."

She saw nothing but sympathy in the official's eyes, which gave her courage. "In Mexico City, Papa held a position similar to that of Señor Felix Moreno. He was in charge of the district's financials. I was ten years old at the time, and knew nothing of the particulars, except that he was found guilty of embezzling a huge sum of money slated for a series of bridges around the city."

"Do you think he was guilty?" Señor Mondragón asked.

"Marco, she was only ten. How would she know?" Paloma said.

Catalina flashed her a grateful glance. "To my knowledge, Papa and Mama never seemed to have any more money than usual. He told me he was innocent and I believed him." *Take that*, she thought, her chin up.

Catalina listened hard for condemnation when the lieutenant spoke, but heard none. "Fifteen years ago, you say? I was in Mexico City. As I recall, the new viceroy had leveled all kinds of accusations at the former viceroy."

"Do *you* remember more?" Señor Mondragón asked.

"That was back when I was drunk more often than sober," Joaquim Gasca said with a shrug. He sighed. "And there was usually a woman or two …." His face turned red.

They all looked at her again, so Catalina continued, startled by the man's honesty. "I … I don't know if there was a trial, but Papa went to prison for five years." She took a deep breath, uneasy after all this time, unwilling even now to remember. "Mama died of shame, I think, and I was sent to an orphanage."

She spoke softly enough, still wanting to skirt around that terrible time, but she saw tears in Paloma's eyes. *I will not cry*, Catalina thought. *I am past that.*

"When Papa was released from prison, he pried me away from the nuns and promised we would get back to Spain somehow," she continued. "We had no money, and the viceroy had other ideas. He sentenced Papa to exile in Santa Fe."

"Prison wasn't enough?" Señor Mondragón asked, with something close to amazement. "Exiled to New Mexico!"

Lieutenant Gasca recoiled in mock horror and Catalina wanted to smack him. He must have noticed the fire in her eyes, because he held up a placating hand. "Don't let it bother you, *señorita!* I was exiled here, too, for numerous well-earned felonies and misdemeanors, in my case."

"Which we will not discuss now," Paloma interjected, and shook her finger at the lieutenant. "Catalina, he has been a rascal, but I believe he has reformed."

Everyone was all smiles again. Catalina could only glance from one to the other in amazement. What kind of lunatic asylum was the Double Cross?

"Papa is sent on audits, as the other *contadores* in the department here are, but everyone in the colony knows he was in prison for stealing money," Catalina said. "He was ruined, and even now has no confidence in adding and subtracting numbers. Gossips say he is a hopeless drunkard, but he never drinks. It's one of many rumors that follow us."

"Why must he continue to be punished?" Paloma asked.

This was the hard question, even though Catalina did not think the *juez de campo's* wife asked it from spite. She could only pick her way through it with what tattered grace remained to her, she who shared his exile and his punishment. "The world is full of bullies and victims," Catalina told her. "You were a victim for a while, were you not?"

Paloma nodded. Her heart wretched with the unfairness of life, Catalina watched Señor Mondragón gather his wife close to him. Why had Felix Moreno sent them to this kind place, where her own injustices felt magnified? She held her head up, determined to ignore their happiness, because to think of it only hurt.

"Times are better here," Paloma said.

Hurrah for you, Catalina thought, and lowered her eyes so that the bitterness would not show, not when these people seemed inclined, for whatever reason, to treat her nicely.

She must not have been fast enough. Paloma grasped her hand. "It's time you had a change of fortune, too. Don't discount us."

Señor Mondragón nodded, his eyes serious, but not unkind, Catalina decided, when she had the courage to look him in the face. "Tell us about your note."

She could have done as he demanded. She could have taken Señor Mondragón's words at face value, but some imp in her, some imp that had been dredging about in discontent and anger, wouldn't let her.

"You tell me first: *Teniente*, do you believe a word of my note to you?"

Silence. Fearless now, or more likely careless because she truly didn't care, Catalina looked at the lieutenant and saw nothing but disbelief.

Catalina started to rise, but Paloma grabbed her skirts and yanked her down. "Don't you move, Catalina!" she admonished, her voice low but intense.

It wasn't so low that the Comanche woman didn't look up and get to her feet in one fluid motion, her hand behind her back where Catalina knew a knife rested.

"No, Eckapeta, this is between Señorita Ygnacio and me. We are in no danger," Paloma said. She lay back again, her hand against her still-swollen belly, and she spoke to Señor Mondragón. "Marco, I know my uncle better than you, and I strongly suspect his hand in this story." She turned a more kindly eye on Catalina now, almost as if asking forgiveness for her unexpected intensity. "Tell us what you are afraid of."

"Why, if no one believes me?" Catalina asked, appalled, even as the words spilled out, that she could not trust even someone as kind as Paloma.

"I was ten years in the Moreno household," Paloma said simply. "*I* believe you."

Chapter Eight

In which Catalina explains herself

No one spoke for a long moment. The silence ended with Juan Luis letting out a sigh that ended in a burp. Joaquim's lips twitched.

"Marco, your son has no appreciation for delicate, overwrought scenes." Joaquim shifted to look more closely at Catalina seated next to him. "Don't get your feathers up, *señorita*." He made a broad gesture. "If Paloma trusts you, then I will too."

"I, too, and for the same reason," Marcos said. "Joaquim, you showed me your note."

The lieutenant reached into his doublet for the folded up paper and handed it to Catalina. "You sent this note to me, fearing that your father would be killed, once the audit was done. Explain it now."

To Joaquim's relief, she did not hesitate. She didn't sound like someone making up a story to get attention, or whatever it was that a spinster, probably in her mid-twenties, wanted. He had no experience with women like this.

"Papa came home one night as usual, and that very evening, quite late, we had a visit from the man who cleans the offices," she said. She looked at Marco, knowing instinctively where the power lay in Valle del Sol. A lesser presidio captain than Joaquim would have been insulted, but Joaquim had always been happy to share his responsibilities.

"A custodian is an unimpeachable source?" Marco asked, sounding as skeptical as Joaquim, had he spoken first.

Señorita Ygnacio took it calmly. "People on the bottom rung have no reason to lie about anything. They have no resource beyond the truth. This

I know from personal experience. Pablo empties wastebaskets and scrubs floors. Men like that don't scheme."

Bravo, Joaquim thought, impressed with her plain speaking.

"Very well," Marco said. "What happened then?"

"He had been searching for something one of the other officers dropped earlier in the day," she said. "He was under a desk, and the door connecting that office to the *contador principal's* private office was open. He heard Señor Moreno promise Miguel Valencia that my father," her voice broke, "and I, I suppose, would not return from this assignment. When that happened, the job of auditor would be Miguel's."

"Did Pablo see either man?" Marco asked. "Why could Miguel exact any favor from the *fiscal*? Who is he?"

Señorita Ygnacio looked directly at Paloma. "He is Tomasa Moreno's husband-to-be. I did not see him that night, but I have heard his name mentioned."

"My goodness. She was barely thirteen when I ...'" she stopped and cuddled close to her husband. "I am certain the story is all over Santa Fe that Paloma Vega stole her uncle's money box."

"Paloma, you would never!" Joaquim said in mock horror.

"Certainly I would never, but my uncle industriously spread that rumor about," Paloma said.

"I would happily gut him from throat to privates," Eckapeta said from her corner of the room by the baby's cradle, "if he has any."

"My dear, what would that solve?" Paloma asked.

Eckapeta shrugged. "He would be dead and I would feel better." She flashed what Joaquim suspected was a rare smile. "You would, too, little mother."

Joaquim smiled inside to see Señorita Ygnacio's wide-eyed expression of horror and disbelief, reminding him that she wouldn't last a week in Comanchería. Probably unaware, she scooted to the edge of her chair, farther from the Comanche and closer to the lieutenant—close enough that he could sniff the sage in her hair.

"All right, you unrepentant souls," Marco teased. He turned his attention to Señorita Ygnacio, more serious. "Do you .... Is there a soldier you suspect?"

She shook her head and ran her hand over her face. In that small moment, Joaquim saw the utter weariness of a woman—a lady—taxed to her limit. He looked at Paloma and saw a similar expression, in her case the memory of a worse time herself, and at the hands of the same man. She turned her face into Marco's chest, and his arm tightened around her.

"Can you do anything to help? No one has ever helped us," Señorita Ygnacio added quietly.

"Someone will now," Paloma said. She folded her hands in her lap and looked at her husband, then at Joaquim.

Marco looked at him, too. "Could you send the escort back to Santa Fe? Have you that authority?"

"I might," Joaquim replied, then spoke to the lady sitting so close to him. "*Señorita*, what is the highest rank among your escort?"

"There is a corporal," she said. "The rest are privates, and the driver practically drools."

I am well-acquainted with privates, Joaquim thought. "I can order them to Santa Fe, and provide another escort for you when the audit is done."

He had never seen a look of relief cross anyone's face faster than Catalina Ygnacio's. When had he been the answer to anyone's prayers? "I'll do it," he said. "We'll keep the driver and send the rest back."

"That might cause more attention and suspicion directed at Señor Ygnacio," Marco pointed out. "Can we send them with something valuable that must get to the governor in a timely fashion? There needs to be a reason."

"Too bad we never found even one of Coronado's seven cities of gold," Joaquim said, after a long silence.

"In New Mexico?" Marco asked, his eyes lively. "The only crop we raise is children."

"What does the governor want more than anything?" Joaquim asked out loud.

"Easy," Marco said. "He wants a treaty with the Comanche. I might remind you we don't have one yet, Lieutenant."

Joaquim shrugged. "Governor Anza doesn't know that. Could we not suggest that he make himself ready for a trip to Comanchería this summer to implement one? You know, word it as a politician would, with just enough vagueness to cover our hairy behinds if it doesn't happen."

"I suppose we could," Marco said slowly. "What do you think, Eckapeta? What have you heard?"

"Much suspicion." Eckapeta sighed. "Everyone wants to talk, but no one seems to listen."

"Sounds like office seekers everywhere," Joaquim teased. "I expected better things from the Kwahadi."

"We are human, too," the Comanche woman replied, with some dignity. "I will go back in a few days to the sacred canyon." She spoke directly to Joaquim. "Scratch your marks on paper to the governor and protect this woman, you two. She doesn't look like a troublemaker."

Eckapeta gazed at the baby sleeping in his cradle. Joaquim looked closer himself, and saw a bit of smudge on his forehead, probably sage put there by the Kwahadi woman, who considered Juan Luis her grandchild.

She stood up, went to the bed, rubbed her cheek against Marco and Paloma's cheeks and left the room. Joaquim listened for footsteps, for an outside door opening and closing. Nothing. The woman had probably come into the house just as silently. Thank God she was a friend and ally.

"Well then," Paloma said. "Write that letter tomorrow, husband, and send those soldiers on their way. Joaquim, it is too late for you to return to the presidio tonight. Sancha will make you a pallet in the *sala*." She lowered herself down farther in the bed and Marco pulled out two of the pillows behind her head. "I will see all of you in the morning."

"We've been dismissed," Marco said as he stood up. Paloma mumbled something and he laughed. "I'll return!"

The three of them went into the hall. "*Señorita*, we can begin the audit tomorrow," Marco said, all business again. "That long table I promised is in there." He turned to Joaquim. "My friend, you must send us a soldier to sit in there, too: orders of the Crown."

"I'll begin it," Joaquim said, surprising himself.

Señorita Ygnacio gave a slight bow and continued down the hall. Marco called quietly after her to leave her door ajar, since there was a charcoal brazier in there now. She stopped. Even in the dim light, Joaquim saw a host of expressions from incredulity to relief cross her face, which now that he looked at it, had some angular beauty to it, provided a man admired tall, skinny women.

Marco watched her go. "I am continually amazed at how a man such as Señor Moreno ever gets a position of importance. How do bad men climb ladders to success?"

"I think it involves considerable ass kissing," Joaquim replied. "I was never good at that." He chuckled. "At least with men."

Marco laughed quietly and slapped his shoulder. "Good night, my friend."

Joaquim stood another moment in the now empty hall, wondering again at his recent good fortune in friends. He walked into the *sala* just as Sancha and Lorenzo put the finishing touches on a pallet with a substantial wool mattress and plenty of blankets.

"The Double Cross is a full house now," he commented as they went to the door. "Noisy, too, I imagine, when the little ones are up."

"There was a time, and not so long ago, when it was empty as Christ's tomb on resurrection Sunday," Sancha said. "I hope never to see those days again."

She crossed herself. To Joaquim's surprise, Lorenzo did, too, which made the lieutenant reflect on the value of a good wife, as he stripped to his small clothes and crawled between sweet-smelling sheets.

He lay there in complete comfort, enjoying the ever-present odor of piñon pine that would always signal the colony of New Mexico to him, as long as he lived here. He smiled into the dark, wondering where all his ambition had gone. He remembered a bad time in his father's *sala* in La Havana, when his father outlined what moves Joaquim needed to make in order to become chief engineer for the entire New World. "Twenty years will do it," Papa had predicted, then shook a finger at him. "Don't disappoint me, *hijo*."

Not for the first time, Joaquim wondered if his father was even alive. After the fourth or fifth of many disastrous alterations in rank and locale, his father had sent him a final scathing letter disavowing him as a son. Joaquim knew his mother had died ten years ago, because his parish priest in La Havana had written him. The letter had been passed around from presidio to presidio until it final reached shabby Santa Maria, only this winter. He had not replied. The priest was probably dead by now.

"I am becoming a better man," he said to the ceiling, yearning to tell someone, anyone.

"I do not doubt that, *señor*," he heard from the doorway, and sat up with a start, his heart pounding. He patted the floor for his knife and came up dry.

Señorita Ygnacio stood in the open doorway. She wore a robe over her nightgown and had braided her long hair, which gave her a childlike appeal.

"*Señorita*, I don't think—"

"For God's sake, don't worry about your virtue," she said, sounding as old and wrinkled as a crone in a village. "I wanted to thank you for believing me, even though I think you would rather not bother with us."

He lay down again, the blanket carefully covering him. "You made some hard accusations, and we have nothing but your word."

"I don't lie."

Maybe it was the single braid over her shoulder. Suddenly she looked so young and vulnerable. Joaquim wondered just how long a person with no power could shoulder another's burdens before melting under the strain.

"Have you no advocate at all?" he asked, when she just stood there. Maybe she was as tired of being alone as he was.

"Not one."

He could think of nothing to say that wouldn't sound condescending or accusatory, so he lay there in silence, half hoping she would go away. A year ago, he'd had not a single advocate, either, until the Mondragóns turned into the best friends a useless man could wish for. With an ache, he felt some pity for the woman standing in the doorway.

He sat up, tugging the sheet around his nearly bare shoulders, and considered his next move. "Señorita Ygnacio, how old are you?" he asked.

"Twenty-five," she replied with no hesitation. If she'd ever had any pride, it was long gone.

He had a hunch. "How long have you been doing your father's audits?"

She gasped as though he had kicked the air out of her, but no matter. She had no business standing there, not really.

"Since I was fifteen," she replied, her voice small now, devoid of confidence. "He … he came out of prison and was sentenced immediately to Santa Fe. You should have seen how his hands shook. I never asked him what happened in prison."

"Just as well," Joaquim replied, thinking of other skeletal men released from prison, blinking in bright light and shrinking from ordinary sounds. "Could he function in his office without you?" He made an impatient gesture. "For God's sake, come in and sit down. This might be important."

She did as he said. She was barefoot, and she kept her legs primly together. He knew how cold the tile was.

"He probably could function, but he relies totally on me."

She sounded even younger, as though she didn't want to be relied on, didn't want any part of this steaming dish of offal fate seemed to have handed her with a spoon.

"Papa always brings home his work from the office, and I check his numbers."

"Are they right?"

"Yes, but he has no confidence. If I tell him I am busy and can't check them, he starts to shake."

Good God, what a shadow of a man, Joaquim thought, disgusted. "If you and he were to disappear over here so close to Comanchería, no one would question it, would they?"

She shook her head. "No one."

"And … what was his name?"

"Miguel Valencia?"

"Miguel Valencia will become the colony's newest auditor."

"He will. *Teniente,* I do not want to die here."

She spoke with some firmness, which made him admire her courage. She had been shouldering big burdens far too long.

"Do you even want to return to Santa Fe?" he asked.

"Not really, but mostly I do not want to be dead," she told him, which made him smile.

He thought for a long moment, considering her presence. He knew her feet were cold, because she started putting one foot on top of the other, then switching feet. They were two lonely people in a happy home, and he suddenly didn't feel so lonely. No telling how she felt, but he could still make her a promise.

"Consider this, Señorita Ygnacio," he said. "You now have three advocates in Valle del Sol. Perhaps four. I will be your friend, and so will the Mondragóns. Eckapeta, if you would allow her."

"She frightens me," Señorita Ygnacio said, and he heard her uncertainty.

"Me, too, but she is my friend," he told her. "No one is going to hurt you, harm you, yell at you, or belittle you here. No one ever does. When the audit ends, we'll get you safely back to Santa Fe or wherever you want to go, within reason." He held out his hand. "Here is my bond and word."

Her handshake was surprisingly firm, even though he didn't think she had even touched a man to shake his hand. She was desperate for help of a kind he had never provided before. She just wanted a friend.

She rose and went to the door, but stopped there and turned around to face him. Ten minutes ago he would have just been impatient. For some reason, he wanted to hear her thoughts.

"*Teniente*, you said you were in Mexico City when my father went to prison. What were you doing there? Comanchería seems a long way from Mexico."

"Indeed it is," he told her, not embarrassed to speak the truth. "I was a royal engineer, sent from La Havana Cuba to rebuild a barracks."

He could nearly see her surprise. "Then why ..." she stopped, obviously realizing how blatant her question was going to sound.

He could help. "Why am I here?"

"Well, yes. It's not polite of me—"

"Señorita Ygnacio, I got very lucky," he said softly, and meant every word.

"I can't believe you," she replied, and he heard all the doubt in her voice, poor thing. She had no idea yet that her own fortunes had turned, none whatsoever. *Pues, bien*, it had taken him time, too.

"Go to bed, *señorita*," he said, "but leave yourself open to the idea that you might be lucky, too."

She said nothing. In a moment she was gone.

Chapter Nine

In which the boring, dull audit might begin—Or not

Catalina Ygnacio woke to two children staring at her. Foggy with sleep, she stared back, then tried something new and radical that her conversation with El Teniente Gasca hinted at. She smiled; these children were not the enemy.

"We have a little brother, and I wanted a sister," the girl said with a sigh.

"He's really quite handsome," Catalina said. Trying something else, she patted the mattress. To her gratification, the girl climbed up and lay down next to her. The little boy followed, and soon they were crowded close together in a bed designed for one person of lean dimensions.

The only way to keep everyone in the bed was to put one child on each side and put her arms around them. They cuddled close, which told her they were welcome in their mother and father's bed. In another place she might have resented their good fortune and turned sour, but not today. She cuddled back and closed her eyes.

"I have a pony," the girl announced.

"No, you don't," the younger boy stated firmly.

"You're envious, Claudito."

"Am not! You're telling a tale and you know what Mama says about that," said the boy, not inclined to back down. Catalina tried hard not to smile at the quarrel. She could hear a familiar firmness in Claudito's reply suggesting that he was his father's son.

"Señorita Ygnacio? I am so sorry."

The sun was up and streaming in the window. Catalina opened her eyes to see Paloma bending over her, eyes full of apology for her children, who glared at each other.

"Don't be," Catalina replied. "We all got warm together. And please, call me Catalina."

"Catalina you are, and I am Paloma."

"Mama, Soledad is telling stories again. She says she has a pony."

Paloma sighed. "Dearest Soli, what has Papa said about story-telling?"

"That I shouldn't do it," the little girl whispered.

It was none of Catalina's business, this little mother-daughter exchange, but Catalina sat up. "I know a lot of stories," she said. "The kind that won't get you in trouble."

The girl clapped her hands, her own misdemeanor obviously forgotten. "Could I tell those kinds of stories, Mama?"

"I believe you could," Paloma said. She touched the little girl's cheek and reached over Catalina to touch her son. "You two are wanted in the kitchen for breakfast." She clapped her hands. "Right now, because *churros* don't keep well."

The little girl gasped and leaped from bed, tugging her brother and urging him to follow her lead.

Catalina watched with interest—she knew so little about children—as the small Mondragóns did as they were told. She had to hide a smile as Paloma called her daughter back and reminded her to fold her hands in front of her waist like a lady and walk down the hall.

"It lasts about ten paces," Paloma said. "Just listen. Ah, yes, there she goes. Soledad loves *churros*." She sighed. "Poor Soledad! She seems to need more attention than I can give her lately, what with a new baby."

"Some of my stories are quite fanciful," Catalina said, already thinking of where to begin.

"So are Soli's," Paloma replied, and they both laughed.

Instead of leaving, Paloma sat down on the bed, her hand to her stomach, which Catalina suspected was more ample than usual. The woman was not long from childbearing. Paloma's eyes followed her glance.

"I press on it and press on it, like the midwife advised, but it seems to be taking longer than last time to shrink," Paloma said. "I ask Marco if he minds. He laughs and says I am finally about where he likes me."

She interpreted Catalina's questioning face correctly. "*Ay de mi*, I was so thin when I came here," she said. "Thin and angry. Well, no, not angry. Maybe I was angry before I met Marco. Or was I confused? I know I was sad at the turn my life had taken." She extended her hand toward Catalina. "As you are now, Catalina Ygnacio?"

Catalina tried to feel offended. She sat there in silence, because she did not know how to respond to Paloma's candor. She swallowed and felt an unfamiliar prickle behind her eyes. This would never do. She had told herself ten years ago when they set out on their exile to Santa Fe that there were no more tears left to cry, not when Papa needed her.

Paloma said nothing, only looked at her with such kindness that Catalina had to swallow again and again. If only her hostess hadn't reached out both hands to her and pulled her close with more strength than Catalina would have suspected …. She let her tears fall.

"You've really been carrying too big a load," Paloma said in that matter-of-fact way Catalina was coming to treasure, after a mere day in her company. "Marco and I talked about this last night, when Juan Luis woke us up. We agreed that you reminded us of each other, a few years ago."

Catalina sobbed harder. She tried to pull away but Paloma held her closer.

"My papa needs me," Catalina sobbed.

"No, he doesn't. Marco is showing him around the Double Cross right now," Paloma said, her voice so soothing that Catalina could only breathe deep and enjoy the warmth of the woman's embrace. "They were even laughing about something when I saw them last by the *acequia.*"

I cannot keep crying, Catalina told herself, and willed an end to tears. She couldn't do a thing about the closeness of Paloma's embrace, and didn't try. "My father never laughs."

"He was doing an excellent imitation of it when I looked outside," Paloma told her. "When you feel better, come to the kitchen and you can have breakfast. I doubt there will be any *churros* left."

"But the audit is supposed to begin today," Catalina said. "There is much to do."

"Not really," Paloma said with a shrug. "El Teniente Gasca had to go back to the presidio. Marco gave him many leaflets to sort out among his soldiers. They'll take them around to the townsfolk who have livestock, and out into the country."

"Why?" Catalina asked. She wiped her eyes and blew her nose with the handkerchief Paloma handed over without a comment. "Surely the *juez de campo* has already accounted for each animal." She put her hand to her mouth. "Oh! I didn't mean that the way it sounded."

"I know you didn't," Paloma said. "My husband does his job quite thoroughly, but not everyone is honest. Marco has noticed that some people need a friendly reminder. He gives them another chance." Paloma stood up and touched Catalina's head. "Everyone gets a second chance here. Take your time."

"But …."

Paloma laughed and touched her head again, giving her a friendly push this time. "This isn't Santa Fe! Things move slower. We can move fast when we need to. Before Joaquim went back to the presidio, he and Marco crafted a wonderful letter to the governor that was a testimonial to vagueness. They signed it and sealed it."

"The soldiers?" Catalina asked, unable to keep the fear from her voice.

"On their way to the presidio to fetch rations for the return trip. El Teniente gave them the letter for the governor and stressed the need to return to Santa Fe quickly. Two of our presidio soldiers will escort them as far as the Dolorosa Pass in the Sangre de Cristos. No one will turn around and come back. Be easy about that."

Catalina let out a shuddering sigh. "I can't tell you what that means to me."

"Just remember what I said about second chances." Paloma went to the door. "I know I hear Juan Luis." She hefted her right breast. "If he squeaks, I flow. We can talk later in my room. The door is always unlatched."

Amazed, Catalina lay back in bed, the handkerchief pressed to her face. It smelled wonderfully of sage and rosemary. She was warm and comfortable and her father was occupied. She tried to think of any time in recent memory when she had felt this way, and couldn't.

Dressing quickly, she walked down the hall to Paloma's room and tapped lightly on the door.

"Do come in," Paloma said. "I'm being held captive by an eating monster."

Catalina laughed and came inside, enjoying again the pleasant fragrance of rosemary and sage. Paloma lay there with her eyes closed, a smile on her lips, as Juan Luis suckled. She opened her eyes and patted the bed. Catalina sat.

"There was a time we doubted I would ever be fruitful," her hostess said in her frank way. "I was so thin and I never had monthlies." She smiled down at her son, who had detached himself and lay there in what looked like a milk stupor. Milk still dripped from her nipple, and he took a lick now and then, which made Catalina cover her hand with her mouth and laugh softly.

"This is the messy time, I have discovered," Paloma said, as she covered up and lifted the sleeping baby to her shoulder. "In a week or so this child and I will come to a meeting of the minds. He'll get more efficient, and I will be tidier."

"And so life goes on at the Double Cross."

Catalina looked around to see Señor Mondragón leaning against the doorframe, his eyes on his wife. Paloma blew him a kiss as Juan Luis burped, then handed him their son for a return to his cradle.

When the *juez de campo* came back to the bed and sat, Catalina stood up in sudden alarm. "Where is my father?"

Señor Mondragón raised a hand to slow her down. "He's in my office, looking over a monumental stack of paper, and smiling like a good Spaniard." He rubbed his hands together. "We do love our red tape, don't we?"

"But I should be there to help," Catalina insisted.

He waved her down. "He's fine. I have a wonderful table I use for audits, with lines painted on it to segment into years. My father, *juez de campo* before me, built it especially for audits. He's sorting the stacks into each allotted space."

"Did … did he ask for me?"

"No. He has it under control, Señorita Ygnacio."

"She's Catalina to us now, my love," Paloma said.

"Ah! Excellent. Then I am Marco. Pleased to make your acquaintance."

Who could not smile at that? Still, she couldn't give up so easily. "He always needs my help."

"I don't doubt that for a moment," Marco told her, his light-brown eyes so kind. "He tells me you are a *maestra* with numbers. He also confided that you work too hard, so we agreed he would organize the papers and let you enjoy a quiet morning with my wife."

Catalina looked from the husband to the wife, wondering what conspiracy was afoot here. She thought again of what Joaquim Gasca had told her last night, how he had gone from royal engineer to private, and had the good fortune—that was good fortune?—to be cast into outer darkness in Valle del Sol. She felt her heartbeat slow down as calm returned. She breathed deeply again of the combined fragrances of piñon from the fireplace, rosemary and sage perhaps from the sheets, a milky odor from Paloma's abundance, and campfire and leather and something else from Marco that she could not identify. Maybe it was his hair oil.

Feeling her shoulders relax, she looked down at her hands, suddenly aware that although they were usually balled into fists, that wasn't the case now. "I really have nothing to do today?" she asked.

Both Mondragóns shook their heads.

"Good," she said, and meant it.

Marco stood up. He kissed the top of his wife's head while she pursed her lips and kissed the air. *How does a person get so lucky?* she asked herself. *Could it ever happen to me?*

"I'll be in the horse barn with Claudito, if you need me," he said from the doorway. "Soledad is helping Sancha plant beans in the kitchen garden."

"Is Eckapeta still here?" Paloma asked.

I hope not, Catalina thought, then felt her cheeks grow warm. Obviously these kindly people loved that Comanche woman.

"She left early, before Señor Ygnacio and I had breakfast. She said something about finding Toshua and telling him of the letter."

And who is Toshua? Catalina asked herself. *Please, please, not another Comanche.*

"It might stir the other Kwahadi to action," Paloma said. "They already spent all winter talking about a treaty."

"You know they love to talk," Marco reminded Paloma. "I almost suspect they will want Governor Anza to come to *them*. You know, to see how brave he is." He sighed, as if thinking of earlier doings she knew nothing of.

Catalina sucked in her breath, and both Mondragóns gave her their attention. Again, that placating gesture from Marco. "Catalina, we have friends in strange places out here beyond the frontier. Better dust off your cradleboard, wife," he said to Paloma. "We might be riding east this summer, and taking along our latest addition."

Catalina looked at Paloma for a sign of fear and saw only calm.

"And I am doing nothing today," Catalina whispered after he was gone.

Paloma winked at her and they laughed together.

WHAT WITH THIS AND that, the audit of the Valle del Sol District, Royal Colony of New Mexico, in the domain of Carlos Rey Tres didn't begin until the entire week had elapsed. "This and that" used to bother Joaquim Gasca. Excessive *aguardiente* and females might have distracted him for too many years, but they never entirely squelched the engineer's part of his brain that cried out for order. He couldn't understand why Marco felt no urgency about the audit.

"The escort never seemed suspicious to me," Joaquim had told Marco, when he brought leaflets to the presidio for the soldiers to deliver for the audit. "Do you suppose Señor Ygnacio is completely crazy?"

"He might be, but his daughter isn't," Marco assured Joaquim. "You should watch her start to relax now, and unbend a little."

"Paloma magic?"

"Of course," Marco agreed, either generously overlooking that hint of wistfulness that Joaquim couldn't quite camouflage with bluster, or unaware of it, because Marco knew he was the sole king of Paloma's heart, damn the man.

"Send your men out with these broadsides, and come back to the Double Cross with me," Marco told him.

Joaquim had no trouble putting his sergeant in charge for the day; spring had come and he wanted to ride. The sun was warm on his back as he and Marco traveled the two leagues back to the Double Cross, with its gray stone walls and guards always on alert. They lazed along, and Joaquim couldn't help but contrast it to last summer, when they had been desperate to stop renegade Grey Owl.

"I was pretty certain we were going to die last summer," Joaquim admitted to his friend as they ambled along.

Marco glanced his way, as serious as Joaquim had ever seen him. "I was, too, and by God and all the angels, I did not want to die." He looked down at his gloved hands, resting on the pommel like a beginning rider. "There was a time I would have given up gladly, but not now, not ever again."

For the life of him, Joaquim couldn't think of anything flippant to say, no phrase to turn with a joke and laugh. He knew exactly what Marco was talking about.

Marco shifted in his saddle to give Joaquim his complete attention. "My friend, find yourself a wife. She will make all the difference."

"I've looked—discreetly, mind you—but Santa Maria's ladies are either married, too young, or too old," he said. "I won't go younger than sixteen."

"Felicia was fifteen, and I was eighteen," Marco said, smiling at the memory. "Greener than grass! Oh, how I loved her."

"Marco, I am almost thirty, nearly as old as you are," Joaquim reminded him.

Marco laughed, the traitor. Why was it some men seemed able to find wonderful wives under each creosote bush?

Marco reached across the short distance between them and touched Joaquim's arm. "Come with me to Santa Fe this fall, when I take my records and wool clip. You'll find someone."

Joaquim nodded, knowing full well he probably couldn't justify leaving the district for such an errand as wiving.

His mood cleared by the time they arrived at the Double Cross. Joaquim breathed deep of the newly turned earth, and watched the sowers broadcasting wheat in one field and planting hills of corn in another.

Through the open gates he saw three children jumping rope, and recognized Cecilia, the Comanche child that Graciela Tafoya had brought to her marriage with Claudio Vega, Paloma's brother. And there by the now-flowing *acequia* stood the three women—Graciela herself, gently rounded of belly, Paloma with Juan Luis to her shoulder, and tall, thin Catalina Ygnacio.

"I thought Señorita Ygnacio would be slaving over numbers in your office," he said to Marco, half wanting her to be working hard because she had caused them so much trouble.

"Catalina? She goes in there now and then, but do you know, I think her father is enjoying himself with my audit. No one is hounding him or belittling him. He hasn't even asked for his daughter's help."

"There's something in the water here, isn't there?" Joaquim teased.

"Nothing except water skippers," Marco said, content to stop Buciro and just watch the scene within the gates. "We're good to each other. It rubs off."

Joaquim watched the family through supper in the kitchen, where all business was conducted in the colony. Paloma felt no shyness about opening her bodice and nursing her smallest, leaning now and then against her husband's shoulder on the bench they shared and gracefully letting him share his supper with her, a bite every other time. She had a beautiful bosom, but Joaquim knew better than to take more than a glance now and then.

Graciela and Claudio had ended up in the kitchen too, sitting close to each other, with Cecilia on Claudio's lap because Graciela's was full of unborn child. Joaquim saw Claudio's contentment, a far remove from the restless horse trader of only last year, who belonged nowhere.

Joaquim had ended up next to Catalina, as he had been shyly informed he was to call her, because no one at the Double Cross stood on much ceremony. Soledad had attached herself to Catalina's other side, and Joaquim watched as Catalina reminded the little girl to finish what was on her plate. She did it gently, barely recognizable as the woman who had paced back and forth in the *sala*, wringing her hands and telling her story of a deprived life and Señor Moreno's cruelty to her father. Nothing could change her height and angular lines, but Catalina Ygnacio's anxious air seemed to belong to someone else now.

Speaking of Señor Ygnacio, Joaquim watched him, too, seeing a certain wistfulness in the older gentleman, fortune's fool. He said little, but let himself be carried along by conversation and good food and warmth that came not so much from the fireplace, but from somewhere deep inside, that tender spot Joaquim was only beginning to discover for himself.

"What do you think of the Double Cross, Catalina?" he asked, when Paloma and Marco were arguing good-naturedly over the last bowl of *flan* and Papa Ygnacio was starting to nod off, despite the murmur of conversation between Graciela and Claudio, seated next to him.

"I wish I lived here," she said, so quiet that he had to lean close to hear her.

She had only been here a week, but her hair and clothes were already starting to smell of sage and rosemary. He took a deep breath of her fragrance and smelled that essence of woman he had been successfully ignoring for months now, since it had not proved beneficial to his reformation.

"I wish I did, too," he whispered back.

Chapter Ten

In which the Mondragóns greet a familiar visitor

Paloma knew it was only a matter of time. Toshua might bluster and look superior, as only a warrior of The People could, but she had seen him tickling Claudito and showing Soledad how to make a whistle out of grass. He would never unbend to admit it, but Toshua was as much the doting grandparent as his wife Eckapeta. He would arrive when they least expected him.

So he had.

She had just returned Juanito to his cradle after a prodigious feeding, and felt the urge to leave the bed she shared with Big Man, who snored now—not loud, but loud enough. She stood by his side of the bed, loving him, wishing there were more hours in the day during his busy spring because he needed the time for planting, but also wishing there were fewer daylight hours, so he would come inside sooner.

The air was cool but not cold, so she didn't bother with sandals. Besides, she liked the feel of clean, cold tile on bare feet. No point in hunting for a shawl, because no one else was awake.

She could have used the sleep, but lately, she had started relishing what few minutes she had to herself. She recognized that awkward time when her baby seemed attached to one nipple or the other and she wasn't even Paloma Vega anymore, just a cow supplying cream, with everyone around her making demands as well.

She chastised herself, remembering the dark time when every thirty days or so ended in a sparse monthly. For a year she had hoped and then prayed with increasing desperation that her body would be receptive to Marco's obviously healthy seed, since he had fathered twins with his first wife. This failure was her failure, and it chafed beyond belief.

Who knew what had changed? Paloma had barely believed it when a month passed, nothing happened, and then another one. In some mystery beyond her imagining and prayers and endless petitions to the Virgin Herself, somehow a baby had taken root and turned into Claudio Mondragón.

And now there was Juanito, which delighted her because his birth seemed to confirm that the path was open for more. All the same, she couldn't help feeling overwhelmed.

She stood in the hall, half asleep, and decided to sit outside on the portal. When she opened the door, she walked to the edge, where she knew the night guard patrolled. One of the archers stopped and looked at her. This had happened several times in the past two weeks, so she knew to wave at him, signaling that all was well.

With a sigh of relief or gratitude or some strange melancholy she could not identify, Paloma eased herself onto the bench by the door. A half smile on her face, she leaned back against the rough stone and let her mind drift to a time when it was only her and Marco. Why had she not appreciated the simplicity of those days before babies, when neither of them thought anything of spending a rare rainy afternoon making love, or even just taking an evening stroll beside the *acequia* hand in hand, with not a childish demand in sight?

"Why am I not satisfied?" she asked out loud. "I have what I prayed for, don't I?"

No one replied, but she knew someone could have. Some instinct told her she was not alone on the porch, not even alone on the bench. Fear gripped her, that first instinct of any settler teetering on the edge of Comanchería. When her heart slowed down to manageable beats, she slid her hand along the bench, certain she was right.

She sighed when a rough hand covered hers. "Toshua, you're too quiet," she said, not even needing to look.

"You have lived among The People just long enough to develop a third ear, my daughter," he said, which pleased her heart. "How are you?"

She could tell him she was fine, and had a wonderful baby to show him when morning came and everyone began to stir. Would he have believed her? That third ear suggested to Paloma that he would not, and no Comanche tolerates a lie, unless he's the one telling it.

"I am tired and a little weary of demands," she said honestly. "I feel ungrateful, too."

"Why, daughter?" he asked.

"I prayed and prayed for God or a saint or someone to open my womb.

Now it has happened, and I am ungrateful. What must the Lord God Almighty think of me?" She wondered how it was she could say such womanly, intimate things to a man living a far harder life than she could fathom. What did Toshua know of God anyway? "A priest would require confession of my foolish thoughts."

"Would he listen first?"

She shrugged. "Some might." She thought of gentle Father Eusebio back in Saint Michael's in Santa Fe's Analco district, the parish church of Indians and servants where she most felt at home. He would listen, suggest, and gently require the smallest of penances, as if those sins weighing on her were lighter than she feared.

"I am listening," Toshua told her, and that was all she needed to throw herself into his arms and weep on his bare shoulder. She babbled about her exhaustion, her gnawing fear that she was torn too many ways to fully nurture her other two little ones, not to mention fill Marco's needs.

"And your needs?" he asked finally, when she wiped her eyes on the hem of her nightgown and her nose, too. "You have some maybe?"

"I suppose I do," she admitted. "I'd like to sit down to a meal without anyone demanding anything of me."

"That sounds within reason," her friend-confessor in the dark told her. "Anything else?"

She shouldn't mention such private things, but hadn't she and Marco spent part of one winter sharing a tipi with Toshua and Eckapeta, and all that meant? "I wish I didn't have to wait until late when I am almost too tired, but after the children are long asleep, to have a little tipi time with Big Man. Oh, I shouldn't say such things." Her face felt hot.

Toshua must have moved closer, because she sensed his silent laughter. She couldn't help smiling. In another moment she was laughing too, but quietly. Obviously the guards walking the terreplein hadn't seen her companion. She didn't want them to hear laughter and think that Señor Mondragón's wife had taken complete leave of her senses and was raving to herself on the porch.

"Daughter, this will pass," he told her. "You two picked the busiest time of the year for a baby to come. Give yourself the gift of summer and fall, when the leaves drop and night closes in earlier, and children get sleepy-eyed sooner."

"Makes perfect sense," she told him, resolved there was nothing she could ever say to this good man beside her that might embarrass her again. "Bide my time?"

"Haa," he told her in Nurmurnah. "Little by little, a small stream turned into that gorge in the ground by Santa Fe."

She nodded; she had seen the place he spoke of. "I should keep coming out here for a few minutes in the early morning hours to have my time alone?"

"That is what Eckapeta did, when our children lived," he said simply.

Why did I whine to this man? she thought, teary-eyed, thinking of his own children dead now, one killed by the Dark Wind and the other by an Apache war party. "Toshua, I …" she began, and could say no more. She leaned her forehead against his shoulder. "Forgive me."

"What is there to forgive?" he asked. "We only do the best we can, on any given day." He chuckled again. "At least that is what Eckapeta tells me, and we know she is smarter than all of us. Rest your head on my shoulder, my daughter."

Silent, she did as he said. When morning came, she was back in her own bed with her dear husband sitting beside her, still in his nightshirt. She touched his leg and he moved her hand higher, underneath the fabric.

"The children …" she whispered.

"Eckapeta and Toshua are walking with them along the *acequia*," he said, pulling her hand still higher until she sighed with her own longing and touched him. It had been months now, since her most awkward days of pregnancy. "Juanito is still asleep and I told Emilio to prepare seeds for planting. We have a moment."

He was extra gentle with her. She moved cautiously at first, then rested her legs on his. The spark caught and lit and she willingly turned herself inside out for this husband of hers who was doing the same thing for her. If she made more noise than usual, what did it matter? She hugged and kissed her man, enjoying him, savoring him.

Even when her milk came, it barely mattered. Marco took care of that, too, and she loved him for it. Finally they lay beside each other, legs entwined, breathing deep until their heartbeats slowed.

"I wondered where you were," he said at last. "I walked outside and found you sound asleep on Toshua's shoulder. We had a quiet talk, we two."

She thought she might feel foolish and awkward to have this conversation with the man she had just nourished as deeply as he had ever been filled, but she did not. "I need you," she said simply, "almost as much as I need some peaceful time. Toshua tells me that is not wrong or silly."

"He's right."

"I have to wonder, though, because I am a skeptic," she added. "I don't imagine women of The People ever have spare time. Was he just humoring me because I am a weak Spanish woman?"

"I am a skeptic, too. I asked him." Marco patted her stomach. "He gave me a smack on the head and told me Nurmurnah women like to sit with each other near healing smoke."

"I remember doing just that with Eckapeta in the sacred canyon," Paloma replied. "I didn't know what it was for. You can smack me, too."

Her husband put forefinger to thumb and made the smallest touch against her forehead, with an accompanying *pop*. They laughed together, but quietly this time, because Juanito was starting to stir.

When Marco sat up she blushed to see fingernail tracks on his back. She touched the marks. "I should perhaps apologize for scarring you beyond recognition," she teased.

"Did I complain?" he asked, amused. "And here I went and swallowed Juanito's breakfast. What kind of father am I?"

They fell into each other's arms and held tight, crying a little, laughing more.

THERE WAS NO POINT in any shyness during breakfast, when Paloma served Toshua and Eckapeta. She passed cornmeal mush to her good friends and sat beside the man who had put the heart back in her during those early-morning hours on the porch. He gave her a wink as he held Claudito on his lap and alternated bites of toasted bread.

Toshua surprised her by sitting there after the meal was done. She knew he was no fan of idleness, no more than her husband, who was probably wondering why *he* still sat there himself, when there was corn to plant.

Toshua wasted not a word, which told Paloma much about what must have been his real reason for this visit. "Marco, I need you to come with me now," he said.

Her husband frowned. "My brother, this is the busiest time of my year. There is planting, and young things are being born." He glanced sideways at Paloma and blushed. "*Our* young things, too. Believe me, if it were another time, I would follow you without hesitation."

It was as if Toshua hadn't heard a word. "We spent the winter talking and talking in the canyon, we Kwahadi and the Kosetekas and even the Yupe and Yamparika."

"Even eastern Comanches?" Marco asked, obviously surprised.

"Even them, little brother. There have been rumors of peace attempts even in that part of Texas where a man is hot and wet all day because the air seems to rain even when there are no clouds." Toshua chuckled. "Even their hands are soft in those places. Babies and sissies."

His eyes turned serious. "We have moved our ever-growing camp north to that wooded place along Rio Napestle that you Spaniards still fear."

"I had heard," Marco said, equally serious. "I think I would be afraid to come with you. Yes, afraid, Paloma," he added. "I'll admit it. It was a killing field of Spaniards fifty years ago. Would I be the only white man among hundreds at this gathering?"

"Thousands, if you add women and children," Toshua admitted. He made a sound of his own. "Well, there are white slaves, too."

"How easily I could become one," Marco said. "I am afraid."

Paloma watched her husband's face, which had gone suddenly pale. "Only a brave man would make such an admission, my love," she told him.

"You're too kind," he replied. He stirred on the bench and put his hand close to her hip. "And there is Paloma."

The two warriors regarded each other. Paloma watched them both, painfully aware how much they must have said to each other last night, when she slept so soundly against Toshua's shoulder and before Marco had carried her back to bed.

"I cannot," Marco repeated. "There is too much at stake right here."

More silence. Toshua broke the stare first. He looked down at the table, then slowly nodded. "The People need to hear from a Spaniard. They need to hear what the governor would want in return for peace. You could tell me before I leave soon, and I will pass along your words. It won't mean as much, but it is better than nothing."

She felt Marco flinch against the flat sound of Toshua's voice, he who was ordinarily so expressive in his colorful and occasionally accurate Spanish. "I will do that, my brother," Marco said quietly. "I will promise right now to go with you at another time. Let us walk by the water."

Without another word, Toshua handed Claudito to her and both men rose and left the house. Paloma got up, too, Claudito in her arms. She went to the window and watched them stroll along the *acequia*, gesturing and talking.

"Eckapeta, I am holding Marco back," she whispered into her son's neck.

Chapter Eleven

In which two drunken idiots are determined to avoid the audit

GASPAR, LONGTIME AND FREQUENTLY abused servant of Roque and Miguel Durán, knew better than to leave the impressive-looking broadside in the room the brothers called their "office." Why they called it that made no sense to him, because the brothers never worked in there. He had seen them open the door and chuck in a document or sheaf of papers, then close it quickly and laugh. Gaspar had a great fear of spiders, and imagined a whole colony of them in that room, multiplying and plotting something sinister.

He wished he could read. The broadside looked important, with letters and curlicues and even a waxed seal with two crosses. Roque Durán had tried to teach him to read once, but that had only led to blows.

Gaspar waited outside the closed door, wondering how wasted with *aguardiente* they were this afternoon. He stared hard at the broadside and nearly turned back to the kitchen, where he could use the paper for fire-starting.

The seal stopped him. This just might be important. He knocked on the door.

Nothing. After pressing his ear against the door, he knocked again. He heard loud, wet snoring, which meant both brothers were in their usual drunken state. He could sneak into the room and leave the broadside in a conspicuous place.

He opened the door slowly and found himself staring into the wide-open eyes of Miguel Durán. As frightening as that was, at least he was not Roque.

"Yes, what?" Miguel demanded. He belched and Gaspar smelled the fumes from the doorway. For the hundredth time, he wondered how different this vile place would have been if either brother had married. Perhaps they had tried, but nothing had ever come of any wooing. Probably the women of Valle del Sol were too smart.

"A … a *soldado* brought this." Gaspar held out the broadside at arm's length. "I thought it might be important."

"You *thought*," Miguel muttered. "Since when do *you* think?"

Gaspar hung his head, silent, while his master laughed.

With more bodily noise, Miguel leaned forward and grabbed the broadside. He sank back against the odorous cushions, read it, then jabbed his sleeping brother. Gaspar stepped back, unwilling to be around Roque when he woke up.

With a groan of his own, Roque sat up and looked at the sheet of paper his brother thrust under his nose. He paled noticeably, and Gaspar saw fear in the man's wasted face. The servant stayed where he was, silent in the doorway. He knew from hard experience that a sudden move might remind his masters he was there.

Roque put down the broadside. "This is serious."

Miguel nodded, his eyes troubled. "Think of all the years we have not been forthcoming to either Marco Mondragón or his father before him …" his voice trailed off, and he looked around.

Gaspar knew Señor Mondragón as a distant powerful figure, the man who counted livestock and registered brands, and assessed his masters' herds and flocks for taxes. The brothers never spoke his name without an accompanying curse.

"Here's what I would do," Roque shouted suddenly. "Abduct the auditor and … and …." Slumping down against the adobe ledge he sat on, he reached for the green glass bottle and drank until wine ran down the corners of his mouth. "I'd keep him for two weeks, or maybe three, or until they give up the audit and go away."

Gaspar knew he wasn't a smart fellow. Hadn't the brothers been telling him that for years? Even so, he saw the foolishness of Roque's idea and wondered just how many more bottles of mescal and wine it would take to ruin his masters' brains forever. You don't kidnap auditors and expect the problem to go away; even fools like Gaspar knew that.

Miguel took a swig from the same bottle and laughed. "Brilliant! We'll keep him here in that old hut, the one that still has a lock and key. Maybe we could send a threatening letter, or even kill him and blame Comanches. Bam! End of audit."

The brothers laughed. Gaspar made the mistake of coughing. Their heads swiveled as one and they stared at him. The servant felt his heart race; he knew that look. They couldn't abduct an officer of the crown—it was the kind of harebrained idea that ordinary men quickly waved aside, once they were sober.

Trouble was, the twins were seldom sober. Maybe they did owe taxes to the government, since their office was an untidy stew of mouse turds, spiders, and mildew. They were afraid of this audit.

He tried to make himself small in the doorway and even took a step back. But no, Roque motioned him closer.

"Sh-sh-should I get you more wine?" Gaspar stammered, telling himself to show no fear.

Moving fast for a drunk, Roque grabbed Gaspar and yanked him into the *sala*, forcing him to squat there on the floor.

"You have an old cousin at the Double Cross, do you not?" Miguel asked. He focused hard eyes on Gaspar, who wanted to crawl away and hide.

"Perla, *la cocinera*," Gaspar whispered.

The brothers looked at each other and grinned in an odd unison that made the hairs on his arms prickle. "You will go to the Double Cross," Roque said, after another glance at his twin. "Miguel, for what reason? Someone will ask."

"Let me think," Miguel said, silent so long that Gaspar began to hope. But no, he snapped his fingers. "Simple! Tell your cousin we need a cook and we'll … we'll pay her ten *reales* a year more than whatever Señor Mondragón pays."

"Ten *reales*!" Roque asked in stupefied amazement. "We can't afford that."

Gaspar looked from one brother to the other. Other idiotic ideas had been strangled at birth, once the two masters started arguing, making him hopeful again. *Let this insanity die*, he thought.

Miguel slapped his brother, a wakeup tap to the cheek. "We're not paying her *anything*! We want Gaspar to look around the Double Cross. You know, see if the auditor has a routine that we can interfere with."

Roque belched, which Miguel seemed to take as approval.

"I knew you would agree," Miguel said, turning his attention to Gaspar. "Go there. Stay a day or two. Look around."

Just agree, Gaspar told himself. *They will see the foolishness of this by the time I return. Maybe.*

He hesitated too long. Out slammed Miguel's booted foot again for another blow to Gaspar's ribs. He curled up tight, hoping for the best, expecting the worst. Two more blows and then quiet, as the snoring drunks leaned against each other.

GASPAR HOPED SOME SENSE would have returned to his masters by morning, but no. He served them their usual breakfast of burned bread and nearly cooked cornmeal, praying they would have forgotten yesterday's lunacy.

"Take the donkey and ride to the Double Cross," Miguel ordered. "Don't return until you know the auditor's habits."

What could he do but throw a blanket over Máximo's bony back and leave? At least the day was mild, with the softness of spring after a winter of shivering from the cold because the twins never allowed much heat anywhere except their own rooms; hunger, because the Duráns thought their servants and slaves could live on air. Strange they never noticed how few servants were left.

The farther he rode, the better Gaspar felt. The sun warmed his back, which was almost as bony as the donkey's. Once off the blighted Durán holdings, he noticed bunch grass and tender shoots of sprouted greenery, first herald of spring. Taking pity on Máximo, he dismounted and led his donkey from patch to patch, thinking how simple it would be to treat animals and people better.

He felt braver, too, deciding to tell the brothers firmly with no misunderstanding that he would no longer work for them. He knew he would forfeit his yearly wage, so small as to be barely noticed. He tried to think what it would be like to serve someone, anyone, without fear, and couldn't. Maybe he was as stupid as the Duráns told him he was. How could he tell?

GASPAR REACHED THE DOUBLE Cross when shadows began to lengthen across the western edge of Valle del Sol. He had been there only twice before, but everyone in the valley knew the Mondragóns, envying the security of their holdings and the fertility of the sometimes-contrary New Mexican soil.

The gates opened to him with a wave of his hand and the words, "Coming to see Perla, *la cocinera*." An old man followed by a silly-looking yellow dog met him at the horse barn and instructed him where to stable his donkey. The old fellow grunted his displeasure at the sight of bony Máximo.

"I come from the Durán *estancia*," Gaspar said, apologetic and embarrassed. "I came to visit my cousin, Perla."

"That explains the donkey," the man said. Perhaps figuring it wasn't Gaspar's fault he worked for terrible men, he loosened up. "I will send a small boy for Perla."

Ashamed of his poor animal, Gaspar tended Máximo, who quickly fell to gobbling far better hay than he usually ate. When Gaspar looked up, his cousin Perla stood in the doorway of the horse barn, her arms folded, as if wondering what he wanted.

He gave her a kiss on the cheek, which seemed to satisfy the old fellow that Perla really was his cousin. Perhaps Perla felt she had been too skeptical. She unfolded her arms and kissed him in return.

Even Gaspar knew she would smell a rat if he blurted out that his masters wanted to hire her away from the Mondragóns, so he looked around the courtyard. He immediately noticed a beat-up carriage with a fading red and yellow royal seal on the door.

"Visitors?" he inquired, hoping to sound interested and not desperate to know.

Perla gave him a swift glance, then softened a little. How often did she get relatives as visitors? "It's the seven-year audit, *primo*," she said. "The governor sent us a meek little fellow who will never inherit the earth." She crossed herself. "His daughter came, too. She and my mistress have struck up a friendship."

"That's nice," he said, as they walked toward the house. He admired the hanging baskets of flowers spilling over along the portal. A little girl rocked a cradle and sang to herself. He knew this was how people should really live. "Is the auditor working here?"

"Yes, in the master's office," Perla said, pointing with her lips.

"Does he stay in there all day?" he asked, hoping it sounded like small talk.

Perla stared at him, and Gaspar suspected he had gone too far.

He shrugged. "Just curious. Nothing ever happens where I live." He didn't dare look at her, afraid she would see his desperation.

There they stood, until Perla must have decided to give him the benefit of the doubt. "Lately, every afternoon after siesta, he and that addled driver take a ride into the countryside."

Gaspar heard Perla's voice soften. "Poor man. From what Señora Mondragón tells Sancha, and what she passes on to me, he's led a miserable life."

Gaspar made a sympathetic sound, hoping she would continue.

Trust Perla to do that, once she had found a subject and an audience. "Señor Mondragón encouraged him to get out a bit. I think it's sweet."

"After siesta?" he asked, and vowed to ask no more, afraid to awake her suspicion.

"Yes, for about an hour. Then he works until dinner."

Perla led him into the kitchen where he began to salivate, because everything smelled so good, from the posole bubbling in its iron pot to what looked like a hunk of beef, turned on a spit by a small child.

His cousin put her hands on her hips. Gaspar held his breath, wondering what was coming next.

"Gaspar, *why* are you here?"

Perhaps he was a better actor than he knew, or maybe he was more of a deceiver than he ever suspected, which didn't soothe Gaspar's immortal soul.

"Cousin, you won't believe what my masters want!" he declared with a laugh and a rueful shake of his head. "They want you to cook for them."

Perla laughed so hard she had to sit down. "You can't be serious!" she said finally. "Only an idiot would leave the Mondragóns." She looked at him in sudden sympathy, which told Gaspar she had some idea of the meanness of his life on the Durán *estancia*. "I trust my refusal will not lead to a beating for you," she said. "Here, let me feed you some of this beef. Maybe I should send you back with *queso* for your awful masters. You know, so they do not take my rejection out on you."

Gaspar nodded, relieved her suspicion seemed to have vanished. She was a simple soul, same as he. He knew of her devotion to the Mondragóns, and he envied her.

"I hate working for the Duráns," he blurted out. "They are mean and drunk most of the time. Do you think … could I ever work here?"

"We can ask," Perla said.

Her kind expression made him feel worse. What kind of a cousin comes to spy and tell lies? Apparently his kind. Pray God that nothing more of the Duráns would rub off on him.

To his relief, Perla invited him to stay the night. Maybe one thing or another could keep him here. He could manage to ride out at the same time as the auditor, and see for himself what the man did. With luck, the Duráns might have forgotten any sinister schemes before he returned.

He could hope, anyway, since hope was the salary of a man poor in wages, character, and courage.

Chapter Twelve

In which Marco makes a not-so-pleasant decision

WITH SERIOUS MISGIVINGS, MARCO said *adios* to his friend Toshua and stood by the gate until he was out of sight, heading north toward Rio Napestle, a place that haunted all Spaniards. He wasted not a moment in rationalizing his decision to stay put.

Never a lazy man, he found it harder every year to throw off winter's lethargy and plunge into spring, that busy time when calves and lambs came into the world—usually during a storm—and when corn and wheat needed to be in the ground at precisely the right time. Valle del Sol was a wonderful place to live, but only when its citizens knew when to plant, and how to plant, to take advantage of every bit of moisture the soil possessed. This was a dry place. King Carlos might not know it, but his subjects did.

Marco could blame Paloma for making it harder for him to move into action. He could also blame his advancing years. A man of thirty-four in the colony of New Mexico had reached middle age. Better to blame Paloma, because this wasn't the kind of blame that made anyone unhappy. He could blame her for being the wife of his heart and soul, a pleasant sort of blame that only made him smile and want to spend another hour close to her in bed, savoring her warmth and that sweet milky smell that he found oddly enchanting.

After his whispered words with Toshua three days ago, he knew Paloma deserved his special attention. That alone made his decision to stay the proper one. His heart had won this mental coin toss, even though his more logical brain nagged him about his duty to his colony and securing its much-desired peace.

Dissatisfied with himself, he leaned back in his chair and looked around his office, pleased at least that Señor Ygnacio knew precisely what he was doing. The little man was out right now for what had turned into his daily ride in the decrepit carriage Felix Moreno had foisted on him. To assuage his own guilty conscience at ignoring Toshua's plea, Marco toyed with the idea of having Santa Maria's wagon maker spruce up the decrepit vehicle before the Ygnacios departed for Santa Fe. Too bad the accountant would be heading back to more trouble and maltreatment, if he returned at all.

He mulled over the strange death threat and wondered—not for the first time—what sort of game Felix Moreno played as *contador principal.* Joaquim Gasca said that his two troopers had followed the four *soldados* for two days and found nothing amiss. Marco then considered the driver who remained here at the Double Cross. He seemed to be what Catalina had told them, a man no more than a halfwit who obeyed orders. Who else was supposed to eliminate the auditor? Perhaps the Ygnacios had misheard the original threat, brought to them by a lowly custodian.

"*Ay de mi,*" he muttered under his breath. He had a bigger concern, one much closer to his heart. True, Toshua had called the matter to his attention that Paloma was simply not thriving. He knew that after she returned Juanito to his cradle following his early-morning feeding, she let herself out of the house to sit in silence on the porch.

He asked to join her once, but she shook her head, and in her kindly way told him she enjoyed the solitude. What could he say? Toshua had told him to let her be.

He finally worked up the nerve to mention something to Sancha, who admitted she worried about her mistress, too.

"There is probably no good time to birth a baby," his housekeeper had said only that morning, when he had found her alone in the kitchen and unburdened his heart to her, as he had done years earlier, after his first family died. "Spring is such a busy time of year and she feels she cannot rest or shirk her duties." She hesitated.

"Go on. Speak," he said, not one to shirk even bad news.

"Sometimes this happens after babies are born," Sancha told him, choosing her words carefully. "A cloud descends."

"How long does it stay?" he asked.

"A week or two. A month." Sancha shrugged. She opened her mouth to speak, but closed it.

"Don't stop now, Sancha," he said. "You and I have been through much."

"I've known it to never leave, this odd sadness," she said.

"What should I do?" he asked.

"Let her rest somewhere peaceful," Sancha told him. "Somewhere quiet."

You have to trust Toshua's wisdom, and now Sancha's, he told himself, then wondered if he could give Paloma more quiet time by sending her on a visit to his sister. That might be just the remedy she needed.

Restless, he went to the door of his office and looked out at the courtyard, where the business of spring was in full swing. Emilio had located all the cloth bags Marco would fill with wheat tomorrow when he led the planting. Two days would see the job done, with beans to follow. At least the corn was in little hillocks of soil.

He remembered dangerous days in his childhood, when laborers went to the field with guards and big dogs, ancestors of the dogs Claudito enjoyed riding now. He remembered sudden alarms that woke him at night, sending him rushing down the hall to crawl into bed with his mother. His father would be on the roof watching, always watching. Sometimes trouble came, and sometimes trouble visited his neighbors, but they all suffered in turn until the Comanche Moon set.

Marco thought of his brother-in-law, Ramon Gutierrez, who had died too young at the hands of Comanches, leaving his sister a widow with one small son and another on the way. Maria Luisa Gutierrez had seen both sons married now, with small children of their own, but she had been alone for many years, her man quiet in another cemetery.

Maria Luisa. Marco sat down at his desk again and took out a sheet of paper. He thought a long time—one mustn't waste paper—then began to write. He told his sister of Juan Luis's birth, and Paloma's strange sadness, and asked if he could send his darling wife and new son to stay with her for a few weeks. *If she remains here, Paloma will work too hard, no matter how I urge her to stop, and never get the rest she needs,* he wrote, even as he dreaded the very idea of sending his wife several hours away. *If she visits you, I know she will relax and put her feet up, which she must do. Her lassitude is starting to worry me.*

He concluded with all the usual comments about home and crops and life in his part of the valley. He promised to come for his wife in a few weeks, bringing his other little ones, and stay for a short visit himself. He knew the planting would be done by then, the calves and lambs frisking about and summer on its way.

He sealed the note with hot wax and his Double Cross stamp and went into the courtyard again, looking for a messenger.

He noticed the poorly dressed man leaning against the outside wall of the horse stable and wondered who he was, as he had wondered yesterday but hadn't taken the time to inquire. Marco watched the man now as the gates opened and the auditor's carriage came into view. He saw how alert he became, and remembered a similar sight yesterday at the same time.

Still watching the stranger, Marco beckoned to Emilio. Marco handed the letter to his *mayor domo,* requesting that he send a rider to the Gutierrez *estancia* and wait for a reply.

Emilio nodded and took the letter. Marco put out his hand. "Before you go, who is that man over there? The one so stoop shouldered, even though he looks young? I don't know him."

Emilio looked where Marco gestured with his lips, Comanche style, and shrugged. "He is a poor specimen, but a cousin of Perla *la cocinera.* I believe he came to visit."

"Does he work for someone?"

Emilio made a face. "Those wretched twins, Roque and Miguel Durán."

"My father never could get them to account for all their cattle properly." He made his own face, wondering how some useless men seemed to hang on, even in a dangerous place such as Valle del Sol. "He told me it was best to ignore them, and I have."

"Perhaps this one should go on his way," Emilio said. "I will remind him that he does not work here."

Marco nodded and returned to his office. Staring at the paperwork before him, he wished for Toshua to appear.

Second best was Joaquim Gasca, who came into the office with Señor Ygnacio.

"Look who I found on the trail from Santa Maria?" Joaquim said. "I told him I would be happy to sit with him this afternoon."

I think you would be even happier to sit with Catalina Ygnacio, Marco told himself, as he motioned the two inside.

True to his observant nature, Marco watched the two men, one old and stooped, and the other confident and capable, after his own years of purgatory. He marveled at the change that had come over his friend since they'd returned from the killing grounds last fall after the death of Great Owl.

Last night Marco had remarked to Paloma on more recent changes, which included heretofore unseen tenderness in that friend's eyes when he looked at Catalina Ygnacio. It pleased him to see Joaquim's attention funneled toward an intelligent but prickly woman long past the blush of youth and well into her twenties.

He had been watching Catalina, too, happy to see a deep dimple in her cheek, she who by her own disclaimer to Paloma had never smiled much or found reason to. Marco also noted that when she laughed or merely smiled, her eyes seemed to grow larger instead of smaller, as was more commonly the case. And what eyes they were, much darker brown than his, and so handsome.

There was no denying Catalina Ygnacio had a sharp tongue and appeared not to suffer fools gladly. Marco couldn't imagine such a shrew in his own household, but he also wondered how much of her quick anger was a defensive move to strike out first before someone had a chance to hit her with sneering words or some other unkindness.

He could almost see why Joaquim might be drawn to such a woman as Catalina Ygnacio. In earlier years he had watched the smooth Joaquim work his magic on other females in Santa Maria. Catalina appeared to have no such interest in coming into the *teniente's* orbit. She was a challenge to him, or so Marco reckoned.

No wonder Joaquim found himself drawn to her. True, she was tall and thin, but Joaquim had made a remark last week about how nice it was to look in her eyes without having to bend down. He had followed that bit of news with a joke, but Marco wasn't fooled.

"You just wait, dear heart," Paloma had whispered to him last night as she handed their well-fed and slumbering child to him to place in his cradle. "Joaquim will realize what Lina is." Then he had snuggled down with Paloma, aware of her sigh as her back came into contact with her mattress, after fifteen hours away from it.

"And what is she?" he teased. "I'm not so certain Joaquim Gasca is a man who will like being ordered about by a thin woman almost as tall as he is, no matter what he says."

Even in the dark, he could almost hear Paloma gathering her innate dignity about her. "There are times, husband, when I look at El Teniente Gasca and see a little boy who wants someone to care enough to order him about."

"How do you know these things?" Marco asked, delighted with her insights, which had proved accurate on many occasions. Even more, she sounded more like the Paloma he knew, and not the woman so quiet of late.

"I just do," she said. He pulled her closer and felt her stiffen. He kissed her cheek, well aware of her next effort to relax, as though life was normal. He saw all the exhaustion in her eyes, even sorrow, as she whispered, "Do you want me?"

"You know I do," he told her, but put his hand over hers as she started on her buttons. "I also know how tired you are."

"That must be it. Give me a little time."

He lay awake until she thought he slept, then listened as she let herself out of the house again, to sit by herself.

Now what, Toshua? he thought, miserable.

*

"YOU'RE NOT PAYING MUCH attention, friend," Joaquim said.

Marco recalled his thoughts to the moment, there in his office, with the *capitán* of the presidio looking at him and the little auditor already rolling up his sleeves to begin tallying figures again. He made himself smile to hear Señor Ygnacio chuckling for no other reason than that he had numbers, lots of them, to add and subtract and check. Marco couldn't imagine such tedium.

"You caught me, Joaquim," Marco replied. "Let us walk outside for a moment and leave this good man to his labor."

It touched Marco's heart to see Señor Ygnacio nod in pleasure at something so simple as being called "a good man." Maybe before he and his daughter left Valle del Sol—*deo volente* all was safe and they were well—Marco could write a letter to Governor Anza and request that the auditor be transferred somewhere, anywhere, away from Felix Moreno. It could happen; the governor had listened to him before.

The two men walked toward the *acequia*, which, next to the kitchen, seemed to be where serious conversations took place. They sat on the low bench where Claudio and Soledad usually played, and he poured his heart out to the *teniente*.

"I have written to my sister, the widow Gutierrez, asking if she will let Paloma and Juanito be her guests for a few weeks," he concluded. "She's not prospering, and I fear for her."

"She doesn't seem quite her charming self," Joaquim said finally. "I think this is a wise plan. Does Paloma?"

"I haven't asked her," Marco confessed. "I know she will argue with me." He thought about last night's conversation with her and wondered if that were really so. "Or she might see the necessity herself."

"Convince her," Joaquim said. He slapped his knees and stood up. "Listen to me giving you advice! I who am less qualified than anyone on your *estancia*."

"You care greatly about her," Marco said simply. "I know you want the best for her." There was no challenge in his voice, but he wanted Joaquim to know that he, Marco Mondragón, was a husband who had eyes in his head.

Marco regarded Joaquim thoughtfully, noting the change that a winter of self-examination and discipline had imposed on a former lecher, drunkard, and all-purpose selfish man.

"I will always care for Paloma," Joaquim said at last. "Marco, you won't mind if I admire her from a distance?"

"Until you find a woman of your own," Marco told him. "Which reminds me: you are busy; I am busy. What do you say we put Catalina Ygnacio in charge of getting Paloma and Juanito to my sister's *estancia*?"

"I have noticed Señorita Ygnacio enjoys being in charge," Joaquim said with a bit of lurking humor in his eyes. "Paloma will be in good hands. Papa

Ygnacio will probably not mind if they take the government vehicle a little farther than a drive around your holdings here. Should I ask her?"

"I wish you would, but let me speak to Paloma first," Marco said. "I will do it tonight."

He nodded to Joaquim at the office door, and remembered Perla's cousin, who had been three days at the Double Cross. He looked around, hoping the man was gone, even as his probably too-soft heart wanted to give him a meal or at least some bread and cheese before he went on his way. Working for the Durán twins had to be close kin to starvation and near slavery.

Thoughtful, Marco walked to the horse barn and saw Emilio. "That man …" he began.

"Gaspar? He's gone," Emilio said. He stood up to show his respect for his master, even though both of them had long settled into casual friendship. "He asked questions about poor Señor Ygnacio's carriage. Not sure why. His questions never seemed to go anywhere." He shrugged again. "Why would anyone work for the Duráns, who was not already a half-wit?"

Gone. Just as well, Marco knew, his mind already on Paloma and then tomorrow's planting. There was much to do on the Double Cross, without worrying about people who didn't belong here.

Chapter Thirteen

In which a storyteller weaves magic and fear

THE YGNACIOS HAD SETTLED into a pleasant ritual each evening. Dinner was its usual pleasant gathering in the kitchen, with the children eating and talking. Marco and Paloma had decided early on that children would always be seen and heard on the Double Cross.

After dinner, Señor Ygnacio would chat in the *sala* for a few minutes, then give a sigh and a yawn and excuse himself.

Catalina usually followed him to his room, where she sat on his bed and visited with him a few minutes. The children waited with barely concealed excitement for the auditor's daughter to return.

Marco admitted to Paloma that he nearly felt the same anticipation, which made his wife smile and touch his face. "Everyone likes a story, dear heart," she told him, and she was right.

Even now, after several weeks of evening stories, Marco wondered how a thin woman with a sharp nature could so completely transform herself into a mesmerizing storyteller. And wonder of wonders, she hadn't repeated the same story twice. Every little *dicho* seemed designed just for his children, which made him wonder if Catalina Ygnacio tailored each little morality play or humorous dialog to his little ones.

He had posed the question to Paloma in a spare moment when she wasn't hurrying from one task to another, even as he wished she would rest.

"Does Catalina tell certain stories for the edification of our own little ones? Some of them seem designed just for Soledad," he had asked. "I love that child, but her own tall tales make me wonder."

"Lina and I had a discussion about Soledad's exaggerations. I told Lina we're trying to teach our little ones that the truth is better, but stories can be fun, too."

Tonight was no different. With no coaxing, Catalina seated herself in one of the two high-backed chairs in the room. He sat in the other, as was his right as master of the *estancia*. Maybe it was a conspiracy with the rest of them, but Paloma made herself comfortable on one of the adobe benches built into the wall. Everyone seemed to pick a seat with the idea that Paloma would have no choice but to occupy the space closest to the corner fireplace, well-padded with Indian blankets and a pillow. Juanito's cradle just seemed to appear there, too.

Sometimes Paloma stayed awake to hear all of Catalina's little stories. Sometimes she nursed Juanito, put him in his cradle and slept, her face so relaxed, while Claudito stayed wide awake and cuddled against her.

Independent Soledad always stationed herself directly in front of the storyteller, sitting with her legs crossed, her anticipation high. Sometimes, before the stories were over, little Soli sat on Catalina's lap.

How was it this woman of no account in Santa Fe could transform herself into a weaver of magic? Her eyes widened, her gaze intensified, and her voice changed, depending on the requirements of the *dicho*. She almost became beautiful.

Even when the little *dichos* seemed aimed at the children's sometimes ornery behavior, Soledad soaked it in. Catalina was telling such a story now, probably because she had watched Soli racing down the hall earlier, unmindful of the servants who had to dodge her as they carried towels and water for Paloma's bath.

"This is the tale of Señorita Rabbit, who never looked where she was going," Catalina began, after a sidelong look at Paloma. "She ran willy-nilly through the countryside, knocking over old Señor Burro, who moved so slowly." Catalina lifted her hands slowly, moved her head from side to side, and brayed an "ee-aa" that made Joaquim Gasca give a snort and turn away.

"She just didn't care," Soledad said.

Catalina added a sorrowful look to Señor Burro's painful gait. Marco listened with appreciation as the story wound on through the countryside, with the thoughtless rabbit finally coming afoul of an eagle that lifted her high into the air—amazing how Catalina could almost take flight as she spoke—and shook the terrified animal a few times until Señorita Rabbit's eyes began to jiggle.

" 'Let me go, Señor Águila!' Señorita Conejo begged, as her teeth began to rattle," Catalina said. She swooped down and plucked up Soledad, who shrieked in terror, trapped now on their guest's lap. "What should the naughty rabbit do?"

Soledad thought a moment, as Marco looked at Paloma, her hand to her mouth, eyes wide and so lovely that his heart yearned for her. Who knew that such simple stories could delight them all?

The girl was no one's fool. Leaning comfortably against Catalina, who had wrapped her arms around the child, Soledad was silent a long moment. "She should be more careful," she said at last, her voice low because Marco sensed some repentance going on.

"If she is not?" came the storyteller's question.

"I think the eagle should eat her," Soledad said. She sighed. "I should walk more slowly in the hall."

"That would be lovely," Catalina said. She kissed the top of the child's head. "But you would never be a thoughtless rabbit."

Soledad shook her head quickly. She sat down on the floor again, her hands carefully folded in front of her. Her innate honesty made her look up with a frown. "I could be, but Mama would not be happy."

"Can you change?" Paloma asked.

Soledad nodded and gave another gusty sigh. "Until I forget. It is hard to be a girl who likes to run."

Marco couldn't help his chuckle. "You could come with me to the field tomorrow while we plant more corn and run all you like, you and Claudito."

Soledad clapped her hands and looked at Paloma. "Could I?"

"You may, if you try harder not to run in the house, especially now that you have a littler brother who needs peaceful sleep," Paloma told Soledad, her eyes kind.

So it went for another story and another, these about little boys and girls who helped their parents and protected small birds and defenseless creatures.

Marco glanced at the doorway to see his house servants clustered there, captivated by the magic of these stories: simple tales of not enough rain, and the promises the foolish landowner makes to a witch for more rain; the story of a dandy who takes advice from a Hopi medicine man who turns him into a ragged coyote for his vanity; the poor girl who finds a gold nugget in an *arroyo* and gives it to a shabby *paisana* who turns into the Virgin of Guadalupe— tales of love and hope and rain that sometimes seemed so far away in poor, dangerous New Mexico.

We need this, Marco thought, as he looked around at all the people under his protection. Suddenly the burden of his responsibilities, sometimes so crushing, grew lighter. He smiled at Paloma, who gazed back at him with so much tenderness that his heart overflowed. *I will do anything to see you happier*, he thought, knowing he could never manage a moment without her, simply because the will to try would be gone forever.

The moment passed. He felt his heart grow strong again. His glance rested on his children, one a child of his body and Paloma's, the other the daughter of a weak man and his vindictive wife, but both little ones equally loved. He watched Juanito asleep in his cradle and then his wife, who was having trouble keeping her eyes open now.

"I think we are done for the night," he whispered to Catalina, who was looking at Joaquim Gasca.

Suddenly he saw them both in a new light, and it warmed his heart still more. Through Joaquim's long winter of personal repair and presidio rehabilitation, Marco had noticed a deepening frown crease the handsome man's face, as the weight of his own sins and his need to redeem both himself and the pathetic garrison entrusted to him bit deep. For a brief time while Catalina Ygnacio, no one's treasure, had spun her tales effortlessly, El Teniente Gasca's load had been lightened..

"Isn't there time for one more story before I must leave?" Joaquim coaxed. "Here, I will carry Soledad to bed and Marco will get Claudito." He stood up and carefully lifted the sleepy girl to rest against his shoulder.

Marco picked up Claudito, breathing deep of the early spring sunlight that he smelled in his son's hair. "It would have to be a short story," he cautioned. "You need to return to your garrison, and Paloma is tired."

Marco followed Joaquim down the dark hall, lit now with only a flickering candle here and there. He looked at the two old paintings of saints, work done a century and more ago before his ancestors were driven from Santa Fe in a terrible uprising that killed hundreds. There was enough of a breeze to set the linen pictures swaying. He couldn't deny a stab of fear, as though cold fingers strummed his backbone. Maybe he should put those old things away. Suppose Soli or Claudito saw them swaying in the hall, moving like wraiths?

He shook off the feeling, grateful Joaquim could not read his thoughts and brand him a weak man, a milk baby.

The men decided that shoes off was enough. In a moment the children's blankets were tucked high against the cold that came with morning, living with thin air at this high altitude.

He stood a moment in silence, then made the sign of the cross over each sleeping body. He noticed Joaquim's smile as he looked at the children.

"Maybe you will have children of your own someday," he whispered to the lieutenant.

"I would like that above all things, but first I must find a wife."

"What do you think of Catalina Ygnacio?" Marco asked, wondering if he was too forward, but curious to know.

They started back down the hall together. "Too thin. Too tall. Too bossy," Joaquim said as they approached the *sala*. He stopped, knowing who waited inside the next room. "And yet, when she tells stories, her whole person changes. How does she do that?"

"Maybe you should ask her," Marco suggested.

"Oh no," Joaquim said with a laugh. "I will leave that to better men than I, the kind who won't do something stupid and break a woman's heart."

Marco thought of both his wives and the numerous times they had forgiven him for being dense and dumb, because that seemed to be a woman's nature. "They are tougher than you think, friend, when it comes to stupid husbands."

Paloma was sitting up when they came into the *sala*. "We have decreed one short *dicho* only," she said. "I must go to bed, and you, *Teniente*, have a dark road to travel."

"There is a full moon," Joaquim said. He rubbed his hands together. "I am a Catalonian from Barcelona and then Cuba, as you know. There is a tale I have heard of here in this New World, but no one has told me—something about a weeping woman, La Llorona."

Paloma gasped and reached for Marco's hand. "Not that one! Never that one!" She stood up, unsteady, and started for the door.

Chilled to the bone by his wife's sudden exclamation, Marco grabbed her around the waist, then picked her up. "It's only a *dicho*, dearest," he said.

She squirmed in his arms to look at his face. "A story of a poor woman who haunts the riverbank, gouging her eyes and calling for her drowned children? No, Marco." She put her head against his chest so he could not see her face.

He hurried down the hall with her to their own room, where he put her to bed, then returned to the *sala*, where Catalina was speaking to Joaquim. They stood close together, as if she did not want her words about La Llorona to travel beyond a few inches, and certainly not anywhere else.

"No, this is not the time or place," the lieutenant agreed. "I should leave now. I ... I'll send my corporal in the morning to sit with Señor Ygnacio."

Still Joaquim remained, and Catalina rubbed her arms. "He was just curious, Señor Mondragón," she said formally, as though he had just broken a spell.

"I know." He heard the sorrow in her voice, as though something—or someone—Catalina Ygnacio wanted was gone from her possession. Her disappointment chafed him.

"I'll save the story for another time and another place," she assured him as she went to the door of the *sala*. She looked down the hall in the direction of Paloma's room. "Such a story would bother any mother. I never thought of it like that before."

Chapter Fourteen

In which Paloma agrees to a journey, because Toshua says so

Marco left the sala for the darkened corridor, unable to shake off his unease at Paloma's outburst. He knew she had heard the sad story of La Llorona, as had everyone in the New World. Some said it came from Indios in the Caribbean. Others traced it to early settlers in Guatemala. Everyone claimed the story was true, told by an uncle or a cousin who knew the woman involved.

He had grown up with the New Mexican version, probably one of many, where a beautiful young woman falls in love with a ranchero, a handsome man who could ride like a Comanche. Marco leaned against the wall in the corridor, which suddenly seemed much darker, except for those slowly moving painted saints. *Dios.* He was taking those down in the morning.

"And they marry," he said softly to himself, remembering how his mother's telling of the story used to scare him enough to keep him indoors at night when he was a boy. "They are happy, so happy, and have three little ones in quick succession."

He closed his eyes, mostly to avoid looking at the paintings. And then the man resumed his wild ways on the plains of eastern New Mexico, not returning for several years, or so the story went.

And when he came back, he was accompanied by a different beautiful young woman, he thought, unable to stop his mind from recalling the sad little tale he had not thought of in years, because he knew that as much as he loved his mother, he would never frighten his children with La Llorona.

They rode through the village in a carriage, and the cast-off wife saw them, as she walked along the riverbank with her children. After they passed, she drowned her children in the river, holding them under until they ceased their frantic struggles.

"*Ay de mi,*" he said out loud, remembering how his big sister, now the widow Gutierrez, held him close as Mama told the story.

She died of grief beside the river, when she realized what she had done. Now her fantasma *walks along the bank, weeping and moaning for her little ones, as she scratches out her eyes.*

"Oof, Catalina just told me the whole story," a voice said behind him.

Marco jumped, then gave a shaky laugh to see Joaquim—or what he hoped and prayed was Joaquim—standing beside him. "Don't sneak up on me! You've heard that beastly tale now."

"I have indeed." The soldier shuddered and inclined his head toward the closed door farther down the hall. "Please tell Paloma I would never have asked for that awful story, had I had any idea what it was about."

"She'll understand," Marco said. "Mamas, especially new ones, must abhor that story." He gave his friend a push. "Go on now. You do have a garrison to run."

Joaquim nodded, his head down. "I've been a little lax there, haven't I? Truth to tell, I like being here, and I think maybe it isn't because I admire Paloma, although I do. You know what I mean. I'm making a mess of this! Somebody stop me."

Marco laughed and gave Joaquim another push. "Maybe you're discovering a heretofore unknown fondness for figures and columns."

"I'm certain that's it," Joaquim replied, humor evident in his voice. "There's really nothing wrong with skinny women, is there? I mean, that's all we see in Valle del Sol."

The two men laughed together. Marco knew that while Paloma could never be called thin again—and thank God for that—she was by no means stout and never would be.

"We all work too hard to be fat," Marco said. "Before you go, help me take down these paintings."

He thought Joaquim might question such an impulse, but he didn't. The two of them lifted the fading linen saints with dowels through the top hem off their wooden perches, each man rolling up the one he held until they were two harmless bits of cloth. Marco leaned them against the wall.

"They should be in the chapel, anyway," Marco said, feeling the need for explanation.

Joaquim was a hard man to fool. "That way they won't scare you anymore, oh brave *juez de campo*?"

"Precisely!" Marco said, wondering why he even bothered to attempt subterfuge. "Ride in safety and come back in a few days. You must at least make sure that your entire garrison hasn't deserted, since you've developed an interest in audits."

Joaquim put his middle finger to his forehead in a lazy salute, then pointed it at Marco, who laughed and opened the door.

MARCO SAID GOODNIGHT TO Catalina as she walked down the hall to her little room, then made sure she had snuffed out the candles in the *sala*. The fireplace gave off only the smallest glow now, as he picked up the cradle with his sleeping son inside and continued down the hall to his bedchamber, where he hoped Paloma was sleeping.

She was sitting up in bed, her chin tucked against her upraised knees, as he placed the cradle close to the fireplace, but not too close. Sitting down on his clothes chest, one stocking off now, he leaned against the wall.

"Goodness, Marco, come to bed," Paloma said.

"I will," he told her. "That story haunts me, too, and do you know what else haunts me?"

"Better tell me, but I think I know," she said in a small voice. "It's what happens now and then, isn't it? Maybe La Llorona reminded you. Or me."

He watched her, wondering if he was intruding on some female ritual he had never noticed when Soledad was an infant. Maybe it just happened with sons. How did she know what he was thinking?

"Paloma, sometimes you wake me up at night, patting around at the end of our bed. Why do you do that?"

"I wish I didn't, but I can't help myself." She lay back against her pillow. "The dream is so real, Marco. I dream I have lost my baby and cannot find him. I pat around the bed, certain he is there somewhere. I start to panic."

"I know. You pat and then you stop and draw yourself into a little ball and go back to sleep. I wondered if *I* was dreaming, the first time you did that."

"No. It's my nightmare," she said. "Why didn't you say anything when Claudio was born and I did that?"

"Because I am a lump-headed husband who just goes back to sleep, happy to let his wife do the nursing and changing and everything else that smacks of midnight work," he said frankly. "I heard a joke once about a first-time father who woke up with a black eye. When he asked what happened, his wife said it was because she hit him with a candlestick, since he was lying there so peacefully with a smile on his face while she nursed their baby."

"*Tonto*! I would never beat you. Haven't even been tempted." She laughed softly. "Well, it *did* cross my mind once."

He took off his other stocking and threw it at her. She threw it back.

"You're looking for a missing child? Why didn't that happen with Soledad?" he asked, curious.

"I wondered about that at first, but remember, she had a wet nurse and did not sleep in here, as our sons do, because I nurse them," Paloma said. "It's as though I have fed them, but they have vanished from our bed." She managed another laugh, but he heard no humor this time. "It stops after a few months." A sigh. "I suppose that is why La Llorona is so frightening to me—that poor ghost, crying and looking everywhere for her children. I feel sorry for her."

She patted the empty space beside her. She hadn't bothered with a nightgown.

His clothes came off slowly, and he smiled to see Paloma watching him. He sucked in his stomach, even though it didn't need sucking in.

"You are a handsome man, for a New Mexican," she teased, and he sighed with relief at the change in her voice. "Please love me tonight. I'm not that tired. Really I'm not, Big Man Down There."

Smiling at his Comanche nickname—what man wouldn't?—Marco did as she asked, loving her carefully. He had come to understand a woman's pride in her body and her role as wife, and knew better than to disagree, especially when he didn't want to, and he didn't.

He was quick to satisfy. His wife surprised him with the ease of her pleasure, although why she should have surprised him, he couldn't have said. Paloma was his equal in everything, including lovemaking.

"Heavenly days, Señora Mondragón," he said when she was nestled at his side, her heavy breasts warm against his skin and dry because she had a towel handy. "You could pleasure me into a coma."

She chuckled and kissed his chest, which meant he kissed her hair and whatever else was close by. Paloma cuddled closer and he pulled the covers higher, mainly because his rump was cold.

While he was working up the nerve to tell her she needed to visit his sister for a while, Paloma toyed with his chest hairs. She finally gave them a little yank, and he tugged back on her hair, glad to find her playful again. He also knew she wanted his attention, and that his wife was a smart woman.

"You already know what I'm going to ask, don't you?" he said. "Heavenly days, Señora Mondragón," he teased again, "have we been married *that* long?"

"We talked about this earlier," she reminded him. "Besides, while you were busy in the field today, your rider returned with a message from my sister-in-law, saying that she would love to see me, her newest nephew, and meet Catalina."

"You're reading my mail now?" he teased.

"Silly! She didn't write it. She told Pablo, and he remembered it." Her fingers, at first gentle on his chest, moved lower to his navel. "I'll go, because I know you're right." She sighed. "So is Toshua."

"You need even more of a rest than an hour on the porch before dawn," he whispered in her ear. "How about in two days? Catalina can go along and then come back with the auditor's carriage."

"Why not ours?" she asked.

"My wagon master is replacing an axle in Santa Maria, and he's too busy with his own spring planting."

"Very well. We can chat on the way there and then she'll return here. You'll come and get me in a week?"

"Nice try, wife," he said, and gave her head a rub. "Two weeks."

Chapter Fifteen

In which the little journey becomes much longer

T HEY LEFT TWO DAYS after Marco begged the loan of the ramshackle little carriage the Ygnacios had arrived in, because his own conveyance was in need of repair from a wagon master also busy with planting.

"Ride with her, Catalina," he said, as they walked toward the office. She said yes, because the *juez de campo* was such a kind man to her father, and truth to tell, she liked him, too.

"Keep Paloma company and stay a day or two yourself," Marco urged her. "Your father is doing well and my sister is a good hostess."

"She needs the rest and I won't mind it, either," Catalina said, even as she wished sometimes that her brain was more disinclined to state aloud thoughts that others left unsaid. "Take me, for example," she said, plowing on. "I have underestimated my father. He is doing so well and he doesn't need my help. Did he ever? Did I render him less of a man?"

"Women try too hard, you are saying?" he asked, giving her a shrewd look that branded him forever as a husband.

"Perhaps we do, and we disappoint ourselves. I will watch over Paloma."

Truth to tell, two days away from Papa might be a good idea, Catalina decided. Lately, she had felt she was getting in the way of his audit. Only yesterday she had come into the office, ready to help, and he had looked up with something close to—but not quite—annoyance at her intrusion.

He had put his hands together and looked at her expectantly, as though wishing she would hurry up and tell him what to do, then leave. She had observed his neat piles of records and realized there was nothing she could do to improve matters. Nodding to him, she had made some comment about Paloma needing help with the children and left him to his audit—*his*, not hers.

What a day of bumbling about that had been. When Joaquim made his now usual appearance before dinner and nighttime stories, Catalina had told him about her father's obvious efficiency that didn't involve her this time. What did the dratted lieutenant do except smile in a most maddening fashion and kiss her cheek?

She turned her face to utter some retort, and he had kissed her mouth. Not just once, which could have been judged an accident because he hadn't expected her to turn her head so fast, but twice. And what had she done but kiss him back? Good God, the man was a rake and a rascal and she had kissed him. Where had her brains gone?

Even as he kissed her that second time—or maybe it was a third time—her own analytical mind tried to convince her this was folly. Easy to think, she decided later, when she had a moment to consider what had happened. For the first time in her life, her heart had overruled her brain. *My word, the man can kiss.* No, it was time for a visit to La Viuda Gutierrez so she could sort out her own feelings.

Leaving couldn't have come at a better time for her, but it wasn't easy, not with two little Mondragóns wearing long faces and wondering why Mama wouldn't take them along this time.

"We *know* that Tia Luisa likes us, Mama," had been Soledad's firm argument. "We promise to behave."

Scrupulous child that she was, Soli amended her statement. "At least *I* promise to behave. I cannot speak for my brother."

Catalina turned away so the determined little girl wouldn't see her smile. Impressed, she had to give Paloma credit for maintaining a serious expression.

"Dear child, Papa wants me to have a real rest, and he fears I cannot do that here on the Double Cross, because we are all so busy," Paloma explained, and probably not for the first time that morning.

"Juan Luis gets to go with you," the little girl reminded her mother.

"He must, or he would not eat," Paloma said. She put her hand on Soledad's head and gave it a gentle shake. "Papa will take excellent care of you and Claudito. When he comes to get me in two weeks, you two may come along. Is that fair?"

Catalina could tell that Soledad didn't think it fair at all, but she gave a sigh, then looked at the auditor's daughter. "Señorita Ygnacio, do you have a story that covers such a sad situation for a little girl?"

"I will think of one and tell you when I see you next, which will be the day after tomorrow at the latest," Catalina promised.

One kiss, two kisses, then one more for Father, Son, and Holy Ghost, from

Paloma on her children's cheeks and forehead. Claudito's lips quivered, but he didn't cry. He had learned well the lesson of silence from Eckapeta, as near to a grandmama as he would ever know.

One kiss and then two more for Marco, who held her close for a moment then helped her into the carriage, with its seat as comfortable as Sancha could make it. He kissed his sleeping son and handed the little one to his wife, who settled the baby in his cradle.

Marco helped Catalina into the carriage and then closed the door. He walked to the front, where Chato sat hunched over, talking to himself. Catalina had already assured Marco that the half-wit understood basic directions, and if he should veer from the proper trail, Paloma could set him straight.

Paloma leaned forward and lowered the carriage's one window. She held out her hand to her husband, who came close, kissed it, and told them, "*Vayan con dios.*" He stepped back and lifted Claudito to his shoulders. Soledad stood in front of him, her hands clasped in front of her stomach in the ladylike posture that made Paloma chuckle.

Paloma watched them standing there in the open gate of the Double Cross until they were mere specks, then leaned back against the cushions. "I'm going to remind myself that Luisa Maria will spoil me and coo over Juanito and I will see Marco in two weeks." She paused. "Won't I?"

"Think of this as a pleasant adventure," Catalina said.

"It's hard for me to even imagine a peaceful room with no one barging in, demanding this and that."

"I think you can imagine it quite well!" Catalina teased. "Start now by taking a nap."

Paloma yawned and closed her eyes. "I'll never get to sleep this way," she murmured, just moments before she did precisely that.

Catalina closed her eyes, too, thinking of years of smarts and slights and rudeness. For some reason she had turned to them for nourishment, letting the sourness of unfair treatment fill her belly. Maybe she lashed out first to keep meanness at bay. She took the idea one logical step forward; it might be time to stop. With a sigh of her own, she relaxed and rested her head against the side of the carriage.

She had no sense of time passing until she felt the spring sun high overhead. But that wasn't what woke her.

The carriage had come to an abrupt halt. Catalina opened her eyes to see Chato the coachman through the small opening, but only dimly, because the overhang of the carriage roof was in shadow.

The shadow moved and she saw a knife sticking out of Chato's neck. The shadow moved again and she saw a horseman, the cause of the shadow, beside the carriage now. She put her hand just above Paloma's mouth and patted her arm.

"Something is happening," she whispered.

Paloma opened her eyes and her own hand went immediately to her sleeping son in his cradle at her feet. She sat up carefully and sucked in her breath when she saw how the coachman leaned.

Both women clung together when the carriage door slammed open and a bearded man with dead eyes leaned inside. To their astonishment, he opened his mouth wide and his eyes wider and slammed the door shut. They listened to shouts of "Idiot! Fool! A mistake!"

Juanito began to stir and whimper. Paloma picked him up and hastily unbuttoned her *camisa*, nursing him to keep him silent.

"Eckapeta and I ... we train the little ones not to cry," she whispered, her blue eyes huge in her pale face. "Juanito is too young for such a lesson." She bowed her head over her child, trying to feed him and protect him at the same time.

The pitiful gesture went straight to Catalina's heart and shoved back her own fears. She reached for Paloma, as vulnerable now as a woman could ever be, and patted her shoulder.

"I'm going to find out what's going on," Catalina whispered, as she wondered at her sudden wellspring of bravery.

With amazing clarity, she knew someone had to protect Paloma and her baby, and there wasn't anyone else around except her. For years her father had depended on her—perhaps too much—but that was nothing compared to this need, growing stronger by the second, to help someone even more vulnerable.

"I do this for you, Marco," Catalina whispered under her breath.

Chapter Sixteen

In which Paloma makes a fearsome decision

CATALINA TOOK SEVERAL DEEP breaths and opened the carriage door. It nearly fell off in her hand, testifying to the strength with which the bearded man had yanked it open, then slammed it shut again.

She saw two miscreants, one the bearded man as he jerked poor Chato from the carriage seat and threw him to the ground. The other, a thin man with a prominent Adam's apple, sat astride his horse, his own eyes wide with amazement. Catalina knew she had seen him before.

To her astonishment, Chato still lived. His hands shook as he clawed at the knife in his throat. She could tell he had not long to live, this half-wit who had sung his five notes and talked to himself all the way from Santa Fe.

I would not want to die alone, Catalina thought as she edged closer and went to her knees. "Be at peace, friend," she said, and traced a small sign of the cross in the blood on his forehead.

Chato opened his eyes, narrowing them as he looked at her. Catalina leaned back, startled at the disappointment in them. "I was just trying to ease your passage," she said. "That's all."

Blood bubbled in his wounded throat and spilled out of his mouth as he tried to speak. Catalina started to wipe his mouth with the corner of her dress when he grabbed her arm.

"It wasn't supposed to happen like this," he said, enunciating each syllable as best he could, all traces of his addled speech gone. "I was sent to protect you both."

"*You*?" She gently pulled him closer. "Tell me more. Please try, please."

His despairing look told her he had a great deal to say and no way to do it. He died in her arms. She lowered Chato to the ground, where his blood seeped into the dry ground. She turned to the source of their troubles, which seemed to multiply like rabbits.

"What on earth are you doing to us?" she raged. If what Chato said was true—and who lies when he is at the point of death?—he might have protected them, given the chance.

The thin man gulped, the sound comically audible, although no one laughed, and said, "You are not the auditor!" He turned to Bearded Man. "Let's get out of here."

"Of course I am not the auditor," Catalina snapped, thoroughly outraged by idiots bent on abducting the wrong people. "When Señora Mondragón returns to the Double Cross, I cannot fathom the trouble you will be—"

Bearded Man grabbed her hands. "*Who* did you say?"

O dios, I have made a mistake, Catalina thought, as fear wrapped her in its clammy embrace. "I misspoke."

Bearded Man pinched the flesh of her upper arm until she felt her knees start to buckle.

"Señora Mondragón is inside the carriage," Catalina whispered. "God forgive me."

Thin Man leaped off his horse. "Pedro, let go of her." He looked toward the carriage, where the door hung half off its hinges. "Señora Mondragón is a sweet lady," he said. "We must release them."

Bearded Man/Pedro shook his finger at Thin Man. "Are you daft?" He uttered a pungent curse. "Of course you are. Why am I asking such a question of an idiot?"

"You are, too," Thin Man said, hands on his hips like an angry housewife. "Don't they tell us that every day?"

"*She* might be sweet, but her husband will kill us. If he doesn't, that Comanche will. We'll be tortured for days. *Ay de mi!* Why do I hang around with idiots?"

Because you're an idiot, too, Catalina thought grimly.

Thin Man started to count on his fingers. "We can't let them go. We can't leave them here. What is left?"

Catalina held her breath and edged toward the carriage. She looked inside to see Paloma, her eyes like coals in her head, staring at her son, who nursed as though this were any ordinary day.

She was shoved aside by Pedro, the bearded man. He reached inside for Paloma, who drew back instinctively, her baby still nursing.

"I will come out when my son is through," she said, speaking distinctly and with more serenity than Catalina knew she possessed in *her* whole body.

How could Señora Mondragón comport herself so majestically, sitting there with her bodice open and her breast exposed?

"That sounds perfectly reasonable," Pedro said.

Shaken, Catalina stood in front of the open door, unwilling to let either of the men gape at Paloma. She wondered what approach to take, since they both appeared simple-minded. "Leave us alone here, and no one will follow you."

"You don't know Marco Mondragón very well, do you?" Pedro said. "And you don't know our masters." He pulled Thin Man away, walking some distance so they could talk without being overheard.

Catalina helped Paloma from the carriage. She had buttoned her bodice and returned a full and sleeping baby to his cradle. Catalina watched her carefully tuck the blanket around him and make the sign of the cross over him, the last resort of a desperate woman.

Catalina asked, "Is this a well-traveled road?"

"Well enough," Paloma said, "except that everyone is busy in the fields today, as is Marco."

At the mention of her husband's name, Paloma began to weep. She cried quietly, then forced herself to stop as Catalina tightened her grip. She took several gulping breaths, then nodded to Catalina, who released her hold.

"Eckapeta would be embarrassed with me for showing such weakness," she whispered. "I have to keep my baby safe, no matter what happens."

"*We* will keep him safe," Catalina said, wondering how either of them could do anything of the sort.

The men came back, walking directly up to them until they stood close enough to smell. There was no place to back up. Catalina glanced sideways to see Paloma clasping her hands at her stomach. As tight as she clasped them, they still shook. Catalina knew how much the woman beside her stood to lose.

"You're coming with us," Pedro said. "If you object, we will …." His face a mask of confusion, he looked at Thin Man and whispered so loud that Catalina almost wanted to laugh. "What were we going to do?"

"I can't remember," Thin Man said. "Something awful, probably."

Paloma nodded. "I will get my son."

She cried out when Pedro grabbed her arm.

"Leave him there," the man said, pulling her into the road.

"But …" Paloma tried to jerk herself from his grasp.

Pedro grabbed her and shook her. "No! He will cry and give us away."

"You can't …" Paloma began. "He'll die without me." She brushed off Catalina when she tried to assist her. Her eyes were focused only on her sleeping son.

"Let's kill him," Pedro said. "I will do it."

Paloma was on the man in a flash before Catalina could stop her. She climbed onto his back and began tearing at his hair, breathing out curses.

"Get her off me!" Pedro screamed, as Paloma started plucking at his whiskers. Catalina watched in horror as Paloma moved closer, her teeth bared. "She's going to tear my throat!"

Thin Man grabbed the back of Paloma's dress and yanked her off Pedro. He tossed her like a rag doll and she lay in a heap at Catalina's feet, but only until she shook her head and scrambled up again, ready to resume the struggle. Catalina grabbed her this time.

"She is a mother defending her child!" Catalina hissed. "Have you never seen a … a … mother bear or … or even a cat? Before God, you have done enough!"

Pedro put the knife down on the ground and backed away from it, as though caught being bad. They stared at each other.

I will die before I look away. You cannot stare me down, Catalina thought, fixing her gaze on him, even as she wondered what had gone so wrong with their harmless visit to La Viuda Gutierrez.

To Catalina's relief, Pedro dropped his gaze and mumbled something that could even have been an apology. He touched his head and came away with a bloody handful of hair.

"She is a witch and must be burned," he said, but his words sounded feeble and confused.

"She is a mother protecting her baby," Catalina said. "Take us if you must—although I do not know why—but let her bring along her son. If no one comes along on this road, he will die."

The two men looked at each other. *Oh please, please*, Catalina wanted to beg, but she knew better. Years of dealing with bullies had taught her not to expect much, but these men were strange in ways she was not familiar with.

"I don't know what to plead for," she whispered to Paloma.

"It could be that where we are going is worse for my son than to leave him right here and hope for rescue," Paloma said, the words coming out slowly, as though she hated to think them, much less say them.

"We don't know that, Paloma!" Catalina whispered back.

"We don't know *anything*," Paloma reminded her.

Paloma held out her hands. "*Señores*, if you must take us somewhere, please leave my baby in the carriage," she said in her kindest voice. "That would be the best thing, don't you agree?"

To Catalina's astonishment, both simpletons nodded their heads. Thin Man stared at her, then looked back at his comrade in stupidity. "She called us *señores*!"

"That is because you will do the gentlemanly thing and leave my son right here," Paloma said in her most soothing voice.

She put her hands behind her back and Catalina saw how they shook.

"Leave him, but be good lads and cut the mules from the traces, so the carriage does not stray," Paloma added.

Without a word, Pedro picked up his knife from the ground and did as Paloma said. Catalina's heart lifted when one of the mules struck out at Thin Man. After kicking out a few times, he ran away while both men cowered in fright. Shaking off what harness remained, the mule bolted down the road toward the Double Cross.

Catalina bowed her head and did something she hadn't done in years, considering her irritation with the Lord Almighty and all his useless saints. She breathed a prayer of desperate petition. *Hurry along*, she prayed. *Let Marco know something is very wrong.*

Chapter Seventeen

In which two fools fool everyone

"THERE NOW," PALOMA SAID, holding her hands in front of her. "We are your prisoners."

The dull-witted companions gaped at each other. For Catalina, they called to mind a mutt she'd observed that scrounged for food on their street in Santa Fe. He liked to chase carts until one day when a cart actually stopped and the driver got out. The dog looked at the man then slunk away, as if astounded he had actually caught one. *They don't know what to do*, she thought, and felt the smallest hope.

Paloma's shoulders began to shake as Pedro bound her hands. She tried to gulp down her tears as the fool stammered an apology, but to no avail. She bowed her head and wept.

Catalina let Pedro tie her hands and heave her onto the back of the remaining mule. She leaned down, willing to try anything.

"Leave Señora Mondragón behind with her baby," she pleaded. "Do what you want with me, but let her stay here with Juanito. You wanted an auditor. *I* am an auditor. I have helped my father for years."

Both men laughed. "Silly! Women can't be auditors," Thin Man said finally. "We are not stupid."

"Yes, you are," Catalina muttered under her breath.

Paloma tried to sniff back her tears when Pedro threw her onto the mule along with Paloma. "Stop crying," he said, "now."

Catalina lifted her bound arms, encircled the smaller woman, and spoke low into her ear. "I fear what they will do if you keep crying."

"But my baby …" Paloma began, then made a masterful effort to stop her tears. "What will Marco think when he learns I have lost our child," she managed to say, "and when he cannot find me?"

"I think—I *know*—he will find Juanito. Someone will find us, too," Catalina said, unsure of how much of her own words she believed.

Paloma shook her head in sorrow. "You do not understand what might happen to my husband when he does not know where I am."

I do know, Catalina thought, as the bleakness of their situation filtered into her whole body like water seeping into limestone. *Sancha told me one night.*

"I *know* this road is well traveled," Paloma whispered. "I *know* this road is well traveled. I *know* …" she stopped and bowed her head.

"Paloma, someone will find Juanito," Catalina said as she felt her own heart break.

"I hope you are right," Paloma said, and then she spoke no more as the men mounted their horses, Pedro pulling the mule behind him. They rode toward the shelter of trees, leaving behind a carriage worse for wear, a sleeping baby, and a dead man.

What Catalina nearly dreaded the most happened next. The two kidnappers drew aside and conferred in low tones, with little glances in their direction.

Pedro drew his knife and sprinted back to the carriage. Paloma raised her head and wailed until Catalina felt every hair on her neck stand at attention. She thought of La Llorona, and knew in her heart that if she ever lived to tell the story again, she would not need to invent a voice for the Weeping Woman, but merely recall Paloma. Catalina tightened her grip on the desperate woman seated in front of her.

To Catalina's relief, he used the knife to rip two dark strips of fabric from the *serape* the dead man wore. He hurried back and held them out to the women, coming close but not too close, as though he feared Paloma would scream again. "We can do this one of two ways. If you choose to scream and carry on, *señora*, I will stuff this into your mouth and gag you. I will also ride back and kill your baby."

Paloma held completely still, silent now.

"Or I can merely wrap this cloth around your mouths to remind you not to scream, no matter what happens." He looked at Paloma warily. "Which would you prefer, Señora Mondragón?"

"I will be silent," she whispered.

Pedro sighed with such relief that Catalina would have laughed, had their situation not been so precarious. He gestured for each woman in turn to lower her head, and bound the cloth.

"Excellent!" he said. "I must put a sack over your head. No need for you to know where you are going, is there?"

"But …" Catalina began, her voice muffled. She stopped talking, aware that these fools knew nothing about how to tighten a gag; this one was already loose.

He held out the dark bag Thin Man tossed to him. "I only have one of these, because we thought to bag us an auditor. You, skinny lady, bend down."

My name is Catalina, she thought as she bent down. The sack went over her head and her world went dark and smelled of mice.

"We only have the one bag. Señora Mondragón, you will have the grain bag. Here we go. Oh dear."

To Catalina's dismay, Paloma started to cough and then wheeze as she breathed in the chaff left in the bag. Still gagging, she struggled to breathe.

"Men—*señores*—please," Catalina said, taking her chances neither idiot would notice how easy it was to talk around the gag, which even now had slipped to her neck. "Take off the bag, shake it, and turn it inside out! Must I tell you how to abduct people?"

"No, *señorita*," Pedro said, his voice full of apology.

Paloma tossed her head from side to side, desperate for air. Catalina heard the whoosh of cloth as the bag came off. Paloma drew a deep breath that ended in one cough, and another and another, until her whole body shook.

Catalina heard the men shake the bag and hoped they were clever enough to turn it inside out before they put it over Paloma's head again. Success. Paloma stopped her struggles and took one deep breath after another. With a sigh, she leaned back against Catalina.

"How is this going to end?" she whispered to Catalina.

"Maybe with us telling two fools how to abduct us," Catalina replied, and was rewarded with a little laugh. Just a little one, but enough to assure her that Paloma still had a beating heart.

The heavens opened like a sluice gate before they had traveled far, with their strange complement of two amateurs at abduction leading a mule bearing women who were now cold and soaking wet and beginning to plot revenge, at least in Catalina's case. She doubted Paloma had another thought in her brain except her son left in an abandoned carriage.

Damn! Catalina thought, *Damn and damn again!* The rain poured down, washing away any tracks the three animals would have left behind on a typical New Mexican day. It was a hard rain, the kind that could last all day and into the night. Every mouse track in the entire colony of New Mexico would be washed away.

"Do you have any idea where we could possibly be?" Catalina asked

Paloma, who had turned her head toward Catalina's breast, seeking comfort as a small child would, or a wounded animal.

"God help us, but we were only an hour from my sister-in-law's *estancia*," Paloma whispered back. "I have seen the slower man somewhere before. *Where?*"

She held Paloma as close as she could, her bound arms looped over the woman. Both of them shivered.

After what seemed like an hour of travel, in what direction Catalina had no idea, Paloma leaned closer.

"Catalina, I simply have to pass water. I am so sorry."

Catalina heard the deep humiliation in Paloma's voice. "No fear there, my friend. I have to do the same thing." She kept her tone as light as she could. "Just think! We'll be warm for a few minutes."

"Hadn't thought of that."

They were warm for a few minutes, even as Paloma's shoulders shook, either with silent tears of shame or from the rain and cold.

Relieved now and grateful, no matter how humiliating the incident, Catalina tried to listen above the rain for something, anything, that might suggest their location. After another hour, she noticed something she almost didn't believe. Her logical mind, that mathematical mind that El Teniente Gasca had teased her about—*Oh, don't think of him*, she scolded herself—told her they were traveling in circles.

She whispered as much to Paloma, who nodded, and turned her head closer to Catalina's ear. "I wondered that, too."

"Why?"

"It means we are not going far, even though they want us to believe we are," Paloma said, after a long pause.

The strange journey continued, and then Catalina felt they were going deeper into a *bosque*, probably one of the many clumps of trees that lined Río Santa Maria. She smelled damp leaves and more darkness, if that were possible. Could a person *feel* darkness? She did. *Maybe someday I will look back on this and wonder at how much I learned*, Catalina thought.

The two fools stopped, so their patient mule stopped, too. Catalina sucked in her breath when Pedro's voice seemed to come out of the ground right next to her. Feeling a cold hand on her leg, she shuddered to think what would come next.

"You behave yourself at once," Paloma said, in that voice Catalina had heard addressed to Soledad or Claudito. "What would your mother say?"

Pedro's hand instantly left her leg. In another moment she heard the creak of saddle leather as the chastened man returned to his horse.

"Paloma, you're amazing," Catalina said, her relief almost a palpable thing.

"I wish Soledad obeyed me that quickly," Paloma said, with some vestige of her former good humor.

Catalina felt the darkness deepen around them when the journey continued. *We must be crossing an open plain now*, she thought. The smell of leaves was gone and a slight wind came up, wind they would not have felt in the confines of a *bosque*.

The disorienting, unpleasant, horrible journey ended abruptly. Catalina heard both men creak out of their saddles. She braced herself for what terror was to come and gasped when Pedro yanked up her arms and pulled Paloma away from the mule they shared.

"Oh please," Paloma whispered, "don't hurt us."

"Oh, no!" he declared. "You said I would disappoint my mama."

Lesson learned, she thought grimly and waited for her turn.

She strained to hear any sound that would afford even the most minuscule hint of their location. Beyond the crunch of gravel, nothing. The rain poured down.

A big door creaked open then shut behind them, and then another door, a larger one. Catalina listened for the sound of a wooden floor, but no, they walked on earth now. Forcing herself to concentrate, she heard drunken singing in the distance, followed by silence. Then she smelled the fragrance of a garden.

Another door creaked open. Her captor ducked down and then threw her from his shoulders onto the ground. She heard Paloma hit the ground, too, and reached for her. She closed her eyes when she heard Pedro draw his knife, then sighed as he sawed through the cords that bound her wrists. The same sound, and then she knew Paloma was free, too.

Free to do what? Catalina steeled herself for the inevitable, then let out her breath slowly as the men moved away. She heard a muttered oath, and then a slap, and then Pedro laughing softly. "Duck your head, you idiot," he said.

Both women remained silent. Catalina could not even hear Paloma breathing.

"You can't escape, so don't try," Pedro said. "We'll tell our masters what fish we have caught. May take us a day, maybe more."

"Please bring us something to eat."

Paloma spoke so quietly and reasonably that Catalina wondered how she managed to sound almost serene, as if this was a visit to a friend.

"*We* barely have enough to eat here," said Thin Man. Catalina knew she was not imagining the embarrassment in the idiot's voice, as if he really didn't want them to suffer.

One of the men was walking around, as though looking for something.

She smelled Pedro's familiar stink as he passed by. He set something beside her.

"Here's a pot to pee in," he said, and laughed at his blinding wit.

He still seemed to be rummaging around. In a moment she felt something in her hand, perhaps a china cup.

"Scoop yourselves some dirt," he said. "We've eaten dirt before and you can, too, if you're not grand ladies."

He laughed then, and that was the last sound from their tormenters as the door closed. She heard a key turn in a lock, and they were finally alone.

Resisting the urge to throw the cup in her frustration, Catalina ran her finger around the rim, finding odd comfort in something as ordinary as a china cup, the sort of thing found in Paloma's kitchen cupboard, or even her own.

She set it down carefully and pulled the bag from her head and the cloth gag from where it had drifted down to her neck. "That feels better," she declared, then burst into tears.

They cried together in each other's arms, until they reached the end of tears. Paloma was no more than a faint outline in the dark room, or shed, or wherever those terrible men had stashed them. She listened as Paloma blew her nose on her dress, then did the same herself, discarding all the lessons on manners taught by the nuns in Mexico City.

"Hand me the cup," Paloma said.

Paloma took the cup. Catalina tried to stand up and discovered how low the ceiling was. She crouched, felt for the adobe wall, and sat down against it, leaning back, wondering what would happen to them now. She closed her eyes, suddenly exhausted. Minutes passed.

"Here. Drink this."

Mystified, Catalina moved toward the sound of Paloma's voice. She felt her friend's extended arm, and then the cup.

"Careful. Drink it all and when you're done, hand it back to me."

The cup was warm to the touch. Slowly, cautiously, Catalina brought it to her lips and drank.

She had never tasted such sweet milk. With deep humility, she understood what Paloma had done. "Oh, my dear friend," she whispered, then drained the cup and handed it back.

Silence for a while, and then she heard Paloma drink. "Not bad," she said. "I let Marco drink once, and he said he liked it."

They giggled together. Catalina felt her face burn with the intimacy of what Paloma had revealed about her husband. She knew she would never ask if he had used a cup.

"I don't intend to die here," Paloma said finally, her voice calm. Catalina shivered at the undertone of fierce resolve she heard. "As God is my witness, I have a vast grievance against these fools."

Chapter Eighteen

In which terror flaps home to roost

"Papa? Papa? See what is in our stable. Is it a miracle?"

The little boy turned to his father, who hurried into the barn out of the pouring rain.

"Ha! A mule." The father came closer, patting the black beast. "Not my idea of a miracle. Odd. Someone has cut his traces. I wonder. Bring the lamp closer, son."

The boy did as he was bid.

"Shine it by his left shoulder. That's right. *Dios mio*, this is the Double Cross brand." The farmer patted the mule. "Paco, we will have to tease our *juez de campo* when we return this handsome fellow to him! He is always chiding us over loose livestock."

"He won't mind being teased?" the child asked.

"Not our *juez*. He'll thank us and invite us into his home for wine and sweet bread." He rubbed his hands together, already anticipating the pleasure. "I haven't been to the Double Cross in years, but there is always a welcome."

The farmer went to the grain bin and scooped out corn for the manger. "Eat your fill, my good fellow. What were you doing wandering about in the dark and the rain?"

"He can't answer, Papa," the boy said.

"I know. We'll take him to the Double Cross tomorrow or the day after, when the storm ends."

His hand on the boy's shoulder, they walked from the barn. "It's a raw night. I wouldn't care to be out in it. I suppose our friend the mule didn't want to be out in it, either. Tomorrow will do, unless the rain stops so we can finish planting. If not tomorrow, then the day after. What does our *juez* need of another mule right away?"

* * *

TWO DAYS AWAY FROM Paloma was two days too many, Marco decided. Nobody could pull a longer face than Claudito, when it came to missing his mother. *Almost as long as mine*, Marco thought, as he endured another meal with Soledad looking daggers at him for allowing Mama and Catalina to just ride away, headed toward a good time with La Viuda Gutierrez.

Even Señor Ygnacio had something to say, he who usually sat silent through every meal, content to listen to the conversation swirl around him. "I'm at the point now in this audit where I would like to have my daughter check my figures," he said, as Marco walked him to the office next to the horse barn.

He stopped, and Marco enjoyed the sudden surprise on his face. "Señor Mondragón, I do believe I have been doing this audit by myself!"

"I wondered when you would notice," Marco replied with a smile of his own. "I'll wager when you recheck your own figures, they will come out right."

Señor Ygnacio chuckled. "Still, I would like to see my testy daughter's face."

And I would like to see Paloma's sweet one, Marco thought. "I believe the plan was for Catalina to return by noon today," Marco said, silently wishing that Paloma and Juanito would come back, too. Why had he suggested she needed quiet time to herself, even if it was true?

Marco brightened when one of Joaquim's two corporals rode through the open gate, ready to sit in the office, because that was what the Council of the Indies demanded. A good meal and light duty probably made the man the envy of his fellow soldiers, although El Teniente Gasca was scrupulous about allowing everyone to have a turn dozing and eating *biscoches* while sort of watching the auditor.

By mid-afternoon, Marco felt doubt fly into the courtyard like a buzzard and flap onto his shoulder, digging in his talons. He and his *trabajadores* had just finished seeding the north field with wheat. Marco found himself looking when anyone came down the road, his head popping up like a prairie dog's. Embarrassed, he vowed not to watch the road like an overeager child.

But there was Señor Ygnacio standing in the doorway now, hands on hips, looking through the open gates, wondering where his daughter was. Marco shivered, as though a *fantasma* had drifted between him and the welcome sun that shone so nicely after nearly two days of rain. Maybe he would ride out in an hour or so, Claudito sitting before him, and they would meet Catalina Ygnacio's carriage.

Or I could declare an emergency and send Joaquim Gasca to look, he thought with a smile. Paloma had made some remark after she was cuddled in his arms and ready for sleep, two nights ago. "I think neither of them needs to search any farther," she had told Marco just before her eyes closed. "What do you think?" Then she'd closed her eyes and fallen asleep immediately, never giving him the chance to say that he agreed, but did *they* know it yet?

"All right, Catalina, where are you?" Marco asked out loud, but softly, because the auditor in the doorway was beginning to droop about the shoulders.

He ambled toward the gate, waving to his guard, who started to wave back then stopped as he leaned out over the parapet and stared. Marco watched as the guard motioned to another guard, who also turned and stared. Alert, Marco hurried up the steps to the terreplein and looked where one of his guards pointed.

"*Indios, señor,* two of them," the guard said. "They're coming fast, but I don't know why. No one chases them."

Marco stared, too, wondering what had happened to his young eyes. He squinted, then started down the stairs. "It's Toshua and Eckapeta," he called over his shoulder, "I think."

His own lance leaned against the inside wall by the gate so he grabbed it and walked out beyond the gate, puzzled but ready.

He yawned, wondering why Claudito had to crawl in bed in the wee hours then push against his back with his feet. He took another look at Eckapeta, then dropped the lance as his heart tried to crawl out of his throat. He recognized the blanket that the Comanche woman appeared to have strapped to her chest. Paloma had wrapped it around Juan Luis two mornings ago because the air had a chill to it.

"*Dios mio,*" he said softly, before Eckapeta nearly slid to a stop in front of him and leaped off her horse, unstrapping the blanket as she moved.

Wordless, her eyes burning into his, she held out his son to him.

Silent himself, Marco held his limp son close to his chest, listening for the smallest breath, for anything to indicate that there was still life within. He felt a little flutter. "Breathe, my son," he whispered.

In another moment Toshua stood beside him, his hand on Marco's shoulder. The firm pressure slowed Marco's own heartbeat to manageable levels again. They watched Eckapeta rush through the kitchen garden and into the house. In mere seconds, Sancha came out, gesturing to Marco to follow her.

Holding his son close, he ran to his housekeeper and understood immediately what she was doing. Hadn't she told him only yesterday morning that one of his laborer's wives had given birth last week?

One knock and she hurried into the little house built against the stone back wall. Marco followed her and stopped, embarrassed and out of breath. Pia Ladero lay in bed, nursing her new baby. Wordless, Marco dropped to his knees by the bed and held out his son. Her eyes widened, questioning him silently for only a moment, before she gestured him to come closer.

In a moment she had shoved aside the fabric covering her other breast, engorged and deeply blue veined as Paloma's had been when her milk first came in. *Don't think about Paloma*, he told himself as he handed her his son. *Don't think about anyone except Juanito.*

With Sancha's help and the aid of a pillow, she draped Juanito across her lap at an angle to her own infant. "There now, there now," Pia crooned as she tickled Juanito's cheek with her nipple. Marco held his breath as he begged in some silent father's language for his exhausted son to suck.

Pia pressed against her breast just above her nipple. Marco held his breath and watched as Juanito's tongue came out and tasted the milk. In another moment he was suckling the kindest, most generous woman in Valle del Sol. Tears rolled down Marco's cheeks as he watched his baby pulling so deep that his cheeks sank inward. The baby tried to raise his hand to touch Pia, but he hadn't the energy. He sucked and sucked and Marco bowed his head and sobbed.

He felt that strong pressure on his shoulder again. He knew it was Toshua and he steeled himself for a Comanche rebuke and reminder to be a man. None of that happened. The pressure on his arm turned into an embrace, two embraces, as Toshua and Eckapeta held him close.

Eckapeta spoke, her voice low and soothing, close to his ear. "We found that carriage belonging to the man who loves numbers. The mules were gone, the driver dead, and there was your son."

"No Paloma? No Catalina?" he managed to say. His nose ran and Eckapeta gently wiped it with her fingers.

"There was no sign of violence," Toshua told him. "We knew we couldn't waste time in getting your son back here. We'll go tracking as soon as we can."

"*You* will," Eckapeta said as she turned to look at Juanito, who continued his struggle to nurse. "I have children to look after here."

Marco nodded and got to his feet, helped by Sancha, who so kindly let him lean for a moment against her shoulder. "I leave it to you to make arrangements for Juanito. Do as you think best." He came closer to the bed and kissed Pia Ladero's forehead, which made the woman chuckle. How often did a landowner and *juez de campo* kiss a laborer's wife?

"Pia, I will never forget your great kindness to me and my family," Marco said. "I am in your debt as long as I live."

Pia smiled down at her son, and then at Marco's son, whose eyes were starting to close. She looked Marco in the face, with no hint of deference because there was no need. "I know from my heart that if the matter were reversed, Señora Mondragón would do no less for me."

Marco bowed his head, unable to meet her glance as a wave of terrible emotion washed over his whole body. He knew she was right, but in God's name, why was this happening to him? To his children? To Paloma herself?

"Thank you," was all he could manage without more tears.

He left the small home, already thinking that Andrés Ladero, a hard-working herdsman, probably needed a larger home, now that his family was growing. There was room inside the wall for one more house. As soon as the spring planting was done, he would direct his carpenters to begin. Or, if peace came, outside the wall.

With Toshua and Eckapeta on either side of him, he went to his office and told the auditor everything he knew. "I assure you, *señor*, we will find your daughter," he finished.

"Will you find her alive?" Señor Ygnacio said, his eyes anxious but his voice steady. Marco knew he was looking at a man well-acquainted with adversity, maybe even a man with more steel in his spine than any of them suspected, including the auditor himself.

"They are alive," Toshua said. "I saw no sign of foul play." He paused then continued, his voice firm, "From Indians or colonists."

"How can you tell me that?" the auditor said.

Toshua gave a snort, and Marco's misery lifted for a moment. *You're a cool one*, he thought. *And a bit too proud of being Comanche.*

"No one among the People would leave a baby behind," Eckapeta explained. "They have been abducted by idiots."

"Name me a self-respecting Comanche who wouldn't have scalped that dead man," Toshua added.

"I'm relieved," Señor Ygnacio said, sounding anything but. "White men did this?"

"Stupid ones," Eckapeta added.

Someone knocked on the open office door and Marco jumped. Eckapeta's hand on his arm steadied him as he turned around to see Emilio, followed by a familiar face. He left the office and nodded to one of the many countrymen who earned a modest living in a holding hardly big enough to feed a family of field mice, let alone a wife and three or four children.

"Francisco, what can I do for you?"

"I'm returning this mule," the *paisano* said, gesturing toward the horse barn. "I think he was part of a team."

"Yes, he was," Marco said, as his heart tried to crawl out of his throat again. "How did—"

"Two nights ago during that big rain, this fellow showed up in my little barn. We fed him and meant to bring him by yesterday, but what with planting ..." his voice trailed off as he suddenly noticed the Comanches.

If you had brought back my mule yesterday, we would be a day ahead, Marco thought, and forced the bitter words to stay inside his head. Marco took in the man's anxious look and knew that although he could bite his tongue, he couldn't control his expression.

"I did something wrong, didn't I, *señor*?" the farmer asked quietly.

"No, you did not," Marco replied. "Thank you for taking care of this animal. I know you had to plant yesterday, just as I did. I would have done the same thing."

He turned to Emilio, who had listened to this whole exchange with his own worried expression. "Give Francisco a generous supply of grain. I know how much my mules eat, and I would pay him back for returning this glutton. And please tell Perla to prepare him a meal before he leaves." He inclined his head toward the *paisano*. "Thank you. Please excuse us now. Emilio?"

The *paisano* made his own bow to the *juez de campo* and followed the *mayor domo* to the horse barn. Marco let out a sigh. "I don't even know where to start," he admitted. "I suppose I should tell the children."

"No," Eckapeta said. "We will find Paloma and the skinny one and have them back here before two weeks have passed."

"And what will Claudito and Soli think when we walk into the house with Juanito?" he asked, adding, "God willing."

A shadow crossed over Eckapeta's face. "I see that we must."

"I don't know a time in my life when I have dreaded anything more than telling my children their mother is missing," Marco said, his voice no more than a whisper, because he felt another wave of misery wash over him. He put his forehead against Eckapeta's and her arms went around him. They stood that way until he had the strength to raise his head.

"I will ride with you to search," Marco said.

"Ah, no," Toshua said. "I came here today to take you with me."

He took a good look at Toshua, the man he knew had returned to Río Napestle. What was afoot? "Why are you even here?" he asked.

"Everything has changed," Toshua said, his eyes not wavering from Marco's face. "There is a war faction led by a man named Toroblanco. He told me if I did not return with a Spaniard with some authority to speak, he would begin a rampage through your settlements."

"I don't care. My wife is missing and my son might not live through the night."

They stared at each other, neither man yielding. "You promised me," Toshua said, his voice so soft, but filled with iron purpose. "Everything hangs on your visit. The People will see a white man with me, or all this talk will go nowhere."

Marco turned away. He put his hands over his eyes, wanting to shut out everything for a moment. The *I cannot* in his heart ran smack into the *You must* in his head.

He raised his head and looked around the courtyard. From the guards on the parapet, to Sancha coming closer with his son cradled against her bosom and Lorenzo beside her now, to Perla standing in the kitchen garden, to Emilio by the horse barn, everyone watched him.

He suddenly didn't want one more second of the crushing responsibility that had been his alone since his father's death. He wanted to search for his wife, the jewel of his heart. He wanted to ride in all directions at once, calling her name.

And here was Toshua, a man as good as or better than a brother, who had never asked him for anything before. Standing there, knowing all eyes were on him and hating every moment of it, Marco forced himself to think rationally. Since the death of Cuerno Verde five years ago, Governor Anza had used his most eastern *juez de campo* to cautiously court the Kwahadi Comanche. He couldn't count how many times the governor ended his letters with, "We must have peace, Marco."

He looked up at the sky, wishing there were a way out of this corner he had boxed himself into, because he was a loyal, though distant, son of Spain, child of the New World, reliable man and devoted husband to a wife in a million. Something had to yield, and Marco knew what it was. Goddamn him, but he knew.

"Very well, brother," he said quietly to the Comanche standing beside him. "*Obedezco.*"

"I don't know that word, Marco," Toshua said in his fairly good, workaday Spanish.

"No one wants to," Marco replied with a touch of humor in his voice, even as his heart broke. "It means, 'I will bend to your will.'"

Toshua was a quick study. "Even against your own will?" he asked.

Marco nodded, not trusting his voice. He took a deep breath, and then another, and turned to Lorenzo. "Ride to Santa Maria and bring back Joaquim Gasca and two or three soldiers." He paused. "No. Just Joaquim."

Lorenzo ran to the horse barn. Marco looked into Toshua's eyes and saw sympathy, but he saw something else, too. He saw duty and honor. Marco could do no less.

"My friend, we will ride to Río Napestle tomorrow. God help me."

Could dread pile itself on top of more dread? Every Spaniard in New Mexico knew Río Napestle, where some fifty years ago a swarm of Yupe Comanches had obliterated a tiny Spanish army of exploration camped near Casa de Palo. The mutilated bodies had been found by an even smaller detachment from Santa Fe. They had buried what they could gather together; then the commander had sowed the killing field with salt, so no Spaniard would ever return.

"No one goes there," Marco told Toshua. "I do not want to either."

"You promised me when I last visited you," Toshua reminded him.

If no one here can find Paloma, what do I have to lose? he thought, of all men the most miserable. *Paloma's brother and sister-in-law will raise our children.*

"I did promise," he said, after another glance around. "Emilio, you are in charge in my absence. We leave tomorrow."

Chapter Nineteen

In which Marco's heart takes another beating

M ARCO STEELED HIMSELF FOR the tears he knew his children would shed when they heard the news about Paloma and Catalina, but he wasn't prepared for the silence.

He and Eckapeta had taken them into his bedroom to break the news, because he knew the *sala* was the wrong place, if not for them than for him. He didn't want to see Paloma's sandals hanging on the wall, just a little lower than the crucifix—the sandals he insisted be placed there to remind him of what a brave woman will do to get a silly yellow dog back to its owner, a reminder of what love looked like.

He didn't want to see the sandals ever again, not if Paloma was gone from his life. Besides, the *sala* had been the room where his papa took him if a lengthy scold was warranted. He wanted the warmth of his own room, to be sitting on his bed with his children close by when he broke the bad news.

After he told them what had happened, and that everyone would soon be looking for Mama and Catalina, his little ones looked at each other in disbelief, then looked at Eckapeta. Claudito's lip quivered, and he turned away from the Comanche woman who loved him as fiercely as a real grandmama would have.

Marco glanced at Eckapeta, too, wondering. He understood at the same time she did, and reached for her as she rose so silently.

"Eckapeta," he called after her, "please stay."

"No. Your children fear to grieve because I have taught them a terrible lesson," Eckapeta said and left.

Her sorrow bit deep into his heart and he asked himself, *What have we become? Have we worked too hard to erase all emotion from our little ones so they will not cry out or weep out loud? Is this lesson too hard? God forbid.*

He pulled his children closer. "Cry with me," he said simply.

The floodgates opened and they wept together. He pulled them down beside him, one on each side, tucking them close, yearning for Paloma with his whole heart, might, and mind. In the early years of their marriage, he had told himself that if something happened to this second wife, he would not keep living.

How wrong he was. He had to live and function and carry on and ride away from the Double Cross with Toshua, leaving the search to others. He reached over Claudito for a stack of handkerchiefs Paloma scrupulously kept beside their bed and handed one to each child.

"Blow your nose, and I'll blow mine," he said. "There is more you need to know."

Dutiful children occasionally, they did as he said, then settled beside him again, even though his shirt was wet with their tears. "First you must know that your little brother is alive and with us here at the Double Cross."

Soledad put her hands on his face and pulled him toward her in that imperious way that he loved, at least under better circumstances. "I want him here with us right now!"

"Soli, he is staying with a kind woman who can feed him, as we cannot. He is in very good hands."

"But not ours," she said mournfully.

For the first time since the awful news of hours ago, Marco felt his heart lift. How wrong *she* was. He had known for years that every soul on the Double Cross was his responsibility. For the first time in his life, when his need was so enormous, he understood the other side of that coin, because he knew he was a good master—his servants and artisans were looking out for him now. He had seen it in every glance and action today, and now he understood it. They had probably been watching out for him ever since the awful day he returned to find Felicia and the twins dead and buried. He hadn't understood then, but he did now.

"Our hands are the hands of everyone on the Double Cross, Soli," he told her. "I'll explain it better some day. We are being carefully tended by everyone on this *estancia.*"

"I didn't know that," she said.

"I didn't either," he said quietly. "We have both learned something good today."

She nodded, not understanding, he could tell. Maybe it took years and trials and right living to understand what he knew now and what was going to put the heart back in his body, once he had a night's sleep. "We'll talk about that later. There is something else you need to know."

"Is it bad, too?" she asked, her eyes fearful. Claudito looked at him with the same frightened expression.

What could he say? His heart, that traitor organ, yearned to stay with his children. His head dictated otherwise. "It will seem so," he said.

"We'll be all alone?"

"Never!" He thought quickly, remembering another resource he had forgotten. "Everyone will be here, and I will summon your Uncle Claudio and Graciela, if need be."

Soledad heaved a sigh that speared his mangled heart. "All right then. Tell us."

"Do you remember when we sat with Toshua a few months ago and he told us how the People were gathering to discuss a treaty with this colony we live in?"

Both children nodded. Even though it had been past their bedtime, he and Paloma—*Don't think about her right now*—had allowed them to listen to what their Comanche friend had to say about peace and better times for the People and the settlers.

"Remember how I told Toshua I would go with him to the canyon at the right time and speak for our governor?"

Claudito nodded, but Soledad frowned. She was older and maybe even quicker than his son, and she knew what was coming. Marco swallowed and plunged ahead.

"This is that time," he said quietly, looking her right in her beautiful Paloma-eyes, because her own mother's eyes had been blue, too. "I must leave with Toshua tomorrow." No need for them to know of even more distant Río Napestle. God Almighty would not mind an occasional omission to avoid greater distress.

"But who will find Mama and bring her back?" Soledad asked. "Papa, no!"

She tried to distance herself from him, but he pulled her back and held her firmly. "No, Soli," he said. "I have to do what I have promised, but Eckapeta and Joaquim will find your mother and Catalina and bring them back."

"You don't care about Mama?" Soledad whispered, even as she burrowed closer to him.

"I love her so much that my heart is tearing into tiny pieces," he assured her, determined not to shed another tear. "My love, there are thousands of lives at stake and I must go." He gently pulled her on top of him so she could see his face, and held his hand under her chin so she had to look at him. "I would not go if I thought Eckapeta and Joaquim could not find her. I trust them. You must trust them, too. And me."

She returned gaze for gaze, then nodded and rested her head on his chest with a sigh. "I hate this but I don't know what to do," she said finally.

"I feel the same way, *mija*," he replied, and never meant anything more.

AN HOUR LATER, MARCO left them sleeping in his bed. He closed the door quietly behind him and just leaned against it, worn down with trying to explain something to children that he didn't even understand himself.

Lingering in the darkening corridor, he noticed Toshua and Eckapeta standing there watching him. He tried to smile and failed.

"I wish I could die," he whispered.

Toshua was on him in a flash. His hands gripped Marco's shoulder as though he wanted to push him through the door. Marco's eyes widened in surprise. His hand automatically went to his waist, but he had taken his knife off before he crawled into bed with his children.

"Don't say that again," the Comanche told him. "My wife and your lieutenant will find the women and bring them back. Don't you dare give up! I won't allow it."

Toshua's words were fierce and to the point. Marco nodded because he didn't know what else to do.

Then it was Eckapeta's turn. Her eyes were deep pools of compassion and something more. She seemed to burn with purpose and resolution that made Marco's current best efforts look puny.

She grabbed his hand and dragged him down the hall to the *sala*. She pushed him inside and made him stand in front of Paloma's bloody sandals.

"Paloma is not a woman who gives up," she hissed. "Don't you dare give up, or I will not know you ever again!"

"Wife, calm down."

Marco couldn't help it. He smiled to hear Toshua's admonition, a sudden voice of reason in a crazy day. He turned around and looked from one to the other. "Very well," he said. "I will not give up." He shook his finger at them both and took heart. "Eckapeta, when you find my wife, *when*, don't you dare tell her what a baby I am!"

Eckapeta's lips twitched. "She is a wife. She already knows."

They left the *sala* and walked to the kitchen, where Joaquim sat. Perla must have given him dinner, but he only picked at it and leaped up when he saw them.

Without a wasted word, Marco told the lieutenant exactly what had happened. Maybe he truly had cried every tear there was, because he had no trouble spelling out the whole horrible day as they knew it. "You and Eckapeta must look for them because I must go with Toshua. Will you?"

"You know I will. Who wouldn't?" Joaquim said simply. He looked at the Comanche woman. "When do we start?"

"At the sun's rising, when these two leave," she said. She put her hand on Marco's shoulder. "Now I will carry your sleeping children into their room, and I will stay there with them."

Marco opened his mouth to protest and she flicked his cheek hard with her thumb and forefinger. "When will men learn to be silent?" she asked no one in particular. "Make your plans, for I've already made mine." She gave Joaquim a look no less menacing than the one she had bestowed on Marco. "You will follow my lead tomorrow, *Teniente*."

Joaquim saluted, and she flicked his cheek, too, but more playfully, and left the room.

"I suppose we have been told," Marco said. "Toshua, did you know Eckapeta was this managing and dictatorial when you paid some man a bunch of horses for her?"

"Certainly not. I would still have those horses."

They sat down with Joaquim, who picked up his spoon again and tried to eat. He threw it down. "Marco, I'm a fool!"

"You're in good company," Marco said. "Why are you a fool this time?"

Joaquim opened his mouth to speak, then closed it, then said, "No, I really am."

People and their problems, Marco thought, so weary now that his eyes ached. Was this awful day never going to end? Were all his days going to be like this? He looked at the lieutenant, a man who had been through much, as had each of them sitting at that table. He shoved aside his own miseries, woes, and doubts and just looked into Joaquim Gasca's eyes.

"*Dios mio*, you fell in love, didn't you? I mean you *really* fell in love. You haven't courted her or bedded her, or even said all that much, but you have fallen in love finally."

"It's a record for me," Joaquim said modestly. "If I tried to bed her, Catalina Ygnacio would slap me silly."

"Probably, and you'd deserve it," Marco replied. "Pa ... Paloma and I have been wondering when you might figure out why you have developed a fondness for numbers."

"I did kiss her before she left," Joaquim admitted. "More than once, I think."

"I do not understand how white men have been able to take over a good portion of this land that extends so far in every direction," Toshua said. He rose with his usual economy of motion. "I am going to lie down far away from idiots."

Marco stared at the table, so Joaquim wouldn't see his smile. Joaquim poked his shoulder. They laughed and it suddenly felt good.

"I mean, *really*, Marco. Catalina Ygnacio is almost as tall as I am, skinny, and maybe even more managing than Eckapeta. Why her? Oh, I like her stories. And have you noticed how her face just glows when she laughs?"

"I have never understood how such things happen," Marco replied, not wanting to be reminded of his own courtships with the two women who grabbed his heart and snatched it away with no effort at all, as far as he could tell. "You're in love, probably for the first time in your long, amorous career. Just leave it at that."

Marco heard a sound at the door to the kitchen garden and looked over to see Sancha standing there, reluctant to intrude, but from the look on her face, wanting to speak to him. He jumped to his feet and she hurried forward.

"No, no, *señor*, Juanito is well," Sancha said, pressing on his shoulders much as Toshua had done earlier, but certainly more gently. "You need to know what we are doing."

"I do, indeed," he said, so relieved that sweat broke out on his forehead. He glanced at Joaquim, who was on his feet, too. "If we have time—"

"We'll talk some more," Joaquim finished. "My sergeant is in charge at the presidio until further notice, and I am at Eckapeta's disposal. "The *sala* for me?"

"No. Take Catalina's little room at the end of the hall."

"I can't," Joaquim replied. "How could I sleep?"

With her hands still on his shoulders, Sancha pressed Marco back onto the bench and sat down next to him. She watched Joaquim go. "Did that one finally realize he is in love?"

"We're all a lot slower than the women on the Double Cross," Marco told her. "What news?"

"Juanito is nursing well and his color is much better," Sancha said, holding his hands now. "There are three women on the Double Cross who will take turns nursing your son. That way, he will not go hungry, and neither will their babies."

"God bless them all," Marco said.

"Right now he is with Luz Montoya in her house. She said she will keep him by her tonight," Sancha said, holding up one finger and then two. "In the morning, he will breakfast at the house of Maria Villarreal, the wife of your chief carpenter."

"Who has a new daughter, if I recall," Marco said.

"Bravo!" His housekeeper held up her third finger. "After a noon meal, he will be back to Pia Ladero. She says she has plenty of milk, so she will keep him the longest." Sancha crossed herself. "We will continue our circuit until … until Paloma is back. I will be with Juanito every step of the way. Perla said she will take over some of my household duties, along with her own."

Marco kissed Sancha's cheek. "Don't tell Lorenzo I kissed you."

"I wouldn't dare," she joked.

"How will I ever even begin to pay back such kindness?" he asked.

"By continuing to be the best master anyone ever had. Go with God, *señor*," she said, and kissed his hand.

She left, probably to continue her own vigil over his son. Marco stretched and walked outside, too, the house suddenly too small. He looked toward the *acequia*, where he heard the water gurgling, as it had flowed and splashed there for years. Only with the greatest effort could he force himself not to think of the many times he had walked there with Paloma, sat on a bench and kissed a little, late at night, if not too many people were about.

He stared at nothing for a long time, then realized that the lantern still burned in his office. *Dios mio, I have said so little to Señor Ygnacio*, he thought with dismay. *He has lost a daughter, and I have ignored his needs.*

He hurried to his office. The door was open, because the day had turned so warm. He looked inside to see the auditor sitting at his desk, hands clasped in front of him, staring straight ahead. Marco knocked on the doorframe to make himself known, even as he dreaded to speak to one more person about anything.

"*Señor?*" the man said as he entered.

Marco came closer, wondering what he could say to make anything better. He was out of ideas and words. His well was dry.

The only chair close to his desk was the one where Paloma sat and knitted when he worked late. He couldn't sit there. He stood where he was. "*Señor*, I have no words left," he said finally. "Forgive me, but I am empty."

"I am, too, *señor*," the auditor said. "Am I destined to be fortune's fool?"

It was a good question, considering the fellow's difficult life, but Marco could do nothing but shake his head. He was drained of all energy.

"I thought not," the older man said in a voice so calm. "Thank you."

For what? Marco wanted to scream, but he remained silent.

"I believe I will not be fortune's fool any longer. Tell me what I can do to help you."

"Oh, but—"

Marco started when the man slammed his hand down on the desk. "I mean it! I have slumbered too long."

Chapter Twenty

In which the matter of honor adds its burden

H AD HE HEARD THE man right? Marco stared at the auditor. "We couldn't ask anything of you. Certainly not."

"Why not?" the auditor asked in a voice nearly serene, as though his outburst had never happened. To Marco's tired ears, he sounded like a fountain of reason in a day gone mad. "Since I heard the news this afternoon, I have been sitting here wondering if I have been asleep for ten years."

"Your life has been difficult," Marco said, not certain how to approach a man suddenly penitent.

"So has yours, *señor*," the auditor said quietly. "You soldier on." He clicked his tongue, as though scolding himself. "What did I do but lean on a young girl I have helped turn into a sharp-tongued woman? I should have been smoothing her path, not tangling it."

Marco was too tired to offer a single platitude, especially when Señor Ygnacio was right. He observed the former convict seated at his desk. Old before his time, he'd been hounded from Mexico City to exile in Santa Fe. Marco saw a man struggling to make some sense out of his life and he took heart.

"You could do me a vast service, Señor Ygnacio."

"Only name it."

"I've sent a rider to my brother-in-law's *estancia*, and I know Claudio Vega will arrive soon. I was going to ask him to keep an eye on things here, but I cannot ask too much. He has his own place to run, there is spring planting, and his wife is about to be brought to bed with their child."

"You would like me to be in charge of your children here?" Señor Ygnacio asked.

Marco strained his ears to hear any pulling back, any retreat into the helpless fellow who had arrived with his forceful daughter weeks ago. He heard only a matter-of-fact question.

"I would, *señor*. My *mayor domo* knows how to run this place as well as I, maybe better. Sancha must devote herself to my new son. I plan to compose a letter this evening, listing some tasks that should be done in the next few weeks, to complete the audit and help around my *estancia*." Marco paused. "Could you help me with those matters?"

"*Sí, por supuesto*," Señor Ygnacio said promptly. He looked around the room, and Marco saw satisfaction on the auditor's face. "I think I've surprised myself." His expression changed, clouding over again. "Pray God that the lieutenant and the Comanche woman can find our loved ones. I have so much to make up for with Catalina."

Marco looked away, needing a chance to collect himself, and knowing the auditor needed a moment, too. He heard Señor Ygnacio blow his nose and waited a bit longer before looking back.

"*Señor*, my desk please," Marco said. The auditor got up quickly, but he did not leave the office. Marco sat in his usual place and found a sheet of paper with writing on one side. He crossed through it, turned it over, and made a list to give to Joaquim Gasca. "I'll leave this here," he said. "Tell El Teniente Gasca to look at it when he returns from his search." He scanned his list, a short one, which advised Joaquim to listen patiently to a widow who liked to complain the crown sucked her blood at regular moments with its demands, and to check on two foolish brothers who never paid enough tax. *Save them for last*, he scrawled, and added, *See that Señor Ygnacio is escorted safely back to Santa Fe before snow falls.*

His shoulders slumped as he stared at the long table with all the documents sorted by year in seven neat stacks. So much has happened in seven years, but not one particle of it was as important as the task awaiting him now.

He took another sheet of paper from his top drawer, a clean sheet, and wrote *Testimonio* across the top. He stared at it a long time, then wrote a formal letter to Claudio Vega, telling him that in the event of his death at the hand of the Comanches on the Río Napestle, and if his sister Paloma did not return, he was to safeguard little Claudio Mondragón's future property by working the Mondragón land along with his own, until his son came of age to run it himself. He added a generous sum to be spent for Soledad's eventual dowry, and gave some thought as to how best to allow Juanito his own inheritance, either in land or money to study for the priesthood in Father Damiano's abbey where the Chama meets the Río Bravo. *And where I married your lovely sister, Paloma*, he thought, as his eyes filled with tears.

Marco leaned back in his chair, recalling all the memories of this room: Felicia sitting in the little chair by his desk, knitting, the solitary years when no one sat there, the happy times when Paloma did as Felicia had done, the room turned over to Toshua and Eckapeta when they came to visit, and now this audit and his will and testimony, should he die soon.

"*Señor*, your greatest service to me will be to watch over my children, until such time as you must leave for Santa Fe," he said aloud. "I need you."

"I'll tell them stories," Señor Ygnacio said. "I'll watch them."

"I thought Catalina learned those from her mother," Marco said, surprised.

"Ah, no, from me, back when I was a man and not a convict and then a shadow," the auditor said.

What could he say to that? Marco knew how tired they both were, but he suspected Señor Ygnacio had no more energy to get up and head for the house than he did. He opened his deep desk drawer and took out two glasses and a bottle of wine.

"Tell me why you ended up in a Mexico City prison," he said, as he handed over a full glass. "I have seen you at work, so conscientious, and I do not believe you were a common thief."

Señor Ygnacio took a sip of the wine, nodded his approval, and took another sip. "It was much as Catalina told you: The Council of the Indies had sent Don Carlos Francisco de Croix Laredo, viceroy of New Spain, significant funds to replace some of the bridges leading from the center of Mexico City to the mainland. You know it was an island."

"Of course."

"When the new viceroy, Don Antonio de Bucareli, was installed, with Croix still in the vicinity, someone altered my records and that money disappeared." Señor Ygnacio sighed and took a deeper sip. "Bucareli accused Croix, who blamed me. I learned later from someone in prison—also jailed by Croix for some offense—that there was bad blood between the two families, going back so far that no one knew why anymore."

"How could the charge stick?" Marco asked, interested now. "Surely others knew of their family feud."

Señor Ygnacio shrugged and took another sip. "Someone planted a whacking sum of money in my house, so why search deeper? I am certain it was Croix, but how could I prove it? I got the blame. I went to prison." He shuddered and bowed his head. "Prison is not a good place for a little man."

Marco remembered tales his father had told of shameful misery that came to wicked men who lied and cheated and went to prison, deserving it or not.

For your own good, Son, stay out of such horrors, his father had admonished, the lesson done. Marco poured them more wine.

Both men were silent a long time, gazing into opposite corners of the room, anywhere but at each other.

"I came out beaten and defeated," the auditor said at last. "I was no man, and even a worse father. Catalina has always been a strong person, rather like your Soledad."

Marco rationed out a smile at that. He knew Soli well.

"At the age of fourteen, she took a long look at me and decided to shoulder all my burdens. I let her." He held up his hand, his voice stronger now. "Don't give me the look that suggests you are going to make excuses for me! I let her, when I should have nurtured her, directed her, and blessed her life."

"I nearly gave up, too," Marco said finally.

"Aren't you listening?" the auditor said, his voice rising. "I gave up!"

"No, you didn't," Marco said, setting down his empty glass. "We would not be having this conversation if you had given up."

No, you never gave up, Marco thought, as he watched the auditor sit taller. *You just needed someone to tell you that.*

"Suppose no one can find our dear ones?" Señor Ygnacio said. "Suppose I never have a chance to make things better? Is this empty talk, fueled by good wine?"

It was a good question. Marco closed his eyes and thought of Paloma patting the bed, searching for Juanito in the nighttime, half in and out of a mother's bad dream of abandonment. Was she doing that now? *O dios.* He prayed she was safe with Catalina.

"I choose to believe we have not seen the last of them," Marco said as he got to his feet. "Toshua said the signs don't point to death."

"You believe a Comanche?"

"*Claro que sí.* Toshua never sweetens any catastrophe," Marco replied with a slight smile. "If the signs had indicated otherwise, he would have told me." He shook off the imaginary buzzard that had roosted on his shoulder all day. "Come on. It's late and we are tired. Probably a little drunk."

He went to help Señor Ygnacio, as he had seen Catalina help him, but the auditor held up his hand and walked from the office under his own power. He stopped. "Even when you first heard my story from Catalina, why did you believe her?" he asked.

"Simple," Marco replied. "When she said that they trundled you off so fast to more punishment by exile in Santa Fe, I asked myself, 'What were they afraid of?' "

"I imagine I disappointed both viceroys by not dying in prison."

"I daresay! They wanted you gone and they sent you to the one place I know of where the senior accountant, my nasty uncle by marriage, would be happy to do either man's bidding, legal or not. It is quite plain to me."

"I know I was supposed to die here," Señor Ygnacio said.

"You have a disturbing facility for ruining a lot of evil plans, Señor Ygnacio," Marco said. "Bit of a talent, perhaps."

"Amazing, isn't it?"

Shoulder to shoulder, they began to cross the courtyard. Nerves on edge, Marco started when one of his night guards shouted, "Rider coming!"

And I know who it is, he thought. *This already terrible day is about to get worse.* "Open the gate," he said. Bracing himself, he stood at the entrance.

Not even waiting for his lathered horse to stop, Claudio Vega threw himself from the saddle, marched up to his brother-in-law, and punched him in the face. Marco staggered, but waved off his guards, who had all drawn their bows. "No, Emilio," he said in a low voice to his *mayor domo*, who had run from the barn, pitchfork in hand. "No."

Claudio lowered his hand, but the anger did not leave his eyes. "How in God's name can you ride from this place with a Comanche when your wife is missing?" he demanded.

"I am bound to do this, Claudio, even if you do not understand," Marco said. He put his hand to his eye, which was starting to swell.

"I will never understand!" his brother-in-law snapped.

Marco could barely meet Claudio's eyes, but he tried. "I have confidence that Joaquim Gasca and Eckapeta will find both women, and soon."

"No, you don't!" Claudio said, raising his voice. "I see it in your eyes."

"All right, I don't!" Marco snapped back, jabbing a finger at his own chest. "A man of honor would never abandon the joy of his heart at such a time. God help me, but don't make this harder, Brother."

Claudio's fierce anger seemed to deflate. "Then ... then ... why, in God's name?"

Marco put his hands on Claudio's shoulders. "A man of honor would also understand that the peace of this sorely tried colony depends on what happens in the next few days with Comanches in council. This entire colony, Claudio. All three thousand souls."

Boot to moccasin, they stared at each other. Marco felt Claudio's shoulders slump and he released his grip.

"I would search, but Graciela is so soon to be brought to bed with our baby," Claudio whispered. "A man of honor would not leave his wife at this time, and I cannot."

Marco flinched at the accusation. Claudio reached out this time, but only to touch Marco's swelling eye. "My brother-in-law, do you ever feel like fortune's fool?"

"Lately, every day," Marco replied. "Come inside?"

Claudio shook his head and turned back to his horse. "No time."

Marco took Claudio's arm gently, not wanting to be punched again. "Claudio, you are as good as a brother to me."

Claudio managed a look in his direction. "One who gives you the black eye to end all black eyes?"

"Yes, that one," Marcos replied, pleased to hear his brother-in-law's lighter tone. "I have left my will and testament in the office on my desk. If nothing goes the way I hope for either me or … or your lovely sister, please read it and follow my hopes and dreams for our children."

Claudio tried to speak and couldn't. He nodded, then stared at the star-filled sky overhead and shook his fist at the heavens. "I will check back here when I can."

Without a backward glance, he rode out of the gates. Marco stared at the ground. He looked at his guards, who still watched, their bows ready, and at Emilio, who was only now lowering his pitchfork. *I wasn't alone*, he thought. *Good to know.*

"I could have killed him."

He peered into the shadows. "Thank you for restraining yourself, Toshua."

Silently, Marco walked the astonished auditor to his room, then went to his children's room.

Eckapeta rose immediately when he entered. He went to one bed and made a sign of the cross, and then the other. He closed the door quietly behind him, not answering her question about his eye.

He left the house again, this time to find Sancha, who must have been watching for him. She led him to Señora Maria Villarreal's house, where little Juan Luis slept, breathing evenly.

"He is fine," Señora Villarreal whispered from her bed. "Don't you worry about your baby, Señor Mondragón. We will watch him as Paloma would."

If only she hadn't mentioned Paloma …. Marco kept his grief inside until he reached his own room and closed the door. He let the tears slide down his face silently. No need for anyone on the Double Cross to know how his insides churned and his heart felt close to breaking.

"Lie down, my brother. I don't care if you cry."

He should have known Toshua would be in his room. Marco took off his moccasins and did as his friend said. He let himself sink into his mattress and knew there was no point in pretending to be a strong man. Toshua knew better.

"Have you ever wept, Toshua?" he asked, when he could speak.

"Certainly." Marco heard a small laugh. "Although no one believes it, I am human, too. But in the morning I get up and no one knows. It must be the same with you."

"I don't want to go to Río Napestle," Marco said.

"But you will."

"Goodnight, my friend, and damn you."

Toshua laughed.

THEY LEFT THE DOUBLE Cross at daybreak, Marco wearing his Comanche loincloth, his bow and arrows slung over his shoulder, and his lance—Kwihnai's lance—across his legs. After a brief moment with Eckapeta and Joaquim Gasca, also mounted, they separated, two headed north to Río Napestle, and the other two on the road toward La Viuda Gutierrez's *estancia* in search of a trail … anything.

Marco looked back to the protecting stone walls of his home, his fortress. Emilio, Sancha, and Lorenzo stood close together, their hands raised in farewell. Close but not too close, he saw the slight figure of Señor Ygnacio, his hands on the heads of Soledad and Claudito. Soledad blew him a kiss, and Marco returned it. Claudito started to follow, but Soledad held him close.

"Look toward the rising sun, Marco," Toshua said, and it was no suggestion.

Chapter Twenty-One

In which Catalina and Paloma consider their dilemma

Morning brought aching bones and stiff necks. They knew it was morning, because there were just enough holes here and there in the old adobe to let in the sun.

Paloma touched her breasts, hefting them, and thought of other mornings when she woke to find herself curled close to the best husband a woman could have, one who didn't mind when she rested those milky breasts on his chest.

You had better be looking for me, she thought, as she squinted in the semi-darkness for that china teacup. She filled it less full this time because there was less milk. Catalina groaned and stretched and yelped.

"Goodness, you make a racket," Paloma teased.

"You would, too, if you were as skinny as I am, and your bones stuck out," Lina retorted. "*Gracias*, Paloma."

Paloma watched with a certain motherly satisfaction as her friend drained the cup. Her heart and soul ached for Juanito, so she told herself again that he was safe somewhere, because that road was well traveled. She pumped milk for herself, dismayed to see so little. She drank, her face bleak, knowing that if she had nothing to eat, there would be no more milk, not for her or Catalina, and not for Juanito when she saw him again. *If* she saw him again.

She couldn't help crying, but allowed herself a few tears only. Paloma blew her nose on her petticoat and reminded herself of a pair of sandals hanging in a *sala*.

"We need a plan," she said. "We need one right now. Catalina, what do you see out of that big hole so high up? I would like it to be an irate husband, an even angrier Comanche and … and—"

"A presidio *capitán* full of fury," Catalina threw in, which made Paloma smile.

"Yes, those three, even just one of those three. I'll even settle for a coachman who isn't—wasn't—as addled as he seemed."

"Someone must do some explaining about that poor man," Catalina said quietly. "I wish I knew who that should be."

Paloma squinted in the dim light to see Catalina feel her way along the wall until she could see through a hole where the wall joined the ceiling. "We're in a garden overgrown with weeds. It might have been beautiful once, but that was years ago."

"Tell me more."

Catalina shifted. "Drat. There is a gate with a lock on it." She slumped down next to Paloma. "Locks everywhere! Someday I am going to have a house with no locks."

"Not if Joaquim remains *capitán* of the presidio," Paloma said.

"He will never marry me, Paloma, but you're nice to say that," her friend replied.

"I suppose he is spending all his time at the Double Cross because he loves sitting in an office while your father adds and subtracts," Paloma said. She moved closer to Catalina, wanting someone's touch. The shed was small, to be sure, but the gloom during daylight made her feel too solitary.

"But I've been dictatorial and cross," Catalina said.

Paloma heard the yearning under the words, the desire for someone to contradict her. "Some men need to be managed, Lina," she said, happy to oblige. "I think that for all his bluster and air of command, Joaquim might be one of those." She took a chance. "When did you decide he might be the man for you?"

"I haven't done any such thing! What about you? When did you know Marco was the one?"

"The first time I saw him. I'll admit it now," Paloma said with no hesitation. "He has lovely, light-brown eyes, and when he smiles …." She remembered the moment in the city street when the stranger from the edge of Comanchería grabbed the little yellow dog that had escaped from Señor Moreno's house. "I knew nothing would come of it because I didn't have much hope left. Maybe like you?"

It was a gently worded question. Catalina took her time to reply, as though no answer would be quite right, not in their present circumstances. "This is odd, Paloma, but I almost forgot what hope felt like until we came to Valle del

Sol. But here we are, locked in a miserable *casucha*, heaven knows where. Is there any point in hoping for anything?"

"People are looking for us," Paloma reminded her.

"When Joaquim said he believed my story," Catalina said so softly that Paloma could barely hear her. "At least, that's when I thought maybe I could like him. You know, a little."

They sat in silence until Paloma felt her eyes start to close. She was nearly asleep when Catalina hissed, "Someone is coming!"

Without a word, they both stood up and put their arms around each other's waists. A key scraped in the lock and the door swung open on creaking hinges.

Thin Man stood there, squinting into the darkness of their constricted world. He held out two bowls. As he edged closer, Paloma suddenly remembered where she had seen him before.

"You are Gaspar, are you not?" she asked. "Perla's cousin. Thank you for bringing us something to eat."

"You are a wretched ... *ay!*" Catalina's own angry comment ended when Paloma stepped down hard on her foot.

Gaspar hung his head. "You were supposed to be the auditor, Señora Mondragón," he whispered. He held out the bowls. "Here. You have to eat this now so I can return the bowls to the kitchen before anyone misses them."

Paloma took both bowls and handed one to Catalina. "No spoons?"

"I didn't think of that," he said, contrition showing plainly on his face.

Catalina took a deep breath and Paloma elbowed her. "We don't mind casual dining, do we, Catalina?" she said. "Let's all sit down while we eat. Tell us something about you, Gaspar. If you are Perla's cousin, you must be a good person somewhere down deep inside. I know it."

I wish my fingers were clean, Paloma thought as she dug into what turned out to be barely cooked cornmeal mush with no salt or pepper or chilis. Her stomach lurched at such ill treatment, but she finished her portion and wanted more.

"Gaspar, could you bring us more in the bowls when you return tonight?" she asked as she ate.

"No ... nothing more until tomorrow morning," Gaspar said. "That's all we ever get, except for what we scrounge."

No wonder you hung around my kitchen until Marco began to wonder who you were, she thought, and surprised herself by feeling sorry for the man, maybe more of a boy, at least mentally. In the future she would eat slower.

"Have you always lived here?" she asked, not so much curious as happy that he had left the door open to welcome sunlight. Paloma knew she would keep him here as long as she could, if he would leave the door open. "What do you do when you don't have enough to eat? When I was hungry like you are now, I used to drink lots of water."

"I do that, too!" Gaspar said, and she heard the pleasure in his voice that someone, anyone, understood.

"We are not so different, friend. Here's my bowl." She handed the bowl to their captor. "Tell us why anyone here would even want to abduct the auditor. He is a kind man who has to work for his living, too."

"I have to hurry back." Gaspar stood up.

"I'm not quite done," Catalina said. "You can talk to us until I am finished."

"I suppose it will not hurt," he said as he sat down again.

There was enough light now in the shed for Paloma to see confusion and unease taking turns on a face that might have been handsome, were it not so thin. His cheeks caved in like those of an old man ready for last rites.

"Think slowly," Paloma suggested. "We have all the time in the world, since Catalina is *such* a slow eater." She glanced at her friend, who began to scoop food into her mouth at the speed of cold honey flowing.

"It's all my fault," he began and hung his head again like the child he was. Paloma wondered if he had ever heard a kind word in his life.

"It wasn't your idea?" Paloma asked, certain it wasn't.

"No! I never have ideas." He scratched his head. "Two soldiers came to the hacienda and handed me a piece of paper. There was a seal on it so I knew it must be important. I took it right to Miguel and Roque."

"Who?" Catalina asked, keeping her voice low like Paloma's.

Miguel and Roque Durán," he said. "They were drunk, as usual, but something in the words on that page frightened them."

He dug deeper into his hair and caught something that he squeezed, then popped into his mouth. Paloma shuddered inside.

"Miguel was shouting about taxes, and Roque screamed that the *juez de campo* would be the death of him yet, bringing an auditor."

"The auditor comes every seven years whether anyone wants him or not," Paloma pointed out. "You can't blame the *juez*."

"Really?" Gaspar said. "Miguel swore on more saints than I have ever heard of that he would abduct the auditor."

"That's ridiculous," Catalina said. "I mean him … not you, Gaspar."

"It *is* ridiculous," Gaspar agreed. "Even I could see that, but Miguel and Roque are barely ever sober." He clasped his hands together. Even in dim light, Paloma observed his black-rimmed fingernails, gnawed nearly to the quick. "I hoped they would change their minds in the morning. I hoped and prayed."

"You came to the Double Cross to look around?" Paloma prompted, when he was silent.

"Perla has lots of food and I stayed as long as I dared." He patted his skinny chest with the first appearance of pride Paloma had seen this far. "I watched the old man go for a ride every afternoon." His face grew solemn again. "Señora Mondragón, *why* were you and this tall one in the carriage? I didn't want to steal *you*."

"We were going to visit La Viuda Gutierrez and show her my baby," Paloma said, fighting down tears again.

"You shouldn't have done that," he said mournfully.

"We didn't know we were going to be captured," Paloma told him, her heart full to bursting. She turned away, unable even to look at the simpleton whose life was too hard.

Catalina leaped to her feet. "That's enough! We need to speak to these Durán brothers," she said. Catalina handed her bowl to Gaspar, grabbed Paloma, and stalked past him into the garden—a woman on a mission.

Chapter Twenty-Two

In which Paloma and Catalina scheme to outsmart a house of fools

"IT IRRITATES ME, BUT I am going to give my special, supreme curtsy to two lunatics who should be locked up," Paloma whispered to Catalina, who towed her relentlessly through a weedy garden, past another gate, and into the main corridor of a house so full of filth that even Catalina stopped her headlong rush to stare.

Catalina looked around, eyes wide. "What *is* this place?" She jumped back. "*Dios*, what did I just step in?"

"You might think about a curtsy, too, Catalina," Paloma said as she stared at mounds of dirty clothes, bits of food in festering mounds, and something both slimy and furry that made her shudder. "We have no other weapon."

"What a poor weapon," Catalina said.

"We can do this together," Paloma said. "Together." She raised their interlocked hands. "We are neither of us alone now. Lead on, friend."

Paloma saw all the fear on the servant's face. "Don't worry, Gaspar," she said. "We will not let you take any blame for what happens next."

She had no idea what was going to happen next, only that the servant pointed toward the end of the corridor. There seemed to be no other servants, unless the rest were so cowed they had fled in terror at the unexpected sight of two women moving with considerable purpose.

Gaspar paused before a closed door. Raising his hand to knock, he hesitated.

Not waiting for Gaspar, who appeared to be a beat behind everything, Catalina opened the door and tugged Paloma in with her. She stepped back at the odor and the filth, but Paloma pushed her forward, ready to do whatever was necessary to let them leave this place so she could find her baby and get home to Marco.

Two men sprawled next to each other on a pile of rags. Paloma looked closer and decided it was another mound of dirty clothes. Did they *never* wash their garments? Bottles lay everywhere, some empty, some tipped over and dribbling wine onto the floor. Somewhere in the room she thought she heard a dog growl, until she realized one of the men had made the sound deep in his throat. Miguel and Roque Durán glared back at her and squinted, as though what little light came in from the hall was too much, so early in the day.

"Who let these silly females out?" one of them asked, in a voice rusty with disuse or ill use. Paloma suspected both. "I will whip you, Gaspar!" said the other.

Paloma nudged the astounded Catalina to move closer. *Twins.* She looked from one unshaved face to the other and wondered how people could let themselves go so deep into ruin, and why.

Now or never. Paloma lowered herself into her magnificent curtsy that had impressed Marco because he loved her, and startled Kwihnai the Comanche because it was so unexpected. What the Durán twins chose to make of her she had no idea, as she gracefully sank toward the floor until her forehead nearly touched tile that hadn't been cleaned in years.

She came up just as elegantly, knowing it mattered somehow that the Durán brothers think her magnificent. She held out her hand and moved forward. "Pray do not blame Gaspar, my lords," she said. "We were impetuous and wanted to see where we were. It isn't often that either of us is taken somewhere with bags over our heads."

The brothers looked at each other, then at Gaspar, who stood to the side and slightly behind Paloma.

"You were supposed to fetch the auditor," one of them thundered, or he would have thundered, if he had spoken more than a sober sentence or two in ages. His words tumbled out like acrobats needing exercise. "You bring us two silly females?"

Catalina gasped and started forward, her hands in tight fists. Paloma grabbed her when one of the Durán brothers tried to leap up, staggered at the sudden exertion, and reached for a Comanche lance propped against the scabby wall behind him. Paloma held her breath as he overset himself and sat down with a thump, his hands white-knuckled around the lance.

Paloma's heart hammered in her breast. "Alas, we were in the carriage instead of the auditor, and Gaspar did not know." She gave a slightly above medium-sized curtsy. "You should know who we are, now that we are your guests: I am Señora Paloma Vega y Mondragón, wife of your *juez de campo*. This is Señorita Catalina Ygnacio, daughter of the auditor."

Catalina managed a credible curtsy of her own. "Charmed, I am certain," she murmured.

The twins looked at each other. Both blinked, and both regarded Paloma and then Catalina, their eyes almost moving together. They even gasped in unison, and frowned together. Paloma felt a shiver start at the back of her neck and travel the length of her spine at this odd brotherhood.

"Wh-which of you is Roque and which of you is Manuel?" she asked. "How is it that we have never met?"

"I am Roque," the man holding the lance said. "This is Miguel. Can you tell us apart?" Both twins laughed, and Paloma felt her shivers deepen.

"No, indeed. How is it that I have lived here for several years now and never met you gentlemen?" she asked again.

"*We* don't pay taxes," Miguel said proudly. "Your husband knows this. He sends us silly forms about livestock and money due, and we just pitch them into our bookroom."

"Everyone pays taxes," Paloma said gently, wondering how to humor these strange creatures. "No one likes to, but we do it anyway."

"We don't! We don't have to!" they declared in unison.

They looked at each other and laughed. Paloma wondered if they were testing each other's mood. "After you," Miguel—or was it Roque?—said to the other.

"We sent this simpleton to abduct the auditor," Miguel said—or at least, the man without the lance, if that was Miguel. "How hard is it to catch an old man?"

Paloma felt Catalina stiffen again and patted her arm. She held her breath when Catalina stepped forward, then relaxed, because her friend was a fast learner.

"If you say you never pay taxes, why would you abduct an auditor?" Catalina asked. "Why not just ignore him, which you seem to have been doing?"

Miguel started to shiver, and Roque put his arm around his twin in a protective gesture. "Because this broadside frightened us, and we do not like to be afraid," Roque said. "Mondragón hadn't sent us one in years, and now this … this piece of Satan's handiwork shows up." He shook the broadside at Paloma. "Your husband plagues our lives!"

"May I ask, what did you plan to do with the auditor?" Paloma asked.

Again they looked at each other. Roque, still holding the lance, shook his head. "We must have had an idea, but now I am not certain."

"We might just keep him a while, then turn him loose into Comanchería," Miguel suggested.

"Or we could kill him and feed him to our hogs," Roque said. He elbowed his twin. "Didn't we do that to someone once?"

"*Dios mio!* Remind me not to eat pork here," Catalina murmured.

Paloma took a step forward and nearly laughed when Roque and Miguel both gasped and leaned back. Roque held out the lance and took a few jabs. Paloma prudently came no closer.

"How long do you plan to keep us?" she asked.

"Until we think of something," Miguel replied, indignant and then puzzled in turn. "We might think of something someday." He laughed and Roque joined in, his laugh identical.

How do I handle these idiots? Paloma asked herself. She thought of her new baby, and her husband frantic with worry and searching everywhere for them, not to mention Soledad and Claudito sobbing themselves to sleep every night.

Don't show your fear, she thought, as she took a deep breath—regretted that immediately—and sat down gracefully on the reeking mound of clothing. She watched as the twins drew back farther and wondered who was more frightened of whom.

"Here is what we will do," Paloma said, clasping her hands tight together so they would not shake. "I will cook for you and make wonderful tortillas, and posole, and flan, provided you have eggs and butter. You mentioned your hogs …." She heard Catalina draw in her own breath. "I can make you *such* a stew. Oh, and bread hot from the *horno*. Butter and honey dripping from it." She heard Roque and Miguel sigh in unison and wipe their mouths.

Roque suddenly laughed out loud. "You will do all that? Why should we ever let you go?"

"We can worry about that little detail later," Paloma said, speaking in her most soothing voice, as she would when Soledad needed cajoling or Claudito pouted. "You can lock us in that hut every night, and let us out in the morning. We will need a blanket each, however, because the nights are still chilly."

She paused and looked at Catalina, who came closer and sat down beside her. Roque glared at her, as though she had interrupted his dreams of glorious food.

"And what can *you* do, besides look like a thin stick?" Miguel asked, then laughed at his own wit.

"I can straighten out your accounts and your books of finance and teach you how to never fear an auditor again."

Silence, then loud laughter, as though the court jester of King Carlos himself had pranced around and told the funniest joke ever heard in the court of Spain. The brothers held each other and laughed until they had to wipe their eyes.

Paloma held her breath as Catalina rose to her full height and pointed at one man and then the other. "You will be …."

Paloma held her breath, praying for her friend not to upset whatever mood had been created by talk of good food, clearly a novelty here. "Please," she whispered, "I must see my children again."

Catalina held out her hands so gracefully to the strange men. "You will be *amazed* what I can do in your office. There will be order and understanding." She held up a single finger. "When we have finished each day, and before you lock me up, I will tell you such stories as you have never heard before."

Paloma saw for a brief moment how the brothers differed, Roque with an expression of extreme skepticism, and Miguel wide-eyed and eager like her own children. Catalina must have noticed, too, because she gave her attention to Miguel.

"Stories about fairies and princesses, and evil *brujos*, and brave knights like you two. I have a story for every occasion." She folded her arms. "*Only* if you let Paloma cook and let me bring some order to your affairs."

Paloma held her breath as the twins looked at each other. She waited for words to pass back and forth, but they were silent, staring into each other's eyes. *Discuss it!* she yearned to plead, in the silence that somehow filled the noisome room. Should she kneel and beg? Should she sob for her family?

The silence ended when Roque set aside his lance. After another look at his brother, he nodded. "You can cook, and you can organize that room," he said, sounding firm and almost thoughtful. "One of us will watch each of you at all times. After the stories, back you will go into the shed." He patted his waist, where Paloma noticed a bunch of keys. "Gaspar!" he shouted, then laughed when Paloma jerked in fright.

"S-s-*señor*?" the witless man whispered.

Paloma looked around to see Gaspar on his hands and knees, his eyes wide, his lips tight. *Pobrecito*, she thought. *Pobrecito.*

Roque patted his keys again. "I will give you my keys to let them in and out, but you will return them immediately."

Gaspar nodded, and slowly sat back on his haunches. He leaned forward again and touched his forehead to the tile. Paloma's heart went out to him as he prostrated himself. He might have been a petitioner to King Carlos himself.

Roque pointed at her. "You, now. I will have your solemn word or we go no farther."

Without a word, she prostrated herself next to Gaspar, as silent tears of shame coursed down his thin cheeks. "You see how we live," he whispered.

Then Catalina lay on her other side, eyes closed.

Roque clapped his hands. "Good for you! Spanish ladies would never go against their word." He tugged Paloma to her feet and pushed her toward the door. "Cook something good," he declared, with an unspoken *or else* in his voice. He yanked Catalina to her feet next. "And you, you skinny one, astound me in the bookroom." He rubbed his hands. "And then a story."

* * *

JOAQUIM GASCA HAD LONG ago perfected the art of sleeping in the saddle. After a day of fruitless searching, he longed to close his eyes and let his horse do the work.

But there was Eckapeta, her frown deepening with every hour that passed, eyes darting everywhere for some sign of their dear ones that had eluded them. Nothing.

Their dear ones. *You really aren't all that skinny, Catalina,* Joaquim thought. *And perhaps it is true that I need someone to manage me, and maybe love me a little.* He opened his eyes, unsure if he was a smarter man yet, or still a smart man in the making. Paloma or Marco could tell him.

And why did he have to think of Paloma, sweet wife and mother probably destroying herself with worry over her baby. He had promised Marco they would find the women, and not to worry about going with Toshua to talk of peace, after years of cruel war. Brave he might be (if he was), Joaquim knew he could not bear to see Marco's agony if he and Toshua returned with news of peace, to find none on the Double Cross. *I will resign my commission and leave this colony,* he thought. *How could I remain, a greater failure than ever before?*

"Where are they, Eckapeta?" he asked.

"Before the rain, we could have found them. Now, I do not know," she said, avoiding his eyes, hers on the distant hill, perhaps wishing the women to materialize. Who knew what Eckapeta thought?

Quietly, he turned his horse around, dreading to face Soledad and Claudito without their mother, but unable to think of anywhere else to look. What would Señor Ygnacio think, when just the two of them rode through the gates? Would the man who knew only misfortune become the face he, Joaquim Gasca, saw when he looked in the mirror? God forbid.

He thought of Claudio and sighed. Each night the good man had met them at the Double Cross, wanting to know if they had succeeded. And each night, Paloma's brother rode home, his shoulders slumped and head down.

"We need a stroke of good luck, Eckapeta," he said, when she bowed to the inevitable and turned her horse, too, to ride beside him.

The Comanche woman reached out and touched his arm. "We will ride out again tomorrow, and the day after."

"But will we find them?" he asked.

"They are brave and smart," she replied, with no hesitation. "If we cannot find them, they must save themselves."

"That's no answer!"

"Do you have a better one?"

Chapter Twenty-Three

In which the price of peace is high

THEY MADE THE JOURNEY to Río Napestle in two days instead of the usual four, riding at an easy pace but not stopping for anything. Each man had a sack of dried meat slung over his shoulder. Marco discovered loincloths made passing water while in the saddle simple.

"When we arrive at Casa de Palo, my friend, someone will probably count coup on you," Toshua said. "They might come at you with knives or big rocks."

Marco wondered for the hundredth time since their journey began just why he was riding beside this reassuring man, when he should be home searching for his wife.

"Better you just duck," Toshua told him. "The Kwahadi know you, of course, but the Yamparika and Yupe, maybe not so much."

Marco tried to swallow his own misery, knowing that once committed on this journey, he could never change his mind; Toshua would not let him. Truly, he would have been a fool not to hear what Toshua was really saying. Yamparika and Yupe, too? He thought of many quiet conversations with Governor Anza, and the letters between them, where he had promised to do all in his power as an officer of the crown to bring Comanches to peace, something no citizen in New Mexico had ever seen and scarcely imagined.

Every step Buciro took toward the river that all Spaniards avoided and away from wherever his wife was now hidden was a knife slicing his heart into strange shapes.

He tried not to weep, but the thought of her somewhere, hoping every moment for him to rescue her while he rode away took a toll so great that he finally reined in his horse, dismounted, leaned against Buciro, and sobbed. He dropped to his knees and then pressed his face against the ground, weeping because he felt so helpless. All the years of happiness with Felicia, followed by years of loneliness so great that he nearly put an end to himself, and then years of more happiness and children and now this.

Marco sat up, ashamed of his unmanly tears when he rode with a man who would never humiliate himself with such a display of cowardice. Embarrassed, he glanced around, hoping like a fool that Toshua had kept riding and wasn't aware of his New Mexican friend's disintegration. What he saw made him gasp.

Toshua knelt beside his own horse. He had slashed both his forearms with a knife that lay beside him. Blood ran down his arms and pooled on the ground. As Marco watched, Toshua raised his bloody arms and chanted something that bore no resemblance to a death song. He appeared to be supplicating some god of his own.

"Toshua ..." he began, not knowing what to say. "Toshua."

His friend looked at him, then down at the knife. With a quick gesture that flicked his blood on Marco, he threw the knife, which landed close to Marco's leg.

Without a word, Marco picked up the slippery knife and sliced his own forearms. He felt no pain at first, because his heart's pain was greater. He watched his blood drip to the ground and soak in. He seemed to be viewing the scene from a great distance, as though he was the all-seeing eye of God and not some pitiful man trying to get through a life filled with danger and heartache.

"Why dare I think I am special?" he asked out loud, but soft. "I am nothing."

With a detached air now, he watched his blood drip until the flow lessened and then stopped. Some sense told him he had done what he could; now God knew the full measure of his despair and his willingness to attempt anything, even this treaty. Some things were simply greater than a man's own family. This was one of them.

He sat in silence, as his heart seemed to rise in his chest again, back where it belonged, to keep beating because his work was far from over.

"I had another wife before Eckapeta and those two awful women you already know about," Toshua said.

Marco opened his eyes, startled at the nearness of Toshua's voice, then realized that the Comanche was sitting right beside him now. *Good God but the man is silent.*

"I paid twenty ponies for her because she was so beautiful," Toshua said, his voice taking on a dreamy quality. Or maybe Marco only imagined that, considering that he felt lightheaded now. Toshua was not a man to dream. Or was he? Marco said nothing, unwilling to interfere with a flow of words from someone he assumed never dreamed.

"I was on a raiding party against the Apache. May they rot while still alive and wander Texas as their skin slips from their bones," Toshua continued, his eyes closed.

"We are both men of misery," Marco whispered. "Tell me."

"Other Apaches came while we were gone. When we returned, *victorious*"— he seemed to spit out the word—"what did we find but death all around, and in ways even more horrible than we had perpetrated."

Marco bowed his head.

"It seemed to take days to gather up all the little pieces of my wife," Toshua said, his voice low and filled with pain. Marco knew that feeling. "Sometimes I still dream that I missed something, and that she wanders in the shadow land, with parts gone—a toe, a breast."

"We live in a hard place, do we not?"

"We do. Let us sit here and howl, and let the great spirit know how we feel," Toshua replied. "When we are done with this, we will cover our shed blood with good earth and ride on. Wolves will howl in their turn, and dig in this spot."

They howled to whatever god they chose, then mounted and rode through wide empty plains appearing mostly level, but full of ridges and gullies, a little water here and there. Marco forced himself to think of nothing except what lay immediately ahead of him, rehearsing what he thought Governor Anza would ask for in a peace treaty: trade rights, return of enslaved settlers, and freedom from deadly Comanche Moons. He remembered his experiences last summer with the ever-helpful Utes, and wondered if the governor would insist upon Comanches allying themselves with Utes (if Utes would agree), colonials, and other friendly tribes to go against the Apache, their common enemy.

So it was that they rode to the Río Napestle two days later, exhausted and wearing their dried blood of mourning. They traveled along the river lined with cottonwoods on either side until they found the encampment. Marco couldn't help his gasp of surprise at the size of the gathering. The dull, undecorated tipis of The People seemed to stretch from horizon to horizon.

"How ... how many?" he asked, eyes wide with fear.

"Maybe three hundred warriors, and that's not counting women and children," Toshua said. "Afraid?"

"You can't imagine how terrified I am," he said honestly, his eyes on the warriors who gathered as they came closer.

"I will do what I can to protect you, but my friend, you are so white," Toshua said.

Marco felt paler than goat's milk, riding beside a friend who could only do so much, circled about by warriors gifted in the art of torture. He tried to duck the rocks thrown at him, but one still slammed into the back of his head and dropped him to the ground.

When he opened his eyes, Kwihnai sat beside him, looking down at him with a frown. Nearly three years had come and gone since Marco and Paloma, named Tatzinupi by Eckapeta, had ridden away from the sacred canyon. Only last summer Kwihnai and his warriors had saved his life when Great Owl had nearly killed their foolhardy little band of mismatched soldiers. Now the Kwahadi chief was an old man. Marco looked past the wrinkles and furrows and scars to see the same kindness in his eyes.

"Kwihnai, will I find my wife?" Marco asked, certain that while he was unconscious Toshua had told the man everything.

To his sorrow, the chief shook his head. Marco closed his eyes.

He opened them quickly enough when Kwihnai smacked his face, took him by the chin and gave him such a shake that his teeth seemed to loosen.

"I have asked my gods this very thing while you were sleeping with a rock," Kwihnai said. "They told me to tell you, oh foolish Spaniard, to trust Paloma to find herself. Don't you *know* the woman you give your seed to when the mood is on you both? She can look after herself. Let her."

Marco realized he lay on a buffalo robe and that he felt comfortable, except for the knot on the back of his neck. He also felt sudden relief at the old man's scold, which sounded very much like the truth. "I trust she knows this, too," he said and held up his hand. "Help me stand."

Kwihnai helped him to his feet, turning him over to Kwihnai's old woman, who washed his face and gave him something to eat that tasted like bugs, but which he was not about to question, because it tasted so good. When he assured her he could stand by himself now, she gestured toward a circle of warriors.

Seeing his hesitation, she chuckled and gave him a push. "No one has rocks now, but sit by Toshua, just to be sure." She added in a whisper, "I personally do not trust Yupes and barely trust the Yamparika."

He knew those tribal names, names mothers in New Mexico told their children to get them to behave and not wander away and fall prey to The People. He took a deep breath and did as the woman said.

"Kwihnai says I may translate for you," Toshua said. "We have talked and talked all winter. Now we want you to listen and take these words to the short, bearded man who defeated Cuerno Verde so many years ago."

"I will do that with pleasure," Marco said. He looked toward Kwihnai, because he knew no other chief in the circle. "Please know that when I have stored your message in my heart I must return home immediately. I mean no disrespect by a sudden departure."

"You will find Paloma waiting for you," the old chief said. "She will not be happy that you left her lost to come here, so good luck."

The Comanches in the circle chuckled and Marco felt his heart slow down until it beat nearly at normal speed. *I am not the only husband here*, he thought, with something close to amusement.

With Toshua translating in a low voice, Marco heard even more names of Comanche tribes than he knew existed, marveling that some had come so far from the east. He ate from the basket of dried buffalo meat that passed from man to man, happy when it came around again.

"This is Ecueracapa, a Cuchanec of The People," Toshua whispered when a warrior maybe at middle age stood up. "He came with good ideas and we have listened. Now you listen to him."

"We are tired of war, and suppose that you are, too," Ecueracapa said, speaking to Marco as though no one else sat in the circle.

"*Haa*," Marco said, wishing he knew more of The People's tongue. "We are tired, too. Tell me what you want me to tell that short, bearded man." He waited for a translation.

"He listens to you?" Ecueracapa asked.

"He does," Marco replied, and felt a quiet pride, the kind that was the fruit of years of hard labor and diplomacy and carrying forth when everything seemed to point in other directions. *I am just a juez de campo*, he thought, *but I am the law in my district, by the grace of God.*

He listened with his whole mind and complete heart as Ecueracapa spoke of moving Comanche settlements closer to the colony of New Mexico, where they could trade in peace. Marco smiled to himself when Ecueracapa insisted on stabilized currency rates so no one of The People would be cheated by New Mexicans. He had known for years just how monetarily clever The People were—stabilized currency rates, indeed. He knew *he* had never been able to cheat one of The People.

His listened as Ecueracapa and others added their requests for freedom to attend the great trade fair at Taos, and perhaps to include another one in mountainous Pecos to the east, a preferred site. He heard nothing that Governor Anza would not welcome, even a request for military aid against the Apaches. Marco glanced at Toshua at the mention of Apache and saw a cloud cross over his normally impassive face.

Everyone looked at him. He was ready. "I believe Governor Anza will welcome your conditions," he said, speaking slowly and allowing Toshua time to translate, even though he was well aware that many of The People could speak his language, too. "He will have conditions of his own, but I know him to be a fair man."

The men in the circle nodded and passed around the dried meat again. Marco turned to Ecueracapa. "I also think the bearded one would prefer you to name one spokesman to talk for all of you. Spaniards are strange that way."

Again the men nodded. They looked to the other men who sat beside Ecueracapa and Kwihnai, probably chiefs as well.

Ecueracapa cleared his throat and the murmuring stopped. "We would meet with your chief in *yubaubi mua*, the Heading-to-Winter-Moon, in this place of much wood."

"You call the Heading-to-Winter-Moon November," Toshua said.

"Whether my leader will be there with me, I do not know," Marco said. "I do know I will be there with … with my wife and children and we will have magic marks on paper from the governor, with *his* conditions. You have my word."

Again there were nods all around, even some smiles. *May I never forget this moment*, Marco thought. *It is worth my lifetime in this dangerous place I love so well.*

Kwihnai spoke in Ecueracapa's ear and the younger chief helped him to his feet. All the men in the circle rose. Kwihnai reached across Toshua and tapped Marco's head, but much lighter this time. "Make sure you bring Tatzinupi. I like her."

"And she likes you. I will bring her," Marco said without a flinch. "I know you will celebrate now and I should celebrate with you, but I need to find that woman of mine, even if you tell me she can save herself."

"Not yet," Kwihnai said. "Your head is too big. My woman will put some hot dung on it for the swelling."

"Then may I leave?"

Marco's heart sank as the chiefs consulted. Ecueracapa spoke to him. He listened, pleased to hear words he knew, then less pleased when he understood.

"I am to accompany you on a buffalo hunt?" he asked Ecueracapa in Spanish, then turned to whisper to Toshua, "Please tell him I am honored, but I can't. I must find Paloma."

"You will go, once you have hunted buffalo," Toshua said. "My friend, this is an honor. Don't fail New Mexico."

There it was again. After years of living in the most dangerous place in all of New Mexico, patiently planning for peace, the whole enterprise finally demanded more than he was willing to give. He had a wife who needed him, but as he looked around the circle of dark and serious faces, he knew he had no choice. Had he ever had a choice?

But no. A man can only bend so far, even in the service of a greater cause.

"I cannot go with you," he said simply. "I must find this wife of mine."

His eyes nearly shooting sparks, Ecueracapa had harsh words for Kwihnai, who listened patiently. Marco stood as tall as he could, wondering whether it would be more rocks to his head this time, or a quick stab in the back, if he was lucky. *Maybe I should have agreed to hunt their damned buffalo,* he thought in misery.

"Toshua, I …" he began, but Toshua put a finger to his lips and mouth-pointed to Kwihnai, engaged in earnest conversation with the man who obviously held the power already.

Moving closer, Toshua motioned Marco to stand beside him as Kwihnai spoke loud enough to include all the warriors. "He is telling the ones who do not know about your Tatzinupi, your little Star, who helped keep The People safe from smallpox."

Marco closed his eyes, remembering his Star and that dangerous journey.

" 'Now he begs to go look for her, she who has been taken by bad men,' " Toshua whispered, translating Kwihnai's compelling words. " 'He must have this woman in his tipi again.' "

Kwihnai lowered his arms and turned to Ecueracapa. " 'He came here, a brave man, to speak for Spain and a king far away. Now he wants to leave because he is a husband,' " Toshua whispered.

The circle of warriors was so silent that not even a bird sang or the air moved in the trees. "*Haa,*" Ecueracapa said at last. "Let him go," he finished in Spanish.

"What should I do, Toshua?" Marco whispered.

"You could kneel," his friend said out of the corner of his mouth.

Barely breathing, Marco knelt before Kwihnai and Eckapeta. He knew how poor his Comanche was, but he had to try. "Hunt buffalo later?" he asked.

"Hunt buffalo later." Ecueracapa repeated the same words but with a smile, telling Marco just how imperfect his Comanche was. "Go on."

Marco staggered from the pain in his head, but righted himself and left the circle, Toshua beside him.

"Wait!"

Marco stopped. *What now?* he asked himself.

"How many horses did you pay for this Star of yours?" Ecueracapa asked.

"Tell him the dowry was one pair of bloody sandals," Marco told Toshua quietly.

Toshua spoke and even Kwihnai gasped.

"Good God, what did you *say*?" Marco asked.

"Fifty horses," Toshua whispered back. "I'm not an idiot, even if you are."

It didn't take remarkable intelligence for Marco to know Toshua was disappointed in him. "I will hunt buffalo with them later," Marco said as they walked away. "I promise."

"I know, but Marco, do not underestimate your woman." He grabbed Marco's arm and spun him around. "You did not see the terror in her eyes when she stared at me in that horrible shed where I had been chained for months! Did she leave me to die?"

"Well, no," Marco said, hating himself for sounding so feeble. All he wanted to do was lie down again because his head throbbed.

"She rolled that rotten egg toward me and went for help," Toshua reminded him, his voice intense and demanding Marco's full attention. "Do not think she cannot help herself. Besides, New Mexico needs you."

"We are different, Toshua," he said, not certain he could talk without tears, unable to guess if Toshua could even understand him. "My heart cannot break into any more little pieces."

Toshua regarded him in silence until his expression mellowed. He pointed toward a smaller group of warriors. "There is a man over there named Toroblanco who does not agree with any of this."

"I should beware of him, too?" Marco asked, dismayed.

"No. He might be dead by morning. We'll see."

"Now you will tell me you can see the future?" Marco said, hating to sound so bitter. He looked around, wondering which of the formidable Comanches Toroblanco could possibly be. "You are a prophet?"

"I claim no such skill," his friend replied modestly. "I know The People pretty well, though. No fear tomorrow."

They left before the hunters at daybreak, their pouches full of dried meat mixed with bugs. Most of the camp still slept; even the dogs ignored them. Sleeping even more profoundly was a man with hair where his face should be. Horrified, Marco looked closer. *Good God*, someone had twisted the man's head entirely around on his neck.

"Toroblanco?" Marco asked, hoping he had not turned as green as he felt.

Toshua dismounted and toed the dead man. "No. One of his allies, though. I suspect they will be picked off one by one, until Toroblanco is looking over each shoulder all day long."

"Toshua, you and your people are masters of fright," Marco said.

"This is news? You are growing more wise every day."

High time, Marco thought. The craziness of his situation reminded him that the crown didn't pay him enough to be *juez de campo*. Perhaps it was time to ask for a raise.

"We'll be home in two days?" he asked.

"Two days."

Chapter Twenty-Four

In which Paloma learns she is not as badly off as she thought

Roque's resolution to sit with Paloma ended when Gaspar brought him another bottle of wine.

"Pedro!" he hollered. "Come here, you worthless lump."

Their other abductor, the bearded man, appeared in the doorway.

"Take her to the kitchen," Roque said, after a long pull on the bottle. "She will cook and you will watch her."

Paloma wanted to protest when Pedro grabbed her arm and tugged her down the disgusting hall again, but she knew better and hurried to keep up with him.

He pushed her into the kitchen. Paloma rubbed her arm and stared in amazement at the filthy, reeking hole with a grease-covered table and a fireplace full of ashes. Turning to Pedro, she gave him her kindest smile.

"Pedro, do you like cornmeal and chilis and big chunks of pork?"

She had him there. She watched his eyes grow big. He swallowed several times.

"And tortillas so light that we have to anchor them to the table?" she added.

He wiped his mouth. "Start cooking."

"Alas, I cannot do a thing until this kitchen is cleaned up," she said, assuming her most mournful expression. "Good food just won't cook in a pigsty."

She almost heard gears turning in his tiny brain.

"What should we do?"

"Are there others here besides you and Gaspar?" Paloma asked.

"Why do you want to know?" he snarled at her.

Patience, patience, she told herself. *Think of him as a not-so-bright child.* "They could help us dust and drag out old chicken bones and—"

"Chicken bones? We've never eaten chicken or any meat from this … hole," Pedro said.

"I was just using chicken bones as an example," Paloma said. For the first time since this man and his equally dim friend abducted them, she felt a kernel of pity. She heard the wistfulness in his voice and it touched her heart. "We can turn this into a room where I can cook good things," she said. "What would you like to eat?"

Her soft heart grew a little softer when Pedro, tough *hombre*, couldn't think of anything.

"Mostly it's just cornmeal," he muttered, and she heard the humiliation in his voice.

"If it must be cornmeal, I assure you I can make it taste much better," she told him. "Do you know anyone who can help us clean?"

"There is an old woman who hides in the barn and only comes out at night," he said, after considerable thought, which involved scratching his chin. This action seemed to remind him that his nose itched, and then another place that made Paloma turn away in embarrassment when he scratched there, too.

"At night? Heavens, what does she do here?" Paloma asked, not certain she wanted to know.

"I think she washes clothes."

"At *night*?"

"Of course. The brothers do not like to be disturbed with any noise during the day," Pedro said, as though it made perfect sense. "She drapes the sheets and things over bushes, then scurries away to hide until they are dry."

"Go get her right now and tell her I need her in the kitchen," Paloma said in the firm voice she reserved for Soledad when her dear one was contrary.

"But I am supposed to watch you here," Pedro said, and started scratching again.

"I am not going anywhere," she assured him. *Not now, at least, until we all eat a little better,* she thought. Pedro lumbered out the door, pouting as he went.

Paloma surveyed her domain, dismayed at what years of neglect could do to a kitchen. "I am going to keep very busy," she muttered. "I will be too tired tonight to cry myself to sleep."

Possibly taking her at her word about good food, Pedro returned in what was likely record time for him, towing a woman scarcely four feet tall. She might have been taller, but she was hunched over.

Too many years bent over a scrubbing board, Paloma thought, reminding herself that when she got home—*oh, please God*, let her get home—she would make certain that the Double Cross servants varied their workaday routines.

"I am Señora Mondragón, sent here to straighten up this kitchen," Paloma said, glossing over an abduction and imprisonment in an adobe hut. No telling how much this old one could absorb, if her life had been spent taking care of the Durán twins. "What is your name?"

"Maria," the old one said. "Just Maria. No other name." She looked through the door she had just entered. "Will we be safe?"

"From what?" Paloma asked, and she started sweeping mounds of dirt toward the center of the room, which set off a fit of sneezing. "Little piles of trouble like this debris?" she asked, when she could speak.

"You shouldn't tease about Comanches," Maria said.

"Except for a minor skirmish last summer by a renegade, Comanches haven't raided here in several years. Here, pile this garbage into one corner. We'll have Pedro take it out and burn it."

Maria stayed where she was, as if rooted to the dirty tile in fear. "They will come and grab us, gut us and eat us!"

"No, they won't," Paloma said gently as she mentally added another black mark to the names of Roque and Miguel Durán. "I need your help," she coaxed.

"Los Señores Durán told me I must wash clothes at night, then hide during the day, somewhere deep in the barn where the Comanches cannot find me," Maria said, her voice low and breathless. "Suppose they come silently while we are working in here?"

"They won't," Paloma assured her. "I'll watch for them."

"You do not know what the Comanches can do!" She looked around, her eyes wild. "There used to be other servants, all gone now. It was Comanches!"

I think it was braver people than you who ran away, Paloma said silently. *Why didn't you run, too?*

Paloma sat the woman down on a bench, after shuddering and sweeping aside either a ratty toupee or a long-dead muskrat. She held Maria's hands, sad to feel her tremble. Maria was even more of a victim than she could ever be. "If a Comanche walks into this kitchen, I will throw myself in front of you, and you can scurry away."

Such a promise seemed to calm the old one. After a long moment, she nodded. "This pile of junk over here?" she asked, looking around.

"Yes, that one, Maria," Paloma said. "I will work here and watch the door for Comanches."

To Paloma's surprise, the three of them worked quietly and well through the morning. By the time when most people would be sitting down to a noon meal, they were still at work, even though Paloma's stomach growled so loudly that Maria looked her way and giggled, hand over her mouth.

"That's it," Paloma said. "I am making cornmeal now. Don't groan, Pedro. You will like the way I do it."

Before Pedro could stop her, she left the kitchen and started down the hall, looking in each room until she found the bookroom and Catalina, sorting through piles of papers. When she stood in the doorway, Roque leaped up, demanding to know what she wanted.

"For heaven's sake, calm down," Catalina said. "It's just Paloma."

"What do you want? Where is Pedro?" he shouted.

Paloma put her hands over her ears. "Señor Durán, you are making this difficult! I need you to show me a storeroom where I am hoping you have some food. We are hungry, and we will eat."

"Not unless I say so," he insisted.

"Then say so," Catalina snapped at him, "or I will not help you get to the bottom of this pile." She flashed a broad smile in Roque's direction. "How will you ever know if the district *juez de campo* and his father before him have been cheating you for twenty years and more? I can't work without food."

"Catalina, they don't ch …" Paloma stopped when her friend gave her a slow wink.

"Very well," Roque said, already reaching for his bunch of keys. "I am beginning to regret that two stupid fools abducted the wrong person. *Ay de mi!*"

He stomped into the kitchen. Maria shrieked, threw her apron up to hide her face, and tried to disappear behind the water barrel when she saw her master. "Forgive me, my lord! She insisted I help clean up this place. We're watching for Comanches!"

Roque stared hard at the old woman, then heaved a sigh of vast ill usage and opened the storeroom door. He groaned out loud, as if Paloma had demanded his treasure and one-half his kingdom—all for cornmeal, flour, some rock-hard sugar, and a few spices. He shook the key under Paloma's nose then flung another key at the surprised Pedro, who had edged his way toward the water barrel with Maria No Other Name.

"Open up the smokehouse, you useless *tonto*! Get a knife from the drawer. I suppose there will be no peace if we do not have something besides cornmeal. Close your mouth. Señora Mondragón will think we have no manners."

You don't want to know what Señora Mondragón is thinking right now, Paloma said to herself as she gave a moderately impressive curtsy and thanked Roque Durán for his all-seeing wisdom and general brilliant sagacity in feeding the starving. She muttered the last of that under her breath, but the man was already on his way from the kitchen so it hardly mattered.

Roque stomped down the hall, hollering something about wanting food and soon. In a few minutes, Pedro staggered into the kitchen under the weight of a slab of smoked pork. He set it on the table most reverently, then opened a drawer with the other key and pulled out a knife. Slicing off a piece for himself, he stuffed it in his mouth. Maria gasped, then came closer, sniffing the mound of meat. The worry in her eyes softened. Paloma had to turn away when the old laundress patted it.

Without a word, and with a defiant stare in the direction where Roque had disappeared, Pedro sliced the laundress a generous portion, and another for Paloma. Within a few minutes, he had slung a large pot over the firewood Paloma had arranged and lit, and at her direction, dipped water from the barrel into the pot. Soon, but not soon enough for any of them, cornmeal bubbled, and bits of pork sank without a protest below the yellow surface, followed by dried chilis and other spices.

"It won't cook any faster if we watch it," Paloma said. "Maria, you wipe down the cabinets in here, and Pedro, you keep sweeping, but do it away from the fireplace."

By the time the cabinets were clean, Paloma set equally clean dishes back on the open shelves. She put her hand on the laundress's shoulder. "Maria, you have done a lovely job here," she said.

To her shock, the woman burst into tears and covered her face with her apron again. "No Comanches anywhere, Maria," Paloma said. "What is troubling you?"

"No trouble," the woman managed to say when her tears subsided. "No one has ever said my name before. It is always 'do this,' or 'do that.'"

"It is '*tonto*,' with me," Pedro added.

Pray I never forget this lesson, Paloma thought. *Such a simple one*. In silence she dished out posole to her helpers, who fell on their food like famished children. Swallowing her own hunger, she prepared three bowls and took them down the hall on a tarnished silver tray that had seen better times, like this entire hacienda and the people within.

Both brothers sat in the bookroom, their interest focused on Catalina, who pored over the documents before her with the same air of interest that her father showed in Marco's office. Paloma stood in the doorway a moment, wondering how Señor Ygnacio was holding up in the face of his only child's disappearance. She thought of her husband and children, searching for Mama. She deliberately tried not to think of her small son, last seen sleeping in a carriage with a dead man lying nearby, and wondered how some people could be so cruel.

Keep your anger, Paloma, she told herself. *Don't start feeling sorry for these miserable people*. She thought instead of Maria, who marveled that someone would call her by name. *I remember those days*, she thought as she went into the bookroom and handed out the steaming bowls of posole.

"Where is Gaspar?" she asked. "May I take him a bowl, too?"

Miguel—she thought it was Miguel—gestured vaguely toward the hall. "Outside somewhere."

She turned to go, not surprised that neither brother thanked her.

"Thank you, Paloma," Catalina said. "You have fixed us a wonderful meal."

"Why, yes, you have," Roque said, sounding surprised.

Paloma nodded, reminding herself it was Roque who had the keys bound around his waist. "You are welcome. Now you can do something for us, *señores*."

Two suspicious faces turned her way, not in any way softened by the food before them. She wondered how long it took for some people to ever understand appreciation. She had been nearly five years in Valle del Sol, subject to nothing but kindness on the Double Cross. Something inside her told her not to completely forget the bleak years of sorrow at her family's ruin, her own subjugation in the house of her uncle in Santa Fe, and the difficulty of life in this poor colony. Better to remember, and in remembering just a little, never turn into Duráns.

"Señor Miguel, would you allow us to have two blankets for the night? It's cold." As hard as it was to tell the twins apart, she had convinced herself earlier that Miguel Duran's eyes reflected something other than hurt and anger. "Please, *señor*."

"Give me another beautiful curtsy, Señora Mondragón," he said and laughed at his own wit. "Maybe one for each blanket, and then I'll think about it. No promises."

Paloma saw Catalina's hands tighten into fists. Paloma looked down at the tiles underfoot, embarrassed to have misread the man's eyes. Without a word, she did as he demanded, one deep curtsy, then another. With tears in her eyes, she left the room without a word.

She dished another bowl and went into the courtyard, looking around, wondering if she had the courage to dart up the rickety ladder leaning against the wall, just for a glimpse of the surrounding land. She started for the ladder, then stopped when Pedro opened the door leading to the kitchen garden.

"Gaspar is in the barn. Where are *you* going?" he asked, his eyes as hard and suspicious as ever.

"To the barn," she said, turning around. She glanced back to see Pedro removing the ladder. *I am the* tonta *here,* she told herself, *if I thought one bowl of posole would transform captors into saints.*

Unwilling to return to the kitchen, Paloma sat in the barn with Gaspar, watching as he wolfed down the food, and wordlessly held out his bowl for more, like the child he was. She reluctantly returned to the kitchen, where

Pedro and Maria still ate, and dished up another bowl for Gaspar and one for herself, filling it to the top. There was no guarantee that any would be left when she returned.

She ate slowly, touched, in spite of her growing anger at her treatment, as Gaspar made little noises while he ate, much as Claudito would make after a hard day of playing by the *acequia*. Why were some children more fortunate than others? Why had she and her brother Claudio been left to find their own precarious way through the dangerous society they lived in? Ultimately, why had they been so *lucky*?

She felt her anger diminish, to be replaced by gratitude and a growing desire to put this place behind her, but never to forget it.

Chapter Twenty-Five

In which Paloma is reminded of all the ways a person can starve

B<small>Y NIGHTFALL, THE KITCHEN</small> was as clean as one Paloma and two addled helpers could make it. While shadows lengthened in the room—shadows that could be seen now because Paloma had washed the two windows—Maria darted from window to window to door, looking for what, only God knew. Paloma mourned inside to see the damage these two brothers had done to keep their servants in line. She thought of her uncle, thankful she had escaped his house before she had turned into Maria.

She managed to put on a smiling face for Miguel Durán when he brought two blankets into the kitchen and set them on the table with a flourish. He stood back, as though expecting all manner of thanks from her, and Paloma did not disappoint him.

"You are kindness itself, Señor Durán," she said, and forced herself to give him a medium curtsy.

He seemed not to mind a medium curtsy. He sat down at the table, looking around in satisfaction at the clean cupboards and dishes, neatly swept and scrubbed floor, and orderly arrangement of the paltry foodstuffs in the storeroom. He beamed at her in odd delight, as though he knew something exquisitely special, something to upset her world. She had been tormented by bullies in Santa Fe, and knew one when she saw one. So much for kindness itself.

He leaned back on the bench and Paloma resisted a nearly overwhelming urge to give him a push and send him sprawling. He laced his fingers behind his head and gave her that all-knowing look, as though he were a little boy chanting, "I know something you don't know."

She waited. She knew he would speak.

"Imagine what that skinny stick has discovered in our bookroom," he said finally.

"I cannot possibly imagine," Paloma said.

"Guess, or I will take back these blankets," he told her, picking them up and heading for the door.

"That my husband and his father have been cheating you for years on payment of your taxes," she called out in desperation, not willing to endure another cold night.

"Ah! You knew all along!" he declared in triumph, plopping the blankets back on the table. He gave her a shrewd look. "Or do you just want me to think you know?"

"You may have it however you choose," she said simply, and folded her arms as a Spanish gentlewoman would. She gazed at him calmly, thinking of all the ways her husband would see to it that Miguel Durán suffered. As much as she disliked Miguel Durán, even Paloma Vega could not bring herself to imagine what Toshua would do to him.

"Your husband, our noble *juez de campo*, has been cheating us out of too many cattle each year," Miguel Durán said. "When we never respond to his broadsides, he sends his henchmen to take four cattle for taxes." He clapped his hands suddenly, and old Maria cried out in fright. "Your friend Catalina discovered all this."

"You need simply to present your records to the *juez* and he will treat you fairly," Paloma said. "That is what everyone else in this district does."

"Or I could demand a ransom for you and make him pay and pay," Miguel countered.

Lord deliver me from imbeciles, Paloma thought, exasperated. "You are in a position to do pretty much as you please, *señor*," she told him.

Paloma could tell from the disappointment in his eyes that she wasn't reacting as he wished. There was something hair-trigger about the man that made her wary. She saw a solution, however temporary, and had no trouble letting tears well in her eyes and slide down her cheeks. All she had to do was think about tiny Juanito in that ruined carriage, and she wept.

To her relief, Miguel threw up his hands and stomped from the kitchen, slamming the door so hard behind him that Maria cried out. Pedro looked at them both and started to tug at the hairs on his beard.

When he turned away, the better to ignore them both, Paloma focused her attention on the knife used to slice the smoked pork, which lay next to the blankets. She had wondered all afternoon how to secure it, and Miguel Durán had given her the perfect cover. Her eyes on Pedro's back, she slid the knife between the folds of one blanket.

Maria gasped. Paloma frowned and shook her finger at the old laundress, who started to cringe and cower. "Please don't give me away," Paloma whispered under her breath. She moved slowly toward the woman, not to silence her—what could she do?—but to touch her shoulder. She placed her hand gently on Maria's back, felt her tremble, then hugged her.

Paloma wondered when anyone had ever touched her in kindness, even though she knew the answer already. She embraced the old laundress, then gave her a light kiss on each cheek.

"Take me with you, when you escape," the woman whispered.

"We will do what we can," Paloma whispered back. "If we cannot immediately, don't despair. I never forget a kindness."

"Nor I," Maria said.

Paloma looked around the kitchen, missing the cheerful blue and white tiles in her kitchen, and the conversation and laughter. Her heart turned over as she thought of Claudito and Soledad, each assigned their little meal-time tasks, and their good-natured arguing about knives and spoons. She recalled her odd darkness after Juanito's birth, and her eagerness to get away from her responsibilities by a visit to her sister-in-law. *What I would give to be overworked in my own house right now*, she thought, with real remorse. *Marco has always been so kind about insisting that I can have more help anytime I want. Why didn't I listen to him? What was I trying to prove by doing it all?*

She had no answers to her questions, only a burning urge now to get the blankets and knife back to the adobe hut. She couldn't be easy until the key turned in the lock.

"Pedro, isn't it time for me and Catalina to return to the hut?" she asked, regretting her question the moment she spoke it. Who in her right mind wanted to be in such a place?

He gave her the skeptical look she knew such a question deserved. Pedro was slow, yes, but not as slow as bumbling, well-meaning Gaspar.

"Why would you want to go back there one minute before *los señores* decree it?" he asked, then shrugged. "Papa told me I would never understand women. Come on."

Paloma let out a slow sigh of relief. She held her breath when he looked around the kitchen and frowned, as if wondering what he had forgotten to do.

"If you are wondering where the keys are, we will have to stop at the bookroom," Paloma suggested.

"That must be it," he replied, then shuddered. "I do not like to spend much time with my masters."

"That is probably true of every servant," she said, making light of the matter, hoping to prompt him to move from the kitchen.

Still, he wouldn't budge, but lounged against the door. "To hear stupid Gaspar tell it, the Double Cross is a palace!"

"I like it there," she said simply, and moved closer to him with the blankets, hoping he would get the hint.

He looked around the kitchen one more time, muttering, "I know there was something …." To her relief, he swore and started down the hall.

She followed him to the bookroom door and waited outside, hoping he could just get the keys to the gate and the shed with no difficulty. To her surprise, he came out holding both keys, his expression triumphant, and if the truth were before her eyes, as surprised as she was.

"*Los señores* want to see you a moment," he said. "I will go ahead to the garden."

Setting down the blankets in the hall, Paloma went into the bookroom, standing still, making herself as small and unimportant as she could. *I am a servant in my uncle's house again*, she thought with dismay. *I am willing myself invisible.*

"Well, *Flaca*," Roque said, making no effort to disguise his own triumph, "show Señora High-and-Mighty how her husband and late father-in-law have cheated us."

Her own expression guarded, Catalina held out many years of livestock assessment. "You'll see that these figures—the ones your husband and his father assigned arbitrarily—don't match any of the actual count of cattle and sheep on this … place."

Paloma looked, remembering the evenings in the office with Marco when he puzzled over what to assess stubborn rancheros like the Duráns, who never admitted to anything. *I can only guess*, he had said on several occasions.

"You must tell the governor about this information I have uncovered," Catalina said suddenly. "March right into his office in Santa Fe and demand justice."

It was surprisingly easy to look wounded and pretend tears this time. "*Dios mio*, I suppose you can! We will all suffer, but what can we do, if you visit the governor?" Paloma squeezed her hands tightly together and looked away, wondering how much drama she could get away with and not rouse suspicion. "Please be merciful," she said.

"Go now," Miguel said, and pushed her toward the door. "Women and their tears! Catalina stays here because after we eat again, she had promised us a story. Poor you."

She glanced at Catalina, who crossed her eyes and waggled her finger in a circle by her ear, since the twins were looking toward the door. Paloma put her fist to her mouth, as though to stop her sobs, then shook her head and hurried down the hall with the blankets. She couldn't help smiling, and put her face into the blankets to hide her mirth from Pedro, who waited for her by the gate.

The gate. She looked up and up and knew there was no way she could ever get over a barrier so tall, even if she did manage to dig a fair-sized escape hole in their adobe prison. *I'll worry about that later*, she thought, as Pedro shouldered open the heavy gate.

He shoved her toward the shed, but she pushed back. "First I must be allowed to empty that … that little bucket the Duráns think will answer our needs."

She took the reeking bucket and dumped it in a far corner of the garden, looking around for a ladder, another gate, or anything that would free them from the *estancia*, once they liberated themselves from the shed. Nothing.

Pedro offered to hand her the blankets, once she had stooped through the low door, but she assured him she could manage. Inside, she set down the bucket and put the blankets beside the opposite wall, which she knew from her brief look outside was overgrown with a sheltering tangle of bushes.

Luckily, the Durán brothers trusted their bumbling servants to lock and unlock the shed, or they might have noticed that Catalina—how rude they were to call her "Skinny"—had cleared away some of the crumbling adobe near the roof to allow in more light. Paloma stared up at the blue sky, as blue as only a sky in the colony could be, and wondered what Marco was thinking as he searched for her.

She knelt on the floor, prayed to Santa Luisa, that gentle martyr who loved the desperate, and began to slice away at the adobe.

Sweating and dirty, Paloma stopped when she heard the key rasp in the lock.

After the door closed and the key turned again, Catalina hurried to her side. "Oh my dear, I wish I could help," her friend said as she smoothed back Paloma's damp hair.

"I'm fine. What do you think?"

Only the final glow of the setting sun cast any light through the small openings near the roof, but Catalina came closer, feeling the opening Paloma had scraped away. "Good work," she said. "We can spread this dirt around in here, and keep the blankets piled in front of the hole."

Catalina sank down and rested her forehead against her upraised knees. "Those odious men made me search and search until I found something that might cause trouble to Marco and Antonio … Marco's father?"

"Yes, and a good man, from all I have heard from others," Paloma said. "Don't worry about what you find. Marco told me a few years ago that

Governor Anza knows what he is doing regarding stubborn, stupid men like the Duráns."

"We have to get out of here as fast as we can," Catalina said, and pounded the earth with her fist. "I know I am thin, but why must they call me *Flaca*? And they stare at me while I work. It's more unnerving than anything my father and I have suffered anywhere else."

She stopped talking and took several deep breaths, then chuckled. "Tell me, Paloma, how was your day in the kitchen? Filled with joy and laughter?"

"Silly!" Paloma told Catalina about Maria, the laundress, terrified for years by the prospect of Comanche raiders, and a woman never called by her only name. "And Pedro … he is a sad one, with never a kind word tossed in his direction, either. Catalina, everyone here is starving, and not just from lack of food. But I think we knew that."

Silence for a few minutes, and then Catalina cleared her throat. "I think I know how we can get out of here. I started tonight."

"Your stories?"

Catalina took Paloma's face in her hands and pressed their foreheads together. "I think I can terrify those men to death, God willing … and Paloma, I intend to."

"When will you start?"

Catalina held up one finger. "I have begun. This was day one. Give me just a little time, and I will scare those monsters to death."

Chapter Twenty-Six

In which Joaquim and Eckapeta
are out of good ideas

"Terrify them into releasing us? I think it will take more than a few stories," Paloma replied. "Although you are vastly talented," she hastened to add.

"Don't underestimate the power of a good ghost story," Catalina said, her expression almost gleeful. "Tonight, after they ate, they started drinking, which they do every night."

"Gaspar says they drink every night and half the day."

"Tonight, I told them a story about an avenging angel sent to spy on two masters who have been abusing their servants."

"Who could those masters possibly be?" Paloma joked. Her arms ached from digging, but even Catalina's second-hand retelling of a story piqued her interest. The woman had a knack. "Don't stop there. You know I like your tales."

Chuckling, Catalina lowered her voice in that conspiratorial way that made Soledad shriek in terror and burrow closer to Marco when she told other, less-frightening tales in the *sala* at home. "The angel turns the bad masters into mushrooms. Then a woman and her daughter go into the *bosque* along the river to pick mushrooms, which they throw into a pot and boil. '*Help me, help me*,' the masters shriek in tiny voices, while the angel laughs from his perch on a beam in the kitchen."

Paloma couldn't help the ripple of horror that darted down her spine. She moved away a little from Catalina, which made her friend laugh. "You're convincing," Paloma said in her own defense. "That was an *angel*? I would hate to hear a story about your devils!"

"Angels? Devils? Does it matter? Believe me, I'm just getting warmed up."

"I wonder why they didn't recognize themselves as the evil masters," Paloma mused.

"Funny, isn't it? People never seem to see themselves as the one at fault."

She tried never to think of her uncle, but Catalina's words yanked Paloma back to those bleak days in Santa Fe. *No, some people never see themselves as the problem,* she thought, then felt another wave of remorse for her dark mood that had worried Marco enough to send her to visit his sister. She looked down at her hands, ashamed of herself.

"What's wrong, Paloma?" Catalina asked gently.

"If I hadn't been so insistent on having some time all my own, we would still be on the Double Cross, and not here in this hut," Paloma replied. "Please forgive me, Lina."

"Nothing to forgive," her friend said. "We're in a bad spot, yes, but you didn't create it." She shrugged, then clasped Paloma's hands between her own. "Sometimes things just happen. I am already planning the story for tomorrow night." She held up a second finger. "Day Two. Want to hear it?"

"Certainly."

"I think they are ready for the tale of two brothers in Taos who keep their servants in line by threatening them with Comanches. Imagine who?" Her voice hardened. "They will be found the next morning, gutted from gullet to privates, with their intestines roped around a tree like a garland, a Comanche lance through their ears."

"You're frightening *me*," Paloma protested, rubbing her arms. "What will be the final terror?" She held up a third finger. "Day Three?"

"Ah, yes, you're catching on. Our favorite story in all the colony," Catalina told her and lowered her voice even more, down into that range where the best storytellers lurk. " 'La Llorona.' I will scare them good."

"Is that enough?" Paloma asked. "I can't see Roque handing over his keys to you, even if you are screaming and wailing the loss of your children."

Catalina poked Paloma's middle. "Hunger is making you skeptical! Let's see what happens when La Llorona *herself* returns long after dark, shrieking and moaning and dressed in bloody rags," Lina said with some satisfaction. "*If* I can squeeze out of that hole.*"

"I'll dig faster," Paloma promised. She sighed, remembering the garden wall.

"Lina, I know just a few more days of digging will get us out, but the garden wall is so high. I doubt either of us can climb it."

"You're right," Catalina said, "but I believe I can get over the wall if I stand on your shoulders. I will snatch the keys from the bunch tied about Roque's waist and open the garden gate, so I can free you."

Paloma nodded. *If, if, if,* she thought, then chastised herself. *Catalina is doing her best. I must try harder.* She thought of poor Maria, and the half-promise she had made to the laundress only that afternoon, pledging her something better *if* …. There was that word again. Better to forget it. She applied her mind and heart to the matter at hand, thinking through several ideas, discarding them, and thinking again.

"If … no, *when* I see Maria tomorrow, I will ask her if she can procure a sheet, or a tablecloth, or something," Paloma said, speaking slowly, trying to convince herself first. "I think La Llorona needs a costume, don't you?"

"We'll need blood for such a sheet," Catalina said.

"We'll find it," Paloma assured her. "Two days, my friend."

* * *

THEIR FRUITLESS HUNT FOR the missing ones had turned Joaquim Gasca into the kind of man he thought not to see again: a man unhappy to look himself in the eye in his shaving mirror.

He looked at himself now—eyes bloodshot from lack of sleep, mouth set in a grim line, the frown between his eyebrows more pronounced than usual. Sunburned, too.

Two days in the saddle had rendered him sore beyond belief, and quite willing to acknowledge that Comanche women were considerably tougher than a Spanish fellow who commanded a garrison. At the end of each long day, Eckapeta dismounted with the ease and grace of a soldier half her age. At least she was kind enough not to further humiliate him with muttered comments in Spanish or Comanche.

"It chafes me, Eckapeta," he said, when they sat by the *acequia* that evening as Soledad and Claudito played. Or tried to play. After only a few minutes, the water, usually so enchanting, lost its appeal to the little ones. They both ended up in Eckapeta's orbit, Soli leaning against the Comanche woman and Claudito on her lap.

If the children of Paloma and Marco were slowly, bit by bit, perishing from the unexplained disappearance of their mother and their father's lengthening absence, little Juan Luis was thriving, nursed to repletion by his Double Cross mothers. Even as Sancha dabbed her eyes over the continued absence of both Master and Mistress, she pointed out that Juanito was a far cry from the wan and listless infant placed in her charge. "We can be grateful for this small favor," the housekeeper had said only that morning before the soldier and the Comanche rode out again, throwing their net wider and wider.

"What chafes you, Joaquim?" Eckapeta said, as they sat by the *acequia*.

"That we know no more than we did the first day we began our search."

Eckapeta pointed her lips toward the children, who had taken refuge with them—a silent warning to watch his words.

Joaquim looked away. He should have known better. Sancha had told him only yesterday that little Soli, usually so forthright and occasionally brash, had taken to sitting on the bench outside her parents' empty bedchamber, staring at the door as if willing them to appear. And more than once, Eckapeta had found Claudito curled up in a little ball of misery in his own room, trying to stifle his tears.

"You taught us not to cry, Kaku," he managed to say.

"I told him that maybe his *kaku* was wrong, and he could cry if he wanted to," Eckapeta told Joaquim as they began another day's ride in the morning. "Joaquim, what are we going to do?"

He stifled his amazement at the normally taciturn woman's unanswerable question; in fact, it shook him to his heart's core. When a Comanche doesn't know what to do, the world only waits for the seventh seal to be opened and the last angel to blow his horn.

"Do? Keep riding. Keep searching."

Joaquim looked up when Perla *la cocinera* came to the door of the kitchen and called the children to dinner. "We have your favorite churros tonight, *hijos*," she said.

Joaquim winced inside to see how slowly Claudito got off Eckapeta's lap. Before his mama's disappearance, the slightest whiff of a churro would have propelled him into a dead run through the kitchen garden to the door. Now he trudged toward the house, head down.

Joaquim looked down at his hands, no more able to raise his eyes than little Claudio. Everywhere they wandered in their increasingly impotent search, they were asked about Paloma. No one mentioned Catalina Ygnacio, so tall and slender (he had thought her skinny at first, but no, she was slender), forthright where she had formerly been shrewish and sharp of tongue, possessing a rare sort of beauty that a certain type of beholder could relish—him, for instance.

"You care a great deal for the auditor's daughter," Eckapeta said.

Joaquim heard no question in her words or voice, only a statement. He might have changed over the winter; it was equally obvious to him that the stern and generally forbidding Eckapeta of first acquaintance had mellowed into a real grandmama, and even more, a mother to Paloma. He knew her heart was breaking for her children and grandchildren on the Double Cross. That she took the time to suspect his own sorrow left him humbled.

"I love her," he said quietly.

He didn't look at her, afraid he would see only skepticism. Joaquim knew his own colorful, destructive past had been the subject of gossipmongers for as long as he had lived in Santa Maria's presidio. Even now, he had no idea how many women he had bedded through the years. To insist that Catalina was different would only have heaped coals of scorn on his head from those who thought they knew him.

"I love her," he said again. He stood up. "Dinner is getting cold."

Eckapeta started for the door, but Joaquim walked toward the office, ready to arouse an equally listless auditor to come to dinner and at least pretend some interest in food.

He found Señor Ygnacio slumped in Marco's chair at the desk, staring into the fireplace. He looked up when Joaquim tapped on the frame of the open door, eyes brightening for a small moment as though he thought perhaps his daughter would come bounding in behind him. The expectation vanished now almost before it appeared, although he did indicate the neat stack of papers on the *juez de campo's* desk.

"You see before you a completed audit, or near enough," he said. "I have found almost everything in order. Whatever questions I have, Señor Mondragón can certainly answer when he returns. It awaits his signature, and yours, and I will be free to leave."

He stopped and stared down at his hands.

"You will stay here until Marco has returned," Joaquim said, then plunged on, "And stay until we find your daughter and Marco's wife. Then, and only then, do you have my permission to leave this district."

"Are we on a fool's errand?" Señor Ygnacio wanted to know, asking the question no one wished to hear.

"Not until we have scoured every inch of this side of the colony," Joaquim replied, hoping his words would put the heart back in his own body. "Not until then. And even then, if you care to stay, I doubt Señor Mondragón would object. Santa Maria could use an accountant. The town is growing, but so many do not read and write. You could compose correspondence for people, and take some of that burden from our priest. There is much you can do here."

"I suppose I could," Señor Ygnacio said, his voice a little stronger. "Would the *juez* agree?"

"More than likely." Joaquim held out his hand to the little auditor, wondering—not for the first time—where Catalina got her height. "Come now. There is food waiting for us."

The auditor rose with some effort, then stopped and rummaged around on the nearly spotless desk. "Ah, here it is. Do you recall Señor Mondragón's list of tasks you were to do, once you … after—"

"After Eckapeta and I found our dear ones?" Joaquim finished, using the blunt words to lacerate his own misery at coming up so short.

"Yes, that." The auditor held out the list.

Joaquim took it, glancing at the words written in Marco's firm, up-and-down writing. The first item caught his eye. *Before Señor Ygnacio is entirely finished, send some of your men back to those houses where they left broadsides, just to see if anyone has suddenly "remembered" animals unaccounted for*, he read silently.

"I'll return to the presidio after dinner and give the necessary orders. Thanks for calling this to my attention. I had forgotten." He heaved a sigh of relief for something else to do. "Let's go to dinner. Perla doesn't like her meals to be unappreciated."

The little man nodded and touched the paper in Joaquim's hand. "It's a short list." He pointed to the final item and clucked his tongue. "And lucky is the man who gets to return to the Durán brothers and snoop around in their barns and corrals and ask pointed questions!"

"That's why it's last," Joaquim said, and smiled a little, knowing that task would fall to him, if Marco hadn't returned by the time the two jobs above it on the list had been accomplished. "Apparently our fearless *juez* is of the same opinion. Personally, *I* never mind putting off dealing with idiots."

"No one does," Señor Ygnacio said.

Chapter Twenty-Seven

In which Paloma misses an opportunity but finds a friend

A ROUTINE IS A routine, no matter how terrible the circumstances, Paloma decided, after her second day in the kitchen of the Duráns. Waking up before Catalina, she had scraped a little more of the adobe from the shed wall down near the dirt floor. If she could cook in the morning and find some excuse to return to the shed, she would have the afternoon to work. The kitchen was not up to her Double Cross standards, but still far superior to yesterday's cesspit.

Or was it the day before? Time was beginning to have no meaning, which worried her almost as much as the weight she had shed every day since their abduction. Four days of hunger was already changing her body. Her breasts were dry sacks now, with none of their usual firmness and bounce.

She needed more than yesterday's bowl of cornmeal and pork to stay alive—all the more reason to retreat to the shed and dig with the stolen knife.

To her surprise, old Maria sat at the kitchen table with something resembling a smile on her face and hefting the iron pot, which she held out to Paloma. "See there? I cleaned it."

The laundress had scraped off the worst of the burned-on cornmeal at the bottom, but Perla *la cocinera* would never have called the pot clean enough for Double Cross purposes. Maria looked so pleased with herself that Paloma would never have asked her to try harder. She took the pot from Maria and smiled her thanks.

When it was filled with cornmeal, water, and chilis, and thick bubbles were starting to plop and wheeze, Paloma added what bits of smoked pork remained, and after searching in the storeroom, an onion. She wanted more meat in the stew. That would only call attention to the vanished knife, so she said nothing.

That knife will haunt us all, she thought, when Pedro came into the kitchen, looking over his shoulder, fearful.

"*Qué es?*" she asked, dreading his reply but needing to know how much trouble was heading their way.

He shrugged and sat down, his hand to his ear as though it hurt. His eyes went to the pot simmering over the fireplace coals, and he wiped his mouth.

"Tell me," Paloma coaxed. "Are you in trouble over the knife you misplaced?" *Which I swiped*, she thought, feeling more than one pang of conscience, because she was generally an honest soul. *It doesn't matter. There are lives at stake here*, she reminded herself.

"That damned knife!" he exclaimed, slamming his hand on the table. "Our masters have said nothing about the knife, but I fear they will."

"Are the knives kept here in the kitchen?" she asked.

He pointed to the long drawer directly underneath the shelves holding dishware and cups. "It's locked, and I don't know how to jimmy it. There is another knife in there that looks like the one I lost ..." his voice trailed away. "I know I left it on the table."

Paloma glanced at Maria, whose eyes seemed to fill with dread and more dread as she watched.

"They can be so cruel," Maria whispered, when Pedro stomped outside.

"I need the knife, Maria," she whispered back. "Have they ... have they ever done bad things to you?"

Maria nodded, and rested her chin against her scrawny chest, unwilling to meet Paloma's eyes. "Don't do anything to make them angry at you, *señora!*"

"I will not," she said, chilled to her bones and more desperate to return to the shed and scrape away. Perhaps she could steal a large spoon, sharpen the edge, and use that instead. She could return the knife, and no one would be wiser, especially those two addled men who drank, and slept, and made their servants' lives miserable.

Paloma went into the storeroom, just to stand there a moment and collect herself, then look for flour and more cornmeal. She could make tortillas—maybe enough to distract the Durán brothers from the paltry amount of pork in today's stew.

Maria knew where the griddle was, and soon Paloma was slapping tortillas between her hands. Maria watched with interest. The two of them worked efficiently, Paloma shaping the dough and Maria cooking it.

By mid-morning, they had accumulated a respectable mound of tortillas—

moist, slightly salted, and steaming in a bowl under a cloth that might have been clean years ago.

"That should be enough for now," Paloma said. "I'll take the griddle off the …."

She stopped, listening to a sudden banging on the main door down the dusty hallway. Maria squeaked like a mouse, her eyes wide with terror, and clutched Paloma, who shook her off and started toward the closed kitchen door.

She opened it a crack to see the Duráns hurrying past. Roque stopped and barked an order to Miguel, who jerked open the kitchen door and grabbed Paloma, clapping his hand over her mouth. He dragged her away from the door and sat down with her, never moving his hand from her mouth.

She knew better than to offer any resistance, even though she wanted to clamp her teeth down on his fingers. She would have, had she not looked at Maria, helpless old woman, who would probably suffer, no matter what Paloma did.

Paloma sat still and listened, forcing herself to hear beyond Miguel's labored breathing. To her dismay, she heard small snatches of sentences. "Has anyone here seen …. We've been ordered to look for …. Missing more than one week and a driver dead …. If you see anything …. *Adios.*"

Paloma closed her eyes and let the tears fall on Miguel's hand. She grieved that she had not leaped up and run into the hall when she heard that first knock, screaming and waving her arms, anything to end this ridiculous abduction by lunatics.

The kitchen door opened and Roque smiled at her in that maddening way, the way a bully would treat a small child.

"*Señora*, I pulled a sad face to hear you and that skinny one had been abducted. Told him to let us know when you were found. I even said I would say a prayer or two tonight for your safety."

Miguel removed his hand. Paloma leaned as far away from him as she could. "You're enjoying this, aren't you?" she said softly.

"We haven't had so much fun in years," Miguel replied. He sniffed the air. "What's cooking?"

"Posole and tortillas," she said, determined to match them calm for calm. She turned to Roque. "Give Pedro your key. I want to return to the shed. I will cook no more for you today."

She started for the kitchen door, which Miguel blocked with his arm. "What will you do when your precious husband winds up in a Mexico City prison because he has been cheating us for years?" he taunted.

"I will go with him," she replied.

"You could stay with us and cook," Roque said.

"Never. Give Pedro the key."

She stared into Miguel's eyes long enough to see uncertainty begin to grow. "Be careful you do not turn into a mushroom. *Help me, help me!*" she said in a small mushroom voice, doing her best to imitate Catalina.

Miguel gasped and stepped aside. She walked past him, pleased to note the change in his complexion from merely grimy to pasty white. She continued down the hall, listening with satisfaction to a rattle of keys and then Pedro loping along beside her.

"Mushroom?" he asked, keeping his voice low.

"Ask Gaspar, if you dare," she said.

When she was locked in the shed again, Paloma leaned against the wall and closed her eyes, weary with fear and hunger and anger now that she hadn't the presence of mind to jump up when someone—it must have been Joaquim Gasca's soldiers—banged on the door.

"You cannot change what you did not do," she told herself firmly. She picked up where she had left off, scraping until she broke through the adobe, which made her smile. The afternoon was passing, so she carefully sculpted a U-shaped hole right at ground level, where no one could tell. Tonight Catalina would tell the drunken fools the story of the evil brothers with their guts looped around a fence and a Comanche lance through their ears. She could almost hear Catalina making all the different voices and recreating the screams of the dying men.

As she scraped and sculpted with increasing intensity, Paloma imagined such a fate for the Durán brothers. Who were they to think they could destroy her husband's life and see him cast into a Mexico City prison? Poor man, he must be searching for her everywhere and out of his mind with worry. "Marco, I will never whine again," she promised as she lay down by the hole and closed her eyes. "Please don't be angry with me for causing all this commotion."

PALOMA WOKE UP AS the puny shadows stretched longer through the gap between the wall and the roof. For the first time, she didn't start and wonder where she was. She knew. Nothing had changed.

Almost nothing, except for an odd odor, which made Paloma long yet again for a bath, or even a damp cloth. She sniffed and wondered. Surely *that* wasn't her.

As she lay so silent, curious now, Paloma heard raspy breathing, followed by a little snuffle. It came from the general direction of her middle, which felt warmer than usual. Curious more than frightened, she gently placed her hand lower and felt the softness of fur.

"What have we here?" she asked, her voice soft. The little kitten or whatever it was started as she began to stroke it, then relaxed again and snuffled some more. She turned her head away from the smell.

Paloma traced her hand down the small creature's back, burrowed so close to her, and felt a fluffy tail. She lay there, petting the animal and letting her eyes grow accustomed to the gloom.

When she could see better, she took a closer look at the animal. It was her turn to start in surprise, which made the little beast rear up and press small paws against her chest.

"And I thought matters could not get worse," she said, when she felt calm enough to speak. More cautious now, Paloma ran her finger gently against the skunk's furry throat and down his chest. "I really hope you will not spray me, because it's been a trying few days."

She slowly reached into her apron, where she had hidden two tortillas. She sat up carefully with no sudden moves and broke one of the corn tortillas into small pieces. Setting them beside her on the ground, she said, "Unlike some around here, I share my food and wouldn't dream of frightening you."

To her delight, the skunk took his paws from her chest and ambled slowly toward the tortillas. She smiled when he nosed about, then began to dine on tortillas. "I know they are good, Señor Zorillo," she said, more interested than repelled. "I made them and no one ever complains."

When the little creature finished, Paloma drew her legs up closer to her body, curious to know what he would do next. "We have any number of worms and bugs in this hut," she told him as he nosed around the dirt floor, snuffling as he went. "You're welcome to stay, I suppose. *Mi casa es su casa*?"

The notion of Double Cross hospitality in an adobe hut with a skunk as guest made Paloma chuckle. She felt her shoulders relax as she leaned against the wall, wondering if he would stay or go. With a pang, she thought of the lives of the saints book she was reading to Soledad and Claudito, and the *dichos* about San Francisco de Asís, that gentle friend of animals.

"Do you know, *mi amigo*, that San Francisco said you can tell the measure of a person by how he treats small animals and children?" she asked. "Or maybe captive ladies? The Duráns do not shine. Have some more. I believe we will get along fine."

Oddly content, all things considered, Paloma watched the skunk make a purposeful circuit about the shed, stopping now and then, with accompanying slurp and crackle sounds, as he encountered worms and bugs. When he finished grazing the constricted field, he waddled close again, turned around several times, and flopped against her leg. Paloma's hand went to his head, which made him snuffle some more and then sigh.

Hours later, he perked up as he heard the key to the garden gate turn in the lock. Footsteps followed, then the next key turned in the lock on the shed.

Paloma rested her hand on the skunk, gently rubbing the back of his neck. Feeling his rapid heartbeat, she prayed he would do nothing.

Catalina crouched into the hut and the door closed behind her. "Paloma, you should have seen their fright tonight," she began, when the garden lock closed, locking them in securely.

"Speak softly, Lina," Paloma told her. "We have a little guest in here and he is wondering about you."

"Paloma, have your wits gone wandering?"

"If you'll move slowly and speak softly, I will introduce you to Señor Zorillo," Paloma teased.

"Good God," Catalina exclaimed, then lowered her voice. "Could our luck get any worse? *Zorillo?*"

"Maybe it just changed, dear friend. I'm going to call him Francisco. We've been needing a guardian saint."

Chapter Twenty-Eight

In which worms start to turn

CATALINA KEPT A RESPECTFUL distance from Señor Francisco, Paloma's patron saint, but did unbend enough to offer him some cooked cornmeal on a tin plate. The skunk snuffled around it, then ate, after what Paloma thought was a reproachful look at Catalina Ygnacio, who didn't seem overjoyed to share their already smelly quarters with the little beast and his eye-watering aroma.

"He'll bring us good luck?" Catalina asked, in a voice of no confidence.

"He kept me company," Paloma said simply. "I needed him." She changed the subject massively. "How did you manage to get a tin plate away from those dreadful men?"

"I scared them thoroughly when the Comanche lance went through the ears of both men, whose entrails were already being spooled from their bodies by an imp of some sort." She gave Señor Francisco a wary glance and edged closer to Paloma. "I've noticed that when the twins are sufficiently frightened, little details don't seem to matter much."

"Are they frightened enough for La Llorona tomorrow night?" Paloma asked. "I've dug all I dare to into the adobe. A wider hole might attract attention. Now I should probably start digging the ground so we can squeeze out. That plate might help."

"They're frightened enough," Catalina assured her. "I've run out of papers to shuffle about and have started over. Roque doesn't seem to notice, but Miguel is a sly one."

"Have … have either of them mentioned a missing knife?" Paloma asked.

"Miguel did, but I exclaimed loudly about something I had found that might implicate Marco or his father in some evil-doing, and I think I distracted him."

"I worry," Paloma said, as she tickled Señor Francisco under his ears. "I worry for old Maria." *Mostly I worry for me*, she thought. Even wasted with drink, the twins would know their servants were too subjugated to steal a knife. "And for me," she admitted aloud.

Lina squeezed her hand. "I worry, too. Tomorrow is the night for La Llorona." She held up her third finger. "Three days of stories, and each more terrifying."

"How long have we been here?" Paloma asked, feeling stupid because the days were blurring together.

Even Catalina had to think. "Five days, even though it seems like a month." She shook her head. "Maybe it is more than that. Go to sleep now. We'll plan tomorrow morning, when our heads are clearer."

Paloma lay down, her cheek against the damp earth, remembering a warm bed with Marco in it and children peeking around the edge of the door in the morning, wanting her to wake up and motion them in. Her empty breasts ached for little Juanito. *Don't think about him*, she ordered herself. *Someone surely found him on the road and he is safe at home. Marco will find me. I know he will.*

In the early hours right at dawn, Paloma was jarred out of sleep by screaming that grew louder and then faded, as if someone was running back and forth, trying to escape any number of the demons Catalina described so well in her dreadful stories. She sat up and reached for Catalina, who clutched her hand.

"What is happening?" she whispered, knowing her friend had no more idea than she did.

To her dismay, the skunk waddled away through the now-sizeable opening in the wall. So much for guardian creatures sent by San Francisco himself. She grabbed the blankets and stuffed them against the hole. So far, no one had come into the shed, so their secret was safe enough, but no one had screamed like that, either.

"*Señoras!*"

"Is that Gaspar?" Paloma whispered to Catalina. "Doesn't Pedro usually get us out?"

"Something is very wrong," her friend replied.

Someone fumbled with the key in the lock for what seemed like a long time, especially when the screaming continued, followed by the shouts of one of the Durán twins.

The door swung open and Gaspar stuck his head inside. "There is a missing knife!" he whispered. "I think Señor Miguel will kill Pedro! Do you know where the knife is?"

"Of course we do not know," Catalina lied, speaking with just enough scorn and indignation to nearly convince Paloma, who grabbed the knife, wiped the adobe clay from the blade and concealed it in the fold of her dress.

"Come! I was told to fetch Señora Mondragón, but you might as well come, too," Gaspar said as he reached for them again. He put his hand over his nose. "It smells as bad in here as in my own room, and you are gentlewomen."

"Not lately," Catalina muttered.

They hurried from the shed and Gaspar locked it behind them. He prodded them down the hall toward the kitchen, where the screaming had turned into a whimper even more frightening.

The door opened and Catalina blocked the entrance, giving Paloma a moment to set down the knife behind the bench in the hall, pushing it partly under a furry mound of something that turned to jelly when she touched it. She shuddered and straightened up in one smooth motion, hoping neither brother had noticed.

Roque stood just beyond Catalina, staring at her, so Paloma reached down and fumbled with her shoe. He turned toward his brother, who had raised a poker over Pedro, kneeling with his head bowed and ready for the worst. Bloody drool cascaded down his shirt.

As Catalina darted forward to stop the man, Paloma looked back at Gaspar. "Find that knife in the hall. Pretend you just discovered it. Don't betray me," she whispered. "We are not your enemy."

Forgetting her own safety, Paloma leaped into the room as old Maria grabbed the descending poker, throwing Miguel Durán off balance. He tried to strike her with his free hand, but he went down in a heap.

"I stole the knife!" Maria said and knelt beside the bloody Pedro. "I wanted to slice off more meat. I was hungry."

Miguel scrambled to his feet, cursing the old woman and striking her with his hands. He had dropped the poker, which Catalina eased away with her foot before Roque could reach for it.

Paloma took a deep breath and stepped in front of Miguel and Maria, who had drawn herself into a little ball and covered her head from further blows.

"We are all hungry, Señor Durán," Paloma begged. "Don't strike someone who has been a loyal servant to you. Please don't."

"Why should I listen to you?" he snarled. "You were supposed to be the old auditor. I was going to … going to …" he stopped and turned to his brother, who had Catalina on her knees now, his fingers tangled in her long hair. "What were we going to do with the auditor? I forget."

"Ruin his life in some way," Roque replied, breathing heavily. "Something we sent Gaspar the Idiot to do."

Now would be a very good time to find that knife, Gaspar, Paloma thought, as she stood over Maria. Pedro lay still, and she wondered if he was dead.

"Stop, stop, here is the knife!" Gaspar said as he came toward them. "I … it must have been … underneath that dead something or other behind the bench. Here."

He held out the reeking knife covered in jellied ooze. "Maybe I should clean the hall so this doesn't happen again." He looked around, eyes wide. "You know how things get away from us."

"I'll help you," Paloma said, thinking of times she had distracted Claudito or Soledad from something undesirable.

Both brothers turned their attention to her now. She saw madness mingled with ferocity in their bloodshot eyes. *I cannot reason with these men*, she thought. *No one can.*

"You have your knife now," she said quietly, trying anyway because she had no choice. "Put it away. The lost is found."

Pedro stirred and groaned. He narrowed his eyes and glared at her. He started to point at Paloma when old Maria grabbed his hand and kissed it over and over.

"Pedro, you have returned from the land of the dead!" the laundress wailed. "God and all the saints be praised!"

"Put the knife away, Señor Durán," Paloma said again to Miguel.

He pointed the knife with its dripping, rotting juices at her. "Kneel down and bow your head, witch," he demanded.

Paloma did as he said. She closed her eyes and told herself how much she would miss Marco and their children. Her mind was filled with sudden peace, relief even, that this misbegotten, foolish ordeal was over.

She waited for the knife to bite into her flesh and held her breath. To her amazement, she felt the blade against her skull as Miguel wiped the disgusting thing in her hair and laughed.

"You are all so careless in here," he said and rested the blade against her neck, flicking the point against her skin. "Are you so careless at your precious Double Cross? I will ask Señor Mondragón that, before they haul him away to prison in Mexico City."

She opened her eyes when she heard the knife clatter into the drawer and a key turn in the lock. Her heart started to beat again.

She watched Roque try to pull his hands, wet with Pedro's blood, from Catalina's tangled hair. He shook her head like a terrier with a mouse, trying to free himself. With a curse, he pulled out the small knife at his belt and sawed through her hair to release his sticky fingers. He looked at Catalina, who had dragged herself upright and glared at him. He turned her head one way and then the other. "It's not even now. What a pity," he declared, as he hacked through the hair on the other side of her head. "That's better," he declared and laughed at the mess he had created.

Miguel clapped his hand on Roque's shoulder. The brothers laughed and left the kitchen. Roque turned back to order Catalina to bring them toasted bread and cheese, and do it quickly.

Paloma crawled to Catalina, who held out her arms. They clung together for a moment in silence, broken by labored breathing from barely conscious Pedro. Paloma looked around the kitchen at benches overturned, crockery smashed, cornmeal ground underfoot and bloody, sticky hair everywhere.

"Maria, do you have a tablecloth?" she asked.

The laundress nodded. With a fearful look toward the open door leading into the hall, she crept on hands and knees to the room off the kitchen with its laundry tub and pile of filthy shirts and socks. Paloma watched her rummage through the reeking pile, gagging, until she found a sheet stained with heaven-knew-what.

"No. I don't dare," she said. She dropped the sheet and shut the door. "They would be so angry."

Paloma untied her petticoat, slipped it off and wiped the front of Pedro's shirt with it, where blood and mucus mingled with broken teeth.

"*You* stole that knife," he accused.

Old Maria pushed her face in front of his, showing a spark of real anger that made goose bumps march up and down Paloma's arms. "I told you *I* stole it because I wanted something to eat! You two fools abducted two harmless gentlewomen and started something terrible."

In silence, Pedro looked down at the tiles, his face a study in confusion. Paloma continued to dab at his wounds, dipping her ruined petticoat in the earthenware water jar that had somehow escaped destruction in the rampage.

Gaspar cleared his throat. "I'll take him to lie down."

"That is kind of you," Paloma told him, all the while thinking, *Keep him far from the Durán brothers. He knows too much.* She wrapped her petticoat around Pedro's head. "He needs his bed."

"No one has a bed," Gaspar told her. "We have piles of rags."

"You deserve better," Catalina said, her voice low, but charged with a fierce anger that Paloma heard from the other side of the room. "We all deserve better."

"Not when you are born with no luck."

"Gaspar, a month ago, I might have agreed with you," Catalina said, calmly and coldly. "We will make our own luck because we must."

Gaspar helped Pedro to his feet. He started for the door, then turned back to Paloma and Catalina, who was fingering her hacked off hair in disbelief. "It started as a silly idea, when the brothers were in their cups. Look what it has turned into."

"I know, Gaspar."

"One thing happens, and then another, and we dig a deeper hole." He brightened. "Almost like the hole you are digging."

Pedro raised his head, and his eyes narrowed. For one shocking moment, he looked to Paloma like the men who had just beaten him. He put his hand to his head and groaned.

Please don't betray us, Paloma thought. *Before God and all the saints, don't.* "Gaspar, *you* won't say anything to …" she whispered.

"Maybe I would have yesterday …" his voice trailed off and he looked around in disbelief, as if seeing the messy ruin of the kitchen for the first time, "not now."

He helped Pedro to a bench and crept closer to Paloma and Catalina. "You had pretty hair, *señorita*," he told Lina. He lowered his voice. "What can I do?"

"Make sure the horse barn is open tonight," Catalina told him. "We want our mule."

His expression brightened, then turned dark again. "No one has good luck here, Señorita Ygnacio."

"We are overdue."

Chapter Twenty-Nine

In which Catalina hatches a puny plan that bears no scrutiny

C ATALINA HATED TO LEAVE Paloma in the kitchen. There had been no time to discuss plans for the evening's terrors, no time to think how to deal with Pedro, who knew who had stolen the knife, and probably how she had been using it.

Now the knife was locked away. All Paloma had to work with, provided she could return to the shed, was a cheap tin plate that would probably bend with the first pressure. Catalina saw their whole flimsy plan crashing down around them. If they could not squeeze out of the shed, how could they ever escape?

While Paloma set a loaf of bread on a plate and looked for something else to serve with it, Catalina fingered her ragged hair. She thought of Joaquim Gasca, who had touched her hair and declared it a masterpiece of nature. At the time, she had called it shallow gallantry, something a man like him might say to get into a woman's bed.

Somewhere, sometime during those few weeks when Joaquim Gasca came more and more often to the Double Cross to sit with her father when he could have sent a corporal as official representative, she had decided her hair truly was beautiful. She knew she was still thin and sharp of tongue, but she had begun to see herself as someone else.

It will grow back, she thought, then smiled inside, thinking what she would have said only a month or two ago, before they arrived in Valle del Sol. *I would have pouted and used this as one more layer of shellac on my heart.* She looked at Paloma, who silently righted the benches then spoke quiet words to Maria, still sniffing back tears and wringing her hands.

You make order out of chaos, she thought. *It's time you were home with your babies.*

"Somehow, a bloody sheet by dusk," she whispered to Paloma as she picked up the tray, took a deep breath, and started down the hall.

She knew the twins would laugh at her when she came into the bookroom. They did not fail her, pointing at her shorn head and slapping their knees with laughter, as if they had never seen anything funnier.

"Did you wander into a sheep-shearing pen, *Flaca*?" Roque asked, trying to appear solicitous, even as he rolled his eyes and snorted.

She ignored them, setting the tray on the desk and seating herself behind it. Roque came closer to eye the bread and bits of dried meat, a skimpy meal by anyone's standards.

"Can't the Mondragón woman do any better?" he asked. "I mean, what am I paying her for?"

His blinding wit sent Roque into another fit of laughter. Miguel joined in. Catalina closed her eyes and told herself to ignore these fools. Easier said than done, when Roque pulled a pair of scissors out of the drawer and continued to snip at her hair, his awful breath on her neck. She couldn't help herself, but her tears only made him cut closer and closer until clumps of auburn hair littered the desk.

She said nothing, willing her tears to dry up, and nourishing herself on the knowledge that hair grows back. True, it was unlikely that Joaquim Gasca would favor her with any attention now, but he probably would have lost interest anyway.

"My hair will grow back," she said, and folded her hands together on the desk. "I need to go through this one last box, gentlemen."

She picked up the first box she had gone through and had wisely never labeled done with a date of completion, as she had learned from her father. To her relief, Roque put down the scissors, after snapping them open and shut a few times close to her nose and chortling like the bully he was.

She glanced at Miguel, who eyed her with more interest than usual. He sat back and folded his arms, his smile benign but more troubling than Roque's antics, because he seemed to know what she was doing. She kept her eyes on the pages before her, suddenly afraid to meet his glance.

"*Flaca*, how many times do you intend to go through the same boxes?" he asked, his voice silky soft and full of menace.

"Only until I am satisfied I have not missed anything," she replied, hoping her voice did not quaver. *What now?* she thought in desperation. *He's wise to me. What now?*

She thought of Paloma patiently digging and welcoming a skunk into their shed, and knew that somehow, some way, even without a knife, Paloma would carve out a wide-enough space for them to escape and begin their bid for freedom. Paloma would never fail her, and she must not fail the kind woman who only wanted to return to her family.

She calmed her mind. "Very well, sir. What you and your brother should do is compose a letter for Governor Anza. Before anything can happen, he must receive your petition to have Señor Mondragón removed from office. Do you know the governor?" *That's right,* she thought, pleased to see confusion take control of Miguel Durán's wine-muddled mind.

"No, I don't know the governor," Miguel snapped. "I suppose you know the governor quite well."

"Better than you do," she said cheerfully, happy to see the pendulum swing more in her favor. "I suggest you write a placating letter, because he holds Señor Mondragón in high esteem." She indicated the cluttered desk before her. "Of course, you and I will work together to make certain that all of Señor Mondragón's faults are laid before him."

"Yes, yes, all of them," Roque muttered. "A placating letter, you say?"

"Very humble, very placating," she echoed. "While you do that, I will return to the kitchen and see if I can find more food."

Miguel gave her an impatient wave with his hand as he sat down in her place and took out a fresh sheet of paper. Catalina left the room and hurried to the kitchen, where she startled Paloma, who held old Maria in her arms, doing her own placating.

"Maria thinks she needs to apologize to me because I was forced to produce the knife," Paloma said. "I have been begging her forgiveness that she took the beating due to me." She raised her eyes to Catalina's face and gasped. "*Dios mio*, what more have they done to you?"

"We will all agree it could be worse," Catalina replied, trying to make light of the ruin that used to be her lovely hair. She touched Maria's arm, and then her face, knowing deep in her heart how it felt to spend a lifetime abused by others. "You, my dear, must somehow procure a sheet for us tonight after it is dark."

Maria turned terror-filled eyes on Catalina. "How can I hide from Comanches and witches if I am wandering about the *estancia*? How can I do this for you?"

Paloma hugged her closer. "There are no Comanches or witches, Maria, only two foolish, evil men who have held you captive with tales of things which will not come to pass, not now, not when peace might be closer than we know."

"I'm afraid!" Maria wailed, and rested her head against Paloma.

Just then, sitting in the kitchen, Catalina Ygnacio, prisoner of fools and madmen and daughter of a beaten-down accountant from Santa Fe, felt a page turn in her book of life. The turn of the page seemed so audible, she wondered why Paloma and even Maria did not hear the rustle of paper.

"I will free us tonight," she said softly, because there was no telling where Roque or Miguel were at the moment. "We will succeed and we will liberate ourselves from this place, Maria."

The old laundress looked more hopeful, but not convinced. Catalina touched her arm again, hoping that somewhere inside that empty shell of a woman a spark still existed. "In fact, you will come with us."

"Oh, no! They will follow us," Maria exclaimed, and put her hands to her mouth.

"I guarantee you they will not," Catalina replied firmly. "In fact, I think it is time you had a last name. I will call you Maria Brava, the courageous one."

"Maria Brava?" the servant repeated. She looked Catalina in the eyes and Catalina saw another page turn, whether Maria knew it or not. "I will have a sheet for you after dark, no matter what."

"It must be bloody," Paloma said. "Find an old chicken somewhere, anything. Throw the sheet over the garden wall, then go back to the kitchen."

"Should I hide in the kitchen?" Maria Brava asked.

"I would," Catalina replied. "Hide and don't come out until we call for you."

Maria nodded and went into the laundry room off the kitchen, murmuring to herself. "Sheet, bloody sheet, after dark. Hide."

As Catalina watched her go, uncertainty circled over her like a hungry buzzard. "She is a weak link to hang our admittedly puny escape plans on."

"She will not fail us," Paloma said, with some of Maria's new-found intensity. "We will grab her and run."

Paloma kissed her cheek. "We found more *carne seca* for the twins. Here, you take it. What a shame we cannot poison it. What a lot of trouble they have been for Marco through the years, I will admit, but what fueled this foolishness? Why do people go so strange?"

"It nearly happened to me," Catalina said, putting words to her thoughts. "One more unwelcome audit for one more distrustful *juez de campo* in one more suspicious district, and I could become such a person."

"But you came to Distrito Valle del Sol," Paloma told her with a smile that belied her shrinking frame, her dirty hair—at least she had hair—and her unwashed condition.

"Paloma, would you faint right now?" Catalina asked. "Immediately?"

Paloma stared at her. "I may not look like much at the moment, my friend, but I don't feel like fainting."

"Faint so I can have an excuse to get you back to the shed," Catalina said, then blew out her cheeks with a great sigh. "Where you must use a tin plate to make that hole big enough for tonight's grand show."

Without a word, Paloma slumped down onto the bench, slid to the floor, and collapsed carefully on her side. "Will this do?" she asked out of the corner of her mouth. "Maria, Maria, don't worry! Just do as we asked for later. I'll be fine before you know it."

Chapter Thirty

In which La Llorona wails for her children and Paloma sees things

Convincing Maria Brava to raise a racket of her own—pleading and begging for Paloma to come around—took no convincing at all. *I swear we will pay you back with kindness evermore*, Paloma thought as she moaned and lay still.

She heard Catalina run down the hall, calling for help, and listened for the heavier footsteps of the twins. In another moment, she was jerked upright by Roque or Miguel. No, it was Roque, because he wore the keys. She stared at the hasp that bound the keys to his belt and felt relief flood her, even as she moaned and let her head loll. It would only be a moment's work to push on the hasp and free the keys, which hung together on their own metal ring.

Someone, undoubtedly Roque, threw cold water in her face. Paloma did what she thought was a masterful display of someone coming out of a faint. She shook her head, then pressed her hand to her cheek. "I don't know what happened to me."

"Maybe the people who live here could feed you a little more," Catalina said, and glared at Roque.

"Just help me to the hut," she gasped, as though worn out nearly to death. "I will rest."

His face a study in worry, Gaspar lifted her more carefully to her feet. She staggered and would have fallen, but Catalina steadied her.

"Here! I can't be bothered," Roque said, and unhooked the keys from his belt, handing the ring to Gaspar. "Bring this right back." He grabbed Catalina by the neck. "You stay here and cook something."

"With what?" Catalina asked, hands on her hips, her stare so militant that Paloma wondered where her courage came from. "Hand me the key to the knife drawer and I will hack off a portion of that smoked pork you squirreled away in your room. I saw you take it."

Roque swore and yanked the keys back from Gaspar. He looked at the keys and stopped at a short key with a triangle head. Taking a knife from the drawer, he pointed it at Maria Brava, who shuddered and tried to hide her face.

"Maria *la loca*," he taunted. "Flaca, get the meat in my room and bring it here!" When Catalina ran from the kitchen, he said to Paloma, "You women are a great deal of trouble, demanding this and that."

Paloma sagged against Gaspar and closed her eyes. When she opened them, Catalina had returned with the smoked pork and Roque was slicing off a hunk. He stuffed it into his mouth while Maria watched his every movement, licking her lips. Roque hacked off more slices for himself and handed the little that remained to Catalina. He put the knife back in the drawer and locked it, then tossed the keys to Gaspar. "Hurry up, you fool."

Paloma felt Gaspar's sigh. She leaned against him for good effect and they moved slowly down the hall.

"Here now, you have to stand upright," he told Paloma as they reached the garden gate.

Paloma pressed one hand against the wall, watching Gaspar find the garden key, a longer key two to the left of the triangle head key that opened the knife drawer. He unlocked the hut and helped her inside, then locked her in. Ear against the wooden door, she listened, hoping he would forget to lock the garden gate, knowing that Maria's part in the escape tonight was questionable. No luck. She heard the other key turn in the lock.

That would have been too simple, Paloma thought as she stared into the gloom until she could make out their familiar prison. She smiled to see the skunk looking back at her, ever optimistic. Taking one tortilla from her pocket, she divided it and ate her share quickly, gobbling it down like Soledad or Claudito, hungry for more.

"This is yours, Señor Francisco," she said as she divided the tortilla again and again, leaving smaller bites for the skunk. She hunkered down and watched for a moment, thinking of earlier times she had sat so close to Marco in their kitchen, leaning against his arm as he shared his bowl of flan with her.

"This isn't getting a hole dug," she remarked to the skunk, who had begun his early-morning circuit around the shed, seeking beetles and worms. She took the tin plate from under her blanket and stared at it a moment, wishing it would turn into a shovel, then began to dig in the dirt below the hole she had so painstakingly carved from the adobe wall. Unwanted tears sprang into her eyes because the opening looked too small for even a child to crawl through.

"I will not fail you, Catalina," she murmured as she dug carefully, hoping not to bend or break the flimsy bit of tin. Why couldn't the Durán brothers have eaten off something more durable?

Ay caray, tears again. Paloma set her lips tight against her own weakness, wondering if it was hunger that made her tears fall so often. Would that she could water the ground and make it softer.

Sitting back on her heels, she stared at the night jar no one had emptied since yesterday, when they were wakened so early with screams from the kitchen. Was that only yesterday? No, it was this morning. Why was she having such trouble remembering things?

I can't, she thought. *I must*. Fighting back more tears, she picked up the night jar and dumped its liquid contents where she needed to dig. She put dirty fingers over her nose until the moisture soaked into the ground, then dug in earnest in the softer soil.

She dug for hours, days maybe—no, hours—her mind free of everything except the faces of her children. She cried when she could not remember if Juan Luis had blue eyes like hers, or brown like his father's. The still-rational part of her brain reminded Paloma that he was only two months old now— was it three?—and eye color might change. Her breathing grew labored as she let the tiniest doubt of his survival filter through the fog of her tired mind before thrusting it aside.

She nearly smiled to recall Soli's persuasive reasons why bedtime should be later, and Claudito's interest in making roads among the squash vines in the kitchen garden. She fought back tears to think of Marco's wonderful laugh and the way he held her so close when they made love. She yearned to tell her dear brother Claudio yet again how much she loved him, and wondered if Graciela had birthed their baby by now.

She dug and prayed for Toshua to give his own persuasive reasons for a treaty to other Comanches. She yearned to feel Eckapeta's arm around her shoulders and hear her often-stringent comments about raising children to be safe in Indian country. She recalled the pride she felt when she earned the Comanche woman's praise for … for what? She could not remember.

She dug and dug until the tin plate bent and snapped, then dug with her fingers until her nails, already brittle, snapped, too. She picked up the sharp fragment of the plate, wrapped a hunk of her dirty skirt around it and kept working. By the time she noticed a difference in the afternoon shadows from the small open space near the eaves, she knew she was close.

Paloma sat back and stared like an addled woman at the hole she had dug. Señor Francisco nestled close to her, full now—how good that someone was full—from the worms and other soil creatures he had unearthed with his steady digging. She rested her hand on his soft fur, tickling him under his chin, because she knew he liked that. She closed her eyes and thanked San Francisco de Asís for the little beast who had kept her company. Catalina might scoff, but Paloma didn't care. Not even her friend was going to convince her that the little skunk wasn't a gift from the saint of simple things.

Señor Francisco stirred when Paloma's stomach growled. She placed her hand on her shrinking middle, puzzled that she felt no particular hunger anymore. Maybe that was what happened when people starved to death. She felt oddly detached from her surroundings, wondering—not for the first time—when she would grub like Señor Francisco among the worms and beetles, if they could not escape tonight.

She sat up, ready to dig some more, when she heard the garden gate swing open. For several seconds, she wondered what to do, before she remembered to cover the hole with their blankets. Stupefied with exhaustion, she rested against the wall. She smiled to think that she couldn't even see her hand in front of her face, and then laughed softly at herself. Who wanted to see such a skinny arm and bloody tips where fingernails had been? She closed her eyes because the lids felt so heavy.

"Paloma? Paloma?"

She wanted—what was her name?—to stop shaking her, so she opened her eyes.

"I dug ... I dug something," she managed to say.

"My God, Paloma, we have to get out of here. You've eaten nothing all day."

"But I dug," she reminded the tall, thin woman. "Catalina," she said with some triumph, remembering her name.

"Yes, you did," Catalina said. She pressed something in Paloma's hand. "Eat this."

Dutifully, Paloma put whatever it was into her mouth, then sighed with the pleasure of a piece of bread. She ate quickly, following the scrap of bread that seemed like a banquet with a slice of smoked meat. "That is the best thing I have ever eaten," she announced. "I can probably dig some more now."

"No need," Catalina said. "I believe you have done it, Paloma." Her arm went around Paloma's shoulder. "I left them so terrified!"

Yes, yes, that was it. La Llorona. Paloma sat up, interested. "I hope you scared those monsters to death."

Catalina chuckled. "Close, so close. I swayed, I moaned, I raked my fingernails down my face, I tried to gouge out my eyes, I wept, wailed, and sobbed for my dead children. I ran around that disgusting room where the brothers live, looking under this mat, and behind that chest for my lost little ones. You should have heard Roque shriek when I grabbed his foot!"

Paloma laughed, but maybe a little too long, because Catalina pulled her close. "We're getting out of here tonight, Paloma. I promise."

"Let's go right now," Paloma said, and tried to rise.

Catalina held her more gently now. "We have to wait a little longer for Old Maria—no, Maria Brava—to toss a bloody sheet over the wall."

"If she doesn't?" Paloma asked, alert, her senses sharp again as the fog lifted from her overtaxed brain. "What will we do?"

She wanted Catalina to tell her that all would be well, wanted to hear some reassurance. Her friend remained silent.

Paloma dug deep into her heart and soul, deeper than she had ever dug before. Every lovely moment of her life since she had come to Valle del Sol seemed to pass in review. Maybe she was just hungry, maybe her mind was beginning to wander again, but somehow she saw more—three little ones playing by the *acequia* instead of two, a fourth baby at her breast, full now and flowing with milk. And there was Marco standing by her, his hand on her head as he ruffled her hair so carelessly as he liked to do. She leaned against his leg and he bent down enough to whisper in her ear. "Happy?"

"Oh, yes," she whispered back.

"What?" It was Catalina, recalling her to a reeking hut and starvation and fear that a beaten-down, worn-out laundress might not fulfill her vital part. "What?"

Paloma tucked the lovely little vision back into her heart. "Catalina, we're getting out. This hole ... you first, or me?"

Chapter Thirty-One

In which Joaquim Gasca finally eats in the kitchen, thank God

"WHAT ARE WE GOING to tell Marco and Toshua when they return?" There, he had said what he knew Eckapeta was thinking. Joaquim Gasca stared at the sandals with the dried blood on them. Marco had tacked them up in the *sala* as a reminder of how brave his wife was. *I can't find that woman*, he thought in shame. Joaquim rubbed his eyes, gritty from yet another day in the saddle.

"It's not good to rub your eyes," Eckapeta said.

He glanced at his constant companion, Eckapeta the Comanche woman, who rode out with him every morning, her back straight, her eyes looking, looking, and looking some more for some sign they had missed, some great key to the mystery of where two ladies could have vanished. Even Eckapeta seemed tired, her eyes heavy, her back not so straight. He wondered briefly how old she was, and what ghastly things she had seen and maybe even done.

Failure settled on his shoulders like mud until he wanted to cry out, "Enough!" He couldn't, though. He was El Teniente Gasca, leader of soldiers, wiser today than he had been for years. If all this was true, why did he feel so desperate right now—so puny, so useless?

"Eckapeta, I was going to get really brave just a few weeks ago and ask Señorita Ygnacio to marry me," he said, lowering his voice simply because the idea sounded so preposterous now. "She probably would have said no, but I was going to ask."

Eckapeta took his hand in hers, raised it to her dry lips, and gently kissed it.

He probably could have withstood derisive laughter, a shake of her head, a snort of amazement, but not that. Joaquim got up and went to the door of the *sala*. He stood in the hall, trying to think of anything except failure. Nothing else came to mind, so he suffered.

Composing himself because he had to, he walked the short distance to the kitchen, where Perla was serving Señor Ygnacio what looked like turkey cooked in chilis. His mouth watered, but even hunger irritated him. Here he was in a comfortable *estancia*, contemplating a good meal, and where were those two lovely women?

The thought of entering the kitchen and sitting down with the father of the lost woman he loved was more effort than he could manage. "Perla, when you get a minute, could you bring some of that to me and Eckapeta in the *sala*?" he asked.

Trust Perla to talk back. "*Señor*, the children are asleep. You can eat and talk in the kitchen. I will leave you alone as I always do."

And trust Perla to be so scrupulous about not interfering with their increasingly unhappy conversation. She knew her place on the Double Cross, a modest one. She never pried; she never eavesdropped.

"I'm too tired," he said. "Just bring us something in the *sala*."

Dios mio, he had angered Perla. She put her hands on her hips. "Señora Mondragón does *not* like food in the *sala*, *Teniente*," she said in a voice that expected no argument from a young pup like him.

"Very well," he groused, succumbing to those narrowed eyes and pursed lips. He called to his companion. "Eckapeta, let's eat something."

They dragged themselves into the kitchen. Joaquim nodded to Señor Ygnacio, not able to look the man in the face, not with his daughter still missing. Here he was, Joaquim Gasca, the weakest link in the colony of New Mexico, unable to find a trace of her. He mumbled a greeting and sat down, weary down to his stockings.

He looked around, still avoiding the auditor's eyes. "Perla, where is Sancha?"

"She is making certain Juanito gets to his last meal of the day, *Teniente*. She will return, and I will leave you all alone."

He made some comment and sat up a little straighter, even though he knew the foolishness of trying to impress someone as practical as Perla. Manners dictated that he should speak to Señor Ygnacio, but he couldn't think of anything to say. Someone so well-versed in life's cruelties would surely give him a trusting look that seemed to say, *I know you are doing your best*. Joaquim knew he was doing his best, but that wasn't good enough. It wasn't finding two women, one dear to his battered heart and the other one even dearer now.

While Joaquim waited for Perla to slice turkey and spoon on chilis, Señor Ygnacio cleared his throat and pushed over a familiar sheet of paper. Joaquim looked at it out of dull eyes, recognizing Marco's handwriting and remembering the list of things to do that the *juez de campo* had left with the auditor.

"Let's see: I did send my men around to remind people to jog their memories about taxes still owed, and ask if anyone had seen … our ladies," Joaquim said. "We did visit that poor old widow—so she claims—worth more than I am probably, and listen to her whine about bloodsucking taxes …." He looked up at Señor Ygnacio. "I don't think I would ever have the diplomacy to be a *juez de campo*."

"Nor I," Señor Ygnacio replied. "Now this last one …."

" 'Save for last,' " Joaquim read out loud and rolled his eyes. "I suppose we can't avoid it. 'Check on the Durán twins one last time, ask point blank about taxes owed, and listen to them breathe out fire about the nerve of auditors to come from Santa Fe to drain their bodies of blood.' Good Lord, no wonder Marco saved it for last." He pushed the paper away.

Joaquim leaped to his feet when Perla gasped and dropped the plate loaded with the turkey meant for him. It was on his lips to scold her roundly when he took a good look at her face, normally a pleasant Pueblo Indian hue, but suddenly drained of all color until her skin looked like putty.

"*Teniente* …" she began, and sank down to the bench before them, something she had probably never done in her life of service to Spaniards. "*Teniente!*"

Joaquim felt Eckapeta grow tense beside him. He took another good look at Perla, whose eyes were wide, her mouth open. "Perla, what do you know?"

She ignored him, addressing the auditor. "Señor Ygnacio, do you remember my cousin Gaspar, who hung around your office for a few days? It was perhaps … perhaps two or three weeks ago?"

"A tall, thin fellow who looked mostly starved?"

The cook nodded, her eyes intense now, as the color returned to her cheeks. "He works for the Durán brothers." Perla turned and spit into the fireplace. "I do not know worse men—drunkards, addled and mean."

She gave her attention to Joaquim now, reaching across the table and grabbing both of his hands. "Gaspar is slow and stupid, but he had so many questions for me about the auditor: how often he went out in his carriage, where he went, when he came back. And then Gaspar left without even telling me *adios*. Ungrateful cousin."

"I didn't know this," Joaquim said slowly, even as his mind raced. He heard Eckapeta rise beside him, her hand tight in a fist in the small of his back, ready to push him from the room if he didn't move fast enough.

"Señor Mondragón calls them his cross to bear. He said they threatened him more than once, and he just laughed."

Joaquim turned to the sound of voices at the kitchen door. Sancha stood there, her husband Lorenzo beside her. "You've heard him say this, Sancha?"

"Often enough," Sancha continued. "It was almost a family joke. In fact it was! Señor Mondragón's father had the very same complaint."

The silence in the kitchen started to hum in Joaquim's ears. "Perla, why didn't you mention this earlier?"

Perhaps he had spoken louder than he intended. The cook knelt on the floor and held up her hands to him. "Before all the saints in New Mexico, *Teniente*, I have never seen this note or heard you talk of these matters! Remember? You have always spoken so quietly in the *sala*, so as not to disturb the children."

Joaquim nodded and helped the cook to her feet. "You have done nothing wrong, Perla. Please don't be distressed." He kissed her hands, which made Perla burst into tears. "Thank you from the bottom of my heart for speaking now."

He ran to the door, Eckapeta right behind him, calling across the courtyard for the corporal still in the bookroom, doing his duty as the auditor's daily observer. "Corporal Gomez," he shouted, "attend to me!"

The corporal came to the door and saluted, his eyes full of questions. Joaquim grabbed his arm. "Didn't you and Private Ramirez go to all the *estancias* near Santa Maria to check on anyone who might still have taxes to pay? It was on the list. And you asked about the lost women?"

"Yes, sir, we did."

Corporal Gomez was a short man. Joaquim grasped him by both arms and crouched enough to look into his eyes. "Did you notice anything different at La Estancia Durán? Think!"

The corporal looked into the distance. *Hurry, hurry!* Joaquim wanted to shout, but he reminded himself that this was a good soldier.

Corporal Gomez spoke finally, hesitantly at first, then with more assurance as the memory returned. "One thing, *Capitán*: Everywhere we went, the *hacendados* invited us inside and offered a cool drink. You know how people are in this valley. Not at the Durán place," he said, his voice firm. "One of the brothers came out of the door, closed it behind him, and walked Private Ramirez and me back toward our horses." He gave a humorless snort. "They weren't exactly rude, but they didn't want us near their house." He shrugged.

"Saddle your horse and follow us," Joaquim said over his shoulder as he ran to the horse barn. "Eckapeta, I …" he stopped. The Comanche woman was already in the saddle, her eyes boring into his, as if she were wondering how someone so slow could ever command a worn-out dog, let alone a presidio in His Majesty's western realm. He wished he knew how to answer her.

Chapter Thirty-Two

In which La Llorona requires a great sacrifice

"A FTER YOU?"
"No, after you, Paloma," Catalina said. "I'm so tall … if I get stuck, you can pull me out."

"How do I do this? Go in on my back?"

"I think so."

Catalina watched as Paloma lay on her back and pulled herself into the dark opening. It touched her heart when Paloma said a Hail Mary then went in head first.

"I'm such a lady, Catalina," she heard from inside the hole Paloma had spent three days digging with a knife, tin plate, and her fingernails. "Good thing Marco can't see me now."

"I remember you told me about adventures once," Catalina said, trying to keep her voice lighthearted. "Are you having one now?"

No answer except a distinctly unladylike snort. She almost feared to watch as Paloma, exhausted and in no shape for much exertion, pulled herself through the narrow opening. She heard Paloma grasping the bushes on the other side of the wall, and then she was free of the adobe hut.

Catalina released the breath she had been holding. Now it was her turn. "Any advice, *amiga*?" she asked.

"I thought of something pleasant like Marco making love to me," Paloma said, and laughed. "You're on your own there. Think of Joaquim Gasca however you wish."

She did and felt her cheeks go red, but it got her into the hole. She eased herself in and held her breath in that same place where Paloma had been silent, that endless moment in the short passage when it seemed a body could not go forward or backward. She felt the beginning of claustrophobia until Paloma grabbed the neck of her dress and yanked. Two more tugs. She dug in her heels, pushed, and was out.

They sat together in silence, just breathing. Paloma started to laugh as Señor Francisco waddled into the hole they had just left.

"Do you think he'll miss us?" she asked.

A blessed full moon lit the unkempt garden. Catalina looked toward the high gate and sighed with disappointment to see no sheet, bloody or otherwise. She felt Paloma's hand in hers and gave it a squeeze.

"Maria Brava will not disappoint us," Paloma whispered.

From your lips to God's ears, Catalina thought. Maybe someday she could ask Paloma Mondragón how she knew the old woman would help them. *She will probably tell me to trust more.*

They were silent, waiting. Pray God they wouldn't still be waiting when the moon set and the sun came up to find them trapped like mice in a cage, scurrying back and forth, trying to find a way out. *Stop it, Catalina*, she told herself.

They gripped each other as they heard a sound much like a moan, followed by a sob. "Maria?" Paloma asked. "*Maria?*"

Silence, then another moan and weeping. Paloma turned to her. "I know what she is doing," she said, her voice filled with urgency. "She has not failed us, and we must not fail her."

"What …" Catalina said, then stifled a shriek as a wet sheet dropped nearly on her shorn head, thrown with not quite enough force to clear the entire wall. It dangled there, until Catalina jumped as high as she could and grabbed it. She held the sheet out in the moonlight, her eyes wide with fright, then gratitude so deep and binding that she knew she would never be the same again.

"It's her own blood," Paloma whispered. "We have to hurry."

Fueled by an enormous desperation to get over the wall and see what they could do to help Maria, Catalina backed Paloma against the wall. She crouched down and waited while Catalina knotted the bloody sheet around her waist, then put her foot on Paloma's thigh and hoisted herself up to the smaller woman's shoulders.

With a grunt, Paloma straightened up. "Hurry!" she begged. "I can't hold you for long."

Catalina grabbed for the top of the wall, groping for a handhold, anything to boost her forward and take the strain from Paloma, who was starting to shake. She found the smallest indent in the thick adobe and clung to it. "Just a little more!" she begged, then put one foot on Paloma's head and swung herself up, to sit astride the wall.

She let out her breath and took a small moment to breathe in and out, calming herself. "Are you all right?" she called down.

"Yes, yes," came a voice from far below. "Toss it down."

Careful to maintain her hold on the sheet—*dios mio*, she could smell the blood—Catalina lowered the untied end to Paloma.

"I have it," Paloma said. "God have mercy, how could one woman be so brave?"

"Hang on tight," Catalina ordered. "I'm going to walk myself down as far as I can."

Terrified, she took several deep breaths then grasped the other end of the tight sheet and walked herself down as far as she could go. How much farther, she couldn't tell, except that she saw more bushes, and slumped over by the gate, Maria Brava.

"You are well named, dear lady," she murmured, then looked up. "Let go now, Paloma. Pray for me."

"Always," came a faint voice and then Catalina dropped to the ground.

It was closer than she thought, which was a blessing unlooked for. She dropped quickly, landing upright, grateful to be on the other side of that pernicious gate. She gathered the sheet together and crawled to the still figure. She touched Maria's shoulder gently. "Please be alive," she whispered. "Please."

The old woman groaned and tried to sit up. Catalina helped her, seeing, smelling and then feeling blood coursing down the woman's arms, where she had gouged herself too deep. A knife lay beside her.

"I tugged and tugged on that knife drawer until I could just get my hand in," Maria said, her voice faint. "You needed blood." She took a shallow breath and another. "Cut some eyeholes. Hurry now."

"First I'm doing this." Catalina raised her filthy skirt and slashed her petticoat into two pieces, which she bound tightly around each of Maria's arms, even as the woman protested and begged her to stop wasting time.

Catalina's fingers shook as she cut eyeholes, then draped the bloody sheet over her head. She looked down through the openings, stunned to see just how much blood Maria had spilled. "I will be *such* a weeping woman," she said out loud. "I will do it for you, Maria Brava."

She knew her way through the dark hallway and moved quickly, thinking of all the stories she had told to others over the years. Most recently there had been Soledad and Claudito Mondragón, their eyes wide as they clutched their lovely parents, all of them held captive by words she wove. For the first time in her life, she prayed she would someday weave that same magic for her own children.

There was work to be done. She still held the knife in her hand, but it was slippery from Maria's blood. She tightened her grip and stopped outside the office door that led into the other room, the one she thought of as the wolves' den, where two old fools drank and plotted. More than fools—madmen.

Holding her breath, she opened the door. The office looked much as she had left it—dark now and smelling of bad odors, failure, and disappointed hopes. She walked quickly through and stood at the closed door. "I am now your worst nightmare," she whispered against the wood as she flung the door open and began to moan and wail.

The brothers were seated as she had left them before Gaspar took her back to their adobe prison. She darted closer and closer, wailing in a high, singsong voice, hoping they would smell the blood. She raised her arms over her head, making herself into an enormous *fantasma*, a Weeping Woman of towering proportions. "If you know where my children are, you miserable worms, tell me now or you die!"

She shrieked over and over, then stopped when she realized the dreadful, addled, half-mad Durán twins were screaming even louder. She clutched the knife tighter, wanting to sink it deep into each man, knowing no one in Valle del Sol would miss them. She raised the knife high and screamed out to every demon who had ever tormented her or scorned her father. She wailed for her mother, long dead of shame and buried in an unmarked pauper's grave somewhere in Mexico City. She cried for her own lost dreams. She wept for her father, who deserved a far better hand than he'd been dealt.

Both men were on their knees now, weaving back and forth, begging and pleading for their lives. She laughed then, louder and higher until she reached the gates of insanity. She lowered her voice to a whimper that made Miguel fall forward and lie still.

She raised the knife high again, then brought it down against the leather belt that held the cowering Roque's key ring. As he moaned and pleaded for his miserable life, she felt along the ring as Paloma had told her to do and pressed on the little hasp. She put the key ring over her wrist, then turned toward the door.

She screamed once more for good measure, ending in a maniac's laugh that made Roque shriek again. She wondered if Miguel had died of fright. "I hope you are dead," she said softly. "How dare you abduct a mother and force her to leave her baby behind? How dare you cut off my hair? How dare you torment a servant and make her dwell in her own dark places?"

After leaving the awful room, she let herself out the office door and ran down the corridor. She stopped in fright as an even taller figure loomed in the kitchen doorway. She shrieked and wailed and pushed the figure back with strength summoned from a previously unknown place in her body, until it staggered and fell down. Pedro stared up at her—no, at La Llorona—his eyes wide with terror. She wondered how he had dragged himself from his bed of pain, or even why. She shrieked at him, waving the knife under his nose, then raced on through the *estancia* until she stood at the garden gate.

Steady now, she counted two keys over from the triangle-headed key, thrust it in the lock, and sighed with satisfaction as the bolt clicked open. She threw off the lock, pushed open the heavy door, and fell into Paloma's arms.

Without a word spoken between them, they turned to Maria. Paloma stopped and grabbed the keys from Catalina.

"What are—"

"I'm going to lock this gate and throw the keys over," Paloma said. "Let them try to find them."

Catalina yanked off the bloody sheet and they used it to carry Maria between them. "We're going out the front door," Catalina said as they hurried along with their light burden. "Pedro may still be in the kitchen."

The moon shone down benevolently as they stood in the courtyard. "Look how peaceful it is," Paloma whispered, "and the stars are so huge. Oh, Catalina, let's get out of here."

Faithful, slow of mind Gaspar stood at the open door. With a flourish that surprised Catalina, he led out the Double Cross mule that had brought the two of them, bags over their heads and terrified, to this place she never wanted to see again.

With Gaspar's help, Paloma climbed onto the mule's back. She held out her arms for Maria and held her close. Gaspar handed her the rope he had used to make a crude bridle and gave the mule a pat. Paloma dug in her bare heels and the animal started for the now-open gate.

"Is there a horse for you, Catalina?" Paloma asked.

"I don't want anything from this place," Catalina replied. "Gaspar, are you coming with us?"

Her heart touched, she choked back tears to see his delighted expression, as though she had offered him a king's fifth.

"Really? I don't have to stay here?" he asked, clapping his hands together like Claudito or Soledad.

"No, you don't," she said. "You may have got us in trouble at first, but you helped us out of it."

He hung his head and toed at the dirt. "Señor Mondragón might throw me in prison."

"Let me handle Señor Mondragón," Paloma said. "Let's get out of this place."

They made a slow procession, following a road that Paloma, dismay in her voice, said she recognized. "Marco pointed this way once, said crazy brothers lived here, and I was never to stop for any reason." She sighed, and Catalina heard choked-back tears. "We are only one league from the Double Cross!"

No words were sufficient after that announcement. They rode and walked in silence, the moon high overhead now and beginning a descent that would lead to another morning in Valle del Sol.

"I could like it here," Catalina said.

"I know I do," Paloma replied. She sucked in her breath and pointed. "Catalina, look … I know them!" She started to laugh. Catalina listened for any hysteria but heard none. Paloma was made of stronger stuff. "They're riding so fast. I see Eckapeta and Joaquim, and maybe a soldier, but who is that other man?" Catalina heard the disappointment in her voice. "It's not Marco."

Catalina strained her eyes, then put her hand to her mouth. "I believe it is my father! My goodness, I have never seen him on horseback before."

"I do believe we are about to be rescued," Paloma said.

Catalina looked up at Paloma's smiling face, grubby and dirty as her own, and started to laugh. "They're too late. We saved ourselves."

"We did, didn't we?"

Chapter Thirty-Three

In which a penitent soul
understands herself better

PALOMA HAD ONLY ONE question as their rescuers rode toward them, and she asked it of the first rider. "My baby?" she said to Eckapeta, leaning toward the woman who considered all little Mondragóns as her special property, too.

Eckapeta grasped her hand. "Toshua and I found him. He is alive and well and drinking deep of three different women on the Double Cross. Be easy, my daughter."

Paloma bowed her head over her patient mule. "I can never repay them, or you," she whispered into the animal's mane, then sat up. "You called me daughter."

"That is how I think of you," the Comanche replied simply. "I should have said so sooner."

The two sat side by side, their knees touching. Maria stirred in Paloma's arms, stared at Eckapeta, then quietly fainted.

"This one does not like to see one of The People riding beside her," Eckapeta observed.

"No. She has been terrorized into submission by those dreadful Durán brothers," Paloma said. "I have so much to tell you." She thought a long moment. Despite her hunger, filth, exhaustion, and uncertainty about her standing with her husband, who was nowhere in sight, there was something more. Call it quiet pride. "We rescued ourselves."

"We looked everywhere," Eckapeta said. Paloma heard all the dismay and anguish in her voice. Who in the world had ever started the massive lie that

Indians were stoic and impervious to emotions? "Too many days of failure."

"Be easy." Paloma hesitated, then knew what to say. "Be easy, Mother. We were abducted by two idiots who somehow made the whole stupid plan work."

They stayed close together, Paloma watching as Joaquim leaped off his horse and ran to Catalina, who stood in silence, her ragged, shorn head bowed, afraid to look at the man, who from the tender expression on his face, didn't care whether she had a single hair on her head or many.

Paloma watched him take the tall, thin woman in his arms and hold her close until her arms went around him, too. Catalina still wouldn't look at him, preferring to nestle herself against his chest. If she could have taken off her head and hidden it, she would have.

"Who would cut off a woman's hair?" Eckapeta asked. She looked closer. "They did a poor job of it."

"Bullies and tormenters," Paloma replied. She rubbed her arms against a sudden chill only she could feel. "Let us go home."

By now, Señor Ygnacio had joined the couple still locked in a tight embrace. Catalina and Joaquim opened their arms and included him in their circle.

"Go on, ask me," Eckapeta said, with what sounded like amusement in her voice.

"Why didn't my husband ride out here with you?" Paloma asked. "I fear I have offended him greatly by whining and complaining. It was a dark time I do not understand."

There, she had said it, putting words to the dread that settled on her when she looked and did not see him, confirming her worst fears. "He is unhappy with me."

Eckapeta leaned close and slapped Paloma on the side of her head. "Silly girl! I doubt you could be more wrong."

"But why isn't he here? I have disappointed him."

"Tscha!" Eckapeta exclaimed, and gave her another slap. "The People in the canyon—the honey eaters, the antelope-eaters, the timber people, the movers—they have been talking and talking all winter." She made a face. "Men! They waste time. We could have ended this endless talk-talk, eh, Paloma?"

Paloma nodded, unwilling to be placated, but unwilling to have another slap to the head that set her ears ringing. She knew it was dark enough that her great good friend would not see the tears on her cheeks.

"Don't cry!" Eckapeta scolded. "Hear what I tell you." She turned her horse to block Paloma's mule, and observed the interesting tableaux behind them, a smile on her face. "The others are far behind. It appears that your lieutenant will not let go of Catalina. He is a smarter man than I thought at first, when he could not keep his man parts in his breeches."

Paloma laughed at that, even as she sniffled and wiped her nose with her fingers. "All of The People got together …" she prompted.

"Yes! Such a gathering I have never seen. The leaders told Toshua to bring the man who saved The People from the Dark Wind. They would listen to him. They had to hear from a colonist, a white man *muy bravo y fuerte.*"

"Marco," Paloma said. Her heart began to lift.

"They wanted you, too, Tatzinupi, the woman who carried a child of The People on her back through the sacred canyon."

"Really? But I couldn't have gone."

"So Toshua told them. Big Man Down There had given you more seed to carry and you Spanish women aren't as tough as we women of The People," Eckapeta said kindly, but with unmistakable pride. "Have a pain on the trail, dismount and bear a child, rest an hour and ride on."

"Not for me," Paloma said. "In this you are my superior."

"But not in biding your time and escaping from bad men," Eckapeta told her. She raised her hand again, but this time it was to caress Paloma's face. "Save that story for when you are washed and fed and in your bed."

"After I have seen Juanito. Eckapeta, I prayed that someone would find him in time."

"Someone did," she said gently. "Your good man took the little one in his arms and went on his knees before the women whose husbands work for him. And let me tell you, he presented every excuse he knew of not to go with my Toshua to the Río Napestle, which is even farther away."

"Why there? That is not a good place for Spaniards."

Eckapeta shrugged. "Good or bad, that's where they rode."

"But there?"

"The buffalo are on the plains, and those men who talk and talk like to hunt buffalo."

"Surely he would not have taken the time to hunt buffalo," Paloma said. She ducked when Eckapeta reached out to slap her head again.

"Don't be so foolish! He wanted to search for you, so desperate he was to find you. Before all the gods and statues you worship, he did not want to leave you lost."

"Then … Ow!"

"If they want to hunt buffalo, do you think one white man among a lot of The People has much say in *anything*?"

"I needed to hear this." Paloma looked away, unable to bear Eckapeta's scrutiny. She tried to laugh and failed. "It was a dark time I do not understand, not when I should have been so happy."

"I know of dark times, too."

Paloma patted Eckapeta's cheek. "Let's go home. I'm tired, and poor Maria here is not getting a moment better."

THE DOUBLE CROSS HAD never looked so welcome to Paloma as it did that night. The full moon lighted their way, the familiar strength of the stone walls soothing her battered heart. She reminded herself how careful her husband was to keep her and their little ones safe, and knew how badly his own heart must have been battered, to leave her lost. And truth to tell, if Eckapeta could not find them, Marco Mondragón would probably have come up short, too.

As much as she resisted the idea, she thought of La Llorona, the weeping woman who lost her children because of jealousy and a broken heart. Like all good colonists, she knew the story by heart. Up until this moment, Paloma had felt the most sorry for the innocent children. Riding so slowly to keep from jostling Maria Brava, Paloma Vega, who knew of dark times, finally understood the Weeping Woman.

"I was the Weeping Woman," she murmured under her breath.

"You may think that, but I do not," Eckapeta said. "To me, and I am certain to Marco, you are who you have always been, Tatzinupi, the Star."

"Star in the Meadow," Paloma said, thinking of the Vega family branding iron, lost those many years and found in a cave in the Sacred Canyon. Claudio had the iron now, as was his right, as well as the title to the brand.

"Star," she repeated. "Eckapeta, I am tired."

"We are all tired," her almost-mother said. "You are whole, though, and you freed yourself. Be proud of that, my Star."

Paloma nodded, close to tears. She glanced back to see Gaspar loping alongside the slowly moving horses. *I should hate him until I die for his part in this fiasco*, she thought, *but what would be the point?* She remembered her own desperate days that turned into years in the household of her uncle in Santa Fe. She understood how easy it becomes to believe you are stupid or ungrateful, if you hear it enough.

She tightened her arms around the old laundress she held, grateful to the core of her body and soul that the woman had shrugged off her own terrors, pounded into her by horrible men, to reach out just enough to help free two women. "Stay alive," she whispered to Maria Brava.

Once through the gates, Joaquim was quick to call for the hacienda's unofficial *curandera*, who took one look at Maria, clucked her tongue, and issued her own orders. In minutes, the laundress was off Paloma's mule and inside one of the little huts within the Double Cross enclosure.

Eckapeta helped Paloma from the mule and toward her house. Paloma breathed deep of the flowers already blooming in the pots and hanging vases that lined the *portal*. Her eyes brimming with tears, Sancha took her arm so gently.

"Just a few minutes and the water will be hot in the bathhouse," she said.

Paloma pulled back. "Not yet. Where is my baby?"

"He is with Luz Montoya, the wife of our beekeeper."

"Take me there, please." Paloma was well acquainted with the stubborn look on Sancha's face. "Yes, I stink and I am more tired than I have ever been in my life, but I will see my son," Paloma insisted as they walked along, her housekeeper's arm about her waist, because she had a tendency to stagger.

"How is it that no one is asleep on the Double Cross?" Paloma asked, looking around at lamps burning in all the little houses.

"We knew you would be returning tonight," Sancha told her. "We didn't know how we would find you, but the wife of Marco Mondragón deserved our whole attention."

Dressed in her nightgown with a *reboza* around her shoulders, Luz Montoya ushered her inside her front room. Paloma's eyes went to a crib in the corner by the big bed where the beekeeper sat, his eyes so kind. She uttered something—it might have been words—and hurried to the crib to see two babies, both asleep and both chunky in the way of babies well fed and tended. Paloma touched her son's cheek. He stirred, opened his eyes, and closed them again.

"You have my heartfelt thanks, Luz," Paloma said, still staring down at her sleeping son. "You and the others."

"It was our pleasure, *señora*, our heartfelt pleasure," Luz replied.

Paloma turned around and sucked in her breath to see two other women standing in the doorway. "The three of you are my saviors," she said simply.

Dropping to her knees, she prostrated herself before these humble mothers of the Double Cross. She spread out her arms and pressed her cheek against the well swept dirt floor. What they had done for Juan Luis Mondragón went far beyond even her most magnificent curtsy, the curtsy for kings and new husbands. She lay flat on the ground before them, even as Juanito's nursemaids began to sniffle and protest. Gentle hands pulled her to her feet, and she enveloped them in her embrace, all the while apologizing for her unwashed state.

Mindful of her as only gentle women could be, they sat Paloma down and told her exactly what she needed to do to get back her own milk. She listened to advice about eating lots of food and letting Juanito suck on her empty breasts first thing in the morning.

"We'll bring him to you three times a day, but we will keep feeding him until your milk flows, and even after, if you need us," Luz said. She dabbed at her tears. "I speak for myself, but I have grown quite fond of Juan Luis Mondragón. He is certainly part of me now."

"And me," "And me," chimed in the other two wet nurses.

Only minutes later she sat in her bathtub, eyes closed, as Sancha scrubbed her hair over and over, then washed her body, all the while bullying her into eating the posole that Perla spooned into her mouth like a mother bird feeding a chick. When Paloma protested feebly that her stomach was starting to ache, Sancha wisely made Perla stop.

"A little at a time will do the trick," Sancha said. "Tomorrow there will be flan for breakfast."

"Breakfast?" Paloma asked, interested, even though her eyelids wanted to droop.

"Breakfast," Sancha said firmly.

In her nightgown now and with her old shawl around her shoulders, Paloma made her way to the house. She could barely manage a smile, but there was Catalina, still in the clutches of her father and a certain presidio captain. Already, one of the other house servants had her eyes on Catalina's ragged haircut. "I can fix this," Paloma heard as she walked by and gave her friend's arm a little squeeze.

Sinking into her own blissful bed, she couldn't help a frown; it never seemed like her bed without Marco waiting for her, maybe with his nightshirt on, maybe not.

Sancha tucked her in. "Please, please, my children …" Paloma whispered. "Let them sleep here with me tonight."

"I'll wake them," the housekeeper said.

In a few minutes Sancha returned with a little girl, her eyes barely open, and a slightly younger boy. The confusion left his eyes when Paloma held out her arms to him.

"Mama, you came back," he said, then crawled beside her without another word. Paloma held him tight, breathing his little boy fragrance, thankful as never before.

Soledad took a moment longer, assessing Paloma in that intelligent way she had of surveying a situation to see how the wind blew. There would never be any flies on Soledad. "Mama, did they hurt you?" she asked, coming close enough to the bed for Paloma to take her by the hand.

Did they hurt me? Paloma asked herself, as time and distance already began their work of smoothing rough edges. "A little, but only a little. Maybe I even learned something valuable. Time will tell. I am here, and I am happy to be with you."

That was all the reassurance Soledad needed. She climbed onto the bed, too, then crawled around to Marco's side and cuddled close.

Paloma's eyes would not stay open. She listened to their deep, even breathing as her children returned to sleep. Tomorrow there would be Juanito to nurse, to bring back her milk and with it, surely her confidence. If she hadn't entirely known her role on the Double Cross, she knew it now: to nurture and mother and keep the heart in her husband. And if that darkness ever returned, it would pass.

Chapter Thirty-Four

In which Joaquim Gasca, noted female expert, learns more about women

WHEN CATALINA YGNACIO WOKE up, her hands went immediately to her hair. Dissatisfied with herself, she fingered the tight curls and wondered how a woman so put upon could ever face public scrutiny. A house servant with definite skills had carefully trimmed what remained last night as she sat in the cooling bathwater and stared at nothing.

And why Catalina Ygnacio, most practical and unsentimental of women, had started crying as the servant dried her and dressed her in her nightgown, she could not have said. She sobbed and sniffled until El Teniente Gasca had knocked once on the bathhouse door, then opened it anyway. She had turned her tearful face toward him, crying and pointing at her ridiculous curls. If he had smiled at that moment, she would have never spoken to him again. To her relief, he simply fingered the silly curls and pressed his forehead against hers.

Of course, nothing else would suffice but that he would take her in his arms and murmur some utter nonsense in her ear about long hair just getting in the way. *Getting in the way of what?* her practical side begged to know, at the same time as her unexpected tender side let him stroke her back and press closer than would have made Mama comfortable. She knew she was skidding toward eternal ruin as she pressed back and maybe even moved her hips a little.

The memory of that shameless bit of grinding made her blush. Joaquim's face had been so serious, and exhausted—every bit as exhausted as she felt. Papa had long since retired to his chamber, a slight smile on his face, so Joaquim walked her to her little room. Since there wasn't much space to carry on a formal discussion, she did not object when he asked to sit on her bed.

Catalina had listened to his outpouring of frustration and disappointed hopes after days of looking everywhere, accompanied by a Comanche just as frustrated as he. She carefully watched Joaquim's sunburned face—testimony to many days in the sun. Already familiar with his casual way of talking to her, she wondered how much of this was balderdash and how much genuine remorse. She ruled in favor of remorse, because there was pain in his eyes.

She told him some of their experiences, knowing Paloma would provide more details tomorrow. She should have been embarrassed when her sentences began to slur together, as if someone had removed the spaces between the words. Her last recollection involved pillowing her head on her hands as she turned sideways and someone patting her hip, even stroking it.

She woke when the sun was high in the sky, with her stomach setting up a racket that made Catalina wonder why everyone in the hacienda hadn't come running. One knock, and Sancha came into the room, carrying a tray of flan—blessed flan, all jiggly and smooth and crackling with a thin layer of burnt sugar. Like a wine taster, she rolled around the texture in her mouth and sighed with pleasure.

"Might you wish a visit from El Teniente Gasca?" Sancha asked later as she cleared away the plates and bowls once containing flan, bread, and fruit, with eggs and chorizo.

"I wouldn't mind," she replied, suddenly shy. "Tell me though, how is Paloma?"

"She woke up long enough to eat, nurse Juanito, say a few words to her children, and drift back to sleep," Sancha told her, relief mingled with satisfaction in her voice.

"Good. This ordeal was nearly too much, especially so soon after childbirth," Catalina said. "I confess I worried about her."

Sancha took her hands. "We worried about both of you, and prayed, and worried some more."

Someone knocked. Catalina recognized his knock, now, and the fact that after that single rap, Joaquim Gasca was coming into the room, regardless. On her way out, Sancha left the door open enough for the commander of a garrison to enter.

He was dressed for riding, which dismayed Catalina. *Stay with me*, she wanted to insist, until she reminded herself that she wasn't so brazen, at least when they weren't pressed hip to hip in the darkness, with only most of the Double Cross watching with way too much interest. Didn't *anyone* sleep after midnight around here?

"I am taking five of my men to the Durán *estancia*," he told her. "Do I ask too much, or would you accompany us? Señora Mondragón is too worn down, but I want to hear your whole story, too. Will you?"

He seemed to want her to say yes. "I will," she said. "Let me dress."

He bowed and closed the door. She dressed hurriedly and started down the hall, only to stop a moment and peer into Paloma's room because the door was open and she felt concern for her friend. What she saw left her at peace.

Both children sat quietly on the end of their sleeping mother's bed, Claudito stacking blocks and Soledad concentrating on cat's cradle. Catalina smiled to see Paloma curled up close to what must be Marco's pillow, hugging it lengthwise to her body. *Hurry home, Marco*, Catalina thought, and not without some wistfulness. *You are missed.* Nodding to the children, she continued down the hall, moving slower than she would have wished, but grateful to be moving at all.

A LEAGUE'S DISTANCE FROM the Double Cross to the narrow, scarcely used road that led to Estancia Durán was hardly enough for her to tell the story of their incarceration in an adobe outbuilding, but Catalina had a talent for condensation.

"It will always be a mystery to me that two fools such as Gaspar and Pedro should hoodwink everyone so completely," Catalina said as the *estancia* came into sight, the place she had vowed never to visit again.

"I think I am always going to smart a bit, thinking how a brilliant commander and a truly astute Comanche saw absolutely nothing," he said. "I don't joke about Eckapeta."

She admired his profile for a moment, wondering if this excellent man would ever forgive himself for a lifetime of being perhaps all too human. She rode in silence, thinking of her own arrival in this lovely valley, all prickly and ready to find offense, weary to her heart's core of rejection and disdain. She thought how Paloma had told her in that dreadful hut how much she, starchy Catalina Ygnacio, had changed. She had poo-pooed the notion, but Paloma had been right in that and in so many other things.

She smiled to think of what she had told Paloma only last evening as they left Estancia Durán and decided to share it with Joaquim. The look in his eyes as he watched her nearly made her forget what she was going to say. *He cares*, she thought, entranced.

"We rescued ourselves," she said. "I will tell you how we did it."

WHETHER UNOCCUPIED FOR A night or ten years, abandoned places have a similar look of sadness. A glance was enough to make Joaquim and his soldiers suspect their quarry had fled.

Discounting a geriatric horse in the barn nosing in its own evacuation for tiny bits of corn, the place bore no resemblance to a working ranch. "Feed that pathetic horse," he told one of his soldiers. "And if you find no food, at least let it out to graze." Joaquim frowned at the ruin of a good horse. "If no grass, shoot it."

The private dismounted and hurried into the barn. Each of Joaquim's nerve endings went into high alert when the soldier shouted in surprise, then came to the door of the barn holding a sheet covered in rust. Catalina clutched his arm and he felt her shake. He dismounted and helped her down as the private held out what looked like a sheet with eye holes.

"I told you Maria cut her own arms to streak La Llorona's shroud with blood," Catalina said. "Our enterprise would have failed without her."

The private dropped the sheet in the dust of the courtyard and led out the old horse, a nag so thin that his legs seemed to knock together.

"Those wretched twins never fed anyone or anything here," Catalina said, unable to tamp down her anger. "Thin people, thin animals, and nothing but cutting words, the kind that wound the heart." She looked at him. "The kind of words I've heard all my life." She picked up the sheet with the long brown splotches, shook off the dust and folded it carefully. "I might keep this to remind myself just how much brave people will do to help others, if they hear kind words."

"Do you need such a reminder?" he asked. "I personally doubt it." He took a deep breath of his own. "I could keep it in my campaign chest … you know, until you decide if you need it."

"You could," she agreed.

Joaquim motioned for the others to follow him. Catalina indicated the kitchen with a nod of her head.

"Pedro surprised me in here. He had been severely beaten the day before by Roque Durán," she said, then turned away her head. "I can't look in there. Miguel started cutting my hair in the kitchen."

Joaquim looked. "No one." He let his gaze travel around the room. "Was there no food anywhere in this place? What did the brothers live on?"

"Some cornmeal and endless bottles of wine. I never saw them entirely sober," Catalina told him from the hall. She pointed ahead. "They spent most of their time in the bookroom, which seemed to adjoin their bedchamber."

She hung back as he moved where she pointed. "I didn't think you were afraid of anything," Joaquim said.

"It was all a show," she told him in her forthright way. "I was terrified." He heard the pain in her voice because he was used to her now. He reminded himself that someone less discerning than the brilliant leader of Presidio Santa Maria would have noticed nothing.

"I told myself years ago to strike first, before someone had a chance to wound me," she said, her voice so soft now that he had to put his arm around her shoulder and bend close. His own heart felt less pummeled when she seemed to blend into him as a soft woman would.

"I've done that, too," he admitted.

She gave him a look of perfect understanding. "Have we both stopped being foolish?" she whispered in his ear this time.

"Perhaps time will tell," he hedged.

"That's not good enough," she said in that stringent way of hers that he was coming to enjoy, because he knew now that it ran so counter to the tenderness within.

He opened the bookroom door. Again she refused to enter, but stood in the hall, directing him to look in the next room, a place so filthy that he didn't want to stay long.

"I told them stories every night, each one more terrifying. I saved 'La Llorona' for last."

"You found it easy to work on wine-soaked brains," he commented, thinking how that could have been him, given enough years and disappointments.

"They were putty, actually."

Joaquim started because she stood beside him now. "Don't creep up on me!" he declared and patted his heart.

She gave him a little jab in his side, which meant his arm had to go around her again. "And … and you came back here in a bloody sheet, wailing and screaming." Just thinking about it made the hairs on his neck stand at attention.

"It wasn't so hard, Joaquim," she said. "All I had to do was think of the many nights when Paloma cried for her infant whom she last saw in a broken-down carriage with a dead man nearby." She shuddered. "I swear I will hear her screams forever! I thought of her and screamed and wailed."

What could he say to that? He held out his hand for her and she came a little closer, holding out her own hand.

"When they both collapsed in a heap, looking for all the world like desperate rats, I grabbed Roque's keys and opened that garden gate. Maria lay nearly dead beside it, so we picked her up and used La Llorona's sheet to carry her to the barn."

Soldiers followed them and looked in each room as Joaquim directed, walking past the kitchen again, down the hall and outside, where the garden gate remained locked.

"Paloma locked the gate and threw the keys over the wall," she said, remembering the determination on her friend's face.

"Break it down," Joaquim ordered his men. His most resourceful private found a pry bar somewhere and yanked the door off its hinges.

"We could have used that," Catalina said, her voice wistful.

When she still seemed reluctant to enter the garden, he tugged gently on her hand. After that first step through the gate, she seemed more at ease, even though she hung onto him with a death's grip. Maybe she wasn't at ease. Two steps, a third, and then she stopped.

"It seems so small," she said. "No one fed us until the second day. Paloma squeezed out her own milk and we drank that."

Resourceful woman, he thought. *No wonder I admire ladies in general and these ladies in particular.*

"Go around to the side. You will see the hole we dug," Catalina directed. "Where are the keys Paloma threw over the wall?"

"I have them," called one of the privates. "Here, *Teniente*."

Joaquim did as she said and walked around the adobe shed. He stared at the hole a long time, wondering how even desperate women could have managed to pull themselves out through such a tiny opening. He sniffed. The air was redolent with skunk spray.

"Good thing you weren't here for the skunk," he commented.

Catalina's sudden laughter startled him. "The skunk found us. Paloma named the skunk Señor Francisco and declared that the saint himself must have sent the *zorillo* to keep us company. She fed him tortillas," Catalina told him. He heard the humor in her voice now. "Crawl inside, Teniente Gasca."

"You're being silly," he teased back. He stood before the door and tried the keys until he found the right one. "After you," he said, gesturing grandly.

Catalina backed away even farther. "Never."

The private stooped inside, swore, and backed out as though La Llorona sat inside waiting to pounce, blood streaming from her gouged eyes. Mouth open, he pointed toward the door.

"I thought you were a soldier most brave," Joaquim joked and bent down to look inside, too. What he saw made him gasp and leap back, too.

A dead man lay there, hands on his throat. The air was thick with the stinging odor of skunk spray.

"Can a man die of that?" the private asked him, amazement in his voice. "I know it's bad, but really, is it fatal, sir?"

Going against every instinct, Joaquim came closer and squatted by the body. He took a careful look, and saw nothing to indicate foul play. His eyes watered against the stench of skunk. A mystery. Could a man die of fear? Perhaps his heart gave out. God knows a steady diet of cornmeal and wine would likely hasten the grave. Still, a mystery.

Joaquim turned to Catalina. "Would you … would you come closer and tell us who this is?" he asked.

He watched resolution replace her own fear. She walked closer and stood by the open door for a long moment, as if steeling herself to look inside the hut she must have thought she would never leave alive. He watched the resolution on her marvelous face as she ducked inside the one place in the world she surely never wanted to see again. One look was all she needed.

"It is Miguel Durán," she said in a voice that held no remorse, not even a grain of it. "He is the one who cut my hair first." She shuddered and turned away.

"It appears he came to a fitting end," Joaquim remarked. "There's no skunk around now, and how did it get in this garden anyway, if the gate was kept closed?"

"Paloma will probably tell you it was sent by San Francisco himself," she said. "I might have laughed at her earlier, myself."

"But not now?"

She shrugged and turned away. Joaquim directed two of his men to drag out the dead man and cover him with the bloody sheet. "We'll come back later for the body," he said. "Maybe."

While Catalina sat on her horse, they searched the house and all the outbuildings thoroughly, finding no sign of Roque or Pedro. They did find endless empty wine bottles, some standing in ranks as tall and straight as soldiers, others thrown against adobe walls to shatter.

Joaquim needed no order to round up his soldiers and get them on horseback again, so eager was everyone to leave such a blighted place. The private he had put in charge of the half-dead horse trailed along behind them, giving the animal time to follow. Joaquim directed his men toward the presidio and food for the horse, and told them he would be along later.

He rode in silence beside Catalina for precious minutes, trying to work up the nerve to speak from his heart before the Double Cross came into view. Whatever glib urbanity from his not-so-long-ago free-wheeling days deserted him now. He felt more tongue-tied than a boy longing after a skinny girl.

Be blunt, he told himself. *Catalina is not one for flowery words.* He thought a moment, cleared his throat, and surprised himself. " 'If I could live on love alone, and prosper all my days, I never would your presence leave, but breathe deep of your ways.' "

Catalina's face colored from the throat up, giving rise to suspicion she had never been addressed in a poet's language before. *She must think I am a stupid imbecile,* he thought in misery.

" 'If, perchance you think of me, and wish to know me more, Just drop a note into the post, or open your front door,' " she continued, blushing in earnest now. She hesitated, then took another breath to say, "It seems we know the same obscure poets, my friend."

It was the "my friend," that made Joaquim Gasca, reformed ladies' man, dismount, take a look to make sure his soldiers were on the road to

Santa Maria, and help Catalina Ygnacio, reformed sharp-tongued auditor's daughter, from her horse.

"I don't remember the rest of it," he said, pulling her close, taking a chance.

"Something about love and kisses and promises," she whispered. "What I used to think was silliness that only happened to others."

"I think it's happening to us," he told her. "Catalina Ygnacio, in some circles—most—I am considered a mountebank and a rascal."

She put her fingers to his lips and he kissed them. "Not here in Valle del Sol. Stop talking and just ask me."

He did, stumbling and stuttering and nothing like the man he used to be. She listened patiently, said yes several times before the good news penetrated, then a louder yes, which made him laugh and start to slap her on the bottom.

He stopped in time, or maybe not, because the woman he was going to marry now put his hand on her hip anyway. He squeezed her, which made her giggle like a much younger lady.

"Should I ask your father?" he said.

"Just tell him," Catalina replied. She let him help her back onto her horse. "He asked me only this morning if you were ever going to get around to proposing."

"And?"

"I thought perhaps you might," she said shyly.

Chapter Thirty-Five

In which a husband redeems himself

Two days resting in bed was Paloma's limit. She discovered it was possible to tire of flan. She also wondered if Marco really felt no irritation with her over her dark mood. Why was it taking him so long to return from Río Napestle?

Don't think about it, Paloma, she told herself, grateful for the early morning distraction of her brother Claudio, who rode back with the servant who had taken the message of his sister's return. He had news of his own, once he had hugged her within an inch of her life and babbled something about giving Marco a black eye and would her husband ever forgive him?

"You did *what*?"

"I smacked him when he said he had to go with Toshua and leave you lost," Claudio said.

"I fear my husband has been pulled in too many directions for most of his life," she said softly. "Pray God he will return soon." She had to change the subject before she started to wail like La Llorona. "What is your good news?"

"Graci was brought to bed with a son last night, or I would have been here sooner," he told her, sitting on her bed along with Soledad and Claudito. "Both Mama and baby are fine, and Cecilia is coping," he added, with a wink at Soledad.

He stayed a few more minutes, but Paloma knew even this short visit was too much for a new father. She sent him on his way after hearing him apologize yet again for blacking Marco's eye, and teased him that the *juez de campo* might not bring charges.

*

ON THE THIRD MORNING after her return from the horrible house of the Durán twins, Paloma rose and got dressed—standing still a moment because the room did spin a bit—and made her way down the hall to the kitchen.

She looked in on Soledad and Claudito first, standing there silently thanking God and all his numerous saints and angels that they were alive and well and much as she had left them.

After greeting Sancha, who knew better than to try to force her back to bed, Paloma let herself out the door into the kitchen garden, where she watched the beans and peppers waving in a surprisingly gentle breeze and vowed never to take even the humblest vegetable for granted. A few days ago, she would have eaten the entire plant, leaves and all.

As much as she dreaded even thinking about the last week, Paloma knew she had changed. *If I feel melancholy again, I know it will pass*, she silently told the garden vegetables. *Please let Marco believe that of me.*

She crossed the courtyard to the little home of Señora Villarreal, who happily handed Juanito to her. She made herself comfortable and opened her bodice to her son, who rooted greedily, then settled into a slow suck, one that soothed her heart. To her infinite relief, she felt that exquisite near-pain as her milk let down.

Señora Villarreal had been watching her face. "You feel some milk?" she asked. "I knew it would return."

Paloma nodded, too overcome to speak.

"There will be even more tomorrow," Señora Villarreal assured her, when Juanito became restless. "Put him to your other breast, then I will finish up."

Paloma did as Juanito's dear nurse told her, handing him back after both her breasts were empty. "I should go drink more milk and eat."

Juanito settled into the remainder of his breakfast with Señora Villarreal, whose own small son slept nearby. "I would say that in two more days, we will turn Juanito over to you entirely, Señora Mondragón."

"I cannot thank you enough," Paloma said, and never meant anything more. She looked around the tidy room, with the Villarreal children's bedding neatly rolled into the corners and the parents' bed made, but pushed against the table and chairs. "Peace is coming to this valley soon," she said, as she buttoned her bodice. "I am nearly certain that Señor Mondragón will draw up plans for better houses, larger ones, outside the walls of the Double Cross."

"Such plans would be welcome," Juanito's wet nurse said. "Will the *juez* return soon?"

"I hope so," Paloma said. "I do hope so, for I miss him." *I hope he misses me*, she wondered silently, knowing such a traitor thought was foolish, but still doubting. "Juanito goes to Pia Ladero now?"

"*Sí, señora*," Maria Villarreal said. She rose and opened the door for Paloma. "Go with God."

"And you."

Breathing deep of her son's fragrance—that delicious baby smell she had missed—Paloma made her way, baby in her arms, next to the home of the *curandera*. She peeked in on Maria Brava, who was beginning to stir. When Maria saw Paloma, she tried to sit up, so Paloma came to her. Maria's eyes never left her face as Paloma told her of Miguel Durán's death by skunk, or heart attack, or divine intervention, whatever would suit the old woman who had dared to help two women who needed her.

"But Roque?" Maria asked, her hand on Paloma's arm now as if entreating her. "He is equally bad."

"El Teniente Gasca could find no sign of him or Pedro," Paloma replied, wondering if Joaquim would authorize a patrol to continue looking for the man. "We pray he is far distant from us," she finished, hoping she spoke the truth.

Her words must have satisfied Maria Brava, whose grip on Paloma's arm lessened. In a few more moments, she slept. Paloma nodded to the *curandera* and ducked out of the low-ceilinged cottage.

She left her sleeping son with Señora Ladero, touched by the kindness of the women of the Double Cross, who had not let her down, or their *juez*. She wondered again at the goodness of some people and the evil of others.

Tired now, and quite willing to lie down again, Paloma made her way toward her house, only to stop at the sound of laughter coming from Marco's office, halfway between the horse barn and the hacienda. The open door invited her to knock on the frame and find herself in Catalina Ygnacio's embrace.

The auditor's daughter scolded her gently for being out of bed, even though Paloma assured her she was quite fit and able.

"You look ready to drop down in exhaustion," Catalina contradicted. She helped Paloma to the rocking chair where she sat and knitted when Marco worked late.

The sight of the familiar room with no Marco in it brought tears to Paloma's eyes. She did as Catalina said, hoping to regain her composure before she came under Sancha's scrutiny in the kitchen. Her shoulders drooped and she bowed her head, starved for the sight of her husband, even as doubts over her reception plagued her heart.

But here was Catalina, eyes bright, smiling at her. "The *teniente* and I ..." she began, then could not continue.

"Good," Paloma said, hopeful that Catalina's own delight left her no room to worry about her companion in the adobe prison. "When?"

"Before he left last night, he said he was going to ask the priest to announce the first of the banns on Sunday." Her face shone with love, a far cry from her brooding, unhappy expression a mere six weeks ago when she had arrived in Valle del Sol. Where had the time gone?

Señor Ygnacio cleared his throat and indicated the bundle of papers neatly tied with red ribbon. "Here it is, *señora*, only awaiting the *juez de campo's* signature." He looked at his daughter with pride. "Catalina checked my figures."

"And found not a single error," Catalina said, returning his look.

Paloma felt that odd disconnect again, wondering, before she caught herself, how life had continued around them as she and Catalina languished, starving, in a garden hut so close to everyone and yet so far. She had to say something; they were both looking at her.

"Señor Ygnacio, will you return to Santa Fe?" Paloma asked. Life would be different for him, now that Catalina was going to become part of life at Santa Maria's presidio.

"I think not," he replied. "I have nothing in Santa Fe."

I didn't either, Paloma thought, remembering her journey here, alone at first and then in the company of the one person who now meant more to her that any other in the world. "I am confident the *juez* will think of something," she said, before returning to her room to sleep because she felt too miserable to face anyone.

We all depend on the juez de campo, she thought that afternoon. Her children came and went, bringing her food, cuddling up for a nap, then running outside to play. She nursed Juanito, grateful down to the depth of her heart for his gentle suck that brought her milk back, then let sleep reclaim her as dusk approached. Before her eyes closed, her one coherent thought was that her husband must return and soon. Everyone needed him, but no one more than her. Perhaps no one deserved him less, despite what Eckapeta had told her about his supreme unwillingness to leave her and go traipsing across Comanchería.

She woke to a darkened room and a quiet house, as though everyone had deserted her. Was she ever going to wake again without sudden fear? She took several deep breaths to remind her she was breathing the sweet sage and rosemary of her pillow. It was late; everyone must be asleep.

She breathed deeper and smelled another familiar odor of wood smoke and leather. She sat up in surprise and woke up completely when she realized her husband knelt by the bed.

With a cry of delight, Paloma touched his familiar face, wondering how a man could sleep on his knees like that, especially with his bed right there, with clean sheets and blankets and her.

"Marco?" she asked, her voice hesitant. "Marco?"

He opened his eyes and she saw the tears in them. She came closer until she had wrapped herself around him as he knelt there. She smelled the dust of the trail on his clothes, his unwashed state, not unlike her own of mere days ago, and held him close.

"Please forgive me," he whispered.

Forgive him? What was he talking about? "Marco, let me help you into bed," she said, tugging on him, wanting him next to her.

"I failed you so badly," he said, the words tumbling out. "I didn't know if you would even want me in the same room, let alone in our bed, but I had to find out. Please tell me you understand. I did it for the colony."

She tugged harder on his arm. "I am certain I owe *you* the apology," she said, her lips close to his ear. "I was so silent and withdrawn and wore you down until you must have been happy to send me to your sister's for a week."

He sat up then, leaning back on his haunches beside their bed, his eyes wide in amazement. "But I did not even look for you!" he exclaimed. "Toshua insisted I ride to Río Napestle, and here you were, lost somewhere. Good God, my wife, the mother of my children, and I rode away!" He leaned forward against the edge of the bed. "Paloma, I only did it for New Mexico."

"That was no offense," she reminded him. Why did he not see the enormity of *her* offense? "I love our colony, too."

Heaven knows she hadn't the strength or the energy to coax her tall husband into a bed if he didn't want to be there, but Paloma tried. She stood up and grasped him under his arms, grunting and straining to pull him up. "You are the most stubborn man I know," she said finally, and lay down on the bed again, worn out with tugging on a dead weight. "Marco Mondragón, get in this bed. Now."

"You really want me, even after I left you lost?" he said, his voice filled with disbelief, but something else now. She had heard that same wistfulness in Maria Brava, in Catalina Ygnacio, and in her own murmurings. It was hope, that tiniest and most fragile flower of the heart.

"Marco, sometimes I think you are an idiot," she said, sitting up and ready to try again. "Take off your clothes because they stink and get in this bed! Right now!"

He still sat there. There was just enough moonlight coming through the closed shutters to show her a ravaged face. Paloma let out a long breath and leaned forward for a better look. The vestiges of a black eye remained, but Claudio had warned her of that. This was more.

She put her hand on his chest, ready to remove his vest. "Marco, you look so worn out, so tired. This was more than a trip with Comanches. What happened?"

In answer, he took her hand and brought it around to the back of his neck, where she gasped to feel a large bump behind his ear. "Marco, my love, what did they do to you?"

"Someone was an excellent shot with a rock," he said. "You remember what it was like when we rode into the encampment of the sacred canyon, with warriors milling all about and throwing stones."

She gently touched the knot on his head. "I remember too well," she said as he traced the small scar on her face from a stone. "I remember Eckapeta and others shielding us as best they could. Oh, Marco."

"I was unconscious for a while, then I pled the governor's case before a highly skeptical audience," he said. "You'd have been proud of me. I'm too tired to tell it. When we left, I could only travel half a day. I would have fallen out of the saddle, if Toshua hadn't caught me."

"He was watching you just for that, wasn't he?"

"Oh, yes. I don't remember a thing for several days," Marco said.

He rested his head on the edge of the bed again, as she stroked his hair. "Toshua built a brush shelter for me, shot a deer, and we stayed there for I don't know how long. I would have been here sooner—truly I would have, Paloma."

He put both hands behind her neck and drew her closer. She forgot about the vest and kissed him. He kissed her back with a fervor that reminded her all over again just how much she loved this *juez de campo*, who bore everyone's burdens, up to and including those of the entire colony of New Mexico and its royal governor. He had worked so patiently for years now to bring the Comanches into the fold of Spain, even as Spain's grasp was slipping.

Never mind that she had prayed and dreamed for those awful days that he would find her, unaware how far away he really was, and in danger of his own. Eckapeta had spoken truly. Only a force greater than all of them could ever have dragged him away. She knew it as surely as she knew every crease and scar on his body.

As she started on his vest again, she explained all that to him as carefully and slowly as if he were Soledad or Claudito. "Let there be no mistake, my love," she said as she helped him from his vest and then his shirt. "I hold no grudge. Juanito's birth was easy enough, but I felt so gloomy. I don't know why, but I did."

He sat beside her now, his arm around her. He leaned his head against hers and murmured something about being so wrapped up in spring planting and events to the east that he overlooked her dark time after Juanito's birth. "All you wanted was some respite," he said. "Believe me, Paloma, I understand that." He gave her head a little rub, a wordless, familiar endearment between them that brought tears to her eyes. "I apologize and you apologize. Let's be done with it. Right?" He took her by the shoulders and looked into her eyes. "Right?"

She nodded and threw her arms around him. He pulled her back with him onto the bed, held her there, and fell asleep. Paloma laughed out loud, which didn't even cause her exhausted husband to stir. She worked her way out of his grasp and took off his clothes, dumping them in a pile by the door. Tomorrow they could argue about whether the nasty things should go to the laundress or the burn pit.

He lay there sound asleep as she fetched warm water from the kitchen, smiled at Sancha with no embarrassment whatsoever and returned to clean him off, gently washing away the grime of travel and with it, her own dismay that she had failed him, or even thought she had.

She scrubbed him gently, marveling at how one man could bear so much for so many. She remembered what Sancha had told her about this dear man carrying their nearly dead son from mother to mother on the Double Cross, begging their help, and then managing to leave with Toshua before he knew any outcome of their son's life or her whereabouts.

She liked to kiss his ear, but she cleaned it first, knowing that a real bath loomed in the morning. She kissed him on his clean ear and let her tongue rove a bit. He woke up.

"There now," she said, her voice gruff, which made him smile. "You'll do for a night in my bed, but tomorrow, it's the bathhouse for you. We'll have the *curandera* look at your head, too." She sniffed him. "No more dung poultices."

"Fair enough," he said, and let her help him under the covers.

His eyes started to close again. She asked him what had been the outcome of his time in Casa de Palo, but he was too far gone to tell her. Shaking her head, Paloma sat beside him until he sank into deep slumber. When he was breathing evenly, she got up, found her shawl and tiptoed through the darkened hallway, hoping someone might still be awake.

A light from the *sala* made her knock on the door, eager to see Toshua.

The Comanche opened the door and took her hand, pulling her inside. "Is he asleep?"

She nodded, pleased to see Toshua. "I want to know what happened." She came closer and held out her arms. "Toshua, thank you for keeping him alive."

"He's tough," Toshua said as he hugged her back. "Almost as tough as you are. Do you know he has not had a good night's sleep since we left? All he did was worry about you, when he wasn't raving with a fever."

"I believe it," she replied as she sat beside him and smiled at Eckapeta, who sat cross-legged on their pile of bedding. "He was certain he had failed me, even as I was equally certain I had failed him. Do you *know* two more stupid people?"

Toshua laughed out loud. "This woman and I have been equally foolish," he said, gesturing to Eckapeta. "And probably every man and woman who ever slept together under the same blanket. Go to bed and be glad you are normal."

Chastened and yet content, she stood up and blew them both a kiss. She looked back at the door. "I must know: will there be peace in this colony that probably even King Carlos himself could not find on a map?"

"There will be peace, Paloma, if not this year, than next. Ask your worthless, good-for-nothing, cry-baby husband you can't seem to manage without. Goodnight, my daughter."

Chapter Thirty-Six

In which some loose ends are tied up, others not

Marco had never been a man to sit in a bathhouse, not when a perfectly good *acequia* flowed through his fortress, easily accessible after dark. He did enjoy washing Paloma in the wooden tub brought to their chamber when it was too cold for her in the bathhouse he had built for her. He had not thought to use the place himself, not such a healthy man as the *juez de campo* of Distrito Valle del Sol.

But there he sat, enjoying the warmth of the water. Leaning back, he rested his arms on the edge of the tin tub as Paloma went over him with a cloth and soft soap. He tried not to smile when she scolded him for worrying about her when she and Catalina had been perfectly capable of rescuing themselves.

He let her carry on, enjoying the scold because he knew she didn't mean a word of it. He suspected she had been afraid for her life, and even more fearful for Juanito's life, because he knew her. He was content to feel her hands on his body and realize that, provided neither of them felt too decrepit tonight, they would enjoy each other as only a husband and wife could.

"Our faithful commander of Presidio Santa Maria is going to become a husband, you say?" he asked, breathing a little quicker when dutiful Paloma seemed to think his private parts weren't clean enough already. "And to a reformed shrew and master storyteller who will keep him walking a straight line?"

"Absolutely," that dutiful wife replied. She worked over his private parts in a most soothing fashion, the dimple in her cheek at play. *Dios*, but he had married a rascal. "She has already started rearranging his personal rooms in the presidio."

"Will she regret marrying a penitent scoundrel?" he asked.

"Not even slightly," Paloma said. "Someone told me once that women like to marry scoundrels, but I never did, Big Man Down There."

She sat back and looked at him, her eyes gentle and filling with unshed tears. "I didn't mean a word of my scold," she told him. "I've never been so afraid."

"I have never felt so helpless," he said. "You pushed back the fear and found a way to freedom, though."

She nodded. He watched the frown leave her face, and the tears retreat. She had more to tell him and he waited.

Finally she spoke. "I'll say this once. I am not one to tempt fate. When things were at their worst, I had a lovely dream. Perhaps it was more than a dream."

"How so?"

She rested her arms on the tub now, close to him. "I saw three children playing by the *acequia*."

"Soledad, Claudito, and Juanito. He was old enough to play with his brother and sister?"

"Yes. And guess what else?" She touched his face, and he could have died with the loveliness of the gesture. "There was another baby at my breast. Just a little one. Whether son or daughter, I do not know." She took a deep breath that caught. "I knew then I was going to live."

He looked deep into the blue eyes of his wife, thankful that a man could be so fortunate twice in his life. He prayed silently that he would be the only husband Paloma Vega ever had, even as he knew without a doubt that if something happened to him, she would carry on, likely remarry, and protect the Double Cross with all of her infinite resources. A man could do worse than know that about the woman he loved.

He rubbed the top of her head and her hand went to his arm. "Paloma, *te adoro*," he whispered.

"*Y yo a ti*," she replied. She tipped his head a little to one side and started in on the dirty creases in his neck. "Tell me again what we are to do this fall, you and I?"

"Juanito, too, of course, and probably Soledad and Claudito," he added. "I am not about to go anywhere again without all of you."

He saw the pleasure in her eyes, followed by a mother's caution. "We are going *where*?"

"A place you've never been. It's called Casa de Palo on the bank of Río Napestle, some four days on horseback from here, although Toshua and I did it in two." He sighed with pleasure when she started on his back. "Oh, a little lower there. Perfect. It will be in the Month-Heading-To-The-Winter-Moon, *Yubaubi Mua*. November."

"There will be so many Comanches," she said, and he heard her fear.

"You can't imagine! Kwihnai specifically requested your presence. Do not fear." He chuckled. "I admit to considerable terror, surrounded by Comanches on all sides, some of whom probably wanted to experiment with new and interesting ways to murder me slowly."

"And you would subject your excellent, charming wife and little ones to such people?" she teased, even though she took his hand in a grip that showed her doubt.

"Certainly," he said, and squeezed her hand back. "A woman and children mean we come in peace." He splashed a little water on her. "Besides, Kwihnai likes you more than he likes me. He said so."

"You're being silly," she protested, but he heard the pleasure in her voice. It reminded him of something else the old chief had said.

"In fact—I hope you believe this, because it is true—Kwihnai told me you could take care of yourself. I confess I didn't believe him, but you and Catalina saved yourselves."

"Maybe we both needed to know we could," his wife told him after a struggle of her own.

She helped him dry off, then walked with him to Señora Ladero's house for Juanito's feeding. She sighed with relief when her milk seemed to pour in this time. Even Juanito opened his eyes in surprise and applied himself more vigorously to his mother's breast.

Señora Ladero watched with the interest of a veteran mother of many. After Juanito emptied both of Paloma's breasts and closed his eyes in complete stupefaction, Pia Ladero gave Marco a shy glance, since he was intruding in the affairs of women, but plowed ahead anyway. "Señora Mondragón, I believe you should take Juanito home now. You have enough milk."

Marco watched his wife's delight in such a homely matter, and reminded himself again that he owed these good servants of his a debt he could not ever repay. He could try, though. Tomorrow, after he finished a lengthy letter to Governor Anza, he would call his servants together and ask their opinion about new homes, just outside the walls this time. There would be more room to expand and no reason to fear Comanches ever again.

Just the thought of such freedom made him suck in his breath as they walked toward the house, Juanito sleeping on his shoulder and Paloma's arm linked through his. He glanced in the door of his office and saw Señor Ygnacio, that quiet, mild-mannered fellow, who according to Sancha had kept

Soledad and Claudito occupied and productive during the time both their parents were away.

"Soledad can add little columns now, and Claudito knows his numbers," the auditor had told him proudly.

Marco stood there a moment, thinking about all the abuse the little fellow had suffered throughout his life, probably because no one, once they learned he was a former felon, had taken the time to plumb his real value. He shifted a little and saw Catalina Ygnacio there, too. They two were engaged in what appeared to be deep discussion.

He hesitated; to interrupt or not to interrupt? He glanced at Paloma, who was watching him with what he knew was unalloyed affection. She was a satisfied woman again, able to feed her baby, her children content, and her husband home. Hopefully she would be more satisfied by morning, because he wanted her with all his heart and body.

And she knows what I'm thinking, he told himself with pleasure, as she held out her hands for Juanito.

"You look like a man who wants to talk to an auditor," she said. "I'll put Juanito down for a nap and see what horrors Soledad and Claudito have gotten themselves into."

"And?" he prompted, certain there was more, because he knew that look.

"You can wait until everyone is asleep tonight, Big Man," she said as he handed over their sleeping son. "I'll keep."

How could a husband not laugh at that? He kissed her cheek and walked toward his office, where the auditor watched him.

"*Señor*, I have read through your audit and can pronounce it excellent," Marco said without any preliminaries as he came into his own office. "Pardon me if I am interrupting anything."

Señor Ygnacio got up from the desk and moved to one of the chairs in front, to sit beside his daughter. Marco sat in his accustomed place. Sancha had already found a small pasteboard box for the entire audit and had bound it with the red tape that all auditors, accountants, and *fiscales* seemed to travel with.

"I've signed it and you are at liberty to return to Santa Fe," he said. "You have my grateful thanks for a job well done, and so I will tell the governor in a letter that I wish you will take along, Señor Ygnacio."

Father and daughter exchanged glances, and the auditor cleared his throat. "With all respect, *Juez*, I would rather remain here."

Marco leaned back in his chair and eyed the two of them, not surprised by the auditor's request. Santa Fe had done the man no favors, and his daughter was not returning. "What will you do here, if you remain?" he asked.

"You mentioned Santa Maria was growing, and that the priest was spending more and more time writing letters for those who haven't the skill, and reading letters aloud to the same folks."

"Father Aloysius *has* complained to me about such a state of affairs," Marco said, smiling inside because he knew where this conversation was headed. "I remember our conversation on this subject. You would like to become a sort of scribe for the village?"

"I would, *vuestra merced*," he replied formally, as if Marco were a Spanish don, at the very least. "My daughter seems determined to marry a rake—"

"Papa …" Catalina began.

"Of whom I greatly approve," he hurried to add with a sidelong look at his daughter, a glance so full of pride and love that Marco smiled at the sheer loveliness of it.

"And when grandchildren come, you would like to spoil them," Marco concluded, then reminded him, "You work for the crown. I do not know the terms which forced you here in the first place."

Señor Ygnacio's face grew pensive. Catalina took his hand and kissed it. "I was sentenced to an indeterminate number of years in exile, *señor*. How does one interpret 'indeterminate?' "

"How, indeed? Let us do this: I will include a separate note to Governor Anza, a man I esteem and who I know esteems me. I will request that you remain here to complete your indeterminate exile, which I will supervise. I do not believe he will tell me no."

Señor Ygnacio clapped his hands in delight, then bowed his head. He started to slip from his chair to kneel before Marco, but Marco was faster. He came around his desk and lifted the auditor to his feet.

"No need for that. I would be unhappy if you left Valle del Sol, for we all have need of you, Señor Ygnacio," Marco said. "Go ahead and make your plans. I believe there is at least one small house available right now in Santa Maria. Since you will be under my authority and still in the service of the crown, there will be a way for the *juez de campo* of this district to pay for such housing and salary as you will require. It will go in my 1786 budget."

Marco wished Paloma was there beside him to watch Catalina's eyes soften. Her tongue was still as sharp as ever, but he didn't mind, because that was Catalina Ygnacio. "Señor Mondragón, will you require him to report to you every six months for a good scold and name calling?"

Marco flinched elaborately. "No! I get enough scolds and name calling from Paloma Vega. Oh! You mean your father reporting to *me*?"

They all laughed. Before he could stop her, Catalina kissed his hand. He admired her short curly hair and told her so, which prompted more blushes and smiles from a woman he thought would never smile. *Everyone changes on the Double Cross*, he thought, remembering what his brother-in-law Claudio had told him only last year. *Even I have changed. I hope I am better.*

He assumed his place behind the desk and waved off both Ygnacios, when the auditor said Catalina insisted on a drive to Santa Maria to visit the presidio. "We will take our old carriage," she told him as she pulled up the hat that dangled on its strings down her back.

"It's Friday afternoon," he warned, then laughed at his own joke. "Look out for drunks."

A half hour later, he was still collecting his thoughts for the governor on this whole crazy turn of events when he sat back, uneasy. He tried to shrug off his vague disquiet, but went to the open door, looking over his courtyard.

Paloma sat by the *acequia*, Juanito beside her on a blanket and Soli and Claudito splashing in the ditch that Emilio had so obligingly dammed. She beckoned him closer, but Marco shook his head, wondering how foolish he was going to appear if he acted on such a flimsy whim. He changed his mind and hurried toward her.

"Have you seen Toshua?" he asked.

"I believe he's in the horse barn. Care to join us?"

"Maybe later." He hurried into the horse barn, all but commanding his eyes to accustom themselves to the dim light immediately.

He heard a sound behind him and whirled around, hand on … nothing. He didn't even have a knife at his belt.

"Brother, you are getting soft," he heard from the shadows. Already mounted and on his equally terrifying masked horse, Toshua had gathered his reins in one hand.

"I'm coming with you," Marco said and looked for his mount.

"There were two of them, remember?" Toshua said.

"One is a fool, and the other a madman," he reminded the Comanche.

"Are you so certain you know which one is the fool? For idiots, Gaspar and Pedro had no trouble diddling two well-trained trackers," Toshua reminded Marco. "Do as I say and stay with Paloma." He left the barn without a backward glance, ducking low, his face intent.

Marco watched him leave. He raced up the steep steps to the terreplein, where his guards stood with lances always ready. He joined them and watched Toshua gallop toward the old carriage, now a distant plume of dust.

Out of the corner of his eye, Marco caught a glimpse of a man in the shadow created by the open gate. He looked closer and squinted, cursing his eyes and wishing they were as sharp as in his youth.

"Call down to Rogelio to close the gate. No urgency in your voice, Manolo," he whispered to the archer standing next to him. "Hand me your bow and an arrow first."

He had trained his men not to ever question him. Manolo casually handed over his bow and plucked an arrow from his quiver, calling no attention to himself. He leaned over the balcony's edge and told Rogelio to shut the gate, nothing in his voice to indicate alarm.

Rogelio moved to do as he was asked, just as the unknown figure by the gate stabbed him. Paloma looked up in alarm when Marco shouted to her. She dragged their sleeping son's blanket behind the bench and jumped into the water to stand in front of their other children.

Quicker than sight, Marco nocked the arrow against the bow, pulled, and shot the man who had yanked out the knife from Rogelio's arm and was running toward Paloma. The arrow went straight through his neck. The man fell to his knees as he grabbed at the arrow. With a wrenching cry, he collapsed face down in the dust.

Marco took the ladder in three steps, waving to Paloma to stay back. By now she had gathered Soledad and Claudito behind her. Eckapeta was running through the kitchen garden to grab up Juanito, still sound asleep.

Breathing heavily, Marco stood over the dead man. Not caring if the stranger was still alive, he yanked him over and grabbed him by his hair, the better to see him.

"Who is this I have killed?" he asked out loud. It had all happened so fast. He nodded to Paloma and pointed at the dead man with his lips. Quickly, she set each child on the bank by the *acequia*, shook her finger at them to stay still and ran to him.

She stopped a few feet from the body, staring down. Marco watched her expression harden and the color rage back into her cheeks. He sat back on his heels in surprise as she gave the corpse a savage kick to the head, then another.

"It's Pedro," she said. "He ran away with Roque. I never trusted him." Her hand went to Marco's head as he knelt beside the body. She pulled him close to her thigh and he felt her tremble. "Thank you, husband. Leave his body outside the gate for the buzzards." She turned on her heel and walked back to their equally startled children.

Chapter Thirty-Seven

In which blood is shed, to no one's regret

IT TOOK ALL MARCO's control to eat dinner calmly with his children, tell them stories—although not as spellbinding as Catalina's—and get them into his own bed, while Paloma, her face a mask of worry, nursed Juanito and bedded him down in their room, too, with shutters closed and bars down.

Marco sat in the hall, Kwihnai's lance in his lap, the lance the old chief had given him last year after he killed Great Owl. Lorenzo and Sancha had taken all the servants into the chapel for safety, and he doubled the terreplein's usual night guard.

"We could go underground," Paloma said, her eyes big in her face. He hated to see her reliving the horrors of her days as a prisoner of the Duráns, but that was life in this place, so close to having no law at all.

"No need. We will wait this way until Toshua returns," he said, and patted the space on the bench beside him.

"I should be with the children," she said, but her protest sounded lame to his husband ears.

"No, you should be with me." His free arm went around her shoulder. "You certainly gave a dead man some sound kicks."

"I wanted to spit on him, too," she said, and he heard all the spark and venom in her voice. But this was Paloma, so he was not surprised when she turned her face into his shoulder a moment later and whispered, "But that would have been really bad manners."

"I had my men drag his body beyond the gate and closer to the river," he said. "We will leave Pedro there for the buzzards." He let out a great breath. "When I think how close he came ...."

She patted his chest, then put her hand inside his shirt to stroke him. "I don't understand this. Pedro feared the Durán brothers, too. Why did he remain trapped under Roque's commands? Gaspar left. Why not Pedro?"

He agreed it was a good question. "Look at Maria Brava. She is pretty much healed and working a little bit now for Alicia, our laundress. You told me yourself that Maria still cringes with every sound."

"True," Paloma agreed. She patted his stomach then withdrew her hand, to his disappointment. "Perla tells me that Gaspar might never be truly useful, because he is so certain he knows nothing and can do nothing. They were so beaten down. So was Pedro. I suppose he felt forced to follow that dreadful man."

"When I think of all the times my father and I laughed over the Durán brothers .... Bumblers, he called them, when he didn't call them something worse." Marco managed a humorless chuckle. " 'They're stupid and harmless,' he told me, on more than one occasion. I wish I had taken them seriously."

"This country is a hard one," Paloma said. "Oh! That sounds so ridiculous."

"It's true, though," he agreed. "Some men it makes, some it breaks." He nudged her shoulder. "And women."

They sat in silence in the darkening hall until one of the guards called out the password, "Santiago!" and Rogelio with his well-bandaged arm continued his duty to swing wide the gate. Marco ran to a rifle port across from the bench where they sat and saw an outline of the auditor's shabby carriage, Toshua riding beside it.

Motioning for her to remain at the door to their bedroom, Marco hurried down the hall to the main entrance. Lorenzo joined him there, hefting a battle ax that might have come to Tenochtitlán two hundred and fifty years ago with Hernán Córtes.

Toshua let himself into the hacienda. He carried a scalp, which he casually draped over a wooden *bulto* of San Isidro, guardian saint of farmers.

"Roque Durán waited to strike until the carriage left the presidio to return here," he said, with no preamble. That terseness alone startled Marco, who knew how well the average Comanche liked to spin out a tale.

"Are the Ygnacios safe?" Marco asked.

"I left them in the presidio with Teniente Gasca," Toshua said. "Roque had no idea." He rubbed his bloody hands together. "I was waiting for him in the carriage. He was surprised."

"I don't doubt that," Marco replied, grateful not to be on the receiving end of even a menacing stare from a Kwahadi Comanche, let alone a scalping. He knew the Comanche preferred to scalp a man or woman still alive and there was no sound like the sound of flesh tearing away from someone's head. Just the thought made him shudder.

"I admit to one disappointment," Toshua said.

"I hesitate to ask, but I will," Marco said.

"His hair!" Toshua exclaimed, pointing to the statue of San Isidro. "I grabbed hold of it to slice around like I usually do, and it came off in my hand. Do some Spaniards have strange hair?"

Marco turned away and laughed. "Some Spaniards wear wigs," he replied, when he could speak again.

"Are we safe?" Paloma asked, hurrying toward them. She gave a wide berth to San Isidro with his new hairstyle. "What's so funny?"

"I'll tell you later, dear lady. Yes, we are safe," Marco said. "Lorenzo, you can release your charges from the chapel. I am carrying two children to their own beds."

"Dismiss the extra guards," Toshua said. He yawned and stretched like a banker or a shopkeeper home after a busy day of toting up columns of numbers or wrapping packages. Scratching himself, he left the hacienda. Eckapeta joined him outside the kitchen garden, where she had been concealed among cornstalks, her knife drawn. Arms around each other's waists, they walked toward the office, their home away from home.

Marco watched them as they stopped, conversed briefly, then turned around. "What is it, friends?" he asked as they came closer again.

Toshua put his hands with their dried blood on them gently on each side of Marco's neck. "You have done a great thing here, my brother." He laughed and released Marco. "Oh, the governor will get all the credit when those men who talk about what happened get hold of the story."

"Historians, do you mean?" Paloma asked, joining them in the center of the courtyard.

"Is that what they are called?" Toshua asked. He looked from one to the other. "There is something I wish to do for you."

"We were wondering that same thing for you. For your part in all this effort to find peace, I cannot offer you land, because it's already yours, anyway," Marco said.

Toshua gave a snort of disgust. "No one but you would ever admit it."

"I have some gold. I have silver. Fine saddles." Marco shrugged. "None of it is good enough for a true friend of the colony."

"I have a better idea," Toshua said as he drew out his knife.

Eckapeta did the same. Startled, Marco stepped in front of Paloma.

"Do you trust me, Marco Mondragón?" Toshua asked.

Did he trust this Comanche? Marco thought through the last tumultuous five years. He said nothing, but he blushed and moved until he was beside

Paloma and not protecting her. "It was instinct," he said, by way of apology. "You know we live with danger."

"And a good reaction," Eckapeta said. "If you hadn't done that, I probably would have slapped you silly, or blacked your other eye. Guard this precious jewel of yours."

As Marco watched, his eyes wide, Eckapeta nicked her wrist until it bled. She handed her knife to Paloma, who stepped forward, this brave wife of his, and did the same to her wrist. Toshua was next, and then Marco cut his wrist. In silence they pressed all four bleeding wounds together.

He felt no shame at his sudden tears, because all four of them wept.

"If you ever, ever, have need of us for anything, only come to the sacred canyon," Toshua said.

"I echo the same thing for you," Marco told him. "Please don't leave us now."

"Just for a while," Toshua said. He looked at his wife with an expression suspiciously like admiration and love. "You think I could keep this one away from her grandchildren and daughter?"

Paloma threw herself into Eckapeta's arms and clung to her, and then Toshua. Marco joined them, not wanting the embrace to ever end.

"I can't let them leave," Paloma whispered as the Comanche couple walked to the office.

"I can't either, my love, but they will be back." Marco replied. "Let's go to bed."

Marco stood for a moment, looking down at his children in their own beds. Pray God they would not remember nights like this one that were burned into his brain from his much more dangerous childhood. Tomorrow it would be back to the *acequia* for more water play while their mama watched, Juanito at her side. He would compose that letter to the governor. He decided to ask Joaquim Gasca himself to deliver it, accompanied by his new wife. A summertime trip through the passes to Santa Fe should give the newly married couple time to know each other better.

It worked for me and my lady, even in winter, he thought, watching Paloma take off her dress in their bedchamber. He smiled to see her stand by the bed a moment, as if debating whether to bother with a nightgown. His smile deepened as she shrugged her shoulders and crawled into bed naked.

He joined her in the same state of nature. Beyond the likely unnecessary comment that he adored her—she already knew—their lovemaking was silent and thorough. He knew this woman well: every curve of her; the feel of her hands pressing down on him, welcoming him inside; the way she tossed her head restlessly when her climax approached; her sigh of satisfaction when it ended.

"I have had enough excitement for a lifetime," Paloma said as she pulled up the coverlet against New Mexico's evening coolness. "I don't need any more adventures." She snuggled close to him. He kissed her hair, ready to sleep because she had worn him out so pleasantly.

As he composed himself for sleep, another thought shouldered its way into his brain, clamoring for attention, now that he had answered the demands of both his body and his wife's.

"Wake up, Paloma."

She muttered something unintelligible and swatted at his hand on her breast.

"No, really. I have something for you."

She laughed without opening her eyes. "You already gave it to me, you scoundrel."

She squeaked and sat up when he dragged the blanket off her. Going to the saddlebags still lying on the floor from his return home several days ago, he rummaged around in them. He came back to bed as she was pulling the blanket up and darting irritated glances his way.

"Here." He held out red dancing shoes. "How many years have I promised these?"

His wife sucked in her breath and put her hands to her mouth. Almost seeming to doubt they were real, she reached out to touch one shoe and then the other. "My goodness, you finally did it. I thought it was just a joke," she said as she took the shoes from his hands. "When did you do this?"

"When Toshua and I rode through Santa Maria on our way north, I left your foot imprint with the cobbler," Marco said. "I've had that paper in my saddlebags for years."

Sitting up in bed, she put on the lovely shoes, their heels higher than she usually wore. She slid to the edge of the bed and stood up, tapping the heels on the cold tile and listening to the staccato sound.

He lay back in bed and watched her do a little *tapatio*, one hand holding her full breasts so they would not jiggle, the other extended as if grasping the hem of a non-existent dress. Ideally, another woman should dance with her, since the church frowned on a man and woman dancing together. Maybe this fall at their harvest fiesta, he would not scandalize too many of his servants and guests if he danced with her.

She was a far cry from the glum woman who had left with the auditor's daughter, or the exhausted, thin, but triumphant woman who had returned, or the woman who had exacted her own vengeance just this afternoon. She was his wife, in good times and bad, and especially now when she danced naked in the moonlight.

Chapter Thirty-Eight

In which justice, sometimes fickle, is sweet, indeed

MARCO MONDRAGÓN'S LENGTHY LETTER to Governor Juan Bautista de Anza, plus the seven-year audit, went on their way in two weeks, following the well attended wedding of El Teniente Joaquim Gasca to Catalina Maria Ygnacio. Marco was convinced the large crowd was there to be absolutely certain the former womanizer and all-around scoundrel contracted legal and lasting vows with a lady they had already come to respect.

The village carriage maker had greatly improved the comfort of the auditor's shabby carriage by adding a real bed, much to the amusement of the *gente* of Santa Maria, who were reticent like most people of Spain, but earthy enough to know the value of a good bed.

Señor Ygnacio, comfortably installed in a combination house and office on Santa Maria's plaza, waved off his beloved daughter and son-in-law with kisses and tears. Marco and Paloma assured La Señora Ygnacio y Gasca they would visit him often.

The Gascas were already too involved in each other to notice a Comanche couple following at a discreet distance behind. "At least as far as the second pass," Marco had instructed Toshua.

THE NEWLYWEDS RETURNED SIX weeks later, as eastern New Mexico cooled down and its farmers began the harvest. Marco left the cornfield to escort the couple to the Double Cross, gates open wide, for their joyful welcome from Paloma Vega, who had a kiss for each of them and two for her own husband, just because.

They talked and laughed over dinner and Soledad exerted all her power to get a story from La Señora Gasca. The lady obliged, telling them of a rancher's spoiled daughter in the colony of New Spain who turned into a horned toad because she would not help her mother.

"Would nothing free her?" Soli had to know.

"Only *un beso* from a *comandante* of a presidio in far distant New Mexico," Catalina assured her, after a glance at such a *comandante*. Soledad squealed when Joaquim Gasca planted a kiss on her forehead.

While the women got the little ones to bed, Marco and Joaquim took a stroll on the terreplein, stopping to drape their arms over the parapet and look across the great plain stretching into distant Texas.

"Governor Anza told me most privately something I was to pass on to you, Marco," Joaquim said.

"I hope I did not overstep my puny authority to keep Señor Ygnacio here for his indeterminate sentence," Marco said, unable to disguise his personal contempt for lawyers and unwarranted punishment of a natural scapegoat like Señor Ygnacio, with his quiet ways.

"Not at all, friend," Joaquim replied. "He applauded your decision and happily washed his hands of the matter. We can expect no further trouble from lawyers." He turned from his view of the prairie and faced Marco. "This concerns Paloma's miserable uncle."

"Who keeps popping up and surviving, where someone far more honest— your father-in-law, for example—sinks," Marco groused.

"Not in this case, God be praised," Joaquim replied. "It turns out that Governor Anza has been suspicious of Felix Moreno for some time. In fact— you'll like this—he planted Miguel Valencia as a suitor for Tomasa Moreno so he could learn more about our friend Felix."

"No!"

"Oh yes. The fool told his supposed future son-in-law about his plans to have Señor Ygnacio killed because he thought the auditor knew too much about his own dipping into government resources. Miguel told the governor, who sent the driver—the one who died at Pedro's hands—to protect Señor Ygnacio from anything untoward."

"And we know how that went," Marco said drily.

"It gets better," Joaquim continued. Even in the dim light of early evening, Marco saw how El Teniente's eyes gleamed. "He told me that years ago, you had approached the *juez de campo* of the Santa Fe district about making some discreet inquiries into Señor Moreno's possible involvement in a land grant belonging to his poor sister's husband."

"Paloma's parents," Marco said. "I had nearly forgotten about that conversation. Don't stop now!"

"Santa Fe's *juez* handed off his suspicions to the *juez* of the El Paso district."
He laughed. "You know how slowly things move in this new world of ours, but
by God, they move. The El Paso official dug deep. The deed had been misfiled
for years, perhaps on purpose by a less-than-scrupulous predecessor. He
found a deed of transfer for that land to one Felix Moreno, *contador principal*
of Santa Fe."

"Just what we thought," Marco said.

"Damn the man, Marco, but in the deed transfer, he swore there were no
survivors of that Comanche raid—"

"While his niece, now my lovely wife, was living under his own roof!"
Marco exclaimed.

"Swore on the holy name of the Virgin Herself," Joaquim finished, then
stood there in triumph. "As we speak, the man is on his way to Mexico City in
chains, to answer for his various misdeeds. I don't expect a favorable outcome
for him."

There it was, confirmation and vindication at last. Marco nodded and
stared out at the big sky before him, wondering why he felt so hollow inside.
He had yearned for this moment for years, and here it was.

"I can't believe I feel sorry for the man, but I do," he said at last. "Why?"

Joaquim turned again to look out across the parapet, their shoulders
touching. "Maybe because you are a far better man than Felix Moreno," he
said, sounding like he was thinking out loud. "Maybe because your life and
Paloma's are much richer than if no Comanche raid that turned Paloma and
her brother Claudio into paupers and wanderers had ever taken place."

"Perhaps," Marco said. "Who can understand the workings of God?" He
crossed himself and started for the stairs. "I had better tell Paloma." He looked
back. "I suppose our governor would like to know what Paloma and Claudio
intend to do with that land which is now theirs again?"

"He would. A letter from Paloma and Claudio will suffice."

THOUGHTFUL, MARCO WENT DOWN the stairs slowly. He walked around the
courtyard, past the flowing, whispering *acequia,* and past the quarters of his
servants, which meant stopping to chat and discuss again his plan to provide
new homes outside the protecting walls of the Double Cross. He stopped
outside his office, wondering what he should tell Toshua and Eckapeta. Were
they even there or had they struck out for the Staked Plains?

It surprised him not at all when Toshua came to the door. Marco had long
given up trying to understand how his great good friend could hear mouse-
quiet footsteps. He told him what Joaquim had just said. Toshua grunted,
nodded, and pressed his forehead against Marco's.

"Paloma will do the right thing, my friend," he said, then went back into the office.

Paloma was reclining in bed, eyes closed, face dreamy, as Juanito nursed. Standing in the doorway, Marco watched his woman and his son, grateful beyond human speech for them and their other children. He thought of Paloma's little vision and knew good things were still to come.

As he sat down beside her, she opened her eyes, reached for his hand, and kissed it. He looked away, unable to stop his tears at such a submissive gesture. "Some days I deserve that; some days I don't," he said softly, not willing to wake up Juanito. "I still regret I was not here to find you."

"And I needed to save myself," his wife said in turn. "Forgive and forget?"

"Done, *señora*," he replied, then told her everything Joaquim had told him about her uncle.

He watched her face for reaction, for visible anger, but all he saw was the same sorrow he had felt. He kissed *her* hand this time.

"Let's go visit Claudio and Graciela tomorrow," he said. "I know he's busy, but this shouldn't wait. Besides, Soledad has been nagging me for another visit to see their cousins again soon."

Nodding in agreement, Paloma handed Juanito to him for a burp. She buttoned her nightgown then folded her arms around her upraised knees. "My first thought is for the land to go to the Franciscan fathers in that district. They found me and took me in."

"Your second thought?" Juanito's burp was followed by a sigh and a snuggle closer to Marco's neck that turned him into mush.

"Why not deed it to Lorenzo and Sancha?" she asked. "She has been so faithful in her service to you and Felicia, and then to me. And you must admit Lorenzo knows livestock."

"Yes, he does, mine and everyone else's!" Marco said, amused. "But he has served us well this past year, and I sense honest reformation, especially if Sancha is there to supervise him. Would you also deed the brand?"

He thought he knew what she would say, and she did not disappoint him. "No, not our brand. It is registered to and remains with Claudio. We can honor our parents right here in New Mexico. Lorenzo will want his own brand."

Bless your dear heart, he thought. "Let's see what Claudio says tomorrow."

"Whatever my brother decides, I will acquiesce," Paloma said. "He is the eldest and I am but a younger sister."

"And my entire life, universe, and galaxy," Marco said.

"As you are mine," his universe and galaxy said quietly.

He put Juanito into his cradle, made the sign of the cross over him as he did over each of his children every night, and over his wife. He lay down next to her, his arm pillowing her neck.

"In his letter, the governor agreed with those terms I suggested to Ecueracapa in the canyon, and added a few of his own," he said. "He wants us to represent him at Casa de Palo in November and encourage the leaders to come to Santa Fe next February or March to sign a treaty."

"Peace at last?" his drowsy wife asked.

"I believe so. We can invite Governor Anza to visit us in the spring, and see our life here on the edge of danger. I know it is too much to ask, but wouldn't it be fun to have the treaty signed here?"

No reply. Marco heard his wife's deep breathing, and closed his eyes, thinking of peace and more children, petty quarrels between his constituents to settle, and squabbles over water, land, and livestock—the crosses to bear of a *juez de campo*. His heart full, he asked God Omnipotent who ruled His universe to continue granting him wisdom to lead his family and protect those who depended on him.

He glanced down at Paloma, she who had borne so much, and who had thought, years ago now, to bring him a little yellow dog through dangerous passes and snow-covered trails, just because she wanted to see the man with the light brown eyes again.

He looked at the red shoes on the little table by her side of their bed. He would dance with her at the harvest fiesta. He wasn't much of a dancer, but he didn't think she would mind.

They had forgotten to close the shutters again. Marco thought about getting up to do it, but that required more exertion than he felt necessary. Looking out the barred window, he watched the moon begin its descent. He prayed for God Omnipotent to bless King Carlos in distant Spain. A pity His Highness would never visit this choice spot in his kingdom, a place maybe not so wealthy as the mines of Mexico, but a place dear to those who lived there.

And now, peace. A *juez de campo* could not ask for more than that. Marco Mondragón closed his light-brown eyes and inclined his head toward his wife's. He knew the children would bounce in early, and a man approaching middle age needed all the rest he could get.

Chapter Thirty-Nine

In which all things meet in one great whole

THE NEXT MORNING, MARCO could barely contain his pride as he rode out of the Double Cross with his wife and children. Soledad sat before him on the saddle and Claudito in front of Paloma, with strict orders not to wiggle about. Juanito slept in the Comanche cradleboard on her back.

They ambled along in no hurry. The harvest was nearly done, all the little creatures birthed and baaing, bleating, or bawling. Hopefully rain would come soon to this parched land, but no one had a guarantee. Marco figured their odds of good weather for crops had increased monumentally when Paloma yanked Roque Durán's nasty wig off the statue of San Isidro, patron saint of farmers. Marching it out to the burn pit, she told Gaspar to stand there and watch it until it was totally consumed.

"Let's take the little ones to the river tomorrow and let them splash," Paloma suggested as they rode along.

"Papa, you've been promising to teach me to swim," Soledad reminded him.

"I have, haven't I?" Marco replied. "Let's do it."

He sent an appreciative glance Paloma's way, always ready to admire her legs when she wore the thigh-high split garb of the People, this latest dress a gift from Kwihnai's wives. She wore her hair in one fat braid down her back, just the way he liked it. Tonight he would brush it for her, which invariably led to much more.

"I know what you're thinking, Big Man," she said, angling her horse closer to Buciro.

"I have no doubt, Tatzinupi," he said. "Takes one to know one."

She smiled at her Comanche name, but the smile turned wistful, and he thought she was remembering her parents. He reached across the shortened space between them and touched her bare knee.

"Somehow I am certain they understand that all has turned out well for you and Claudio," he said. "I feel it."

"I used to ask you that over and over, wanting you to tell me if they knew of our happiness and our children," she said, wonder in her voice. "I don't anymore. Why is that?"

"You know it to be true," he told her.

She nodded, then rode a little to one side, wanting some alone time, as much as a mother carrying two children on her horse can expect. She dabbed at her eyes, then straightened up and squared her shoulders, her posture erect and her manner dignified.

If only they could see you, my love, he thought. *Please, God, let it be so, even if only a glimpse.*

He had sent a rider ahead yesterday evening to warn Claudio what was coming his way. When they arrived at Estancia Vega, the gate was open in welcome and Claudio stood there, Cecilia dancing around and eager to see her cousins. Daughter of Graciela and an unknown Comanche, she and Soledad were already fast friends. In no time Soli and Claudito had vacated the parental horses and Marco was helping Paloma dismount.

Paloma kissed her brother's cheek and grabbed him in a warm *abrazo*. "I'm sorry there was no opportunity to speak to you and Graci at Joaquim Gasca's wedding," she said. "We've been busy; you've been busy."

"Haven't we? Come inside, you two. We have wine for us and milk for the children, *biscoches* for everyone and a beefsteak for your eye, Marco."

"It is long since healed," Marco said. He laughed, which gave Claudio permission to at least smile, even though he apologized again.

"*No me importa, hermano,*" Marco said. "You have a champion there, Paloma. If I mistreat you, he'll punch me again."

Laughing together, they walked toward the house. Marco was pleased with what Claudio and Graciela had done with the raw adobe dwelling they had built in quick time over the winter. Flowers bloomed in earthenware bowls, and there by the front door was a carved bear, symbol of Graci's Ute nation, although some of the Bear People had moved farther west toward the setting sun.

Graciela herself sat in a chair in their *sala*, Rafael nursing. Paloma kissed the newest arrival among them, then sat down beside her sister-in-law and opened her deerskin bodice, too.

"Two beautiful mothers," Claudio said, and Marco heard all the love, satisfaction, and pride in a man who last year would never have said anything remotely sentimental. "Lorenzo told me all you went through at Río Napestle and after. I'm truly sorry I added to your burden."

"I've thought about this, Claudio," Marco said. "You did not add to my burden. You were my conscience."

"I don't understand," Claudio replied.

"I don't either, really, except your passionate demonstration of what I owed your sister reminded me what I also owe this colony." He patted Claudio's arm. "Leave it at that and speak of it no more."

Paloma put Juanito to her shoulder. "Claudio, what are we to do with Papa's land?"

Claudio nudged Marco's shoulder. "My sister is somewhere in her twenties—I never can remember where—but she sounds the same as when she was little and skinny and already had her mind made up."

"I do not!" Paloma protested, then had the grace to turn a bit rosy, to Marco's delight. "Maybe I do, but it's a good idea."

Claudio sat down beside his wife and indicated the other end of Paloma's bench to Marco. "Let's hear it."

"Deed the land to Sancha and Lorenzo," she said with no preamble. "Lorenzo and *his* brother kept you alive, and Sancha has been a most loyal servant." She tried to look dignified, but Marco saw the intensity in her eyes. "Tell me what you think."

"Graci, if ever you needed proof that Paloma and I are brother and sister, you have it now," Claudio said to his wife. "We were wondering this morning what *you* would think if I proposed the same thing."

Marco watched his wife's expressive face pass through stages of delight and introspection, followed by a single tear down her cheek, and then another. He flicked them away with his finger, and she clung to his hand.

"The brand stays with me," Claudio said, his voice so tender, as if he spoke of a living being.

In a way it was; Marco knew that better than either of them. Through the years he had recorded many a brand for the tough citizens of the Valle del Sol District. He knew the price paid for each brand far exceeded any monetary amount derived from the sale of cattle and sheep. There had been years when the brand might well have been dipped in blood, as settlers struggled to stay alive in a place both inhospitable and beguiling in turn, a place not easy on friend or enemy. *These brands of my district are nearly sacred to me*, Marco wanted to say out loud, but he refrained. Holy Church would probably frown on such a statement. He would keep that to himself, or maybe tell Paloma.

He could say one thing. "I have learned a valuable lesson in these past few months that I probably should have figured out sooner," he said.

"That your brother-in-law has a wicked jab?" Claudio teased.

"That, too," Marco told him. He put his arm around Paloma. "My love, when I was taking our son from mother to mother, when I was relying so heavily on sweet Señor Ygnacio to watch our children, when Emilio told me not to worry about the planting ..." he stopped, unable to go on.

Paloma patted his knee, her expression kind.

He took a deep breath. "What a fool I was to think that nothing mattered in my life except the discharge of *my* responsibility to every servant, guard, herder, and artisan on the Double Cross. They were my stewardship."

Paloma was already nodding. Trust his wife to have figured this out much sooner. "All these years, I had no idea they were watching out for *me*. Toshua and Eckapeta, too." He took another breath, and another. "And I was their stewardship. I was never alone, was I? Even in those darkest days. Never."

Paloma turned her face into his shoulder and he held her close until Juanito squeaked in protest. Everyone laughed, breaking the moment, or perhaps making it sweeter. He could think about that some time.

It could keep. Marco Mondragón, *juez de campo* of the Valle del Sol District, rancher, farmer, father, husband, and all-around idiot at times, breathed deep of the aroma of piñon from the small fireplace in the corner. He noticed the inside of the fireplace was already black with resin from many fires this winter and spring. Piñon would always mean New Mexico, and struggle, and home: his colony's refiner's fire.

He kissed the top of Paloma's head, anticipating brushing her hair tonight and feeling blessed beyond measure, his cup full.

Bryner Photography

A WELL-KNOWN VETERAN OF the romance writing field, **Carla Kelly** is the author of thirty-seven novels and three non-fiction works, as well as numerous short stories and articles for various publications. She is the recipient of two RITA Awards from Romance Writers of America for Best Regency of the Year; two Spur Awards from Western Writers of America; three Whitney Awards, 2011, 2012, and 2014; and a Lifetime Achievement Award from Romantic Times.

Carla's interest in historical fiction is a byproduct of her lifelong study of history. She's held a variety of jobs, including public relations work for major hospitals and hospices, feature writer and columnist for a North Dakota daily newspaper, and ranger in the National Park Service (her favorite job) at Fort Laramie National Historic Site and Fort Union Trading Post National

Historic Site. She has worked for the North Dakota Historical Society as a contract researcher.

Interest in the Napoleonic Wars at sea led to a recent series of novels about the British Channel Fleet during that conflict. Of late, Carla has written two novels set in southeast Wyoming in 1910 that focus on her Mormon background and her interest in ranching.

You can find Carla on the Web at:

www.CarlaKellyAuthor.com.

Books 1-3, The Spanish Brand

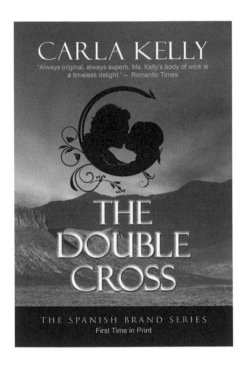

The year is 1780, and Marco Mondragón is a brand inspector in the royal Spanish colony of New Mexico whose home is on the edge of the domain of the fierce Comanche. On a trip to Santa Fe, he meets lovely Paloma Vega and rescues her from cruel relatives. Now he is determined to find out if they stole the brand belonging to her parents.

At the end of the 18th Century, during the decline of the Spanish Empire in the New World, Marco and his wife Paloma fight the scourge of smallpox by bravely venturing onto the Staked Plains, stronghold of the Comanche. As part of a devil's bargain, they must put themselves at the mercy of these dangerous enemies and try to inoculate them.

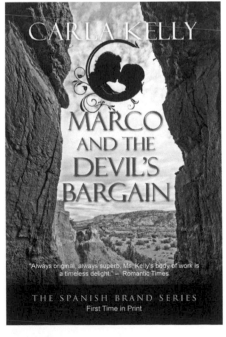

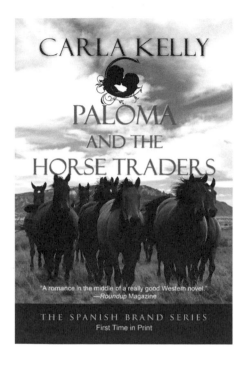

As the 18th century ends, the Comanches have made peace with the Spanish colonists in New Mexico. No one is as relieved as Marco and his wife Paloma, who live on the edge of Comanchería. Then a new threat emerges: a renegade Comanche. Flanked by a disgraced lieutenant, a band of horse traders, and a slave girl, Marco and his friend Toshua venture north to defeat Great Owl or die trying.

If you loved The Spanish Brand, you'll also love Carla's very first novel,

Daughter of Fortune

Maria Espinosa is "La Afortunata." First she survives the 1679 cholera epidemic in Mexico City, then an Apache raid on the caravan transporting her to Santa Fe. Rejected by her sister, Maria goes to live with a ranching family living uneasily among the Pueblos and inspires a rivalry between Diego and his half-Indian brother Cristobal. When the Indians revolt, will Maria's good fortune hold?

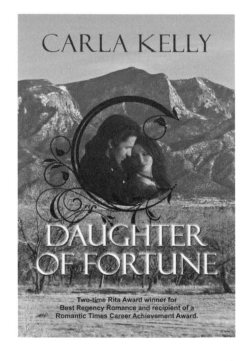